I WAS UNDER A WITCH'S SPELL

He stood in the doorway, a figure so striking that the room went dead—tall, thin, with the graceful, tough beauty of a tomcat. His face was the perfect face of Prince Charming. But most arresting were his eyes, the bluest eyes I'd ever seen.

He saw me and stared. I was overwhelmed but the stare was remorseless. It was as if I'd been fed a secret love potion. I had never experienced such an intense reaction to a perfect stranger. All the time I was conscious of those eyes, those marvelous eyes staring at me.

He sat down next to me and tilted my chin so that I was forced to look at him. His eyes were very deep and very sad. I was lost . . .

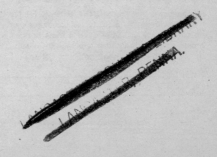

Other SIGNET Gothics You'll Enjoy

Chapter I

The first time I saw Stonehaven I sensed that demons were at it, twisting it into a brooding pile of stone. The house was on a hill, overlooking a lake. Its gray stones leaned, perhaps to catch the whispers of elves dancing on the lake in spring-time, driven by a faery wind. It was no spring evening now; instead it was a cold and gloomy morning. The snow fell soft as sifted flour on a baker's board. Staring at the massive old bones of the house I thought it possible that I had come to the dark side of the moon.

Although I was about two hours away from my world of New York City, a magic clock must have tricked me and sent me back into time as the car propelled me forward through space. Drawing near Stonehaven the landscape became alien, consisting of vast, deserted forests. The house itself was found at the end of secret roads and was hidden from sight by hills and snow-covered pines. It made its appearance abruptly, a haphazard creation, an architect's hideous, grim joke. After parking the car I paused to steel myself and then I began the long march up the path. Correction, not I, but we. We moved unswervingly toward the house. Two taut figures walked together to face the house that day.

Myself and Andre. Andre was my new husband; Stone-haven was his ancestral ... domicile, I hesitate to call it a home. He had looked at it a thousand times, knew its every angle and twist, but he too was stunned by the sight of it. We walked mechanically, our boots crunching the snow. The house drew us remorselessly on. It was careful to suppress its shock and show only a slight expectancy as we approached. I tried to tell myself that the mantle of snow gave it the look of an eccentric Father Christmas. But this was pretense. The

5

snow really made Stonehaven look a hellish invention of Viking myth.

We arrived at the huge arcs of rock fronting the house. Once past them, we stood on the broad stone porch. I took a deep breath as the heavy wooden door swung open on its hinges and the house received us. The door slammed shut, the slam reverberating through distant rooms. Was it the wind outside or a sigh of satisfaction from the house itself I heard? And I wondered if the house, having let me in, would ever let me out again.

It was a quirk of fate that finally brought me to Stonehaven. I often contemplate what would have happened if I'd run a fever or been hit by a car the night of that party in Greenwich Village. Would everything have been different or would I have met Andre anyway, the next day or the day after that? Who can say? But I still perceive my life divided into clean halves. If I ever really do become a painter, that's how museum directors will describe my work: "And here we have a splendid example of the artist in her cheerful pink phase, the pre-Andre period, and here we see her work in the more mature post-Andre period."

Of course, the night of the party I knew nothing of this. No trumpets heralded the impending changes in my life. I walked along under the smoggy skies of New York City, clear of conscience and supremely untroubled. I was one of the many young art students who, bursting onto the New York scene every year, are immediately swept up in a kind of ecstacy. For let them talk about crime, pollution, and whatever else, New York still boggles the mind. Sooty and no longer in her prime, she is still the queen city, magnificent as Venice in decline. I loved her.

So as twilight fell, I walked the hot, dirty pavements, taking it all in. A small boy rolled a ball across my path and mumbled something in Spanish. A chic woman at a window in a restaurant caught my eye as I passed and instantly glanced away. Two taxi drivers honked and cursed, driven to a frenzy by traffic, heat, and grime.

I was so fascinated by the city I forgot where I was going. "Whoops," I thought, "I've missed it," so I retraced my steps to an old narrow building, scrolled and embroidered, which was wedged between two modern skyscrapers. The twin doormen standing before these chrome, glass, and steel wonders gave me only a cursory glance. I had to smile. Perhaps it was my dress, obviously run up on a home sewing machine. I shrugged and intersected them as they paced, which startled them, for the narrow brownstone I entered had very expensive apartments.

I didn't belong here; the doormen were right. I didn't really belong in New York at all; I was here by accident. My grandmother, a woman of iron-gray hair and iron-strong character, had raised me, and very properly too. She did her best to drum the old-fashioned virtues into my reluctant head and to some extent she succeeded. If she pitied me for being an orphan she never showed it. I was no Oliver Twist. My grandmother's house exuded security, sound judgment, and solid affection. Growing up under her protection in the quiet, pretty streets of Osborn, Illinois, I had had a childhood to be envied.

My sheltered upbringing did have one unavoidable negative side; it didn't prepare me to take my place in the modern world. My grandmother saw to it that I was accomplished in a dozen trivial ways and even in one important way: as a painter. I was reasonably independent but by no means emancipated. Even the 1920s had scandalized my grandmother. She was not one to compromise and she raised me in conformity with her remorseless Victorian ideals. So here I was, twenty-three years old, shy, unsophisticated, and thoroughly out of kilter with my generation. In short, my grandmother had succeeded all too well. I was a lady, alas, a member of a vanishing species, second cousin to the dodo bird and soon to be extinct.

Oddly enough, it was my ladylike appearance that got me invited to the party that night. I'd met Robin Rouen (yes, the famous painter) through one of my art teachers. He came to visit a class while I was doing watercolors. I was practically tongue-tied with awe at meeting him and this amused him, as if I were some sort of strange insect he'd discovered. He decided to make my acquaintance, perhaps to learn if I were real or merely an actress who'd hit on a good pose. Robin is an expert at poses. Having concluded that I was genuine, if a bit ridiculous, he invited me to the party. It was an act of kindness, like feeding a stray cat. No doubt he also planned to present me as a little bibelot he'd found: Tamara Lewis, genuine anachronism.

I suppose it was to escape just that image that I'd made an impetuous dash for New York when my grandmother died. I couldn't see either of the two future roads open to me in Osborn: gentle maiden lady or marriage to one of the local boys on his way up. I'd had enough dates with the latter to consider the former. In any event I took courage and my small inheritance in hand, quit my secretarial job at the law firm of Rollins and Rollins and came to New York! Stimulation, anonymity, freedom, and a fourth-floor walk-up all my own. I had never been happier.

Here I was, about to attend one of those notorious New York parties I'd read about in secret at my grandmother's house; an intermingling of strange and eccentric people, of successful and glamorous people. I fought down the nagging fear that it would probably turn out to be prosaic and dull, a better-dressed crowd of Shriners on a spree, not very different from back home.

I rang the doorbell and was buzzed into the ornate vestibule. I located Robin's large duplex apartment and waited until the door opened. One glimpse of Robin and I knew that this party couldn't possibly be like any back in Osborn.

Robin Rouen filled the entire space of the doorway, an enormous Falstaff with spade-shaped black beard. "Little red fox," he shouted, waving an arm expansively. This was his nickname for me because of my hair; it is extremely red and extremely long. Grandmother had once feared that it would make me vain but she'd never had the heart to cut it, even when I was a small child.

I blushed at Robin's effusiveness and followed him into the apartment, feeling like a minnow trailing a whale. The duplex was everything I could have asked it to be; high ceilings with elaborate moldings and spotless white walls covered with Robin's enormous paintings which made the rooms glow with color and life. The living room was so filled with people milling and talking that I caught my breath. "Everyman, this is Tamara Lewis," Robin shouted above the din, gesturing grandly. "Maid Marion escaped from the thirteenth century." He shoved a gold goblet of something bubbly into my hand and vanished.

Fortunately, everyone was too busy to pay any attention to me and by wedging myself between a bookcase and a huge porcelain vase filled with yellow roses, I was able to observe without being seen. I felt thoroughly intimidated, for I recognized faces I'd noticed on magazine covers or on late-night talk shows. A strikingly dressed middle-aged woman laughing loudly at some private, and I suspect, malicious joke stepped backward, almost pinning me to the wall. Turning, she stared at me in surprise and then distaste. Her eyes took in my cheap dress and went blank.

In a nearby corner, an earnest conversation was going on about nuclear disarmament. To emphasize a point, one of the speakers bent forward gesticulating, saw me and stopped momentarily. Then he returned to the discussion. I decided that it might be safer to hide in the midst of the crowd and began weaving my way across the floor. A curving cardboard armchair painted cobalt blue caught my eye and I tried to reach it, tripping over a girl with an enormous Afro hairdo. We smiled curtly at each other and I moved on.

Robin suddenly emerged from a kitchen blazing with appliances, bearing a tray of food. He was followed by half a dozen white-coated caterers, each carrying an identical silver tray heaped with delicacies. "Victuals aloft," Robin shouted, in a fog-horn voice capable of drowning out the cheers of fans in a football stadium. He planted his tray down firmly on a long oaken table near the twisting stairway which led to the upper floor. I could hear muffled whispers and giggles filtering down from the bedrooms.

The food looked suitably exotic. In true Rouen style, however, there was an abundance of plebian food for those who were really hungry. A number of trays held pastrami sandwiches, pickles, and chopped liver. Since my budget was severely limited, I decided to forego the delicacies and dove for a satisfying pastrami sandwich. Caviar could wait.

I was busy sampling desserts when the doorbell rang for the last time that evening and I just happened to glance at the door in time to see the latest guest enter. He stood in the doorway, a figure so striking that the room went dead. Only for a second, it's true, but you could have heard a pin drop. It was a man, or rather a boy, my age, not fully a man as I was not yet fully a woman. He was tall, thin, and strangely cat-like. Not at all feminine, he had the graceful yet tough beauty of a tomcat. His hair was worn long: it was light to the point of silver. His face was the perfect face of Prince Charming in every fairy story. But most arresting were his eyes, the bluest eyes I'd ever seen, hard, opaque sapphires, looking at the world out of a pale and troubled face, a medieval face. Clearly another time-traveler who had blundered into the wrong century.

Robin was standing on the other side of the room. When he saw his latest guest, he looked annoyed, even fearful, but quickly and with bravado he crossed to the door. I watched him speak to the new arrival, the guest's eyes looking round the room, searching for someone. He seemed to be questioning Robin and, at one point, became angry. Then his face turned ugly and, like a bully, he grabbed Robin's arm. Robin pulled back, appeared to plead, and then rubbed his arm. The newcomer became impatient. He seemed indifferent to the crowd, frankly ignoring the admiring smiles of a number of women. For a moment I thought the guest was going to leave. Then he saw me and stared. Making the decision to stay, he reached for a glass, still staring. I was overwhelmed, but the stare was remorseless.

If I didn't know better I'd swear I'd been fed a secret love potion. I would never have believed that I could experience such an intense reaction to a perfect stranger. I told myself to stop behaving like an idiot. Yet all the time I was conscious of those eyes, those marvelous eyes staring at me. Without looking around I could feel their pronounced blue flame piercing me like a laser beam.

The party continued. I ate and drank without tasting. People tried to initiate conversations with me but I couldn't respond. Finally the sofa and turquoise chair on either side of me were permanently vacated. I had succeeded in driving everyone away and was probably identified as the bore of the party. I sat in anxious silence and waited.

I had to wait a long time. Guests began to leave, the party slowed to a lower gear. Fascinating conversations went on around me. Still I sat. Finally he stood next to me. I couldn't bring myself to look at him. I averted my eyes. He sat down next to me and tilted my chin so that I was forced to look at him. His eyes were no longer opaque but had melted. They were very deep and very sad. Reason didn't stand a chance; I was lost.

"It must be a witch's spell," he said quietly in a deep voice, surprisingly out of keeping with his boyish appearance.

"Witch's spell?" I repeated. As soon as the words were out of my mouth I realized that I sounded like a parrot.

The eyes twinkled briefly and then the light went out and they were sad. But the twinkle had given him away. He was aware of my feelings and probably amused by them. "Do you think I do this at every party, sit and stare at a beautiful woman?" he asked sarcastically.

That finished me off. The words, "He thinks I'm beautiful," kept racing around my head. "You can believe me, I don't," he said seriously as if he wanted to convince me. "But don't you feel it too, like a spell?" he whispered.

I nodded.

"Do you ever ask yourself," he continued, "if you come from another time, that somehow you've taken the wrong turning and arrived here, in this century by accident." He took my hand casually, unaware of the electricity this simple gesture generated.

"Andre," a voice said, startling us. The stranger dropped my hand and I looked up. His bulk implacably barring the way, Robin stood with his arms crossed. "Andre, his name is Andre," Robin said jovially, but his smile was false and his eyes wary. "I thought you two would get on," he added, a supreme understatement. "I see, Maid Marion, that you've found your Robin Hood."

"Jokes are unappreciated," Andre growled.

Robin brushed this remark aside. "No relationship should start without a formal introduction," he said. "Red fox, allow me to introduce you to Andre Piedmont. Are you reeling under the impact of the name Piedmont? It's quite famous, you know."

For a moment I thought that Andre was going to hit him. I said hastily, "Piedmont, no, I don't believe I've ever heard it before." As soon as I said this, I felt stupid again. "Another gaffe," I thought. To me Piedmont was a region in Italy, although I hadn't the faintest notion where. North? South? But obviously it was a name every New Yorker had heard of, except me; I really felt like a small-town girl.

Robin laughed. "She's never heard of the Piedmonts, Andre."

"Little fox," he said to me, "ask him to tell you about them some day. You are sitting next to the heir to the great but declining Piedmont fortune, scion of one of America's oldest and most eccentric families."

The remark sounded innocent, even flattering, but Andre leaped up, instinctively graceful, like a wildcat. "Let's get out of here," he muttered to me.

"Now Andre," Robin said placatingly. But Andre merely looked at him with contempt and pulled me up from the sofa. His "Come on" was peremptory. I didn't have to go, dragged off in this unseemly way. I looked sheepishly at Robin. He had invited me to his party, had treated me with kindness. It was rude to abandon Robin and follow this Andre Piedmont, whoever he was, but I couldn't stop myself.

As I walked past Robin, he whispered, "Take care, Tamara, be careful." Andre heard and paused a moment, on the verge of speaking. I had the horrible feeling he was about to push me away. His face was somber and he watched me for a long minute. Apparently, he was equally helpless, for he grabbed my arm again and hurried me out of the apartment.

"Andre," Robin shouted urgently, as we rushed to the street. "It isn't fair, Andre. Oh damn," he said quietly in frustration as the door clicked behind us. The hot night air hit our nostrils and we paused on the noisy street. A dog barked in a nearby apartment. An elderly gentleman out for a stroll gave us a disinterested glance. The doormen from the neighboring buildings looked at us with open curiosity. They decided we must be rich and straightened up instinctively. They were right about one of us; heir to the Piedmont fortune. I decided that I didn't care about that in the slightest. I would love him as fiercely if he told me he was on the dole. "Andre"—I said the name over to myself, rolling the two syllables in my mouth. It suited him. His parents must have been perceptive people who knew that their baby deserved an extraordinary name. Then he looked at me and all thoughts of any kind simply vanished.

"Taxi?" he asked. "Or walk."

I answered, "I love to walk."

"I knew that," he said, "for I prefer walking; but in the country, not here."

"The country," I said quietly, pastoral memories from childhood turning me nostalgic. I remembered lilac bushes. Briefly, I rejected New York. Then Andre took my hand again and there was nowhere else I wanted to be, no other person I wanted to trade places with.

We walked in perfect silence. New York City had become, for us, a holy cathedral. But as lovers do, we were really worshiping ourselves. A witch's spell? "I may as well believe in magic," I thought. "It's as good an explanation as any for falling in love at first sight."

It was after the snow fell, gilding stoops and garbage cans

with marshmallow, that I became a bride. It had been an odd courtship. In all honesty, it hadn't really been a courtship at all. Through the pleasant autumn months, Andre and I had walked silently through the streets, gone to movies, or listened to music. We rarely talked, showing none of the usual self-absorbed garrulousness of lovers.

I quickly learned that Andre had "moods"; he sulked when we were together. But it didn't matter. During these months the things that had once seemed important in my life now meant nothing. The fixed star in my universe was Andre. When he was present I was happy, when he was absent I was miserable. When he asked me to marry him (something I'd never thought possible), I didn't think twice; I went hopping off to the marriage bureau at once. My grandmother literally must have shuddered in her grave. I knew that it was idiotic to marry a man one knows nothing about, to throw caution and common sense to the winds, and although I repeated this wise advice to myself, it didn't make the slightest difference.

Andre and I spent one month in my apartment like a normal married couple. Every morning I'd make breakfast and while we ate, Andre looked at the newspaper and I looked at him. Then we'd play records and sit on the small couch, staring out the window at the traffic. We'd light a fire in the tiny fireplace which upped my rent shockingly. Then we'd read or take a walk. It was amazing how little I knew about Andre; his past, his interests, his family. But I quickly learned that any probing sent him into an irritable "mood." I didn't dare risk this so I asked no questions.

For all I knew our New York life was to continue forever, but one night the inevitable occurred. Andrew threw a book aside and leaned back, closing his eyes. "I wish we could stay here forever," he said, and then sat up sharply. "However," he said with a crooked grin which distorted the symmetry of his face, "tomorrow I must return home to Stonehaven. Coming?"

I was astounded. "What do you mean, am I coming? Of course, I'm coming." After a while it became clear that Andre didn't intend to explain further. "Perhaps I ought to pack," I said moronically, as if I were going around the corner for an hour instead of setting off to my permanent home.

"Don't bring much," Andre said. "Stonehaven has everything you'll need." There was an ironic cutting edge to his voice. For the first time I felt a twinge of discomfort, a re-

minder from my critical faculties that I'd ignored them for
some time now.

That night was the last time I slept in my poor but loved
sanctuary. As I drifted off to sleep I imagined I saw Stonehaven; an ESP bolt. I pictured a beautiful stone house, surrounded by flowers, with painted shutters and a chimney
pouring out smoke, a charming house, a caressing house.
Home. I smiled to myself as I fell asleep; so much for ESP.

The next morning found me sitting next to Andre in a
small red sports car I had never seen before. A minimum of
luggage had been piled in. I left the key to my apartment
with a downstairs neighbor. She promised to guard my flat
from prowling addicts and lunatics. The car roared, I fought
down tears, and we were off.

"Good-bye, New York," I whispered as we drove through
nearby streets and past adjacent neighborhoods. There were
crowds and dogs and playgrounds and children. Ethnic food
markets tempted us to stop. But Andre drove on competently, turning on the radio. Its mechanical voice filled the
space between us. "Andre always keeps a wedge between us,"
I thought, feeling annoyed with him for the first time. That
made two twitches of normal feeling in two days. Could I be
returning to my old self?

We were bumping along the bricks of the West Side Highway. There was the George Washington Bridge, suspended
magnificently over the once mighty and now reeking Hudson.
We crossed the bridge to the Palisades beyond, still beautiful
and deceptively indestructible. Now there was real snow, the
mildness of a New York City winter was behind us. The sky
was no longer yellow. We turned off onto the throughway in
heavy traffic. Cars exited for suburban villas and develop-
ments, or palatial shopping centers.

The small, ancient mountains were ahead, beyond the com-
muting suburbs. I waited expectantly. The house of my
dreams should lie just around the bend from this streamlined
modern highway which had replaced the old Route 17 to the
Catskills. The house would be far enough to escape noise and
soot but close enough for convenience. Any house in these
parts would be frank and open, with neighbors on either side,
for our road led to popular resorts and hotels. The region
was not at all mysterious; it was still within the orbit of New
York City.

Then the strangeness began. Past the exit marked Middletown we turned off into a snow-covered pastoral scene, followed a back road, and drove from this back road to another. For miles we climbed hills and passed frozen streams. I could have sworn we remained on this planet, but I wasn't at all sure we remained in our own time. Somehow we were driving through an American wilderness gone these two hundred years. Narrow dirt roads twisted through the trees like a maze; I saw many deer and once glimpsed a black bear lumbering along. Occasionally we passed a small house. Rocks were everywhere, placed to form huge quartering walls, walls which kept the cows in and the intruders out.

The roads became ruinously icy. Still Andre drove competently as ever. It began to snow. I glanced at him. He crouched lower in the seat, the melancholy lines of his face deepened. "Why is it so deserted here?" I asked myself. Suddenly, Andre braked the car, throwing me forward. We were at the crossing of two roads.

"Look," he said in a voice bleak as the scene around us. We had arrived at our destination. My heart sank, for above us stood Stonehaven, intimidating the surrounding countryside.

Chapter II

━━━━◄━◆━►━━━━

Stonehaven stands on a hill at the confluence of two country roads in the rural district of Woodlands. Who would imagine that a house of such magnitude would stand here, has, in fact, stood here for two hundred years. Even after I grew accustomed to Stonehaven there was an inevitable moment of disbelief when I returned; from town, the market, or visiting. I never failed to approach it carefully, either by car or on foot. I was never so foolish as to take it lightly.

I finally decided that Stonehaven appears formidable because it was conceived by a graceless mind. It has grandeur and stature but is somehow off-center, square where it should be rounded, illogically cornered and angled. Actually squat.

An abandoned sawmill lies at the base of the hill just across the road. This mill is part tree again, a crumbling ruin which straddles a clear stream. Yet the mill looks unnatural, as if quickly crushed, not slowly eroded. I had the bizarre fantasy that the house had destroyed the mill.

To the left of Stonehaven is a lake. It looks perfectly charming until one of the local people reels off the drownings. These untimely deaths have given the lake a proud place in local history. The most famous victim was a poet who used to vacation in Woodlands until the summer of 1912 when he went for a midnight swim and never returned. The local inhabitants like to show tourists where the poet lived. His summer cottage has disappeared but the crumbling foundation remains. Some day it will be an archaeological site and it waits for the spade to dig up shards, fragments, and maybe an old skeleton or two.

To the right of Stonehaven is a small pond, which should be precious because it is fed by a mountain spring, but long ago a caretaker with a sense of humor filled it with catfish. They found the environment ideal, were fruitful, multiplied, and grew monstrous big. There is no pleasure in sitting beside the pond now.

I have heard people say that the house looks at its worst in winter but improves in springtime. I don't agree. To me the perfect forms of flowers only accentuate the distortions of Stonehaven; irises and day lilies, no matter how profuse, can't erase the impact of the pines. These huge wintry trees grew close and protective around the house, grazing its windows, keeping it dark, imprisoning it behind a natural wall. The pines dominate all rivals, including the maples which were planted to ignite the grounds into a fire of red and gold in the autumn, but it never quite works. Even in the fall the primary color is dark green, for the pines march back and to the sides of the house and then become an enormous wooded army for thousands of acres.

On that first winter day, the pines provided the only reminder of the color of growing things, for the earth was bleached white by snow and the house and the sky were the same dull gray. The exterior of Stonehaven prepared me for the vast gloomy rooms inside. In keeping with the style of the house I expected a formal confrontation with servants. There they'd be, like characters in an English novel, lined up in two even rows, waiting for the first social gaffe of their new mistress. But these were American servants who had the pride of independent country people settled for generations. Therefore, there were no fawning retainers to greet us, just employees seeing to their work. They were too busy to do more than nod and smile as they passed. So it was Andre who escorted me through the downstairs rooms, Andre who showed me to our bedroom, and Andre who mumbled bits of historic lore. He made a grim and mocking tour guide.

By the time we reached our own bedroom I was stunned. My grandmother's house and apartment were all I had ever known. They were modest dwellings. In order to absorb the scale of Stonehaven I tried to erase my impressions of enormous fireplaces and high, beamed ceilings. Most of all I needed time to adjust to the portraits, portraits of the lofty Piedmont ancestors. There were endless tiers of them; their eyes followed me as I walked. These paintings made Stonehaven a house dominated by the dead.

Since our bedroom was much too grand for either intimacy or comfort, a showplace to be roped off and displayed to tourists, I knew I'd have to find another room for myself where I could be comfortable. In this room I would always feel that architecture students were peering into corners, that voyeurs waited outside in the hall to get a peek. Dismally, I sat staring at the fireplace and occasionally glanced out the window at the snow, falling in thick, damp clots.

"Why didn't you tell me?" I asked Andre very quietly.

"Tell you what?" His voice was creaky as if Stonehaven made it difficult for him to speak.

"What it's like here. I suppose I should have guessed but it was beyond my imagination to conceive of it."

He looked at me. "You feel like that already."

And for the first time since I'd met Andre, he talked about himself. "If you feel this immediately, Tamara, imagine what it was like to live here as a child. I was born in this house. It was always too big, too cold. There were too many objects for a child to break: too much noise echoed in the big rooms. There was space and freedom only in the woods. Friends, too. As a child, I never had a human companion, only wild animals that I tamed myself. That's why I love the forests of Woodlands but I hate Stonehaven."

For a moment I was too startled by the intensity of his feelings to say anything. Finally I asked, "Why stay, Andre?"

I walked to him and took his arm. "Let's go away. We could go anywhere you want."

"I might lose my inheritance."

"Then lose it; we can both work."

"Unfortunately, it's not that simple. I have obligations, responsibilities. Many families depend on me to keep things in order. Did you think I lived a life of total idleness, Tamara? Sorry to disillusion you, but the estate, Father's investments, the house itself all take a great deal of work. I am a Piedmont and I was raised to take my place as my father took his before me, so please don't talk like a child. I can't cut and run just because I don't like the life I must live."

The cutting tone of his voice upset me. "Please don't blame me, Andre. I was trying to find a solution . . ."

"What did you think when you married me, Tamara, what fantasies did you have? That I was a rich motorcycle racer or an arch criminal on the run, that life with me would be romantic. I am what I said I was, a man who belongs to an earlier time, a steward shackled to my estate. In marrying me you married Stonehaven, too. You've been here only an hour and you're already whining to leave."

He slammed out of the bedroom while I cried. Later someone brought me a cold supper which I couldn't eat. Time passed. When it was very late I climbed into the huge bed alone. It was unfamiliar, too soft for my taste and the caressing satin sheets seemed a wasteful luxury. Sometime after I was asleep, Andre joined me, but I pretended I didn't know he was there and we slept with a wall of ice between us while outside the night winds howled, with nothing in their way except Stonehaven itself.

Of course we patched it up the next day, and Andre did try to keep his temper. As a peace gesture he introduced me to Crispin. Crispin is a white Persian cat with red eyes and a luxurious tail that expresses what he thinks. Crispin was clearly Andre's cat and wouldn't come to me. I'm ashamed to admit that I was jealous of Crispin because Andre treated him with a tender gentleness he rarely showed me.

Andre offered to continue our tour of the house by showing me the portraits and although he tried to joke about them, he radiated tense anxiety. I humored him to prevent the onset of a black mood by joking too, and pretended that we were having a lighthearted good time. Crispin snaked his way between Andre's legs as we walked.

"Who is that?" I asked, staring at a large Wagnerian woman with dark hair. She seemed to watch me as closely as I watched her. "That," Andre said, "is Anne Piedmont, dowager and snob who moved to Berlin in the twenties with her husband, an industrialist. She was one of the few aristocrats who admired Hitler uncritically, and she became a German citizen when World War Two broke out. They say that she worked for the Gestapo."

This biographical sketch depressed me and I changed the subject. "My goodness, some of these pictures look just like you, Andre. You really are a time-traveler."

For a moment his eyes went dead. "The family resemblance, what you might call the Piedmont face," he explained.

"Who is this one?" I asked, interrupting because I'd found a portrait of a woman dressed and bejeweled in the style of the sixteenth century. "She's posed like Anne of Cleves. But how funny, Andre, she's got your face. It looks like you peeking out from behind those jewels."

"That," Andre said, "is a painting done by Holbein." He poked it affectionately and I winced. "You don't treat her very formally," I said.

"Why should I?" he answered. "She's no stranger, I've known her all my life. She was French, of royal blood. Henry the Eighth had this portrait commissioned so he could decide whether to marry her or not. One look at the illustrious Piedmont visage and Henry said no, loudly."

"I'd say she was lucky."

"Not too lucky. She died in childbirth two years later. Even Henry might have kept her around that long."

"Henry the Eighth! How far back does your family go?"

"Henry is quite recent. None of our portraits go back any further but there are old records and legends. One antiquarian has seriously suggested," Andre laughed, "that the Piedmonts can be traced back to the Crusades. He claims we rode with Counts Raymond and Baldwin. Imagine seeing this face pop up in Jerusalem, that must have given the heathens courage. What, all the way from Europe and that's the best you can do?"

"Sounds like you go back to the Flood?"

"At least."

"But not all of the paintings look like you. Here's one that's dark. A totally different type. Somber."

"Old Uncle Ebeneezer, one of the capitalist Piedmonts. Made fortunes for the family, which were rapidly lost by the profligate Piedmonts. We're not nearly as rich as we once were and we owe this decline to scoundrels like Cousin Horace here. Turned orphans and widows out penniless into the cruel Edwardian world, and seduced every chambermaid he met. He was one of the English Piedmonts; they're the most dissolute lot of all."

"Did he come to a bad end?"

"Not him. Everybody he cheated did. No, he wound up dying at nearly ninety in a brothel with his boots off. I rather admire him myself."

"I hope you haven't inherited his bad habits."

"No, not his," Andre said and his voice went grim again. Then he laughed. "Oh, the stories that are told about the Piedmonts. Old families attract rumors like magnets attract clips." His eyes slid sideways, giving him a sheepish look. "If you hear any silly old wives' tales about Piedmont scandals, you won't believe them, will you, Tamara?"

"No," I lied, "I won't believe them." I lowered my voice so the house couldn't hear me. The house always grew quiet when anyone laughed, as if intrigued by the novelty of the sound. If the Piedmonts could make Stonehaven their family seat, they could be guilty of any crime attributed to them.

I became interested in the portraits and in the following weeks paraded solemnly past them. The Piedmonts were a remarkable lot. Like geometric shapes, their faces were distinct and persistent. It was a little disconcerting to see so few elderly Piedmonts represented, a mere sprinkling of gray-beards, but I reminded myself that until modern times most people were lucky to reach middleage, much less to surpass it.

The reason I studied the portraits so conscientiously was to take my mind off Andre. Despite an occasional gesture of friendliness he grew more distant and aloof each day. Every morning when I left our bedroom I'd think, "Why did he marry me?" and I wondered if he were asking himself the same question. To be fair, he was busy; they were constantly asking him to see to this or that. I saw him working in his study often enough but I practically had to request a formal interview to get in. He was lawyer, landlord, CPA, tax consultant, and IBM computer all rolled into one, and instead of rushing to his new bride when his work was done, he paced the upper floors of the house or played music in the nursery. I was never invited there, although it was his favorite room.

So with nothing to keep me busy, I was in everybody's way. Being lonely, I cultivated Crispin's friendship. He twitched his tail sympathetically while I waited for Andre's attention, but I rarely got it. I'd stare at the snow and think wistfully of trading this opulence for my New York apartment, but it was no use. I loved Andre and, if anything, he was even more fascinating at Stonehaven than he'd been in the city. I forgot my pride. If Andre decided he wanted me to leave, he'd have to hire kidnappers to remove me. I couldn't give up the improbable idea that "things would somehow work out."

I explored the main sections of the house and located a charming circular room. I moved in my books, my grandmother's favorite trinkets, and a comfortable chair. I had to live with the elaborate silver and crystal and I could do nothing about the Victorian furniture someone had chosen for the room, for I didn't have the courage to rearrange Stonehaven yet.

My one achievement was discovering Woodlands. Because the region is so uninhabited, it is an ecological miracle. I love walking in the woods and I went out every day; the snow didn't stop me. Forests are at their most beautiful in the winter and I found trails, climbed over stone walls, and went bushwhacking with only landmarks to guide me. When the snow was deep I went cross-country skiing or wore snowshoes, Indian style. On icy days I attached grippers to my boots. The clearer it became that I was persona non grata at the house, the more I went into the countryside. I was gone until nightfall on warmer days. I came to agree with Andre; it was easy to love Woodlands, and easy to hate Stonehaven.

I first noticed the portrait when I came in from a long walk. I was out of breath and on my way to have tea when I decided to go to the bedroom to get an extra sweater. Despite central heating and roaring fireplaces Stonehaven is cold. A damp chill never leaves it. Too big to heat properly, I suppose.

I saw the painting as I left the bedroom. Clearly it had been here for ages but there were so many pictures around it, under and over it, that I had never singled it out. Now that I noticed it, I couldn't ignore it and I stopped to look. It was the portrait of an eighteenth-century American gentleman. I don't know how I recognized that he was American except that the painting was primitive, even distorted, and an English country gentleman of the same period would have had access to a better draftsman. The portrait's face was the basic Piedmont face again, and yet it was not. The lips were too thick, the nose highly arched, and the brows over the eyes were heavy. But the eyes were right, blue and electric. It was hard not to look at the eyes; they seemed to want you to.

The picture wasn't that different from the others; maybe this artist just had a better knack of catching the sitter's personality. But it stayed with me and I found myself going back to the painting often. Once I tapped it, half-afraid that my hand would touch flesh.

I couldn't resist asking Andre about it one night, when we were together in my special little room. From time to time Andre would find me and take me walking, or he would lie with his head on my lap, while we both watched the flames in the fireplace. Such times were rare but they kept hope alive.

"Who is that woman with the red hair in the portrait near the library?" I asked. "Red hair is so unusual in your family that she's got my curiosity aroused."

"Ssh," Andre said, grabbing my wrist. He wanted quiet.

"Answer me," I coaxed, growing confident.

Andre sighed. "Why do women always want to talk? Okay. She was my aunt Helena Piedmont, widely loved in Woodlands. She tended the sick, taught the children, and was generally believed to be a good witch practicing white magic. The people here are superstitious; they're mountain folk, not urban types."

"They can't be that naïve; it's the twentieth century. I've noticed some modern little houses around here with new cars parked in the driveways."

"Surface dirt. Scratch below and you'll find they still believe in impossible things."

The subject was changing itself and I had a leading question to ask. Casually, I inquired, "Speaking of portraits, what about that odd-looking eighteenth-century gentleman in the hall outside our bedroom. Do you know who I mean?"

There was a pause and it went on so long I realized that Andre knew perfectly well who I referred to. He stared at me intensely and I flushed, thankful for the dim firelight. His face was serious.

"Naturally, you'd have noticed him," Andre said flatly. "Well, you might as well know. He's the black sheep of the family. Piedmont history is riddled with scandal but he was the absolute worst. His name was Geoffrey Piedmont and he lived here at Stonehaven before the Revolutionary War. This was wilderness in those days and the house was spanking new. Woodlands was a frontier: there were Indian raids; scarlet fever epidemics. It was sparsely settled, although here and there the tired traveler could find an inn. This area and those around it were divided into huge estates, copies of European models, owned by rich, landed families who lorded it over the peasantry. As it turned out, this peasantry was really a yeomanry. The farmers and laborers were no serfs and the landed gentry never got away with what they did in the old country.

"Which brings us to Geoffrey. He was literate, a graceful dancer, and handy with a gun. In short, he had all the virtues of an American gentleman of his time. But he was insane; there's no other explanation. As a child he was supremely willful. Later he became sadistic. He liked to maim horses and beat servants. In those days maiming horses was considered the worse crime. Men felt an affection for horses then that they reserve for cars now. That made hurting a good steed all the more fun for Geoffrey."

"Monstrous! What happened to him?"

"He went too far and got caught. He was a rake, not in our modern comic-opera sense of the word. He was no lovable MacHeath out of *The Beggar's Opera*. In those days the word 'rake' had cruel implications. A rake wasn't a seducer, he was a rapist. Fathers locked their daughters in the house when he came round, and no girl with any sense would walk alone in the woods."

"This couldn't have gone on long."

"It didn't. One summer, Geoffrey's father, a decent, honorable man, sent his son up to the Manor, about forty miles from here, in a last-ditch reform effort. The Manor was the seat of the richest and most important New York family of its day: the Remingtons. If a change of scene didn't cure the boy his father was prepared to send him to the madhouse. This may not sound unselfish to you but the rich weren't expected to follow the same rules of conduct as the poor and Geoffrey was heir to a major eastern estate. If he'd confined himself to his usual brutalities he might have escaped scot-free.

"But a strange thing happened. The incorrigible criminal underwent a metamorphosis. He fell in love with a farm laborer's daughter. Rumor has it that she was very beautiful. She was also virtuous. Though he did his best to woo her and behaved impeccably for the whole summer, Geoffrey never succeeded in seducing her. Marriage was out of the question, for it was unthinkable that a farm laborer's daughter could become mistress of Stonehaven. Since she couldn't be his wife, the girl refused Geoffrey's other offers. He was broken-hearted and everyone hoped grief would reform him. The girl became a heroine for curing him of his evil."

"Did she? Did she cure him?"

"A delusion. One hot rainy day shortly before Geoffrey was to return home to Woodlands a new man, he kidnapped the girl from her father's house and took her into the woods. He raped her repeatedly, tortured her, and cut off her head."

"That's a horrible story. I hope he was punished."

"He was, with a rope around his neck. But not until he'd sent the girl's head to her childhood sweetheart, a poor, hard-working farmer. The shock sent the farmer into a rigid trance, what we today call a catatonic state, and he never came out of it."

"And Geoffrey?"

"He rode home perfectly cheerful, feeling proud of himself. He thought he could sneak back into Woodlands, secretly collect a few followers, and ride off. Now that he knew what evil he was capable of, he was confident that he could make his way in the world. There's always a market for professional killers. As a hired murderer he would have the money and leisure time necessary to perform an occasional act of . . . curiosity or impulse. But he underestimated the underground chain of gossip which is amazingly effective in rural districts. By the time he got to Woodlands, a crowd of angry men were waiting for him. They hanged him right then and there, in the woods, at his favorite trysting place.

"The grisly incident destroyed his mother and made his father a recluse. It cast a cloud over Stonehaven for decades, which may account for its unpleasant personality. But at least the fair maiden was properly avenged and that is the end of the story."

Andre got up and stoked the fire with an iron poker.

"Then why have his picture up?"

"He was a Piedmont; he has his place on the wall with the rest. Some day I, too, will be embalmed there, one of the gallery. Not a very pleasant afterlife to look forward to. Perhaps I'll never have my portrait painted and they'll be forced to stick up a photograph."

Andre paced up and down, restlessly. I bit my lips but I couldn't keep the words back. "Andre, are you sure that's all?"

"What the hell does that mean?" he asked, spinning around.

"An ancient story is like a plant that sends off shoots. All kinds of weird legends and addenda get attached to it. I can't believe there isn't more. Besides you're agitated. It upset you to tell me that story. Why? I know it's hideous but it happened over two hundred years ago. Yet you act like it's fresh, recent."

Instantly I knew I'd said too much. A screen of frost was between us. He stood still and stared at me with eyes so troubled I looked away.

He said quietly, "You're too perceptive, too smart. You're right. There is more. While they were hanging him, Geoffrey laughed. The pain didn't bother him. They had to retie the noose and hang him all over again to get him to die. But before he strangled, he cursed the Piedmonts and that curse has followed us down the centuries. We're an unhappy family with those among us who like to blame the curse instead of themselves for their unhappiness. But damn it, do you have to drag it out of me like this? Can't you see that I don't want to talk about it or think about it?"

"Why is everything I do wrong?" I said, putting my head in my hands. Silently Andre watched me, but he didn't comfort me. Instead he said quietly, almost in a whisper, "I sometimes wonder if I didn't make a mistake, marrying you." Then he walked out of the room.

Each word hit like a slam and I wept luxuriously. I could picture the judge in the divorce court, allotting me alimony payments. There I'd be, holding a sheaf of legal papers, all I'd have left to remind me of my marriage to Andre. I had behaved like a fool from the night I met him and my grandmother was right: a fool gets what she deserves.

Chapter III

In the end I went to Mrs. Parsons. Mrs. Parsons was general housekeeper at Stonehaven, an aging girl Friday who had risen to her position by outlasting everyone else. She was a local woman who had come to the house as a kitchen maid in her early teens and had simply stayed on, doing any work, pitching in for any person. This included the baby nurse, for Mrs. Parsons had helped raise Andre.

She was friendly to me because she was generous and kind and because I was mistress of Stonehaven. She had devoted her life to the Piedmont family. When I felt depressed I would talk with her, for the atmosphere of the house didn't seem to oppress her; she was invariably pleasant and a little silly. She'd bustle about, a round, white-haired woman, just this side of old age, and wherever she went, uniformly dressed in white blouse and black skirt, she banished chills and cobwebs.

I decided to ask her about the Piedmont curse. She was dusting delicate ceramic figures when I found her, looking like a fairy godmother waving a feather duster in place of a wand.

"May I trouble you for a moment, Mrs. Parsons?"

She looked up, courteous yet curious. I hesitated. How could I ask about the Piedmont curse? It was a distinctly melodramatic subject. "She'll probably laugh at me," I thought.

"I want to talk to you about Geoffrey Piedmont," I said, getting right to the point. "Isn't there some story about a curse connected with him?"

Mrs. Parsons liked to gossip. She chuckled with delight. Apparently, she considered Geoffrey a local treasure: Woodland's own Loch Ness monster. She wasn't at all reluctant to talk about him.

"So you've heard about him at last," she said with satisfaction. She put her feather duster aside and settled down for a

26

good long talk. "The Piedmonts are a remarkable family, ma'am. A branch of the Piedmonts came over to America early, not on the *Mayflower* but on the next boat out. They were mainly rich merchants, but one was a nobleman, not very high up but important enough; I can't imagine what he gained by leaving England. Like the rest of the family he broke away from the Anglican Church. Eventually, the Catholic Piedmonts arrived in Maryland, while the Puritan Piedmonts went to Massachusetts. Whatever the different reasons, they were all in trouble with the authorities in England and they all got out fast.

"Geoffrey Piedmont was the first child born at Stonehaven, a direct descendent of the English nobleman. The family had owned an estate here in Woodlands for generations before Geoffrey's birth. But until Stonehaven the houses were all built of wood and they burned down. Geoffrey's father was an ideal master. While he lived, the people prospered. He worked hard, lived quietly, and treated his tenants decently. Woodlands was a model community, an example of what life could be in the New World.

"Then the master had a son, and what a son. You wouldn't believe the things he did, ma'am. When he was a child no animal or baby was safe near him. His poor father was in despair. The boy grew up so cruel, he was accused of practicing witchcraft. Understandably, for besides committing evil sins he did strange things. He was seen in the woods at night picking herbs and flowers. He was caught dancing with twelve naked women in a circle. Once, past midnight, a man went out searching for his daughter and found Geoffrey in the cemetery practicing necromancy."

Mrs. Parsons was skeptical. "I'm not convinced about the witchcraft myself." Her voice was grim. "What Geoffrey did was worse than black magic. His father would have been relieved if his son did nothing more than sign a pact with the devil. The Piedmonts were rich and powerful and they protected Geoffrey for a long time. But even they couldn't save him forever. Geoffrey was caught and hanged here in these woods."

"Isn't that when the curse started, Mrs. Parsons?"

"Yes," she answered, "and it's hung over the Piedmonts ever since, like a dagger. The hanging was bungled. That was common enough in those days. And, to give him his due, Geoffrey was brave, he never showed fear. He laughed to scare everybody and said that his death would haunt the Piedmonts. He cursed them, saying that he was leaving them his evil nature as an inheritance. It would reappear in each generation. One male and one male only would become another Geoffrey. Nobody could predict when or whom the curse would strike."

"Horrible," I said and meant it, thinking of Andre.

"You can imagine what it did to the family. No man or woman was ever at peace, for the curse could afflict any son at any time. Sometimes the evil didn't show until a boy was grown. No wife could be sure of her husband, no mother be sure of her child. No man could trust himself, his sons, or his grandsons. And the horror is that the curse won't end until the entire line dies out."

"Why do they have children?"

She looked at me disapprovingly. "You can't expect a whole family to be celibate, ma'am. That's not realistic. Besides, the curse is tricky. One man might never marry and still the evil would blossom in him. Perhaps not until he was past forty or fifty. Another would marry young and his wife bear eight sons, each free of the curse and each happy. Happy, that is, until each became a father in his own turn and had to fear for his own boys. I tell you the curse has corrupted the family, sowing fear, suspicion, and jealousy. It's like a disease carried in the blood or through the genes. Geoffrey knew what he was doing when he made that curse."

"Perhaps the curse really is a disease," I said, "and has nothing to do with Geoffrey. He may have known that he had a hereditary illness which would afflict other members of the family. He probably cursed the Piedmonts just to be dramatic. Or there may be no disease and Geoffrey's curse set off a hysterical chain reaction with people acting cursed because they believe they've been cursed. There's undoubtedly a medical or psychiatric explanation which fits the facts."

Mrs. Parsons looked at me without expression. "Those ideas have been suggested before. But whether the curse is real or not, the Piedmonts have had many disasters. The family's seen insanity, murder, incest. Ironically, through it all, there have been Piedmonts who lived normally as there are Piedmonts living normally today. Some of these lucky ones scoff at the curse, say that it's nonsense, and insist that every old family has skeletons in the closet. To me they sound like people trying to convince themselves, people who can't silence nagging doubts."

"Why do they leave Geoffrey's portrait up?" I asked.

"I don't know, ma'am, and I've often asked myself the same question. But no member of the family has ever ordered any portrait removed. Each hangs in its own place unless it's being cleaned or lent to a gallery. That's the one iron-clad rule at Stonehaven."

"Then I'll be the first mistress of the house to break that rule," I said. "Please see that the picture of Geoffrey Piedmont is removed at once, Mrs. Parsons, because I don't want to see the face in that portrait again. I'll explain to my husband if there are any objections." I sounded confident, but it took all my courage to assert my authority.

Mrs. Parsons was shocked. "None of the paintings have ever been removed, ma'am," she repeated. Tradition thrives unchallenged at Stonehaven.

"Please do as I ask," I said, more forcefully than necessary because I felt insecure.

"Very well," she acquiesced, "I'll see to it now," and she left. I avoided my bedroom until I was too tired to stay awake. At 3:00 A.M. I walked along the corridor half-expecting to find the portrait still in place. I was immensely relieved to see an empty rectangular space where the picture had been.

"And that's the end of that," I said decisively. And prematurely.

Chapter IV

It was at dinner that Andre said quite casually, "I see that Geoffrey's picture has been removed from its accustomed place. Was that your idea?"

"Yes. I don't want to see it again."

"In that case, you did the sensible thing. Though I doubt that you'll feel any more at ease. Stonehaven has never allowed anyone to banish its ghosts. You can turn your back on them but then they just hide behind you, waiting for you to turn around and look."

When Andre mocked me I could never think of anything to say. So I dipped my spoon into the chilled cream soup and ignored him. Inside, I raged. My feelings were imprisoned in an ice cage, which they couldn't melt. On the outside, the entire room, including me, formed a winter scene. The table was long, its cloth sparkling white. The chandelier sparked dazzling cold glints of light. Even the heavy silver spoon in my hand felt cold. I must have looked very composed, like a statue crafted of snow, and Andre, so blond, looked like a pale elf out of a forest of fir trees, way to the north.

My emotions, however, pounded to get out. I wanted to ask, "Andre, do you care for me in any sense, do you even like me? Do you want me to leave?" But I didn't dare ask. I was afraid. What, for example, if he said, "Yes, go now. I've been wondering why you didn't ask me sooner." What would I do? I would probably have to leave. So I simply continued eating, course after course, while Andre remained aloof and preoccupied. What is that famous Shakespearian line about conscience making cowards out of us? Apparently love has the same effect.

The arrival of dessert made me realize that I had consumed an entire meal without tasting a bite. I launched a miniature rebellion against Stonehaven by stabbing the fine Piedmont linen napkin crumpled and soaking in my coffee cup with my fork. With luck, I could put a few holes in it.

"Stop that, that's childish," Andre snapped.

I looked up, surprised. After dining with a silent mannequin, you hardly expect it to turn on you and shout.

"Tamara, I am frankly getting sick to death of your moods."

"My moods?"

The Piedmont eyes turned on full power, glowing like a Siamese cat's do, when caught in the glare of headlights. "I've tried to be patient with you. I know that I'm difficult to live with, that Stonehaven is no place for you, but it would help if you would stop treating me as if I'm some sort of monster. You always look as if you're waiting for the next blow."

"I can hardly believe that you're finally talking like this to me."

"Are you angry with me?"

"Angry! Andre, I'm delighted. You have no idea what morose thoughts I had all through dinner. You barely seemed to notice that I was here."

"Listen, Tamara. Tomorrow, let's get out of Stonehaven for awhile. Let's walk in the woods the way we used to walk in New York City. Remember?"

"Vividly."

"I'll put off all my work and we'll pretend that we're a thousand miles from Stonehaven." He pushed his chair back and stood up. "There are things I must get to tonight. But I promise tomorrow. Pray for good weather."

I recited every prayer my grandmother had ever taught me.

And perhaps they worked, for the next morning was perfect. A thaw had come. In the country a thaw is an event. It's like finding an oasis in the desert. The air takes on the smell and feel of springtime. A springtime crueller than April, for winter will be back. But while it lasts this false spring is beautiful. The small animals of the woods, the squirrels and raccoons, move again. The deer are sighted, leaving the woods and taking to the open fields again where the snow has melted off and the good green of earth is seen again.

Warmly dressed, with Crispin following us part of the way, Andre and I soon wandered deep into the woods, away from roads and people, and most of all, away from Stonehaven. The sun was so bright that diamonds sparkled in the snow. Yet this cold and distant sun was in a sky as blue as the Mediterranean Sea off the south of France. On the earth itself, the holly and the ivy defeated winter's plan: to turn Nature into a Harlequin of shadow and snow.

What a day we had! We were like two children, let out of school for Christmas vacation. We told each other idiotic jokes, laughed for no reason, threw snowballs, even played King of the Mountain along ancient stone walls. Stonehaven was a dictatorial nanny and we were cleverly evading her powers.

So we went farther into Woodlands, hacking our way through shrubs, winding in and out of trees, blazing our own trail. Like Hansel's breadcrumbs, our footsteps in the snow showed where we had been and how to return.

Instinctively, we stopped when we came to the heart of the forest. Except for an occasional chickadee, all was silent. Even here there were stone walls. Once they had enclosed open fields. Now they looked artificial, useless and silly. Stones dividing the forest into square segments. They made the woods look like a Bonsai garden created by giants.

"Don't tell me they once farmed as far as this?" I asked.

"Woodlands was once fairly populous. Many an old wives' tale predicted that it would be lumbered and farmed until every tree was gone."

"Perhaps the soil was too rocky."

"Perhaps. The farmers were a hardy and stoic lot, though. Not likely to be driven out by a few rocks in the soil."

"Well, whatever the reasons, I'm glad Woodlands survived. I love it." I rubbed my hand along the dry bark of a young birch tree the color of pewter.

"Poor Tamara, imprisoned in Stonehaven. It's turning you into a Snow Queen. It does that to all the mistresses of the house, fashioning them in its special image."

"I don't want that to happen."

"It wouldn't suit you. You remind me of Ceres, the Roman goddess. No matter how final winter seemed, she always returned to resurrect the earth."

Standing still made us conscious of the cold, still air. Tentatively, Andre touched my hair. "Or perhaps you're more like a nymph. It's hard to say. But you do look like you belong here, a native species of Woodlands."

"A firebird?"

"That's it. A ruby-crowned firebird, bringing the springtime, by magic. Next, you'll be sprinkling flowers and melting the ice."

"You make it sound very tidy. You've conveyed the image of a supernatural housekeeper."

"Mother Nature is very tidy. She looks exactly like Mary Poppins."

"Ridiculous. I think the cold air has gone to your brain."

"Not the air, Tamara, but the lengthening shadows. I'm afraid we have to go back."

And so we did, reluctantly. And the nearer we came to Stonehaven, the more unreal the day became. By the time we reached the edge of the woods, I couldn't trust my own memory of it. Had we really forgotten about the curse? Did we really romp and joke and have a good time? And had Andre been friendly and kind? I could feel him shutting me out, locking himself into his own thoughts again before we reached the house.

We arrived there just before nightfall. It would be a night for star-gazers. Only in winter are the stars bright over Woodlands. In the summer a slight haze obscures them. Tonight they would dominate the frozen sky, flecks of ice in a cold sea. Springtime suddenly seemed very far away.

Inside the house, I realized I was freezing, and it was very pleasant when Crispin flopped into my lap. He gave me a mysterious, impassive cat look. "You have firebird eyes," I said, rubbing his warm white fur.

The delicious fire in the fireplace awakened thoughts of arson. I looked around the huge cave of a room and asked myself if I shouldn't just burn down Stonehaven. If the house read my mind, it didn't seem concerned. Undoubtedly, it was impervious to merely human attempts to destroy it. Others had probably already tried and failed.

I also reminded myself that eliminating the house wouldn't eliminate the curse. The curse transcended Stonehaven, Woodlands, even Time. The curse. Superstition. I would not let myself believe in it. Andre half-believed it. He was certainly afraid of it and so it was destroying him, slowly working at him, an undetected cancer.

The luck of the Piedmonts. And here Andre remained, heroically, Dr. Jekyll waiting for his alter ego to erupt. Why not at Stonehaven since he probably believed there was no escape? Superstition. If only there were some way to counteract the conditioning which had made Andre believe that the curse was real. And that he was its target.

For he must believe it. What else could explain his strange moods, his contradictions? What did it matter if the curse had no real power. Hadn't I read somewhere that there were natives who would actually die because of their faith in a witch doctor's power to put a fatal curse on them. Andre had that kind of irrational unconscious faith. Was there any way the light of reason could penetrate it?

"I'm getting very philosophical, Crispin," I said. But it took my mind off the sight of Andre, entering Stonehaven with the look of Atlas taking on the weight of the world. I would do whatever I could to help him fight his own fears of the curse. For the curse was taking him away from me. My strong elf of the winter sunlight had withered as soon as he returned to his own house.

Chapter V

No memory can sustain you forever. And it isn't easy to keep good resolutions. Andre's continuing rebuffs, his apparent indifference soon made me feel angry. And injured. It was all very noble fantasizing to myself that I would come to Andre's rescue, save him from his fears, stand by him in his hour of need, and all that. In reality, I couldn't get near him. He not only rejected my help, he rejected me. I felt like a psychiatrist pursuing a patient who wants no part of the therapy, who refuses the treatment that would cure him.

As the weeks passed I began asking myself again why Andre had bothered to marry me. When I reached this miserable state, Mrs. Parsons took pity on me and decided to help.

"You look glum," she said forthrightly, shoving a cup of tea into my hand. "You're much too young to sit around looking grumpy all day."

"I can't help it, Mrs. Parsons. It's this house. It makes me jumpy."

"People often say that, ma'am. I can't understand why. Look at all this beautiful wood." She knocked loudly on the woodwork next to her. "They couldn't build a house like this today. Couldn't get the materials or the craftsmen. It can't be the house."

"Maybe not."

Boldly she said, "There's an old saying in Woodlands that when the bride's unhappy the groom's to blame."

"I don't think that's an appropriate subject for us to discuss, do you?"

"I'm not one to say a word against any of the Piedmonts, especially your husband, ma'am. I raised him from a baby. Cutest thing, full of the devil." She paused, trying to be tactful. "But he's never been easy to get along with."

When I stared at her, she was looking away, radiating innocence. Only a pompous ninny could rebuke her. I had to laugh. "You're right, Mrs. Parsons, Andre is temperamental. I see that you have my best interest at heart and also that you've been plotting something. Out with it. What are you getting at?"

"You've had too much idleness, ma'am, and too much time alone."

"One of the idle rich, that's me," I said bitterly.

"It isn't good for people to mope, to worry, and concentrate on their troubles. No one gets through the world without troubles." Her voice, speaking these clichés, was sad. This surprised me. She had always sounded cheerful.

"That's true enough, Mrs. Parsons. But what can I do?"

She glowed. "I've thought it over and I have a suggestion." This was Mrs. Parsons at her finest, offering good advice. It was her greatest pleasure. Second only to giving out the juiciest of gossip, of course.

"If your husband has no time for you, Woodlands does."

"What?" The Piedmonts in their portraits were probably sneering at Mrs. Parsons' insolence now.

"The locals would be glad to meet you, ma'am. There isn't much going on here, I know. We're such a little community. But they're trying to raise money for a hospital in Orinville. And the school board's in hot trouble over outspending its budget. You, being from Stonehaven, you'd be listened to. You might be able to do some good things for Woodlands. And it would benefit you too. You'd get out and meet people, make friends. It's better than being locked in the house alone all the time, isn't it?"

A vision of my grandmother, looking self-righteous, rose before my eyes. Grandmother was no doubt in complete agreement with Mrs. Parsons. Since coming to Stonehaven I had spent all my time absorbed in myself. I had behaved like a pampered selfish child. I had been so busy brooding I hadn't even thought about my obligations as mistress of Stonehaven.

"You're right, Mrs. Parsons. As a member of the first family of Woodlands, I will henceforth drown my sorrows in good works. At least it will get me out of gloomy Stonehaven. Since it was your idea, where do you want me to begin?"

"With my good friend, Celia Gordon. She knows all about everything. A very capable woman. She'll see that you meet people. You needn't take on too much at once. Just talk to Celia. She'll get you started."

"Get me started. Well, why not?" But Mrs. Parsons was finished with our conversation. She had spotted her chief enemy, dust. Like a hunter, she moved to the kill. Fully engrossed in polishing a mahogany table leg with her apron, she barely noticed me leave the room.

Miss Gorden, never one to waste time, arrived at precisely ten o'clock the next morning. She was preceded by a flustered Mrs. Parsons who had forgotten to remove Crispin from the room. Miss Gordon's one weakness, apparently, was a severe allergy to cats.

Everything about Miss Gordon seemed to point accusingly. Her long nose, her sharp elbows, her chin. Even her knees. Sitting bolt upright directly opposite me, Miss Gordon gave the impression that her knees were making rude remarks. Her nails were long and triangular, her hair short and straight. Despite her age, it was fully black. No gray hair would dare ruin the perfect symmetry of that head.

Miss Gordon's eyes kept making sharp, quick jabs in all directions. There was nothing about my precious little room that went undetected or unanalyzed in Miss Gordon's, no doubt, geometric brain.

Mrs. Parsons, having removed a complaining Crispin to a distant part of the house, returned to make the proper introductions. Miss Gordon, I was informed, had been chief visiting nurse in the district of Woodlands for forty years.

I said that this was a record to be proud of. Miss Gordon agreed. The formalities over, she began to talk in a sharp voice.

"Minnie Parsons tells me you hate it here at Stonehaven."

"That isn't quite how I put it, Celia," Mrs. Parsons said feebly.

"You know that's exactly how you put it, Minnie," Miss Gordon countered. She returned her full attention to me. "Personally, I don't blame you. This house is nothing but a big pile of rocks. Sitting in it, you feel like you're trapped in a cave."

"It's not cozy," I said.

Miss Gordon looked even more distrustful. Was I making fun of her? I assumed my most angelic appearance. Appeased, she got right down to business.

"I came to find out about you. Did you meet Andre in

New York? It's odd I never heard he was even thinking of getting married. Then, bang, one day he's back up here with a bride."

It was easy to see what Miss Gordon had in common with Mrs. Parsons. They both relished other people's business. Miss Gordon's nose had a tendency to twitch just before she asked a snooping question. This active nose made her appear more animal than human, as if she could smell out news the way a dog smells out bones.

"I'm sorry no reports of me reached you from New York, but then you must consider that Andre and I had a very short engagement."

There was a pause while Miss Gordon waited hopefully for me to continue. Knowing the Piedmont talent for bringing misfortune onto themselves, she probably suspected that Andre had found me in an East Village white slavery ring. Or was uselessly attempting to cure me of a fatal heroin addiction. Since I wouldn't confirm her impressions, she tried another approach: talking instead of asking. Perhaps she thought this would break down my reserve.

"I understand you like our woods. We're all very proud of our scenery. You'd be surprised how far back some of the families here go. Now we Gordons have been here almost as long as the Piedmonts. That's why I call all the Piedmonts by their first names. Just because we were poor and they were rich doesn't make them any better than us. Of course, I've always been an independent woman. Not like some of the ingratiating shufflers around here with their 'yes, sir' and 'no, sir.'" She looked pointedly at Mrs. Parsons.

"Don't you start on me, Celia," Mrs. Parsons said indignantly.

"Shut up, Minnie. Some people have a servile mentality and others don't. It's nobody's fault but that's how the world has always been."

Mrs. Parsons looked as if she might cry. "Would you like some coffee?" I quickly asked. Miss Gordon nodded. "Would you please get some for us, Mrs. Parsons?" I asked in what I hoped was a soothing way. Mrs. Parsons did her best to exit with dignity, not quite bringing it off. She looked slightly wilted.

"You don't look rich," Miss Gordon resumed conversation.

"I'm not rich. That is, I wasn't rich before my marriage." Nor did I feel yet that I had any right to the possessions of the Piedmonts. I didn't believe that I owned Stonehaven, for example. Instead I felt like a guest.

"Where are you from?"

"Osborn, Illinois."

"Nice little town. I was there once years ago. Just as well you're not rich. People around here have no use for putting on airs or snobbishness. If you want to get along with them, you won't pull any milady stuff. Except with the shufflers, like Minnie. She's got some idea you're going to form a committee for doing good. Going to organize charities. Minnie thinks anybody connected with Stonehaven and the Piedmonts wears a halo."

I felt honor-bound to put in a good word for my only friend. "Mrs. Parsons is a dear lady and I frankly think you're awfully hard on her."

Miss Gordon snorted. "Minnie and I have been friends since we were schoolgirls. She's used to me." And without a further thought for poor Mrs. Parsons she returned to the subject of the Piedmonts.

"Yes, the Piedmonts were always rich. But even though we Gordons barely scraped along, we had reasonably good luck. Only a few skeletons in the closet. But the Piedmonts, with all their money, have had nothing but misery. So I say, let them keep their money. What good has it done them?"

"Perhaps they would have been just as unlucky if they'd been poor."

"Perhaps. But I doubt it. Don't misunderstand me, I'm not suggesting that the Piedmont luck is a punishment for being rich. I'm not superstitious. Minnie's always got her nose in the astrology column of the *Orinville Gazette*. I don't for a minute hold with that kind of nonsense."

I decided not to admit that I never passed up the astrology column myself.

"What I mean," Miss Gordon continued, "is that the Piedmonts wouldn't be so identifiable as a family if they weren't rich. With their portraits and genealogies. They know all about themselves. From all over the world. I've got kin that started out in Scotland, a whole line of Gordons, and for all I know they have the luck of the Piedmonts. But I'll never find out because they've moved all around and broken contact. And I could never afford to hire detectives to trace them and track them down."

"I see what you mean."

"There are definite advantages to poverty. For example, I'm going to take you around and introduce you to the finest person you can know in Woodlands. Her name's Jenny Hooper and she grew up poor and it didn't hurt her at all. Gave her character."

"I'd like very much to meet her."

"Fine. Company is what you need. I'll take you over there next Tuesday morning. You'll like her husband too. He's a policeman in Orinville. They're both young and they have a pretty baby, a year old."

"It's kind of you to do this for me, Miss Gordon."

"Call me Celia. I intend to call you Tamara. You don't have to thank me. People are neighborly in the country."

We were interrupted by Mrs. Parsons. She was unwilling or unable to look Miss Gordon in the eye. I hardly blamed her, for Miss Gordon glared at her mercilessly until she left.

"I don't want Minnie to hear what I have to tell you. It's about the curse. There are two schools of opinion on that subject. Silly fools like Minnie believe in it. They won't always admit it if you ask them point-blank, but they do. Then there's the scientific point of view, mine. There's nothing mysterious or frightening about the Piedmonts. They've just had exceptionally bad luck. Don't you listen to half-truths and innuendoes from people like Minnie. Go and find out about the Piedmonts. Their history is on record at the Orinville library."

"The Orinville library?"

"I'm Woodland's amateur historian and I once did some research into the Piedmonts' land holdings. I came across plenty of material on the curse. Once you have all the facts, you'll see as I did that's it's just a superstition. There's no such thing as a curse. Supernatural fiddle-faddle. If you take my advice, you won't listen to another rumor. You'll get to the truth. Woodlands is peculiar, but not so peculiar that we have ghosts and reincarnation, and transmigration of souls, or whatever. People make up the wildest stories."

"In what way is Woodlands peculiar?"

"It's underpopulated. In the eighteenth century, around the time of the Revolution, there were several thousand people here. We had a real town then. I know because the county Chamber of Commerce asked me to write up a pamphlet on it once. To attract tourists. It was a waste of time because the tourists never came here anyway. I don't understand why.

We've got the most beautiful scenery in the county. But all the resorts and motels are way west of here, practically at the other end of the county."

"That's odd."

"Peculiar. That's what I said. Woodlands is peculiar. Nothing ever thrives here. Never seems to take. Nobody knows why the town died two hundred years ago. Or why another one never grew up. The farms all failed, the businesses went broke. The lumbering died out. Woodlands today looks exactly like it did a century ago. Wilderness. With a small number of residents, mostly descended from the original settlers. Settlers who came at the same time as the Piedmonts. But the Piedmonts got rich and the rest stayed poor."

"And nobody knows why."

"No. But nobody resents the Piedmonts. Stonehaven has provided a living for generations of locals. Take Minnie. Or her husband. Have you met him?"

"I somehow had the impression she was a widow. Probably because I've never heard her mention her husband."

"She'd be better off if she were a widow. He's a grouchy bitter old man. Not at all like Minnie. He spent years working as a laborer, a jack-of-all-trades, at Stonehaven. Like me, he's semiretired now. We're both getting on."

She had decided that it was time to leave so she stood up. "I've got a patient to look in on. Mary Alder, having her fifth baby. On welfare, too. Lots of people around here work for the county, do odd jobs, or run a small farm. Nothing much, a cow, vegetables, keep chickens for eggs. Raise pigs for meat. More than ought to be are on welfare. If it were up to me, I'd cut them all off. I don't know what this country is coming to when people are too lazy to do a day's work for a day's pay."

I walked with her to the door of the room. She opened it and looked carefully in all directions to make sure that Crispin wasn't anywhere near. "I've enjoyed meeting you, Tamara. And you go on being nice to Minnie. She deserves it. She'd have been on welfare years ago if she'd had to rely on her husband Tom. Shiftless. And he's not aging well." Her lips shut tight in a line of intense disapproval. Then she snapped, "It's a sad thing, when the old don't mellow." And, with a sharp click of her heels, she turned and left.

Chapter VI

———◦×◦◆◦×◦———

The town of Orinville is ten twisting and wooded miles from Stonehaven. In the springtime the drive is restful as long as one remains on the alert for squirrels and migrating turtles who like to sun themselves in the center of the road. In winter, however, the trip is treacherous and sometimes impossible, especially if the snow-plow driver decides it isn't worth the trouble to keep the road clear.

He may be right, for Orinville is a disappointment. It is not really a town, it is scarcely a village. It lies in a valley with hills on all sides. At one time Orinville was a fairly prosperous little railroad town. But its inhabitants deserted it, its tracks became rusted and overgrown when the railroad went bankrupt. Now it consists of a single main street, with old houses at one end and a business district of sorts at the other. The street is never crowded. Orinville sleeps in the summer and broods in the winter.

But Orinville does still sport a few reminders of its once, if not glorious, at least adequate past. The office of the *Orinville Gazette* remains, with a staff of three, including the receptionist. The mansion of railroad tycoon Slocum P. Orin still stands at the other end of the street, although painfully in need of repairs. Its once famous garden is now an open field, usurped by small boys for softball games in the springtime.

And there is the library, a gift of Andrew Carnegie for the edification and uplift of the citizens of Orinville. It is located between the supermarket and the launderette. Mr. Carnegie apparently did not take philanthropy lightly. The library is the largest building in the business district; massive steps lead to ornate carved doors. It is little used and on this day was deserted. Surprisingly, for such a gray winter day the library was dimly lit. Perhaps to save on the cost of electricity. Maybe Mr. Carnegie didn't bother to provide funds for light-

41

ing. Ample money had clearly been left for staff and books. Four underworked librarians stood around silently in the gloom. The walls were packed with books whose function seemed mainly ornamental. No competition for television or snowmobiling, the chief interests of the Orinville citizenry.

I asked one of the librarians where to find the section on local history. Immediately, I wished I had asked someone else, for the woman stared at me severely from a slightly crooked face. Her hair was pulled back into the tightest bun I had ever seen. It must have been painful, for it stretched her skin, somewhat like a face lift. Her thick glasses gave her the appearance of looking through a telescope. She studied me and then said, "Material on the Piedmonts can be found on the farthest shelves down that hall." And she pointed the way I ought to go.

Slowly, listening to my own footsteps, I walked down the long corridor. I stopped for a moment and looked back. The librarian was watching me, rotating her head slightly to keep me in view. I had the feeling that if I weren't careful, she would tiptoe behind me, hide, and peer at me to observe my reactions while I read. So I turned around again. She was still behind her desk. She glanced quickly down at her book when she saw that I was watching her.

After a few false starts, I located the proper shelves. The Piedmonts could hardly complain of going unnoticed. I found references to them in mammouth volumes and slim, decaying pamphlets. I released piles of trapped dust into the air, moving the books about, trying to find something concise, written in a style that wouldn't put me to sleep instantly. It occurred to me that somebody should write a doctoral thesis on the Piedmonts. There was certainly enough information. Then I realized that in all likelihood, somebody already had. Right now at some honored university, there was probably an elderly professor who had come upon these obscure records in his youth. A treasure of original sources, he had made them his magic road to an academic sinecure.

It looked like I might have to follow in his footsteps, coming back to the library every day, tracking down references, wasting time, following leads which turned out to be dead ends. I was on the verge of abandoning the project when I came across a slim nontechnical book. The dust jacket described the author, Emma Piedmont, as a noted historian and scholar at an outstanding eastern women's college. She was also interested in, and knowledgeable about, anthropology and comparative religions. This book was a labor of love, the result of Dr. Piedmont's curiosity about the origins of her own family. She sounded a reliable woman. She had also written a three-hundred-page book on the architectural significance of Stonehaven. At this I shuddered.

I glanced at the copyright date. Dr. Piedmont had done her research ten years ago. The book was, therefore, somewhat dated, but clearly it was the best I could do. I took it with me to the reading room.

The room was shadowy and smelled musty. It was difficult to get comfortable, sitting on the lone bench provided for readers. I wondered why it was so dark. Then I looked up and saw that the light bulbs burning in the high dome of the ceiling were coated with dust. My eyes were already feeling the strain and my head began to ache. I had no choice but to make the best of things, for all the material on the Piedmonts was firmly stamped, "Reference Room Only."

I opened the book. Dr. Piedmont wrote concisely, carefully defining terms to avoid even the suggestion of bias. She stated flatly that she planned to expose the myths that surrounded the family. She began by scoffing at the theory that the Piedmonts extended back to antiquity in an unbroken generational chain. It was impossible to take seriously the suggestion that members of the family had lived in Constantinople during the six-century reign of the Emperor Justinian and his wife, the Empress Theodora. She found it equally ridiculous to assume that the Piedmonts, using a different name, of course, had wandered across Europe with barbarian hordes in the eighth century, sailed as Vikings, or took Jerusalem from the infidels in the First Crusade.

The only substantial evidence on the subject showed that the family had been founded during the time of the English king Henry the Eighth. There was nothing mysterious in this. An obscure English family with French connections began its rise to power and wealth through intense loyalty to the House of Tudor. The family, named D'Arcy, willingly lent large sums of money to Henry's father who built up an impressive royal treasury. They continued making loans to the son, who enjoyed depleting the royal treasury. Clever investments in numerous mercantile projects, including wool production, certainly did them no harm. Their absolute devotion to Henry's version of Protestantism won them a small place in the nobility.

It was during the Catholic portion of Henry's rule that the family managed to marry off an illegitimate daughter to the impoverished third son of an illustrious Italian family. The Italian family had inherited its magnificent titles from its forefathers, a group of notorious Renaissance noblemen who had acquired stature and fortune through a well-mixed blend of intrigue and poison. The D'Arcys continued marrying their daughters off into the same family, always equipping them with solid dowries. Eventually, some of the daughters returned to England, bringing husbands and children with them.

The new family evolved into something different from either its D'Arcy or Italian antecedents. It had come to be called Piedmont and was divided into an Italian and English branch. For political reasons, the English Piedmonts severed all ties with their Italian relations after the death of Mary Tudor. The Italian Piedmonts were strict Catholics, loyal to the Pope, to whom they were distantly related. The English became strong supporters of Good Queen Bess.

It is the English part of the family that interested Dr. Piedmont. This side of the family boasted one minor Cavalier poet and two fanatic Puritans. But for the most part, they seemed a dull lot, preoccupied with making money. It is strange then that they were always whispered about. Accusations were made against them. Unfortunately, Dr. Piedmont, despite intensive research, could not find out exactly what these accusations were.

Then came the American Piedmonts. And they produced Geoffrey. Impassively Dr. Piedmont gave Geoffrey's history. She added little to what I already knew. Apparently Geoffrey was born tongue-tied, with an unusual growth of hair on his cheek. This birthmark was later burned off. But the local farmers interpreted it as a sign that he was the devil's own child. Even as a small boy he talked for hours in a language that nobody could understand. He insisted that it was a make-believe language he had invented himself. He used to joke about the Piedmonts, claiming their respectability was a sham, that their real lives were subterranean and secret.

I paused because my headache was growing worse. This was due to more than the dim lights. Reading about Geoffrey made me remember his portrait. That face. It required an effort of will to read further. Dr. Piedmont was objective. She deliberately avoided drama. None was necessary. Even told in a straightforward way, Geoffrey's story was hideous. In detail Dr. Piedmont described Geoffrey's childhood, then his later influence on the local boys, which turned them into criminals. His Herculean attractiveness to women. His favorite trysting place in the woods. The rape. The murder. The beheading of the victim. The execution. And finally, the curse.

The curse was the only part of the story that interested Dr. Piedmont. She discussed the tragedies that kept the curse alive, emphasizing that she included only proven case histories. As a scholar, she deleted all incidents that were based merely on gossip. For instance, that Judge Crater had really been Rudolph Piedmont all the time, leading a double life.

There were several documented suicides within the family during the early part of the nineteenth century. And a few cases of melancholia. But the first bizarre tragedy occurred somewhat later. Jeremiah Piedmont was an adventurer who lost fortunes as quickly as he made them. Late in life he became obsessed with spiritualism, searching New York City at night for prostitutes and pickpockets. He believed they had special powers and brought them back with him to his Lower Manhattan mansion. There Jeremiah held long séances until daybreak. One Halloween morning, after an especially grueling séance, the butler entered Jeremiah's study and found him dead, his throat slit, his body mutilated. It was decided that the crime must have been committed by one of the thieves Jeremiah had found on a nocturnal tour of the city. The butler stated that his master continually bribed and enticed "riff-raff" from the poorest and most dangerous parts of the city to return home with him for a séance. Odd then that none of his beautiful antiques were missing from the study.

Then there was William Piedmont, who had lost all his money. He gained it back when he discovered gold in California. Unfortunately, he was gunned down in the street before he had a chance to enjoy it. He was now a legend in the West because his ghost had been seen wandering in the desert. And seen, not by the gullible, but by highly reliable witnesses.

After this the Piedmonts became tragedy-prone. In England, Lord Norris Piedmont, a well-known Victorian surgeon, was imprisoned and actually hanged for conducting extreme experiments on living victims in his London laboratory. He was most anxious to establish at exactly which point a human being dies of sheer pain.

Roger Piedmont was a brilliant architect at the turn of the century. He was also a gambler and a dandy. His career was cut short before World War One when he was shot by a jealous husband. In the 1920s Thomas Piedmont and his sister Virginia moved to a quiet southern town. They were practically lynched when the town's residents discovered that their relationship was incestuous. Their house was stormed, but Thomas and Virginia were found already dead. The authorities could not determine what had killed them.

Allen Piedmont, star of the silent films, was found guilty of sex crimes against children. After his arrest, a series of unsolved ghastly child murders came to an end. Olympic swimming champion Norman Piedmont died during the 1930s Depression in disgrace. He had become addicted to cocaine. Sir Charles Piedmont, the famous Egyptologist, became a traitor during World War Two. Leaving his wife and children behind, he fled to Germany. He believed Hitler to be a modern counterpart of the Pharaohs and committed suicide in 1945 when the Nazi regime was destroyed.

There was more, much more, but I had read enough. Grimly, I asked myself if Celia Gordon had been kind or malicious in sending me here to the library. The search for truth had not been consoling. I skipped the rest of the chapter.

But then I noticed. The last two pages of the chapter were missing. Curious. They had been ripped out carelessly by someone who obviously had little respect for books. I ran my fingers over the ragged edges of the missing pages. I felt enraged. Destroying a book is an especially nasty form of butchery. At least to anyone who loves to read.

I couldn't imagine who would do such a thing. Maybe a small child, rebelling against too much homework. But no child would read this book. Certainly, there could be no damaging information in the book itself. Everything about the curse was widely known. Dr. Piedmont's little volume would probably sit on the shelf for another ten years before anyone looked at it again. Why bother to rip anything out?

I went on to the next chapter. This consisted of a persuasive argument by the author that the curse was simply a superstition, no more. She considered it repugnant that anyone would actually believe that the Piedmonts were in the grip of an evil spell. This, after all, was the scientific age.

I could visualize Celia Gordon nodding vigorously as the author made her points. Dr. Piedmont compared the curse with other related beliefs. She suggested that the curse was a relatively recent manifestation of an ancient myth common to agricultural peoples. Geoffrey was an allegorical symbol of winter with its associated evils of hardship and cold.

Dr. Piedmont introduced elaborate statistics to show that the Piedmonts had only a slightly higher number of misfortunes than any other well-documented family of equal age. However, even Dr. Piedmont had to admit that these "misfortunes" were rather gross. She explained this unavoidable fact as the result of chance.

In conclusion, Dr. Piedmont stated that the family really victimized itself. It inculcated the curse into each generation of children, at the same time resorting to lies and creating taboos to protect them. The poor confused children thus internalized the curse in the same way that led Victorian youth to repress sexuality. This caused untold psychic damage, with the result that a significant percentage of male Piedmonts believed in a hereditary doom and acted out their fate accordingly. The effect was circular. Belief equals behavior equals belief.

Dr. Piedmont thought that the entire situation could be remedied through education. From toddler stage on, Piedmonts should be given a thorough scientific indoctrination. This total absorption of scientific method and principles would immunize them to the counter-attraction of supernatural explanations. Thus the family would be saved. Dr. Piedmont closed what she called "this lengthy essay" with a plea for her colleagues to take up the study of residual superstitious mythology in the atomic age. It was, she sadly noted, a neglected field.

Fini. I closed the book. Did I believe it? It was all very logical and undoubtedly would have convinced Dr. Piedmont's learned colleagues. I found her arguments thin and inconclusive. So it had come to this. That I was seriously arguing with myself as if in a court of law whether there were supernatural forces at work in the universe or not. But that horrendous list of tragedies which Dr. Piedmont had so carefully put together seemed better explained by the curse than by her psychological mumbo-jumbo. The curse made more sense than any theories she offered. It certainly fit the facts more elegantly than chance or probability.

A supernatural force sounded unreal in the modern world, an insane black thing left over from the primeval swamps, defying all known laws of the nature of matter. How it must hate physics! How would it work anyway? Not on sheer will. I could sit here in the library and curse Stonehaven for the next decade and go home and still find it ogling everything from its damned hill.

Okay, I couldn't create an efficacious curse. But what if it could be done and I just didn't know how? What if there were funny little tricks that didn't seem to make any sense because they had nothing to do with our concept of cause and effect? Maybe a curse wouldn't just be empty words if someone whispered it under a full moon, in springtime; say, by a brook where the deer came to drink. Maybe the thing, the force, whatever it's made of, would respond just because it liked to be asked in that particular way. It might decide arbitrarily to put the curse into action. Primitive peoples could have been on to something when they realized that there was a power out there that would work all kinds of evil in your favor if you knew how to reach it, get it on your side. Propitiating the gods. It had sounded quite innocent in high school anthropology. Not anymore.

I felt as if I had just learned that the earth was flat. There would be no further trips to the library for me. Much more of this and I would greet Miss Gordon with a voodoo doll full of pins on her next visit. I put Dr. Piedmont's book back in place, and began walking back along the corridor.

Then it hit me. So hard I had to stand still. If the curse were real, it was of more than academic interest. Andre wasn't just imagining things. He might be turning into another Geoffrey Piedmont. I felt terrified, literally terrified. I didn't want to believe it could happen, but it might be true. Andre insane and spending his life in a psychiatric hospital would be heaven compared to our future if the curse proved to be real.

I forced myself to calm down and walk again. I lectured myself. Woodlands was just getting to me. I had become introverted and isolated, living in that dreadful house. The loneliness was beginning to have its effect. Curses were ludicrous. Science had triumphed ever chaotic magical thinking three hundred years ago. Tomorrow was my day to meet Jennie Hooper. A nice normal day was just what I needed. By tomorrow night everything connected with the Piedmont curse would be back in proper perspective. I loved Andre. He needed my help and I was no good to him in this hysterical, irrational state of mind. There must be a diner in Orinville or a lunch counter. I would stop off, have a cup of coffee, and read the *Gazette*. I would feel better instantly.

The librarian was still sitting at her desk. She looked up as I approached. This library would bring out anyone's over-wrought imagination. Creepy place. I made myself smile at her. Just to break the tension.

She didn't respond in kind. Instead she said, "I walked over to the bench while you were reading. But you were so absorbed in Dr. Piedmont's book you didn't even notice me, though I stood behind you for quite a while."

My headache moved from my forehead to my sinuses and began to thump.

She continued. "Interesting woman, Dr. Piedmont. Did you know that she got to be president of Merriweather College? Not long after she'd finished the book you were reading. Sad, isn't it?"

"Sad? Being President of a college?"

"Of course not. I mean it's sad that her career was cut short. Such a waste of talent and energy."

"What happened?"

"I assumed you knew. But you were probably quite young at the time. There was a good bit of publicity. She was kid-napped. The ransom note requested a very large sum of money. It was delivered. The kidnapper escaped. But it was too late. She was found dead. Somewhere in Vermont. Poor woman. The kidnapper wasn't a professional, although that's what the police originally thought. The crime was carried out in a most efficient manner. The kidnapper must have been a maniac. She had been tortured and died of starvation. The luck of the Piedmonts, as they say."

And now she smiled, a contented, humming smile. Behind the thick tunnels of glass, her eyes twinkled merrily.

The headache was no longer simply in my sinuses. It was in back of my eyes and banging hard at the temples. Yet I was delighted with every blow. Otherwise I might have screamed, a loud, panicky scream. Which would have made at least a small Piedmont scandal. The new mistress of Stone-haven standing in the Orinville library, screaming hysterically, out of her wits in fear.

Chapter VII

Miss Gordon arrived promptly the next morning. The sky looked like the earth does after a snowfall. The snow was suspended overhead and within a short time would begin to fall. Miss Gordon interpreted the weather as an evil spirit out to persecute her.

"You can never rely on the weather in Woodlands. If you plan a picnic, it rains. If you decide to ski, it melts all the snow. Now look what it's done. The roads are covered with a thick sheet of ice and we'll be lucky if we get to Jenny's without smashing up the car."

"Maybe it would be better if we stayed here and arranged to visit her another day."

"Absolutely not. The weather never tells me what to do. Jenny expects us and Jenny's going to get us."

I saw immediately that it was useless to argue. It was easier to risk death in an auto accident than to try to change Celia Gordon's mind. I sent her ahead to get her car and went to feed Crispin. Mrs. Parsons had already given him a bowl of milk. He drank neatly, as he did everything, lapping the milk with his quick, darting pink tongue.

"You look like a frog, Crispin," I said, "sticking your tongue out to catch flies on a summer day." This remark got what it deserved, a stare of total disdain from the cat. He wiped his long whiskers with a paw the color of milk glass. For comment, he gave me a throaty, condescending mew, then walked to the nearest chair, jumped onto it, and went to sleep.

Andre was off in the nursery, that room he so dearly loved, brooding. Perhaps he found the nursery soothing be-cause it took him back to childhood, that charmed time of life when the curse would have had no power. It would have made a marvelous game, something out of Buck Rogers, Kidnapped, or Cowboys and Indians. Whoever catches the curse is It until he tags you. Home free could be nana's rocker or the toy chest. Perhaps childhood had nothing to do with it. Maybe Andre chose the nursery because it was way at the top of the house and therefore provided maximum solitude. And maximum security, especially from me.

There was no reason to seek him out in order to say good-bye. He would only resent it as an intrusion, an unauthorized attempt to cut a hole in the wall he had erected between us. My beloved schizoid Andre. How could I half-understand what went on inside his head. Sometimes tender, more often remote. A dual personality. Siamese twin brains sharing one body.

Why analyze it? I would just have to learn to live with this chronic pain. Millions of other women probably did. Ironic. I could face anything the Piedmonts conjured up, as long as Andre was loving. But I couldn't stand his coldness, his withdrawal, his indifference. I would pay a price for learning to put up with his inevitable rebuffs. In a few years I would look like that particular kind of embittered woman one sees so often, the sort with taut mouth, dead eyes, and a perpetually sour expression.

By the time I reached Miss Gordon's cranky old blue Chevy, she was quite rightly annoyed with me for keeping her waiting. I made my apologies as best I could without telling her the truth. I couldn't very well admit that in my unhappiness I sometimes lost track of the time. Besides, Miss Gordon would never consider this an acceptable excuse for tardiness.

"I wouldn't have thought you the type to be late, Tamara. Bad habit. Particularly on a day like this when that damned weather wants to keep us all homebound. Fasten your seat belt. The driveway's more like a roller coaster than a road today."

Hiccoughing and coughing, the car resisted Celia Gordon's commands, given ferociously via steering wheel and brake. It continually tried to go right or left into a snowbank. The more she threatened, the more it defied her. After a particularly unpleasant swerve across an icy patch, she began to swear loudly. This had some effect on the car. Perhaps it was afraid of being abandoned altogether, for it inched slowly down the rest of the driveway, keeping its mind on its business.

We were a good ways down when I noticed a workman I had never seen before. There was nothing extraordinary in this. What made the man conspicuous was his calm, unhurried walk toward the house. In weather like this, the local people never walked. If they didn't own a car of their own, they were always free to use one of our pickup trucks. Andre saw to it that every employee at Stonehaven had access to a car.

Yet here was this man, with a heavy armload of wood, strolling along as if there were a hot spring sun in the sky.

"Who is that, Celia?" I asked.

She was engrossed in the car. "Snow tires are shreds. That's what I get for buying on sale. Brute of a car, I've a mind to send it to the junk heap tomorrow. You hear that!" she shouted, banging it on the windshield, "it's the glue factory for you."

"Celia," I tried again. "I've never seen that man before."

This time she heard and looked out the side-window quickly. "Wouldn't you know it. It's Tom Parsons."

"Mrs. Parsons' husband?"

"Of course. Who else would walk around in this weather. It's raw, it's damp, but there he goes. He loves it. You can't get him to stay inside a house, summer or winter. Sometimes I think he's part bear, the way he likes to go off in the woods. And at his age. He's even older than me, if you can believe that's possible. Well, he won't die of exertion, anyway. Always complaining about his arthritis. Imaginary complaint. He'll go on to be ninety, Tom will. Poor Minnie."

Slowly the car drew up to Tom Parsons and then passed him. It gave me an opportunity to watch him. He had a strong, square body. From even a slight distance, you'd never guess his age. Up close I saw that his face was red and weathered, criss-crossed by tiny lines. Despite the condition of his skin, he still looked surprisingly youthful. There was little gray in the black hair, the hair of a young man, thick and shining. But it came low across the forehead. The bones and features of the face were blunt. With the slight forward tilt of his body he presented a Neanderthal profile. The hunched form of prehistoric man. Our eyes met as the car reached him. Stone Age man never had such eyes. Very small, but intelligent, inquiring. He summed me up in the moment when he could see me clearly. I don't think I made a flattering impression. For the look he gave me was one of total contempt.

"I don't like his face," I said to Celia.

"Who could?" she answered. "Ugly, isn't he. Like something that crawled out of a primeval swamp."

A primeval swamp. I remembered my morbid speculations yesterday in the Orinville library. Tom Parsons looked as if he would find it easy to get along with any supernatural force, as long as its intentions were evil.

If names were truly descriptive, then Jenny Hooper would have been called Jenny Wren. Her tidy little starter house reminded me of a nest, constructed affectionately but efficiently, with a sharp eye for economy of resources.

The house was brand-new, made of wood, and painted an honest no-nonsense white. It stood alone in the woods on one cleared acre, facing a county road. A rail fence enclosed the house, defining the property's boundaries.

It was the sort of house that would have a pleasant backyard in the springtime. The lawn would always be neat. There would be a small vegetable garden because homegrown tomatoes and rhubarb are better and cheaper than what the supermarket sells. The windowsills would have geraniums in flowerpots; stiff, starched blue curtains would move with the wind when the window was open.

Jenny Hooper was ironing precisely the right curtains when we came into the house. No one would ever describe her as pretty. "Plain," my grandmother would have said. She was very young but more mature than girls of comparable age in the city. As if she had skipped adolescence, becoming an adult the day childhood was finished.

A hard but decent life had made her strong, unspoiled, and free of self-pity. She projected inner beauty. Her face, because it was hers, looked lovely.

She greeted me with friendliness, said all the right things to Celia, made coffee, and set out fresh-baked brownies. Miss Gordon immediately told her that I was miserable at Stonehaven. But Jennie knew how to cope with tactlessness.

"It's just that you've had to be here first in the winter. Everyone in Woodlands becomes sad at this time of year. The roads are icy and you have to stay home when you want to go out. But we local people know that the spring is coming, and spring makes the winter worth living through. You'll love the long days. And the wildflowers! Our Woodlands forget-me-nots are the bluest color. I don't believe they're as beautiful anywhere else in the county. The gardens at Stonehaven are magnificent. Just wait. It doesn't feel like it today but springtime will come."

It was kind of Jenny to pretend that my unhappiness was caused by the climate. A warm sun, a merry breeze, and the Piedmont suffering would melt along with the snow.

"If you live here long enough," Jenny continued, "you find ways to use the winter. I do all my sewing projects for the year now and collect recipes. If the inside work is done in the winter, the outside work can be done in the summer. You'll find me in the garden for hours on a sunny day."

"That's all right for you, Jenny," Celia said. "You're a hard worker. You'd find ways to be busy, instead of bored, if you were confined in a cage."

Miss Gordon was probably right. The house was spotless. The furniture was obviously as well tended as Stonehaven's precious antiques. Jenny's handiwork was everywhere. Even the dishtowels were embroidered with the letter "H," a task she had probably finished in-between knitting a sweater and upholstering a chair.

Thought had gone into acquiring things. Jenny and her husband must have spent hours studying the Montgomery Ward catalog; planning, budgeting, adding furniture one piece at a time. Dreaming about the future when they could afford to add new rooms to the little house. For clearly the house wasn't meant to stay small. It was supposed to grow and grow, until it would comfortably hold all the children who would be born there.

The miniature kitchen was the heart of the house. In addition to the usual appliances, it held a washer, a dryer, a net playpen, a chrome and plastic high chair convertible into a youth chair, and the kitchenette set. I would have preferred to visit there. But the room was reserved for family and friends.

Special guests like myself were taken into the living room, which had a slightly formal atmosphere, reminiscent of a parlor in an old-fashioned Victorian home. It was the storeroom for Hooper treasures.

Honeymoon souvenirs were exhibited on the coffee table. The family heirlooms, two carnival glass candy dishes, were displayed on end tables. A few pieces of open stock "company china" were visible through the glass door of the china closet. A silver-plate tea set was conspicuous.

Jenny herself had made the slipcovers for the furniture, a pleasant floral pattern that helped drive away the mood of winter. She had chosen colorful landscape prints for the walls. These were interspersed with numerous photographs of relatives, all smiling the same "say cheese now" smile for the camera. The family's prize picture was shown off where it couldn't be missed, on top of the enormous color television set.

An adorable baby girl, carefully posed, smiled out of a silvery frame. The pastel tints of the photograph made the child appear embalmed, with the artificial look usually accomplished best by an undertaker.

"A charming little girl," I said.

"Thank you," Jenny said, literally beaming. She was the sort of mother who is unassuming herself but wildly partisan when it comes to her children.

Miss Gordon said, "Don't be fooled now. Stacy Lynn looks like an angel in that picture but she's already a hellion."

"Celia's right. Stacy's napping now," Jenny said, "but wait until she wakes up. Since she learned to crawl, I don't get a minute's peace. I'm really going to be run ragged in a few months, because I've just found out that Jack and I are going to have another baby."

Miss Gordon obviously thought such timing disgraceful. In her view Jenny's respectability quotient dropped. I thought it was marvelous, and said so to Jenny. Unhappily, I considered the curse of the Piedmonts. Would Andre and I ever dare risk having a baby?

Jenny sensed that my mood was deteriorating. But perhaps she assumed it was just a return of the winter doldrums because she changed the subject back to the glories of springtime in Woodlands.

"Winter is harsh but you'll like it better when you've lived here through all the seasons. Then you'll understand that winter has its place. It rounds out the year. I'd hate to live where it was always springtime. Then spring would be commonplace. But it seems like magic after winter. Who could believe now that our bushes, dead in the snow, will produce purple lilacs one day. And our trees, naked and barren, will sprout wonderful white blossoms. It doesn't seem possible, but it happens every year."

"Along with the black flies," Celia said.

"They are a nuisance, Celia, but bugs beat the cold."

"I agree with you, all right, but I wouldn't want Tamara to expect spring to be perfect. It has its faults, like everything else."

Miss Gordon's cynical observations were interrupted by grouchy noises from one of the two bedrooms opposite. Jenny went to see what was the matter.

I could hear her speaking mildly to a baby. Its face was washed, diapers were changed, and Stacy was presented to us for approval. She had no trouble getting it. She was delicate, a figurine of a child; in truth, the photograph didn't do justice to her.

Jenny put Stacy on the floor to crawl, and tried to chat with me. Miss Gordon's presence made this difficult. I talked about New York. One thing led to another and I found myself telling Jenny about my painting. She listened courteously but also with interest.

Since I'd come to Stonehaven I hadn't had the energy even to think of painting. Sometimes I'd forget that I had ever had ambitions to be an artist. It was delightful to talk again about my aspirations. It made me feel like Tamara Lewis once more, that reasonably pleasant young woman who had never heard of the Piedmont curse. I found this so refreshing that I felt guilty. Was Andre such a handicap to me? Underneath my powerful surface emotions, did I just wish he would go away?

I realized that I was getting like Andre, sliding into a private world no matter where I was. It required an act of will to concentrate again on my surroundings. Jenny was talking rather quickly, to protect me. Apparently, I hadn't answered the last two questions put to me. Celia's nose twitched. A probe was in the offing. I interrupted Jenny and talked steadily for five minutes until all twitching stopped.

But I had underestimated Celia. She wouldn't be circumvented. "Absentminded and you keep people waiting," she said to me. "Interesting. Have you always been dreamy or is this a trait you acquired at Stonehaven?"

I was resigned to being interrogated when Stacy provided a diversion. She actively investigated the television knobs. Jenny hurriedly removed her. This supreme injustice could only be met with irate tears and kicks. Jenny held and soothed her.

Miss Gordon couldn't concentrate further on questioning me when such a splendid opportunity had arisen for informing Jenny that she had spoiled Stacy irrevocably. Then Celia triumphantly announced that Stacy's father was even worse. Miss Gordon found Jack Hooper's devotion to his daughter practically criminal.

Jennie rebuked Celia gently. "All first babies have a right to be spoiled. We'll be tougher on the next one."

"I doubt it," Miss Gordon sniffed. "You'll be just the same."

Crisis over, Jenny went to the kitchen for more coffee and brownies. With mother gone, Stacy was more attentive to us; the two curious humans she found somewhat in the way. She coaxed a game of patty-cake out of Celia, and won me over by solemnly presenting me with her teddy bear.

"Little witch," Jenny said when she returned, smiling at Stacy and setting a tray down beyond the baby's reach.

"Bewitching, definitely," I said.

Celia felt she had been polite long enough. She had put up with tedious conversation about painting and New York City, hoping that at least one useful piece of information would slip out. She had endured maudlin cooing over the baby. The morning was nearly gone and there had not been one iota of gossip obtained.

She set about salvaging the visit by asking Jenny about her cousin Edna Flint's goiter trouble. Celia's cross examination was brilliant. She would have made an excellent trial lawyer. But Jenny was uncommunicative. Soon she had Celia doing most of the talking.

If Celia couldn't get information, she could at least impart some. Jenny heard all her opinions politely. Although Miss Gordon would have liked Jenny to pass on at least a few details to the neighbors, I felt certain the gossip would go no farther than this room.

At least, as far as Jenny and I were concerned. Celia herself would see to it that the entire county heard everything. Vigorously assisted by Minnie Parsons.

"Jenny, can you believe that Julia Sampson's graduating from her nurses' training course this year? That silly thing. She'll never hold a job. Giggly type, only interested in boys. What can you expect? Her mother's got no sense. Look at the way she keeps going back to Dr. Henry to cure her varicose veins. For twenty years he's been treating her. Can you see any improvement? I can't. Throwing good money after bad, as far as I'm concerned. That's typical of your family, Jenny. Your cousin Tad's just lost his third job this year and his wife's pregnant again. Only good news is that Donna's cow calved last week. She'll have no time on her hands now. Not with that lazy, do-nothing husband of hers. He'll——"

"Excuse me, Celia, I hate to interrupt you but Stacy will cry in a minute if I don't prepare her bottle," Jenny said. Feeling conspiratorial, I followed her to the kitchen. I didn't want to abandon Miss Gordon but at times her personality made me feel as if I were stuck between floors in an elevator. Claustrophobia had set in.

Jenny opened the refrigerator and took out the milk bottle. The milk was from a nearby farm so she gave the bottle a good shake. Local milk is unhomogenized, and the cream forms a yellow band at the top.

Jenny poured the milk into a plastic bottle, twisted the nipple on, and called to Stacy. But Stacy had charmed Celia into opening her purse and the baby was ensconced in the living room, happily examining its contents.

Jenny whispered, "Don't pay any attention to Celia. She's really a kind person underneath her bossy ways. When she can do you a favor, she will."

"She already has. I've enjoyed being here today."

"It's been nice for me too. There aren't many people our age here. Mostly children from a few big families and old people live in Woodlands. The rest leave. They have to. There are so few jobs up here."

The sound of the front door opening made us turn toward the living room. A masculine voice greeted Miss Gordon with deference. Jenny, bottle in hand, led me out of the kitchen, calling as she walked, "Jack, I want you to meet our new neighbor."

A tall man, with one of those nondescript faces you never remember, was standing awkwardly in the doorway. The policeman's uniform he wore did not give him stature. It made him look like a giant child in costume for Halloween.

He seemed embarrassed, almost bumbling, and couldn't look me in the eye when we were introduced. His face relaxed when he spoke with Jenny. Then he smiled at Stacy, picked her up and tossed her gently in the air, catching her surely in his large hands.

"Like I told you," Celia snapped, "the father spoils her worse than the mother does."

Jack Hooper blushed but didn't stop playing with Stacy. Jenny smiled an amused, tolerant smile, watching Stacy's delighted face. Parents and child formed a charmed circle, excluding Celia and me.

They did not mean to insult us. They were scrupulously polite. But we were no longer welcome guests. We had become interlopers, gate-crashers.

It was a precious hour of the day for Jack Hooper. As usual, he had driven all the way home from Orinville just to see his family. And, in a little while, would have to drive back. So the Hoopers wanted their privacy. Celia and I were most emphatically not invited to lunch.

Everyone said good-bye. Celia had her coat on and was opening the door. I bent down to say a special good-bye to Stacy Lynn. The room was suddenly quiet. Activity stopped. The Hoopers and Miss Gordon froze like statues.

A beautiful child. But there was something strange about her appearance, something that had nagged at the back of my mind all morning. I rubbed her cheek and she smiled. A pale little face, a face out of a storybook. Blond hair, light to the point of silver. A merry smile. A darling creature, a kitten, an elf.

And then I realized. At Stonehaven, there were portraits of children. Stacy's face was an exact replica. The Piedmont face. She stared at me innocently from eyes like opaque sapphires. Eyes I had grown used to. Andre's eyes. Stacy didn't look like the Hoopers at all. She was the image of Andre.

Chapter VIII

The snow which hung suspended in the sky all morning had finally begun to fall. It came down in damp, soggy clumps, for it was late in the season. Miss Gordon urged her stubborn car slowly up the driveway toward Stonehaven. The car was unequal to the task. Halfway up, Celia braked.

"I can't make it any farther, Tamara. They won't have this driveway cleared for hours."

"Can you back down from here?"

Miss Gordon frowned, then nodded.

"Then don't worry about me," I said, "I've got strong boots on. I can walk to the top."

"Are you sure you can do it?" Celia sounded concerned. "The storm's turning into a blizzard."

"Don't worry, I don't want you to get stuck. Remember, I love to walk in the woods. A little snow doesn't scare me."

Apparently Celia decided I had pluck, for she honored me with a rare smile. I opened the car door on my side and stepped out, smack into a mound of snow. I braced myself, bent my head, and walked slowly. The snow was unnatural, more like a diseased rain. It was gray instead of white. Very different from the dry crystals of a sunny day. Within minutes I was wet through and shivering.

I kept to the middle of the driveway. It was filling with snow but tire tracks were still visible. I walked in the grooves.

The sight of tire tracks set me thinking. Could we have guests? Had some friends driven up a few hours ago for a visit? Silly idea. Andre and I had no friends. And who would want to come to Stonehaven anyway. Hardly the most cheerful place to spend a gloomy afternoon. The tracks were probably made by one of our own cars.

I was close to the house now and I glowered at it. It glowered back. Something seemed wrong. Two people stood casually at the top of the driveway, chatting. Wearing no hats, coats, or gloves, they were like two snowmen brought to life. Completely comfortable in weather that would have driven any natural mortal indoors quickly.

The wind blowing in my face made it difficult for me to identify the men at first. I hoped they were strangers. But unfortunately I soon recognized one of them. Andre. Quite suddenly he turned and saw me. There was a moment when he didn't move, when he seemed to be making a decision. Then he waved, a friendly useless wave, and walked away, apparently without a care in the world. He was probably whistling.

I called out to him but the wind threw his name back in my face. I was infuriated, and muttered to myself that he might at least come and help me. Particularly since moving through snow was easy for him. He was like a seal or a snow leopard—a member of a species perfectly adapted to the climate, while I struggled along in a clumsy, elephantine way.

As an added humiliation, Andre's companion stood and watched me approach, making no move to help, although it was obvious that I was straining to finish the climb. I was panting, my legs were tired, and I was growing warm from exertion. The wind hurt my face and my toes were numb. They would ache painfully when I finally did get inside the house.

"Some gentleman you are," I said, staring at the man ahead. I don't think he heard. He merely waited, indifferently, for me to reach him. Now I could see him clearly. Tom Parsons. I wanted to tell him off, to insult him, to dismiss him from his job. How could Minnie stand to live with the man? What a cross to bear.

Then we were face to face. And I couldn't say a thing. I sensed danger. As if I were alone at night in Central Park, confronted by a mugger. I wanted to run. I told myself to cut out the nonsense. I was very close to the house. What could happen here? I avoided looking at Tom Parsons by staring after Andre. He was beyond the house. He turned and I had the impression that he was walking toward the woods. Absurd. No one sane would go into the woods on a day like this. Unless they were suicidal.

I decided to brazen it out with Tom Parsons. "I believe you are Mr. Parsons," I said. "I am Mrs. Piedmont." I had meant to put him in his place but the words came out overstressed. I sounded insecure. His eyes were wary, like an animal's, always on the watch. But he looked insolent.

"I know who you are," he said, in a harsh, gravelly voice that sounded not quite human, issuing no doubt from vocal chords somewhere back on the evolutionary scale. He waited to see if I had anything further to say. Not that he cared. He was being polite. Like a master tolerantly hearing out a servant.

Because I was afraid, I became obsequious. I smiled as best I could and said that the snow was dreadful. This seductive little ploy would never have worked. But it did get his mind off me and onto the weather.

For a long time he stared at the sky, lovingly. "Beautiful, the snow's beautiful," he said. "Most people don't like it.

Spring's what they want. Well, spring's coming soon. Woodlands is different then. Whole different world." He leered. "You'll find spring very interesting."

The leer only frightened me more. Despite my heavy winter clothes, I felt nude, exposed to hostile excited faces. Now it was like being trapped in Riverside Park by a street gang.

I forced myself to keep calm. In reality, I was fully dressed and talking to one lone man. In front of my house. And the man was an old family employee. Suddenly I felt very cold. If I didn't get into the house and warm up, I might get sick. I said that yes, the spring would be interesting, and left abruptly.

Mrs. Parsons was relieved that I was home. She had grown worried and was considering calling out the volunteer fire department to rescue me in case I had fallen into a ditch somewhere. She helped me off with my coat and boots and promised to bring me a cup of hot coffee. I hobbled off on my miserable, burning feet. What I needed was a complete change of clothes.

I opened the bedroom door and there stood Andre. It was a shock.

"What are you doing here?" I asked.

Andre was in a good mood. "Stop staring at me as if I were a ghost, Tamara. After all, I do live here, you know." He laughed and I resented it. Ignoring me in the snow and teasing me now.

"It isn't funny, Andre. It's not a cute little joke. Did you and Tom Parsons find it amusing, watching me freeze out there on the driveway. Moods are one thing but sadism's something else again. I am your wife. I don't expect to be subjected to adolescent tricks by my own husband."

Andre's face was impassive. He said nothing and his silence made me furious.

"How did you get up here so quickly?" I shouted. "You were disappearing into the woods a few minutes ago. While that hideous old man made not the slightest effort to help me. What's going on in Woodlands? Curses, and portraits, and all the rest of it. Things that go bump in the night. Now you and your vanishing act."

The blue eyes were totally without expression. Then, slowly, as if explaining why grass is green to a child, Andre answered me. He spoke gently. So gently that I felt guilty for having screamed at him like an outraged harpy.

"I would never play cruel jokes on you, Tamara, and I would hope that you'd know this without being told. I was going to go down the hill and help but Tom said that he'd assist you. There was an emergency in the kitchen. One of the maids, Mrs. McKinney, had fainted. Tom had been sent to get me. Since Mrs. McKinney has had a coronary, I was naturally concerned. I did not go near the woods. You had an optical illusion. Understandably; it's not easy to see in which direction someone walks in a snowstorm. I walked past the house because the snow drifts most heavily right alongside it. Then I turned and was headed toward the kitchen when one of the servants intercepted me and told me Mrs. McKinney had revived. A special crew was going out to plow the driveway and she would be taken to the doctor immediately. I came up here to get warmer clothes in case I was needed."

"Andre, I feel terrible. What can I say?"

He held me. His sweater smelled of damp wool. "Forget it, Tamara. I'm no saint when it comes to temperament. You've excused my anger often enough." He changed the subject. "Tell me, how did you like Jenny?"

"Very much."

"Another conquest for Jenny. People generally do like her. She's a decent sort."

I mimicked Miss Gordon. "That Jenny Hooper hasn't got a mean bone in her body. Where she got all that goodness, I can't imagine. Half the Hoopers are in jail and the other half are drunkards."

Andre laughed. "You sound just like Celia. Take care you don't get like her. I'd have to divorce you."

"I wouldn't want that."

Andre became serious. "You know, Tamara, in your own very different way, you're as strong and as honest as Jenny. And, of course, I find you much more lovable."

Was there an ironic twist in what Andre said? A little knife dig masquerading as a compliment. Stacy's blue eyes. Perhaps at one time Andre had found Jenny quite lovable. And what did he feel toward her now? Platonic love? Brotherly affection? Good old Jenny? Or something more intense?

Eventually I talked myself round. And concluded that Stacy had probably inherited the Piedmont face from an ancient liaison. Most likely Geoffrey and a scullery maid.

Then I forgot about Stacy. Once again my world was reduced to Andre. I was reminded of the day we walked in the woods together and he told me I was like a firebird. Briefly, the obscure corners of Stonehaven radiated light.

Chapter IX

Andre insisted that we have luncheon in my special room. For once we had a cosy domestic meal, snacking together in a little space, like most young married couples. It made the difference between eating and dining. The dining hall at Stonehaven was truly suitable only for a squadron of medieval knights.

Outside our windows the snow continued to fall, creating false mountains in the woods and fields. The wind did indeed howl. Andre poured tea from a china pot, the booty of Captain Piedmont, who went down with his ship one hundred and twenty years before. The tea was good and strong. It thawed muscles and sinews. I began to forget my long hike up the driveway.

Andre had fallen into a sleepy holiday mood. He put a record on the phonograph. We listened to Domenico Scarlatti's harpsichord music. Its Spanish rhythms helped me imagine that we were far from the cold of Woodlands. I closed my eyes and pretended that we were waiting for the afternoon heat to lift in the tropics.

A scratching noise interrupted my fancies. I opened the door and Crispin came in. He waited politely for the music to end and then began his own concert of purring. I had achieved the impossible: a sense of peace and well-being at Stonehaven. The house didn't like it. Quickly, it put an end to our comfort.

Mrs. Parsons barged in and said that there was a telephone call for Andre. He asked if it were urgent. She couldn't say. It was a Mr. Wenzel or Wessel, an attorney from New York City, but she couldn't take a message because there was excessive static on the line. Due, no doubt, to the storm. Rural electricity. Not what it should be.

Andre was irritated. He wanted to stay with me but, as usual, duty came first. Off he went while I was left with Crispin again.

"Old friend," I said, petting him and rubbing his fur first wrong way and then right way. He rolled over on his back, stoplight eyes aglow. "What do you think of all this, Crispin?" I asked. It seemed to me that his answering purr sounded most commiserative.

Mrs. Parsons waited. When she had my attention she said, "I want to apologize, ma'am. Elsie, the young maid—no, I don't think you do know her—told me that my husband Tom was rude to you this morning."

All lingering hopes of punishing Mr. Parsons vanished. If I hurt him, his wife would suffer. "He wasn't polite," I said, a massive understatement. "But I'll just ignore him. No need for you to apologize. You're never rude."

"I'm most relieved you took it so well, ma'am. Tom can be a shock. He's stubborn, does just what he wants. I've never been able to bring him around to behaving sensibly. Honey catches more flies than vinegar, I tell him. But he doesn't listen. I'm glad you didn't dismiss him on the spot. He deserves that, but he's been here for years and he loves the old house in his own way. Then there is the money; we do need it."

"For your sake, I won't take him seriously if he gets hold of me and insults me. But I'll avoid him to prevent any unpleasant confrontations."

She smiled. "Merciful, that's what you are. I won't forget it, either." As if to make immediate amends for her husband's behavior, Mrs. Parsons began straightening up the room. As she examined the heavy velvet drapes for dust, she talked, allowing me to comment noncommittally from time to time. Her one-way conversation covered the week's menus, plans for next summer's garden, and the local assessment of Jenny Hooper. "A paragon, ma'am." Such was the general opinion.

A necessary pause for breath gave me the opportunity I needed. I had made a decision. This afternoon, instead of brooding, I was going to read. I would force myself to concentrate, for I was just plain sick and tired of wasting time.

Mrs. Parsons asked me where I was going. I answered that I was finally about to explore the library at Stonehaven. Normally, she would merely have asked if I wanted tea or coffee sent ahead. But she said nothing for a full minute. She didn't return to work. She stood quite still.

"What is it?" I asked.

She jumped, the way people do when they are alone in a room and an unexpected visitor startles them. Or when they are deep in concentration and someone interrupts them. She must have realized that she was behaving strangely because she smiled, a silly, false smile. It made her look like a carnival kewpie doll. Then she hurried to the closet and returned with a cushion.

"You put your feet up and slip this behind your back, ma'am," she said, an artificial twinkle sliding into her voice.

"But, Mrs. Parsons, I don't want to lie down. I must go and choose a book."

"You must still be tired and chilled from your walk. Just tell me what you want and I'll be glad to get it for you."

"Don't be silly, I don't know what to read. I'll have to see the library before I can decide."

She had suddenly become as tenacious as Celia Gordon. Her jaw was firmly set. But she couldn't carry it off. She was like an obsequious bulldog or a determined pussy cat. I walked right around her.

"Mrs. Parsons, dear guardian of the library, I am off to see for myself what you are hiding."

"It's not that I'm hiding anything." A note of desperation had crept into her voice. "It's just that I hate to see you wear yourself out. How about a love story, a nice love story. I'm sure I could find you one you couldn't put down, it's so interesting. The one I read last week. Just like a daytime television serial, it was. Beautiful."

I left before I was subjected to a synopsis of the plot.

Poor transparent Mrs. Parsons. She couldn't hoodwink a four-year-old. Because she was funny, I was convinced that the library itself would somehow be funny. A comic rendezvous place for lovers, perhaps. With Mrs. Parsons sentimentally covering up secret meetings between a Romeo and Juliet from the kitchen.

I should have known better. Stonehaven would never tolerate love. As soon as I had opened the thick double doors of the library I knew that no one would ever choose it for a trysting place. The atmosphere was wrong. Totally wrong.

The room was eerie. Which was strange, really, because

unlike the Orinville library, it was brilliantly lit. No corner was unilluminated. There were no hidden shadows. A magnificent chandelier blazed colored light.

But the room looked peculiarly old. The sort of room that might once have housed the Inquisition. Or the executioner. Or, worse yet, the royal torturer. Perhaps the room had been brought lovingly, piece by piece, from Europe and reconstructed here.

The walls were hung with scarlet silk. Oaken bookcases, some fronted with glass, filled the room. Heavy ladders were available, for the shelves wound their way up to a towering ceiling, just under the top section of the house. I had never seen so many books. Not new, brightly covered books either, but massive leather-bound volumes with titles embossed in gold. Had I stumbled on the missing collection of the great Dr. Faustus himself?

At least there were no portraits here. But Stonehaven had more than made up for that, for weird carvings of gargoyles ornamented the shelves. The plunder from a thirteenth-century cathedral. They laughed and stared, stuck out their tongues, rolled their eyes, and curled their forked tails. Or ominously pointed at you with sharp claws. I knew they were rigid wood, immovable. But like a child's fantasy of living toys, I was afraid that they came to life when the lights went off.

In the center of the room two men were talking. The man facing me was Tom Parsons. I had not expected to see him again so soon. The other man had his back toward me. I was frankly afraid to see his face.

Then he slowly revolved his body and looked directly at me. I wanted to dance. It was Robin Rouen. I ran up to him, hugged him, kissed him. It was dear old wonderful Robin. A teddy bear, not a monster. I almost cried with relief.

"Little red fox," his deep voice boomed and echoed throughout the great room. "What's the matter? Did you expect to see a ghost?"

"At the very least. Robin, why didn't you come sooner? I should have invited you but I've been preoccupied."

"With the curse of the Piedmonts?"

"Yes. You tried to warn me, didn't you, that night in New York?"

He stared at me. "What's this I see? A drawn, peaked, little face. And you're thinner, too. Would you like to cry on my big broad shoulder. Come, tell Uncle Robin all about everything."

"No, I don't want to waste our time together with unhappiness. It's so good to have a friend. I need your jokes today more than I need your shoulder. I want a few hours of cheering up."

"Don't fib to me, Maid Marion. You're afraid Andre will think you're disloyal if you confess to me. Well, at least you still love him. That's a good sign."

"But why didn't you tell me you were coming. Mrs. Parsons acted as if she'd hidden a cobra in the library." I was suddenly very conscious of the other man in the room. Tom Parsons. "Is there some reason for sneaking into the house like this?" I asked. I took one step back. Now I wasn't touching Robin.

Tom Parsons didn't look at me. He stared at Robin. As if awaiting a signal. Perhaps he received it. For he turned and left.

Robin took my hand. "Have no fear, madame, you can trust me," he hissed in his best stage-villain voice.

I couldn't help smiling. "I can't possibly believe that you are linked to Tom Parsons in any way. My faith in the scientific method has been badly shaken here at Stonehaven. But I could more easily accept that angels dance on the point of a pin than suspect you of evil, Robin."

"I always said that you were a very perceptive young lady. As usual, I'm proven right. I didn't 'sneak' into Stonehaven, as you put it. I planned to make a surprise grand entrance this evening, burst in on you dramatically at dinner or some such thing. My dear old friend Minnie Parsons was all for announcing my arrival the moment I appeared. But I managed to talk her into keeping me a secret. I hope she's not going to get into trouble because of our little game of collusion."

"Absolutely not. Besides, she can't keep secrets. Her attempt to keep me away from the library was a complete failure. The expression on her face gave her away. I knew she was up to something."

"Poor old Min."

"This room is hardly hospitable. Come along and let's find Andre. He'll be delighted to see you."

"I wouldn't be too sure of that, Tamara."

I remembered the tension between them the night I'd met Andre.

"Anyway, red fox, Tom Parsons will inform Andre of my whereabouts. No need for you to bother. You don't want to deny me a few moments alone with you." And he ostentatiously kissed my hand.

Robin. Next he'd probably bow, a sweeping eighteenth-century courtier's bow. The library was a superb stage for him. It had the proper dimensions for his size and grandeur. Only Robin could have looked underdressed, a dun-colored Benjamin Franklin, while garbed in flaming ascots, capes, or sporting a top hat. Only the wardrobe of Henry the Eighth would have done him justice. Tights, jewels, and an earring in one ear. That's what he needed.

Tactfully, Robin did not press me about my life at Stonehaven. He discussed his work, his next show at an uptown gallery, his evolving style. He spoke to me as one artist to another, which was certainly flattering. Then he told me about his latest party. Apparently it had been a tremendous success.

"If only you had been there. It was a costume party. Presumably underwater. We pretended the living room was one huge sea. I had the walls hung with blue satin for the occasion. Blue carpets were put down. I festooned the entire apartment with chains of false pearls."

"Did anyone think they were real?" I asked.

"Many people did. I caught someone stealing a rope of my best translucent pink. Silly fool could have bought it at Bloomingdale's for next to nothing."

"Did you call the police?"

"I considered it, red fox. But I let the culprit off with a warning. You would have loved the special brew I concocted. Secret recipe from the lost island of Atlantis."

"I wish I had been there to drink it."

"With your marvelous tresses you could have come as Venus, rising from the sea, or a burning phoenix, reborn from the waves."

"What were you?"

"I was Neptune, naturally. Naked from the waist up. I carried an immense gold paper trident. You would have laughed at the girls. Couldn't resist being mermaids; wanted to show off lots of bosom. They had to be carried in by their escorts because they couldn't walk on their fishtails. Once they were put down on the rug, all they could do was lie there, sulk, and talk to each other while everybody else had a splendid time. What price vanity!"

"I don't think we could reproduce the merriment here."

"Why not? Stonehaven has had some good parties in its day."

"Really? I would imagine that an evening with the neighborhood mortician would look raucous in comparison to a party at Stonehaven."

Someone behind me said, "Sorry you're so unhappy here. Woodlands must have clouded your judgment. You'll talk to anybody."

I turned. "Andre," I said, "what an unpleasant remark. Is that the way to greet an old friend?"

"It is when the 'old friend' is Robin Rouen. Grand opera's own Friar Tuck."

"Andre! Cut it out. It cheers me enormously to see Robin again, after the gloom and doom of this house. The least you can do is to behave like a gentleman."

"All right, I'll be very proper. How long are you planning to stay, Robin? Tom Parsons didn't seem to know. Which surprised me, considering your close friendship with him."

"Your husband is being a little foolish, Tamara. I barely know Tom. Old Min now, we go way back. Since my first visit to Stonehaven. A dear lady. Of quite different character than her husband."

"You still haven't answered my question," Andre interrupted. "How long are you planning to stay?"

I was angry and I shouted. I felt like a ventriloquist's dummy, controlled by the ceiling of the library. It threw my words down with a reverberating echo. My voice sounded flat and unreal, the voice of the echo, real. "I hope Robin plans to stay days, weeks, forever. What did Robin ever do to you that gives you the right to act like a boor?"

Curiously, after I said this, both men stood quiet. When they spoke, they were scrupulously polite. Robin apologized for arriving unannounced. He planned to leave shortly to return to his latest painting. No time for vacations, an artist must be disciplined.

Andre then asked that we excuse his bad temper. He went on to say that I needed company and Robin would undoubtedly provide necessary entertainment. He had Crispin brought to us because he knew that Robin was a cat fancier.

Both men spent a few minutes complimenting the cat. Then Andre said that he had work to attend to and left.

I was flabbergasted. Ceremonial courtesy. Respectful bows preceding a judo match. I asked Robin what had happened. He evaded my question. Effectively. By bringing up the curse.

"Andre's imagination is kept vivid by that damn curse, Tamara. It makes him suspicious, hostile. He's got it into his head that I'm a double agent, a spy, interlinked with his enemies."

"Enemies?"

"Enemies, red fox, whom he has created inside his brain. Will-o'-the-wisps. Chimeras. One of these days he'll be seeing 'the little people' at twilight."

"Is this a clever way of telling me that you believe Andre is insane?"

"No, it's my brilliant way of telling you that the Piedmonts live under the threat of the sword, despite their wealth and their beauty. They are subjected to constant fatigue, stress, and anxiety. It affects them. Makes them appear paranoid when they're not. Be patient with him, Tamara. Try to overlook odd quirks. He needs your help very much."

"If only I could prove that the curse doesn't exist. That is, if it doesn't exist."

"Ah, you're begun to believe in the power of the supernatural, haven't you? You're not quite prepared to admit it to yourself, yet. But your skepticism is weakening. It still glows but it is flickering. Then you'll appreciate this library. It has one of the finest magic collections in the world, the result of generations of questing Piedmonts. And their wives."

"Probably starting with Jeremiah Piedmont who took up spiritualism in the nineteenth century. I read about him at the Orinville library."

"Doing homework on the subject? Don't bother with Orinville, then. Bet you didn't know that Jeremiah tried spiritualism in order to contact the ghost of Geoffrey Piedmont."

"No, I didn't."

"The library at Orinville can't provide the juicy details. You'd do better to look right here."

"Why would anyone want to contact Geoffrey?"

"To control him and perhaps, ultimately, to control the curse itself. Did you read Dr. Emma Piedmont's little thesis?"

"That's all I read."

"She's a good example of the scoffers. That's the name I

have given to those Piedmonts who refuse to accept the possibility that the curse and its legends are real. They collected volumes on magic in order to prove to the rest of the family and the world at large that magic is superstitious nonsense."

"And those who believed in the curse? I suppose they studied magic to find an antidote to the curse, a way of circumventing it."

"The true believers? Not necessarily. Some developed a psychotic identification with Geoffrey. There are cases of Piedmonts studying magic to insure that they would personally become the victims of the curse."

"Sounds to me like they already were."

"Admittedly, by the time they reached that state, it's doubtful that Geoffrey would overlook them. Although there is one rather gentle Piedmont, a former college dean, who resides in a padded cell. The hospital staff has been trying desperately for years to get him to think he's Napoleon. Apparently, this would be considered a step toward mental health. But he absolutely insists that he's Geoffrey. Although he doesn't do anything that Geoffrey would approve of. The poor fellow's one hobby is making dolls for orphanages."

"Then you think I ought to use this library in the future."

"Definitely. I'm surprised that you didn't go rummaging around here earlier, Tamara. It's quite fascinating."

"Unlike Bluebeard's wife, I'm not tempted to explore any unknown rooms in Stonehaven. Can't tell what you'll find."

"Then what you need, red fox, is a magician's guided tour. Here I stand, ready to offer you the tourist's special." He performed a graceful pirouette, his cape swirling out behind him. It was jet black. He took a pointer, tapped it on a bookshelf, and waved it like a baton. I observed that he was wearing soft gloves of pure white. Saying, "Follow me!" he led me to an enormous wall of tightly packed books, rising steadily, a mountainous mass, to the ceiling.

Chapter X

Robin cleared his throat and began to lecture. His customary twinkle was gone. He looked dead serious. As if starting a prayer, he mumbled the ritual abracadabra. For the moment I had become his student.

"Magic is a very ancient subject, Tamara. It has managed to find a niche for itself even in this so-called scientific age. It ought to have become extinct, but just as reptiles survived into the age of mammals, magic, too, has continued past the time of its great ascendancy and power."

He ran the pointer across a row of books. "These contain a history of that magnificent age when everyone accepted the existence of supernatural laws. The ancient occult traditions are saved. Nowadays, we don't believe what these books tell us. We file them away and try to forget them. In the past, these books were considered works of the devil and people tried to burn them."

"But because of the Piedmonts, I assume, the books survived."

"Correct, Tamara. The Piedmonts are unusual. Most people are indifferent to the devil. They wouldn't know him if he bit them. Which must please him greatly. Makes his work easier to accomplish."

"But the Piedmonts didn't underestimate him."

"No. They were never allowed to forget his existence. Thanks to Geoffrey. The Piedmonts were rich. They went where they wanted, bought what they wanted, and did what they wanted. Inherently eccentric, they were indifferent to conventions. So who could stop them if they wanted to study about the devil? We don't have autosdafé any more."

"I imagine the Piedmonts managed to avoid being burnt at the stake even when it was relatively common."

"Yes, Tamara. Usually, they were rich enough to escape punishment. And they were adept at dramatic escapes. No prison could hold them. Diabolical traditions are their eternal light. They've kept them alive even through the darkness of our modern period."

"The way medieval monks preserved the classics."

"In a sense, the Piedmonts are satanic monks. Although, to be strictly accurate, we should drop the concept of the devil altogether. As this library will teach you, Tamara, 'devil' is just a name we in the West have given to a cluster of functions greater and older than the concept of Satan. There is no evil being with human weaknesses. There is an evil force. It's far more dangerous, powerful, and sinister than any devil could ever be. The Gnostics understood this better than the Christians ... maybe that's why the Christians called them heretics."

"And the Piedmonts, I take it, went about the world collecting data on this force."

"Everywhere. They went to Haiti, to Africa, to the Orient. Look at these books! They're written in Greek, Latin, Chinese, Bengali, several are in Tibetan dialects. All instruct on the universal evil principle. The names for it are different. In different places it uses methods adapted to the specific culture to get what it wants. But it generally wants the same things."

I lifted a book off a nearby shelf. It was beautifully bound in Morocco leather. The text was in Latin, which I couldn't read. But I could make out the title. *De Occulta Philosophia* by Henry Cornelius Agrippa von Nettesheim.

On a bookstand, carved to resemble an eagle or some more ominous bird of prey, a huge volume stood open. The language was completely unknown to me, though the curlicue script reminded me of Arabic or Hebrew.

"Little red fox, you are viewing one of the rarest books in the world. It's *The Necromitian* by that mad Arab, Abdull Latief. I know half a dozen scholars who would commit murder to get hold of a copy. Many learned men don't even believe the book exists, but it's here."

"Fantastic!"

"As I told you, nowhere in the world is there a library like this. It does indeed contain the lore of centuries. Do you want the history of magic? Then find a ladder and investigate those rows just there." He pointed to shelves inches above his head. "You'll find the Greek and Roman mystery religions well represented. Care to study the rituals of the Illuminiti?

No problem. There's excellent material on casting spells, prophesying the future, necromancy. There's even a modern side to the library. It's complete on the subject of ESP. From Hermes Trismegistus to Rhine, it's all here. See, a whole section on Aleister Crowley."

I raised my eyes and saw a gargoyle watching me closely. Its wooden mouth was pursed in an "O" shape, as if amazed itself by the number of books surrounding it. I wondered if it approved of Robin's didactic manner.

"You sound cold, Robin. Like a technician who experiments with animals and feels utter indifference to their pain. Do you realize the implications of magic? If there's any truth to it, then none of us are safe. All the scientific facts we have carefully constructed over the last three hundred years are meaningless. A gigantic something is waiting to knock them over like building blocks."

"Or use them for its own purposes, Tamara. Concentration camps and nuclear bombs might strike it as amusing toys. But you're wrong if you think I feel no passion on the question of magic. I'm like a mouse, staring fixated into a snake's eyes. Terrified, but unable to run, while the jaws open. I've been using the occult in my work. My painting is in transition, growing more bizarre."

For the first time I was aware that I was alone with Robin in a room with walls so thick that screams might not penetrate to the hall outside. Robin's size no longer seemed humorous. I had always thought of him as a living stuffed toy, a child's panda come to life. I had never realized before quite how strong he was.

He was no longer talking to me, he was really talking to himself.

"Everything I paint now comes out in the colors of magic. I've become obsessed with satanic red. I'm doing an immense canvas in just that one shade. It was this library which first attracted me to Stonehaven. I've delved. I've sat here for hours devouring words. I've learned. I know quite a bit about witchcraft. I've thought about becoming a warlock. I know what it would do to me. But I may not be able to resist. Like drug addiction or alcoholism. I crave it. I've played little games with white magic. Mixed herbs. Done palmistry. Tea readings. Petty stuff. But I'm getting more expert."

"Not black magic?"

He ignored me. I don't think he even heard me.

"The Key to Solomon. I located that volume nearly at the top of the collection. Then I went on to spells from the Black Books. Andre let me spend hours over those. Alas, he is suspicious of me these days. Even tried to forbid me the house once."

"Why? Did he feel you were getting too absorbed for your own psychic health? If so, I think he was right. Please snap out of this mood, Robin; you're frightening me."

"But I got back in anyway. I know I'm only an amateur, I've barely gotten beneath the surface. Even talented students spend years at these studies. Dr. Dee sat over his books sixteen hours a day for half a century. But then he didn't have 'the gift.' I do. Given time, I could accomplish marvels. I'm no longer ever sick. Do you realize that? Never ill at all."

Slowly, I began to back up. If I kept my eyes on his face and moved carefully step by step, perhaps I could reach the door. Robin might not even notice. There must be no sudden movement, no panicky reaction. But, as if unaware of his own body, Robin moved with me. He continued to talk, his face close to mine, his eyes now focused on my mouth. I kept my lips closed tight. We were like stilted ballroom dancers, the roles reversed. I led, he followed.

"I've held séances. In my apartment. One time we were too successful. I'm not sure, but we may have conjured the ghost of Geoffrey. It was dark . . . I couldn't see clearly. But there was a face, it looked like the Piedmont face. There was a mark on the cheek. At the time I thought perhaps it was that hair birthmark. I know it was burned off. But, like a starfish, it must be able to regenerate itself."

Now Robin's feet were moving independently of mine. We were still walking backward toward the door but he had quickened the pace. I was no longer in control.

Robin changed his voice. His speech became sibilant. He spoke almost in a whisper. I had heard that odd, hissing voice somewhere else. In a moment I remembered. When I was fourteen, a man had phoned. Several times. I never found out who it was. But he threatened to perform certain acts with me. I was terrified. Grandmother finally informed the police. They advised changing our phone number. We did. I never heard the voice again.

Until now. The words were different but Robin's voice sounded the same. It reawakened dormant terror.

"The Black Mass. I am tempted to explore the Black

Mass. Dare I risk my soul? I am humble before the unknown. Wiser men than I have been lost. All the work, the concentration, preparing the mind; that's the hardest part. And the danger. The elements are powerful and unpredictable. No one ever really conquers them. That old saying about supping with the devil, it's true. I don't know where my damnable insatiable curiosity is taking me. Where . . ."

A ripping noise on the heavy door stopped Robin in midsentence. Another ripping sound. Robin listened. The gargoyles above looked amused. Perhaps it was one of their own kind outside. Had it gone for a walk and come back only to find the door shut? Or was the resident demon of the library clawing to enter the room and begin its studies?

The scratching could not be ignored. Most likely it had already left narrow lines in the wood of the door. And for all I knew, the door might be a valuable antique, imported from a monastery in Spain. It certainly looked it.

But what would Robin do if I went to open the door? I stared at him. His cheeks had begun to quiver. I expected a mad assault at any moment. Unexpectedly he rushed past me, threw open the door, and started to laugh. A roaring voluminous laugh, head thrown back, spade-beard trembling.

"Crispin, my comrade of a cat, come in!" he shouted. Daintily, taking prissy little steps and fluttering his tail, Crispin walked to me and licked my ankle.

"See, red fox, how futile is the vanity of man. Here I stand, building a cathedral of magic, and there you stand, scared to death that I'd gone mad. And here we both are, conjuring Beelzebub and Ashtoreth in our imaginations, when this little animal walks into the room and the world is restored to its normal proportions again. A triumph for realism. I think I'll give up magic altogether!"

Robin was his old self again. Had he really looked menacing a few minutes ago? Perhaps it was merely the result of the atmosphere of this room. Nevertheless, I scolded him for a good ten minutes for giving me a scare.

"Forgive me," he begged. "It's the drama. I can never resist. I began thinking of magic and became overly exuberant. I imagined myself to be a great magician with immense powers."

"You appeared to be in a trance. I've never seen you like that."

"Then you've never seen me working, either. Similar

moods come over me when I paint." He looked worried. "I really had you frightened. What an idiot I am. A fool. See, I smite myself in wrath." He struck his forehead with his fist.

"Stop it, Robin. You'll only hurt yourself and silly antics aren't going to make me forgive you. I don't know if I can ever trust you fully again."

Robin looked like a disheveled urchin, caught with his hand in the cookie jar. "Little red fox, you are one of my favorite people. And I promise very solemnly to redeem myself someday."

His voice shook with emotion. Any moment a crocodile tear would probably ooze out of his eye. All I felt toward him was disgust. I changed the subject back to painting. Robin was never irritating when he talked about his work.

"I must confess, Tamara, that I did not come into the library unannounced today simply because I wanted to make my grand entrance later. I came in here to search for some old engravings. I need them for my next project. I was afraid that you'd think I was antisocial, spending a few hours in the library alone. You'd consider me a tired old bookworm, and never invite me back."

I stifled my weariness. "Feel free to spend as much time in the library as you want, whenever you visit, Robin. However, it would make things easier if in the future you'd let me know when you've arrived."

"I shall inform old Min of our conversation, dear lady. She didn't like deceiving you at all. She will be relieved to know that I shall never expect her to do so again."

"Did you at least find what you were looking for?"

"Indeed. I located exactly what I wanted."

"I'm glad of that, anyway." I left because I couldn't bear Robin another minute. The house was very quiet as I walked down the hall to my special room. Stonehaven was digesting the emotions released in the library. My fear must have made a tasty dessert for it.

I passed the gargantuan stairway leading to the upper floors. A blooming young girl, fresh as a shepherdess or milkmaid, knelt next to the great banister. She was cleaning the steps. I had met most of the servants already. But I had never seen this girl before. She must be the one Mrs. Parsons had mentioned earlier.

"Are you Elsie?" I asked.

She nodded.

I didn't like her. I had no use for tattletales. Apparently Tom Parsons had boasted that he had put me squarely in my place this morning. And Elsie had wasted no time carrying the tale right back to Mrs. Parsons. I decided the girl needed a little lesson in good manners.

"I understand, Elsie, that you received the impression that I consider Tom Parsons rude and unpleasant. Actually, when I met him today, I found him extremely polite. He offered to help me up the driveway to the house. But I like walking. So I refused his help. I must have been rather brusque with him. I hope I didn't hurt his feelings." That would burn the old buzzard when word got back to him. The servants would probably tease him for days. Christians, one point; lions, nothing.

Elsie had the good grace to blush. Maybe she'd think twice before engaging in malicious gossip again backstairs. But she was so young. I didn't want her to feel crushed. I decided to be friendly.

"Would you mind doing me a favor, Elsie? Please find my husband and tell him that Mr. Rouen will not join us until dinner tonight. You might not have known, but we have a guest staying with us."

"I did know that, Mrs. Piedmont. At least, I figured he was a guest. He certainly doesn't look like anybody from around here."

"Did you see him passing on the stairs?"

"The big bearded gentleman? No, I saw him very early this morning. While you were at Jenny Hooper's house. He was standing outside at the top of the driveway, with your husband. They were laughing and talking, having a great time for themselves."

"My husband? Andre? But that can't be, Elsie. My husband saw our guest for the first time an hour or so ago, in the library."

"It was Mr. Piedmont all right. You can never confuse him with anyone else, not with that hair of his. And I was very close."

I started to argue and then caught myself. Elsie was looking at me with open curiosity. If I said anything more, she would tell everyone that the master had lied to the mistress. Wouldn't that lead to snickers and sneers.

"Never mind, Elsie. I'm sure you're right. I probably misunderstood. It's not important."

Elsie was telling the truth, that much was clear. She had no reason to lie. She could lose her job if she were caught. But Andre. Why didn't he tell me that he'd met Robin this morning? And why were they buddies on the driveway and enemies later in the library.

It seemed such a trivial lie that I was shaken by it. I felt like a blind swimmer passing close to poisoned anemones. Something evil was right around me. But my senses were too limited to comprehend it.

By the time I reached my bedroom I was too confused to think clearly. There had to be a connection between Robin's obsession with the occult and his meeting with Andre this morning. But what could it be? Whatever it was, it meant trouble.

I put my hand on one wall of the room. It trembled very slightly. As if somewhere within itself Stonehaven was chuckling with pleasure.

Chapter XI

Conversation at the dinner table that evening was something less than sparkling. Robin chattered, doing his best to be witty, but succeeded only in being annoying. Andre sat at the head of the table. I sat at the foot. It was like being at different ends of a long tunnel.

I was preoccupied with worry and kept losing track of Robin's conversation. Andre was in a sulk to end all sulks. Dutifully, he ate his food. But he was with us in body only. He sat mute, his face totally expressionless, like the legendary handsome prince turned to stone.

Mrs. Parsons had done her best in honor of that rarity: a guest at Stonehaven. She had seen to it that the table was set with the family's exclusive pattern of Spode china, its best sterling, its finest embossed napkins.

The snow had stopped, the wind had died, and the stars were as bright as Christmas. It made a beautiful scene. Unfortunately, the view went unappreciated by the observers. I, for example, could barely eat. My wineglass remained untouched. For all I cared, the champagne bottle could have stayed in its silver ice bucket all evening. But Robin wouldn't hear of it. Thanks to his gargantuan appetite, a respectable quantity of food and drink was consumed.

Andre and I approached our superb dinner as if it were an act of penance to eat it. I managed a bit of the dessert, a delicious Genois cake, elaborately iced. Iced. It was appropriate. Andre and I were frozen blocks at either end of the table.

Because it was expected of us, we had coffee together. But I insisted we drink it in my special room. Starved for warmth, I sat close to the fire. Andre chose a chair as far from me as possible, and Robin flopped onto the sofa. Insensitive to others at the best of times, he talked on and on. Dinner and drinks had left him feeling sentimental and he clearly expected a warm evening of auld lang syne.

Finally, it occurred to him that he was not the life of the party, that in fact there was no party at all. This depressed him.

"I feel," he bellowed gloomily, "that I have been presiding over a wake. Chief pallbearer."

"The pall is emanating from you," Andre said.

"An unkind cut, old man. Would you care to fill the time with a few card tricks or sleight of hand? We could take turns telling jokes. Anything would improve the evening."

"Robin, you're so provoking," I said. "We're very fond of you but we don't have the patience to humor you tonight."

Andre laughed. "Tamara is very tactful. What she really means is that you're boring us to exhaustion and since you're an uninvited guest, you ought to climb back into your car and return home."

"Stop it, Andre," I snapped, losing my temper. "I'm tired of your self-pity and self-indulgence. What makes you think you can say whatever you want, whenever you want, to anybody. What gives you the right to hurt Robin and embarrass me?"

"Never mind, little red fox, I have a thick skin. But she's right, you know, Andre. The only reason I haven't left is because I'm snowed in. Once morning arrives and the roads are plowed, I will depart with speed. Therefore, since we're stuck with one another for a few hours, we ought to make the best of it. But you can't do that, can you? You've got to be on stage every moment, suffering in noble silence, pretending to be a character out of the Brontes." Robin cupped his hands around his mouth and called, "Heathcliffe! Heathcliffe!"

Andre shouted, "Damn it, I don't have to put up with this nonsense in my own home."

"It isn't precisely a suburban bi-level, old chum, and it isn't exactly your home. It's the Piedmont estate." And Robin smiled unpleasantly.

"What do you mean by that?" Andre asked, with that icy calm people sometimes show when they really feel intense anger.

"You know what I mean, don't you, Andre? You understand perfectly. But you would prefer me to keep quiet, under the circumstances."

"I can't stand any more of this," I said. "You're playing verbal Ping-Pong, exchanging messages, flashing each other signals. Why? Because there's something you don't want me to know. But I mean to find out. So let's get it over with. Tell me!"

Andre stared at Robin a long time. Then he looked at me and said quietly, "Your grandmother would approve of you, my pet. You've absorbed all her values. Including a high-minded suspiciousness. You think people are keeping secrets from you, plotting behind your back. Next thing, you'll decide the soup's poisoned. Better watch out."

When I answered Andre, my voice was no louder than his, and I was just as angry. "When I married you, Andre, I assumed I could trust you to be truthful with me. Even when it came to unpleasant truths. I know you have secrets. I know that something odd is happening at Stonehaven. The house exudes an evil force."

"And you suspect that I am somehow in league with this force?"

"At one time I would have thought such a possibility ridiculous. Now, frankly, I don't know. Let's start with the lies. You told me that you first met Robin in the library today. Yet, Elsie told me in all innocence that you and Robin first met on the driveway this morning. Apparently in high good spirits. Why? Were the two of you planning to perform an occult service before lunch?"

Andre's face seemed to shrivel while I watched. He looked

old. Unhappy. I knew I was creating a crisis between us, forcing things to a head. But I couldn't stop.

"I saw you being very friendly with Tom Parsons, a man I'd hardly expect you to consider a chum. And I saw you walk toward the woods, quite casually today, in winter weather which kills. Yes, Andre, it's true; people who go into the woods during a blizzard often die. And there's one more thing."

"Yes?"

"Jenny Hooper's little girl. Why does she look exactly like you? Everyone says that Jenny is marvelous. And I agree with them. Do you find her marvelous, too? If so, why did you marry me? Why didn't you marry her? Did you choose me because of some twisted motive? Did I seem a likely victim? Is Geoffrey Piedmont resurrected from death again, this time through you?"

There. I had said it all.

Andre's voice had aged. In minutes. Boyhood was on the other side of a dividing line created by my words. He did not look at me when he spoke.

"The curse is true, Tamara. I'm convinced of that. I had hoped when I married you that you would change my mind, make me see that the curse is a foolish superstition. I had also hoped that you would assume that I was radically different from Geoffrey, an unlikely heir for him. Instead, you consider me his logical successor. You see, since adolescence, I've been waiting for Geoffrey to arrive. To suck out my mind and replace it with his."

Robin interrupted. "I know I don't belong in the center of a domestic squabble. But Tamara is a clever girl and this might be the right moment for 'the whole truth and nothing but the truth.' Instead, you're using self-pity as a shield."

"Damn you," Andre shouted. "You charletan. You sham of a sorcerer's apprentice. You insist on directness, on truth. You, who came sneaking in here with stupid incantations and worthless charts. Caught hiding in the library! Keep out of my business! I'll tell Tamara everything, but in my own way. Without your innuendoes and sly digs."

Now Robin was angry. "Watch what you say, Andre. I'm on your side, trying to protect your interests. But don't push me too far. I might decide to become explicit myself, without measuring the impact of my words. And the result could be brutal, especially for you."

"Who cares what you could say, you pompous fraud!" Andre faced me. "Tamara, I'll tell you the truth. We'll bring everything into the open. But you'll be disappointed. I can't offer you any elaborate confessions. You'd like me to tell you that I'm a werewolf, or a warlock. Sorry, no such luck. You're stuck with me as I am. A morose human being. That's all."

"You're not answering my questions."

"All right. I've never hidden anything from you; the truth is quite dull. I have known Tom Parsons since I was a child. I'm not fond of him but I do speak to him civilly. Because I don't kick him whenever we meet doesn't mean that I seek him out for secret orgies when no one's around. Nor do I perform miracles. I can't remember the last time I walked on water. And I'm no better than anybody else at surviving blizzards. I never go into the woods in the midst of one."

"Andre, I saw you doing just that."

"Then have your vision tested, dear one. Or accept what I told you before. The snow creates strange effects. You've heard of mirages in the desert. Snow, too, can cause an optical illusion. As for Elsie, she lied. It's her word against mine and I hope that you don't hold me in such contempt that you believe her, not me. After all, you just met her, while I am your husband."

"But why would she lie?"

"I have no idea. When you've lived here for years you'll understand that the local people gossip and lie without giving it much thought. They lead uneventful lives and inventing exciting incidents or exaggerating everyday events makes the world less monotonous. I never talked to Robin this morning. I never talk to Robin at all if I can possibly avoid it. Did it ever occur to you that Elsie might have chosen to lie about Robin and me just to get back at you."

"To get back at me?"

"For breaking a cardinal rule: the lady of the house never lets herself get drawn into the servants' gossip. If Elsie wants to carry tales about Mr. Parsons to Mrs. Parsons, that's up to her. Under no circumstances should you take notice of it. Your rebuke to Elsie is the talk of the kitchen. The servants are so shocked at your behavior that they've taken her side. I overheard them discussing it. They think less of you now. Better be careful to hold your tongue in the future."

"I had no idea I'd done anything inappropriate. I'm sorry."

"Now to Jenny Hooper. Not my type. Never has been. I've always been attracted to red-haired girls. But perhaps I've been foolish. Evidently, they're not very loyal. There's nothing extraordinary in Stacy's appearance. Look around the county. It's a fact of life that the Piedmonts, in days of yore, took full advantage of a master's bed rights. Even in the New World, where it wasn't strictly legal. If you think I'm exaggerating, observe Minnie Parsons. She has Piedmont eyes. As blue as mine. And I can assure you that I never bedded Mrs. Parsons' mother."

"All right, I've been imagining things. I'm sorry that I've hurt you. But, often you're very distant, Andre, and it makes me unhappy and suspicious."

He was at the door. I could see that he was eager to leave. "If I am distant, wife, it's because I am waiting. For the Devil Incarnate. But I assure you, he has not yet come. I would find it a comfort if you'd take my word for it. Meanwhile, we can both watch for signs of his presence. But please be subtle when observing me. I hate to be treated like something viewed under a microscope."

The door slammed; Andre was gone.

Robin took my hand. "It was a mistake, forcing Andre into explanations."

"I see that."

"Are you satisfied with his answers?"

"Yes. But so what? My marriage is finished. I've been harsh, instead of kind, judgmental instead of trusting."

"Don't be so hard on yourself, little fox. Andre expects too much of you. He wants you to save him from his fate. You don't have the power to do that."

"What should I do now, Robin? Drive back to New York with you?"

"You'd hate yourself if you did. Hold on here, Tamara; Andre will come round eventually. What he needs is time." Robin gazed ahead, abstracted. Then he repeated, "What Andre needs now is plenty of time."

Chapter XII

The next morning dawned bleak and gray, following a night to match. My head ached and my throat was dry. Too many aspirins. I had needed them to get to sleep. For the bed had seemed extraordinarily large last night. It had been half-empty. Andre had gone upstairs to the nursery after dinner and never returned.

The air coming in through the slightly opened window was softened. Outside, winter still controlled the world. The earth was covered with snow. But the depth of the snow was deceptive. Winter was losing its power. Spring was asserting itself.

The Catskills are cold for a long time and winter would produce many an icy morning yet. But this was the last real snowfall of the year, winter's farewell gesture. The scene outside my window looked permanent. But it was as ephemeral as a rose garden on a June morning.

I lay in bed a long time, staring out the window. Too depressed to get up. Mrs. Parsons, with her marvelous sixth sense, surprised me with breakfast in bed. She even allowed me to save face by pretending that I had a cold, and so should take my time about getting up.

On the breakfast tray was a note from Robin. It said, "Sorry, little fox, but I'm taking my leave at an early hour. I think it's best if I don't return for a while. But, like a bad penny, I'll turn up. You'll see. Love, Robin."

I ate breakfast with the same indifference I had eaten dinner the night before. I pretended that I was back in my apartment in New York. What would the view be like from my window today? Rain instead of snow. People I would never know walking back and forth across the street. And I would watch them for an hour or so while the fireplace warmed the little room and kept it cozy. And the radio played pleasant wake-up music.

It's possible that I would have done what I had never done before: spent the entire day in bed. But Mrs. Parsons interrupted me.

"Jenny Hooper's dropped in to see you. Are you well enough to see her, ma'am?"

"Of course. Tell her I'll be right down."

Jenny and Stacy Lynn were waiting for me in my special room. One look at Jenny and I couldn't believe that I'd actually suspected her of having an affair with Andre. The accusation seemed ludicrous in broad daylight.

She was leaning protectively over Stacy. "She feels a little insecure," Jenny said. "This is her first visit here." There was nothing furtive about Jenny. Nothing dishonorable. An honest woman. Andre had told the truth; they must be, as the saying goes, just good friends.

"I'd like to paint the two of you someday," I said. "American Madonna and Child."

Jenny blushed. "Sounds sacrilegious."

"It wasn't meant that way," I said.

"I'd be flattered if you painted a picture of both of us. But I'd prefer you to paint Stacy alone. We'd hang it where everybody who comes to visit would see it."

The idea unnerved me. Stacy alone. It would look like another Piedmont portrait.

"Let's decide on that when the time comes," I said, and reached out to the baby. Stacy crawled up to me, stared solemnly, and then plunged into a friendly game of peek-a-boo.

"Want some cake?" I asked Jenny, while Stacy took time out to chew her shoelace.

"No, thank you. Have to get Jack up and off to work every morning. And the only thing that will do it is coffee cake or pound cake."

"And I suppose you bake it yourself everyday?"

"Of course. I couldn't afford store-bought."

Cheerful, efficient Jenny. I would gladly have traded Stonehaven for her little starter house. Hers was a decent, hardworking life. Very much in order. No grim tragedies from the past polluting the present. No labyrinthine complexities. For Jenny, existence was neat, simple, cubed, and clean. Not surprising that she was an optimist about her future and I was a pessimist about mine. Mine was cluttered with Piedmonts.

"This morning I had to stuff Jack with coffee cake. And

naturally I ate my share, too. He's got a Police Benevolent Society meeting tonight in Orinville. It's a regional meeting and he's got to attend. But what he really wants to do is work around the house."

"He wants to be with you."

"With me and with Stacy. He'd carry her off to work if they'd let him. If you want to see my husband happy, then see him on a weekend. You can hear him humming for hours when he's in the workshop in the garage. Especially if he's using safe tools and can keep Stacy with him."

A chuckle of joy from Stacy focused our attention on her again. She was reaching for a deliciously shining object. A Sandwich glass candlestick. Jenny literally swooped down on her and brought her back to me.

"I guess it's time for more peek-a-boo," I said. "Must protect the precious Piedmont treasures. I hate to sound grim but I wish Stacy would break them all."

Jenny looked around. "Stonehaven is more like a museum than a real house, isn't it?"

"It certainly is. I didn't grow up surrounded by such riches. And I'm not sure that I'll ever be comfortable with them. This room is simplicity personified compared to the rest of the house. We have a dining hall which could have held the Knights Templar. And bath tubs the size of Noah's Ark."

The bitterness in my voice surprised me. Jenny looked uncomfortable. Politely, she changed the subject.

"I came to invite you to the annual Woodlands party. We hold it in Orinville every spring. That's because we've so few people. If we didn't let everyone in Orinville come, it wouldn't be much of a party."

"Do the Piedmonts usually come?" I asked, hoping that I sounded tactful. I didn't want to commit Andre to a social gathering where he'd feel out of place. I'd used up my allotted quota of gaffes yesterday, when I bungled the interview with Elsie. It wouldn't soothe Andre if I made a similar error this soon.

"They're always invited. And they're always welcome. Sometimes they act as if they're doing Woodlands a big favor by showing up. But I know that you would never behave like that."

I could well imagine how some of the Piedmonts had viewed the locals. As social inferiors. They would have attended the parties out of a sense of lofty duty. Doing their bit for a worthy cause. The arrogant sneers in the portraits made this abundantly clear.

"I'd like to come, Jenny. And I'm sure Andre will, too."

"We always have a good time. There's all the food in the world and plenty to drink. I'm never sure which attracts people the most. Woodlands has more than its share of hard drinkers."

Considering the climate, I could well believe that.

Jenny continued. "And there is dancing. Plus politicking. There's no election this year but anybody who's thinking of running for office next year has to start wooing votes now. Out here, you get paid for being county assessor, road supervisor, or whatever. The money's not much but every little bit counts. There's plenty of competition so you'll meet lots of would-be candidates at the party."

"Is there anything I can do to help?"

"I think the planning committees are already formed. It never occurred to anyone to ask you to join one. But I'll talk to Celia. She'll find something for you to do."

An irritated meow made us look around. Stacy had a firm grip on Crispin's tail. Apparently she had decided that he would make a good addition to her stuffed animal collection at home. Crispin, his dignity severely impaired, managed to extricate himself and jump to a safe shelf.

"This is Crispin's first encounter with a child," I said. "Well, cat, I guess you'll have to learn to keep out of her way." Insulted red eyes gave me a royal stare. The feline monarch of the house wasn't about to change his habits.

"On the other hand, maybe you'd better keep away from him, Stacy. He could be dangerous for you. Very sharp claws."

Stacy pouted; her lip quivered.

"Tantrum on the way," said Jenny. "Sorry but the kitty cat lives here, baby. We can't take it home. It's time I got you in for your nap anyway, little grouch."

"Do you have to leave so soon?"

"Tamara, I'm ashamed to admit that I need sleep as much as Stacy now that I'm pregnant again. Maybe she could skip her nap but I can't skip mine. I'm tired."

"Well, come again soon. And I promise to clear a room of treasures so you won't have to keep close watch on Stacy. The people who've lived in this house haven't liked babies. They were the kind of people who never dropped cigarette

ashes, kept dogs, or scratched table tops." I thought again of
Andre spending his childhood here. Hardly surprising that he
was moody.

"I know all these things are expensive," said Jenny. "And
some of them are very beautiful. But I don't understand the
kind of people who prefer objects to babies."

"Neither do I. Oh damn. Crispin's attacking the drapes. If
they're torn, Mrs. Parsons will never forgive me. Take Stacy
and I'll meet you in the hall." There was a brief but violent
struggle and Crispin was disentangled from the drapes.

"Instead of scratching the drapes, Crispin, you've scratched
me." He was puffed with pride as if to avenge his recent humiliation at Stacy's hands.

"I see you feel you've asserted yourself," I said, as I
rubbed the ruptured skin on my hand. Apparently I had been
punished enough. Crispin patted me gently, claws retracted.
Stretched out, his tail gracefully looped, he looked as if he
were made of white taffeta.

"You'd make a beautiful ornament for a mantelpiece," I
told him, rubbing his head. Crispin purred, thoroughly molli-
fied. I picked him up and carried him out of the room.

Then I stopped dead. Ahead of me stood Jenny. I could
see her profile clearly. She had a tight grip on Stacy, who
was nearly asleep. Jenny stood absolutely still and stared into
the room in front of her. Her face was pale, her eyes did not
blink, and her mouth was open. Was she seeing a ghost? A
crime being committed? A corpse? For she was on the verge
of a scream.

I hurried. When I reached her, seconds later, I touched her
arm. She turned her head and looked at me. Her eyes were
slightly out of focus. Then, after an effort, she returned her
face to normal.

"What's going on in that room?" I asked, afraid to look.

"Nothing," Jenny said, a slight tremor in her voice. "Nothing's wrong." And, forgetting to say good-bye, she walked
away from me and left the house.

Stunned, I forced myself to examine the room. It looked
exactly the same as it always did. There was nothing unusual
about it. Only one person was there. A person you'd expect
to see at Stonehaven. It was Andre. He was holding a portfolio. Just Andre alone in the room. And that was all.

Chapter XIII

"What frightened Jenny?"

Andre's mouth bent sour. "Was Jenny here? I didn't notice her. Too absorbed in these pictures. Most likely the sight of me reminded her of our nightly revels in Hell."

"Please don't be sarcastic. She was really upset. Did something happen?"

"Not as far as I know. A ghost may have materialized behind me, of course, and made threatening gestures. Tamara, are you convinced Jenny was scared? Or are you imagining dramatic events again?"

"She was going to scream."

"Just the sight of my face. Often affects women that way. Forget it! Take a look at these engravings. Our recent guest removed them from the library and forgot to put them back. They reveal his character. What sort of man would enjoy seeing them, Tamara?"

I picked up the top picture. It was a woodcut showing a horned figure. Half-man, half-woman. Simply done. But something about the curving lines made the picture grossly erotic. I averted my eyes.

"What, you don't like pictures of Satan's familiars?" Andre asked, mockingly. "I don't blame you. This is the most innocent picture in the portfolio. I'll spare you the rest and return them all to the library, where they belong. Perhaps you now have some insight into why I don't care for your friend Robin Rouen. His soul has rotted."

"Are you coming back here when you're finished with the library?"

"No, not just now. If I'm going to metamorphose into Geoffrey, I'd rather it happened in private. So I'll go off by myself and listen to music. I'll call you if the hair birthmark materializes. Wouldn't want you to miss that part of the transformation."

91

I was alone again. Back to my early morning mood, which though dreadful was not one of black despair. Instead, it was as if the weather outside had seeped into my mind, leaving it cold and gray.

I put on my boots, my coat, and a winter scarf. If walking didn't cure my depression it might satisfy my curiosity. I went to the front of the house and then started walking toward the woods. A line of footprints headed straight into them.

Could they be Andre's? Was this the path he had followed yesterday, after talking to Tom Parsons? Then I reminded myself that the snow had continued late into yesterday. It would have obliterated any footprints. These must be fresh.

Andre was right. I was a suspicious woman. Last night, I had accepted his explanation completely. This very next morning, I was dubious again. Poor Andre. He ought to have chosen someone more loyal. Or more gullible.

I had reached the edge of the woods. No end yet to the footprints. Where did they ultimately lead? Probably out again to the road. But I felt like following them.

Sometimes, when walking in the woods, I liked to move alongside the hoof prints of a deer. It made me feel that I was somehow participating in its private existence. I would follow the meandering trail for a long time. Perhaps tracking human prints would give me the same sensation.

I stepped into the woods but a squat figure imposed himself between the trail of footprints and me. Tom Parsons, his face rough as bark, barred my way.

"What do you want here?"

"The snow's stopped, and I feel like walking in the woods."

"Well, don't do it. The snow's deep in there; you'll never make it. We'd have to send a rescue party out for you."

"But you've been in the woods. And nothing has happened to you."

"I'm different. You haven't been here long. I've spent years in these woods. Winter and summer. I can find my way in them at night, without a moon. There are landmarks. I know where the rhododendron patches are. And where the big rough hickory stands. I can't get lost. But you can."

The Piedmonts might own the woods on paper, but Tom Parsons looked like the real proprietor. The woods were his by squatter's right. For he had lived in them and loved them. I was an interloper. Perhaps I should have turned back and left the beautiful wilderness ahead to him. He understood it better than I ever could.

But a rebellious, stubborn impulse stopped me. The woods were magnificent; Stonehaven a nightmare. Why should I return to the house?

"What if I won't turn back?" I said.

"You'll wish you had. There are hidden places in the woods where you might fall. No one would hear you scream. You'd die there, of fatigue and cold, during the long night. It would make an awful death."

I tried to stand my ground, to exert myself and dominate this infuriating old man. But I wasn't strong enough. I might have won, if we'd been inside the house. But out here, in his world, I didn't have a chance.

In my mind I saw a deep snow-filled hole, deceptively covered by a thin layer of ice. The snow was warm and melting. I visualized myself finding that hole in the woods. I would put my foot on the ice and feel it give way beneath me. Then I would tumble, my leg would twist, making a cracking sound. And I would lie there, struggling to crawl, until night fell, and exhaustion destroyed me.

Tom Parsons smiled. "I think you'll go back now."

He was right. For I would spend my time in the woods waiting for that fall. Or that push. Tom Parsons, I observed, had hands as strong as tree roots.

I turned around. What was that old saying about being caught between the devil and the deep blue sea? I decided to opt for Stonehaven. It was the lesser evil.

I spent the following two weeks, hiding in Stonehaven, like an animal trapped in a cage. But winter grew weaker by the day and finally I couldn't stand being indoors another minute.

At first, I crept out, skirting the perimeter of the woods. There was no sign of Tom Parsons. The next day I grew bolder; I went farther into the forest. I met with no accident. Saw no ghosts. Then I stopped being cautious. I went walking whenever I wanted, stayed in the woods all day, if I felt like it. For spring had altered Woodlands.

Not in the way most people expect. There were no bursting blossoms and brilliant skies. Not yet. Early spring, like late fall, is an amorphous time, a tug of war between two seasons. In place of snow, rain falls. The ground snow melts. Nature's raw landscape appears, with slopes and valleys exposed, looking exactly as marked on a surveyor's map.

The pine trees lose their dominance as dried leaves and grasses, the brown residue of last year's glory, are seen to cover the earth. There is water again as ponds and lakes fill and run, no longer buried under a static coating of ice. What ice there is becomes paper-thin, cracks as a mirror breaks, and falls away in chips at the slightest touch.

Mud is everywhere. It sticks to your shoes, gets on the tires of your car, is tracked through every room in the house. It is the result of melting snow and constant rain.

Rain comes down on the roof, runs off into the river. It drenches animals and people. The sound of the rain becomes background music. The day's tasks are performed to the monotony of its rhythms.

Only in the city does the poet's springtime arrive overnight. Thus it is to city people that spring owes its fabulous reputation. Country people know that early spring is the ugliest time of the year.

I had experienced the coming of spring in New York City. One day the dawn was soft and warm. Peddlers turned florists and sold daffodils from pushcarts. Crowds were happier. People strolled, looking in store windows. Or sat on stoops, drinking beer. Guitars played Spanish music in the warm night.

I understand the urban worship of springtime. How can it be otherwise when the mere change of season brings instantaneous beauty and light. But in the country, a full six weeks after the death of winter, the air is still cold and the earth is damp.

Still, I loved walking in the woods, even in wet weather. Although I couldn't see anything growing, I knew that the earth was rich with life. Someday plants would appear and then the natural contours of the land would be disguised again. This time with flowers instead of snow.

The early spring air, impregnated with moisture, had lost its winter clarity. By late afternoon, I could no longer see my breath become mist. I found something new every day. One morning, I came upon a skunk cabbage, large with fuzzy leaves, growing in a field.

The birds returned, one species at a time. Red-winged blackbirds usurped the feeders placed under the windows of my special room. A robin was seen. Ducks and grebes borrowed the pond. They are tourists who will fly farther north in the morning. And startled chipmunks now darted from one rock crevice to another in dry stone walls.

Slowly, the earth will lose its moisture. The strength of the sun will increase. Until finally, a day will come when the air will be mild and hazy. The sky, bleached of its intensity, will look almost powder blue. The barn swallows will dip for insects on the surface of the pond. At night, the stars will blur in the warm air. And a springtime will have arrived which rivals anything the city has to offer.

In the meantime I was consoled by waking each morning to birdsongs. And I needed consolation, for too many nights I slept alone. I was marking time.

Andre didn't bother with pretenses any more. He barely spoke to me. Common sense told me that now was the time to leave him. He didn't want me around, that much was clear. But I was still incapable of finalizing the break between us. I was waiting for an outside event to do it for me. If only a giant governess would come for me, pack my bags, settle me in a car, and drive me back to New York.

So, to keep sane, I took woods walks everyday. They provided my only escape from inertia. I became quite proficient at finding my way around.

Tom Parsons would have been proud of me, for I learned where the landmarks were. The old hickory he had told me about was near a fire trail, ten miles into the woods. I found two impressive boulders, resting in an open field. There was a secret lake, where pilated woodpeckers liked to come. I could hear them hammering at the sides of trees at the other end of the lake. And I found mountain laurel. Acres of it. I promised to myself that I would return for a visual feast in June.

So it was that I happened on the cottage in the woods.

At first it reminded me of Hansel and Gretel's gingerbread house. It was small and rustic, with a sloping alpine roof. Wedges of blue and gray stone had been used to face it. These looked like mouthfuls of hard candy. A topping of confectionery snow on the roof would have provided a delicious finishing touch.

But there would be no more snow this year. On this colorless spring day the cottage looked like a leprechaun's home. Surrounded by moss-covered walls of rock, and with the soft rains touching it, it had the air of a mysterious relic of Ireland, transplanted in the New World. At twilight it must look enchanted.

It was deserted. Probably uninhabited during the winter season. I felt extremely curious. No one had told me about a shelter in the woods. Yet everyone knew I walked here even on frigid days when this cottage would have been a Godsend, a resting place, offering refuge from the icy winds.

What was it doing here so far from the main roads. Obviously, it lacked all the amenities of civilization such as plumbing and electricity. It was situated in the oldest and darkest part of the forest. An odd choice of location because the little house would never get light.

And it would certainly be damp. It was wet throughout the surrounding forest but in this one place it was positively humid and warm. A modified version of what I assumed a tropical climate would be.

What caused the weather to be different right here? Was it somehow the trees? They were thick and close. Lumbering had never been tried in this section of the woods.

The trees were so tall that their first branches began well above my head. They blocked the sky and filtered the light thinly, forming a roof that pressed moist air down and held it trapped in this one small area. Peculiar, trees making their own weather, rather like the sea does.

I climbed the wall and entered the clearing around the house. But I felt like a trespasser. Someone must own the little house. They might not like intruders. And the house itself looked like it didn't want visitors. It was shut tight.

The air grew more oppressive with each step I took. By the time I reached the cottage I was panting. The door, as I had expected, was locked.

There was no crack in the mortar between the rocks, no way I could peek in. The windows were unshuttered but old curtains were drawn across them from the inside. They weren't transparent.

There was nothing I could do but go home. I turned my back on the cottage and got the strangest sensation. Someone was watching me. Immediately, I thought of Tom Parsons. I spun around. Nobody.

I walked on. Again, an overpowering sense that I was being stared at. More than a stare. Someone was devouring me with his eyes. I turned around. Still nothing.

I continued walking. It was very quiet. Yet the semitropical air cried out for intricate animal calls. Jabbering monkeys. Roaring jaguars. If I closed my eyes I could believe that I was in a Brazillian rain forest with lush green plants all around me. So I kept my eyes firmly open.

The wet air grew increasingly sensual. I remembered the picture Robin Rouen had found in the library at Stonehaven. It shot to mind, vivid in every detail.

I climbed over the wall, welcoming the coolness of the stone under my hands. I set my feet on the path which ran next to the wall and forced myself to walk. The air grew drier. Eventually the trees thinned. The day became lighter.

I couldn't shake off the irrational idea that it was the house itself which had watched me, that it was intensely alive and hated its immobility. Trapped, all it could do was stare jealously at moving objects, through the lidless windows that formed its eyes.

Chapter XIV

"Who owns that little house in the woods?" I asked Mrs. Parsons, when I'd returned from my walk.

"You mean the stone cottage? It belongs to the Piedmonts."

"The Piedmonts! Why didn't anyone tell me about it?"

"Didn't I mention it to you once? No, I guess not. It's so rarely used nowadays that people probably forgot to tell you about it. My husband goes there quite a bit. But he's the only one. He takes care of it."

"I'm curious about it. Why doesn't anyone go there?"

Mrs. Parsons underwent her usual brief struggle over whether to tell all or keep her mouth shut. Then, unable to resist, she said dramatically, "It's haunted."

"What?" I pretended to be shocked.

"People think it's haunted anyways. Rumor has it that the cottage stands on the exact spot where Geoffrey Piedmont was hanged."

This was rather worse than I'd expected.

"Isn't that unlikely? Geoffrey was killed in the eighteenth century. Yet the cottage can't be more than twenty or thirty years old."

"Less than that. But locals have always known exactly where Geoffrey died. He'd had such a way with the young rowdies of his own time that night after night they'd return to the hanging tree. It was their shrine. They kept coming back to honor Geoffrey and to do mischief."

" 'Mischief' doesn't strike me as quite the right word, Mrs. Parsons. They weren't boy scouts on a spree."

"I don't think they did anything very bad. Geoffrey's death knocked the wind out of them. But they did keep Geoffrey's legend alive. Met to tell stories about his prowess. Eventually, the tree and the land it was on got a terrible reputation."

"Because of Geoffrey's death? Or was there something more?"

"Some of the boys claimed they'd seen Geoffrey's ghost in the woods. No one believed them. But no one was brave enough to make sure the boys were lying."

"I can understand that."

"Adults stopped going anywhere near the tree. But the spot was irresistible to children. Each generation of small boys proved themselves brave by sneaking off to the tree after dark. The parents tried to stop them."

"Even years later?"

"Because of the ghost. Over a hundred years after Geoffrey's death, boys came home with the tale that they'd seen a man in funny clothes walking near the tree. The man wore a wig and tights. He appeared on warm nights."

"Do you think the children were making the story up?"

"Maybe. Each group of boys could have passed the story on to the next. You know how children hand down games and songs. But the parents were scared. They weren't about to take any risks."

"Were they able to stop the children from going to the tree?"

"No, the boys still managed to sneak into the woods sometimes. But they were watched closely so their nocturnal visits became less frequent."

"Then the place was abandoned?"

Mrs. Parsons blushed. "Not really. Adolescents discovered

it. They made it a lovers' lane. After all, they were safe there. No one was going to interrupt them."

"It seems an eerie choice."

"It was dark and private. That was all they cared about. None of them ever admitted seeing a ghost. Perhaps they were too preoccupied to notice."

"Or maybe there had never been any ghost. Just a little boy who had found storytelling a clever way of getting attention."

"One day the hanging tree was gone. Nobody knows why it was removed. But it was chopped down one night. I suspect it was done by some children up to a prank. The tree stump was left to mark the spot."

"Until it was bulldozed to clear the ground for the cottage?"

"That's right. It was Andre's father who had that built, let's see, about eighteen or nineteen years ago."

"Andre's father!" Sometimes it was hard to remember that Andre hadn't been spawned in the pond outside Stonehaven, that he had an immediate family, like everybody else. Recent Piedmonts tended to blur and merge with their lengthy chain of predecessors. I knew absolutely nothing about Andre's father and mother. I'd never even sought out their portraits.

"Your father-in-law, Edward Piedmont, never did believe in ghosts, ma'am. He was a skeptic. But he built the cottage because as a boy he would find his way to the tree stump and hide. It made him feel wicked. And I imagine that later he had his share of adventures with girls in that very spot."

"You mean that he had the cottage put up out of a sense of nostalgia?"

"He wasn't a very happy man but he'd had a delightful childhood. I suppose that spot in the woods reminded him of it. He liked to escape from Stonehaven and go off to the cottage to read or think."

"Like father, like son," I found myself saying.

"What?"

"Never mind, Mrs. Parsons; please continue."

"The cottage was simple but Mr. Piedmont liked it that way. He found it refreshing. Stonehaven was always too ornate for his taste. So he'd spend days, and sometimes even weeks, at the cottage. He especially liked it at night, when the kerosene lamps were lit. Sometimes he'd take my husband Tom with him. They were both great outdoorsmen.

And Tom was stronger then. So he was a big help to Mr. Piedmont. They'd hunt and fish. Tom gets sentimental about those outings. He was very attached to your father-in-law."

"It all sounds very chummy and peaceful. Where was Mrs. Piedmont during this time?"

Mrs. Parsons neatly ignored my question. "After Edward's death, the cottage was neglected. For a while, teen-agers used it as a trysting place. But they soon stopped. It's been abandoned for years."

I couldn't believe it. The cottage wasn't dilapidated. Someone lived there. At least part of the time. There was no point asking Mrs. Parsons if she knew who it might be. Clearly, she hadn't the foggiest idea. She'd attribute the decent condition of the cottage to Tom.

Then again, she might be right. Perhaps it was Tom and only Tom who lived there. What had I heard about him? That he was like an animal of the woods. That he felt caged inside a house. Then the cottage might suit him perfectly. A sturdy den surrounded by Nature.

Someday I'd explore that cottage. My curiosity would leave me no choice. But it would take time to gather the courage to face it. I'd have to wait for the right moment. Preferably, when Tom Parsons was busy elsewhere.

I asked Mrs. Parsons to show me the portrait of Andre's father. She led me up the staircase and stopped in the hall.

"There's Edward Piedmont," she said.

I looked. There, under a 1950s crewcut, was the inevitable Piedmont face. The portrait had nothing to teach me. I may as well have spared myself the climb upstairs.

"And where is Mrs. Piedmont's portrait?" I asked.

Mrs. Parsons seemed surprised. "She wasn't a Piedmont, ma'am. No more than you are. Her picture doesn't hang in the house."

"That's right, she wasn't a blood relative. But I am disappointed. I wanted to see what Andre's mother looked like."

Down the corridor, the phone rang. Elsie came to tell me I had a phone call and I went to answer it.

It was Celia Gordon. Her voice crackled.

"That you, Tamara? Jenny Hooper told me you want to help with the annual party? Is that true?

"Yes, Celia."

"I can't believe it. A Piedmont willing to do some work."

Crispin, his sixth sense in perfect working order, had discovered that I was on the phone. This meant that I'd be sitting still for a few minutes. Taking advantage of the situation, he leaped into my lap, and merrily kneaded the material of my clothes.

"Ouch!" I said.

"What was that?" Miss Gordon asked.

"Never mind. It's just my cat. Scratching away."

"Ugh, don't say the word 'cat' to me. Even the thought of one makes me itch and swell."

"What would you like me to do for the party?"

"You're an artist, aren't you. Then you belong on the decorations committee. That's Jenny's. Get together with her and decide what you're going to do."

"Okay."

"Everyone's cooperating and the party's going to be a big success. Which is fine. Except that every drunkard in the county will be out on the road, risking all our lives."

Any drunk in his right mind would faint at the thought of driving the same road Miss Gordon was on.

"I'm glad the party's going to be a good one," I said.

"Just pray we don't get a fire. It'll ruin the celebration. I'm proud of our volunteer fire department. But they'd rather go to a fire than a party any time. If the alarm bell rings, all the men will take off and won't come back for hours. The women will be left behind."

"Fires are dangerous, Celia. Somebody has to put them out."

"The men don't all have to go. And believe me, they take off with gusto. Imagine a bunch of grown men acting like small boys. Racing around in a big red truck, ringing bells, splashing water. Watching things burn."

"Sounds exciting."

A loud, disdainful sniff was her only comment.

There was a sharp click and the phone was dead. I debated whether to call Jenny now. Would she even come back to Stonehaven after the bad fright she'd had on her last visit? I wanted her to return. Just to spite Stonehaven. It would like nothing better than to keep her away. But I intended to fight back.

If we had to hide in a broom closet, I would find some corner in the house where Jenny, Stacy, and I could be safely together.

Chapter XV

It occurred to me that the logical place to put a child is a nursery. Would Andre object if I invaded his precious sanctuary for a few hours? Only if he were in a totally unreasonable mood. And even Andre would soften when confronted by Stacy Lynn, little imp that she was.

A few days later Andre went off to Orinville. It seemed a propitious time to explore the nursery and see if it would be appropriate. At Stonehaven even a nursery might be dismal.

It was on the top floor of the house, just beneath a cavernous attic. I had no idea why it was in so inconvenient a section of the house. I could only conclude that upper-class parents liked to keep their children well out of the way.

I climbed the central staircase to the upper floors of Stonehaven, where doors opened onto rooms dusty in the afternoon sunlight, and lumps of furniture were ghostly under shroud-like sheets. There was an occasional laugh or loud comment, when I passed a floor where servants lived. Once, a woman holding a hairbrush, stepped out of her doorway as I passed. Blushing, she ducked back into her room, mumbling excuses. Actually, I should have apologized to her since I was the intruder.

I felt as if I had found that part of the hive where the working bees lived. The drones (and I was one) dwelled below. Perhaps the Piedmont children had been lucky, after all, to spend their lives up here, among the servants.

I was prepared for the worst by the time I reached the nursery. No doubt, it would reflect the conventional Victorian attitude to children. I would find a gray, shabby room, straight from Dickens, meant to turn children into sober adults, quickly and ruthlessly.

I was amazed to find a charming room, brightly painted. Tall windows admitted a flood of sunshine. If this room were haunted, it was by the spirits of children. Merry poltergeists. Nothing more ominous.

I couldn't blame Andre for spending time up here. It was like being in a high tree house, overlooking the woods below. Marvelous old children's toys were scattered helter-skelter. There were wooden chairs and tables, an old blackboard, turn-of-the century dolls with china heads. An Edwardian rocking horse stared at me pleasantly from a round glass eye. Smocks and rain slickers were hung from wooden pegs along the wall. A miniature tea set of real silver had been placed conveniently next to a dollhouse complete with running water and lights.

Only Andre's stereo unit looked absurdly out of place.

Obviously maids came up here from time to time. Everything was dusted and the worn linoleum was washed and waxed. The glass in the windows sparkled.

All I had to do to make the room ready for Stacy was to see that all valuable or dangerous toys were hidden in cupboards. Balls and blocks were left temptingly in view. I found a big panda and put it accessibly on the floor. A quiver of sharp toy arrows was within reach. I shoved it into a closet, well out of the way.

Now I was ready to phone Jenny. But I couldn't break away from the room.

I was attracted to an orange bookcase in one corner, filled with books owned by Piedmont children, little boys and girls who sat up here on rainy days absorbed in adventure stories. How many of them later lived tragically and died prematurely?

It was a wonderful collection of books. *The Bobsey Twins,* my grandmother's old favorite, was well represented. There was a beautifully illustrated volume of *Anderson's Fairy Tales.* I found a ragged copy of *Peter Pan,* with Tinker Bell sprouting butterfly wings and antennae.

The girls in the family had done their share of reading, for there was more than one copy of *Rebecca of Sunnybrook Farm, Alice in Wonderland, The Little Princess,* and *Little Women.* Toddlers had *Winnie-the-Pooh.*

All the Oz books were there. And Mark Twain's *The Prince and the Pauper.* There were a few penny-dreadfuls. And old pulps of *The Shadow* and *Fu Manchu,* with lurid covers, promising thrills galore. There was even a copy of *The Rover Boys at the Seashore!*

I picked up a Dr. Seuss book. Inside, laboriously printed in sprawling childish letters, was the name: Andre Piedmont. I had to smile.

I could have stayed there, browsing all day, but I noticed a package on one of the shelves. I reached in and removed it. It was a rectangular shape, with cloth wrapped round it. I unfolded the cloth. It was a lovely old sampler, worked by a child. The words "Bessy Piedmont, age 10," were embroidered in the center, above a motto. The borders had been decorated with forget-me-nots and fancy stitches.

It was badly wrinkled and would have to be ironed. Poor sampler; winding up a substitute for wrapping paper.

The rectangular shape inside turned out, appropriately, to be a book. Robert Louis Stevenson's *A Child's Garden of Verses*. I had loved the poems when I was little: "The Land of Counterpane," "Where Go the Boats," and "The Swing." I used to recite them for my grandmother.

I leafed through the pages, admiring the old-fashioned illustrations. Then something fell to the floor. Photographs. One showed a young boy with golden curls, dressed in a Lord Fauntleroy suit. He was riding a hobbyhorse. Next were two pictures of women, circa 1925. Another was of a girl about twelve, probably taken a decade later. None were particularly interesting.

However the next picture was. It showed a slim, dark woman. She wore the short skirt and padded jacket of the early 1940s. And she smiled for the camera. But her eyes didn't smile. Thus the smile looked false, as if sketched over a mouth about to cry. I turned the picture over. It said, "Laura, 1944."

She was in the one remaining picture, too. Now dressed in the style of the late 50s. But I glanced at her only long enough to notice the possessive way she gripped the shoulder of the boy in the picture.

A boy of ten or so. Andre; with a look on his face which didn't please me, a look that was sly and smug. The boy in this photograph was a spoiled brat.

Had I found the key to Andre's character? I had made the assumption that his childhood was unhappy. But what if instead, he had been Mama's precious darling? Raised to be indifferent to others, indulging in emotional binges just because he felt like it. Without the excuse of early trauma.

I looked at the picture again, and felt very angry. The

door opened. If it was Andre in a grouch, there was going to be quite a row. But it was Minnie Parsons.

"One of the cooks told me you were up here, ma'am. She saw you on the stairs. I came to see if you needed anything."

"No, I was just straightening up."

"Lovely room, isn't it?"

"Enchanting."

"Your husband's fond of it too. It was never meant for adults, though. I remember when there were lots of children playing here. I liked the house better then. It was livelier. Too quiet now."

I showed her the sampler. "This would look pretty on the wall up here. If it were cleaned and pressed."

"I'll see that it's done, ma'am."

"Remember when you told me that there was no portrait of Andre's mother in the house. Well, I think I've found a photograph of her."

"Let me see. Yes, that's her."

"An unhappy face. I assume that she had the luck of the Piedmonts."

"She was a lonely woman. Edward Piedmont was a good man and he loved his wife. But unfortunately, he liked to be by himself much of the time. She was only seventeen when she married him. Too young really. He was forty, his character was set. He had no friends so there weren't many visitors. And she hated the house."

"Sounds awful."

"Not all the time. Her husband let her give parties. He hated them himself. Sometimes he wouldn't even come. But he knew his wife needed a social life. So he let her give elaborate parties from time to time."

"I suppose he thought he was being enormously generous."

"And then she had her children?"

"Children! Isn't Andre an only child?"

"There was a girl, ma'am. Born when your husband was five. He adored his baby sister. But she died of pneumonia when she was six. It was very sad."

"Poor Mrs. Piedmont."

"It killed something inside her. She remained correct and proper. A brave woman. She went on living for a while but she was like a zombie."

"Did she have any family of her own to help her?"

"She was a Blake, ma'am. Didn't you know?"

"Who are the Blakes?"

"A very old family that has intermarried with the Piedmonts off and on for generations."

"Oh?" This sounded ominous. "Were they as unlucky as the Piedmonts?"

"No. They've got no curses hanging over them. But the Blakes got plenty of bad luck whenever one married a Piedmont. Maybe marrying Piedmonts was their curse. They never seemed able to resist them. There are people who say that what we consider the Piedmont face ought really to be called the Blake face. It doesn't stem from the Piedmonts at all. It started when a Scandinavian woman came to England and married an Augustus Blake, sometime in the sixteenth century. Their children had silver hair, blue eyes, and fairy-tale beauty."

"But Laura Piedmont was dark."

"Not all the Blakes are fair. Anymore than all the Piedmonts are. There just seems to be a dominant type."

"You mean a recurring replica. But I take it the Blakes are resigned to their fate and so Laura simply acquiesced to marrying Edward Piedmont."

"In part. But I think she married for love. In later years she thought about leaving her husband. But by then her parents were dead, her relatives scattered, and she had nowhere to go. Besides, she was a lady. She decided that it was her duty to stay on at Stonehaven with her husband even when things went very wrong."

"For better or worse till death do us part," I said.

"That's right. She took the wedding vow seriously. She was old-fashioned."

"My grandmother was exactly the same. She would have applauded Laura Piedmont."

"I admired her myself."

"Mrs. Parsons, do you think we could arrange a small luncheon up here. Nothing fancy. I'd like Jenny and Stacy to come."

"What a good idea. I'd love to see a baby playing up here again. You leave it all to me. I'll see that you get a good meal. And I'll make sure there's ice cream for Stacy. She's an adorable little thing, isn't she, ma'am. Just tell me when you'll want the food."

"I'll go down and call Jenny right now. Then I'll let you know." I left the nursery with regret. But, since Mrs. Parsons went downstairs with me the house stayed leashed, obedient to her personal brand of protective magic. I was brought safely to a telephone.

Before Jenny had a chance to refuse my invitation to lunch, I quickly explained to her that I had discovered a delightful room way at the top of the house where we wouldn't be bothered. And Stacy would have lots of toys to keep her busy. We would be free to talk about ornaments for the party.

Jenny was less than eager but she accepted. We arranged a date and rang off. I waited for Stonehaven to signal its displeasure, but the house was quiescent. I couldn't help feeling a furtive sense of satisfaction. I'd outwitted the house at last.

Chapter XVI

Jenny arrived at Stonehaven with Stacy Lynn dressed in her Sunday best, all frills and ruffles. Apparently, an invitation to Stonehaven was still considered special in Woodlands. Poor Jenny. She'd probably agreed to come today because she felt under royal command.

I did my best to make her feel comfortable. But the climb up the formidable staircase didn't help. Only when we arrived at the nursery were we able to relax.

"This is quite a room," Jenny commented.

I bounced a red ball to Stacy. "Here, sweetheart, this is for you," I said as Stacy laughed and crawled off after it.

Jenny and I settled in and started eating sandwiches and potato chips. I talked about my Midwestern childhood. Jenny told me that she had grown up on a farm and had fallen in love at the age of twelve. With a horse. She had then spent the better part of the next six years in a stable.

Until Jack. She had known him all her life but had never given him a second thought. Then one day he dropped in to chat with her father about buying a pig. That evening, Jenny went to the movies with him. Within a week they were in love. Two years later they got married.

"My first and only boyfriend," Jenny said.

"Weren't the horses jealous?"

"They took it well. My kid sister came to the rescue. She reached eleven and then it was her turn to take care of the horses."

"I guess Jack took up all your time."

"Only about half of it. I went to work after school in the Orinville drugstore to earn money. Jack got a job at the garage. We saved our earnings for two years. Otherwise, we'd have been broke when we got married."

"You certainly do seem to manage well."

"You learn fast on a farm. I cooked all the family's meals from the time I was ten. Raised six younger brothers and sisters, because my mom had to go to work to make ends meet. I started sewing for pin money when I was nine."

"Caring for one man and one child must seem a cinch after that."

"At least it's no harder." Stacy climbed onto Jenny's lap. After receiving a solid hug, she was put down on the floor again and handed a rag doll.

"Have you ever traveled, Jenny?"

"Never been outside the county. Someday Jack and I want to see Florida. But I don't know when we'll be able to spare the money. At one time, I thought we'd have to move since Jack wasn't sure he could get a job here. Then there was an opening on the police force. Luckily."

"Are you glad you stayed?"

"I couldn't bear to leave Woodlands. It's in my blood. My family's been here for over a hundred and fifty years. Most people nowadays don't have roots. But we do. When we say 'home' we mean it."

"Perhaps I'll get a sense of that at the party."

"If you're not too bored to notice it. After going to parties in New York, ours will seem dull and mediocre. Not that you'll be neglected. Every politician running for office will court you. Influence at Stonehaven is worth a lot."

"I bet I'll enjoy the party more than you might expect. Don't forget, I come from a small town myself."

"It's probably a metropolis compared to Orinville."

"Yes, it is. But the parties at the Methodist Church were tame and yet I always had a good time at them."

"There have been parties in Woodlands that could match any in New York. They were held right here at Stonehaven."

"I understand my mother-in-law gave those."

"I remember her as a hostess. I was just a child at the time. Everyone in Woodlands was invited. And people came from as far away as Boston. Some even flew in from California. Mrs. Piedmont had food brought up from the city. There were musicians and singers. Her parties were the talk of the county."

"I can't believe that they succeeded. Stonehaven is too depressing."

"The house was never gay. But Mrs. Piedmont was imaginative. She held parties on the lawn in the warm weather. Had flowers strewn everywhere. She had costume parties at Halloween and there were Twelfth Night masked balls in the winter."

"I see, Jenny. In a sense, she kept the house disguised. Did it work?"

"Everybody seemed to think so. I don't know anyone who attended the parties who didn't love them."

"Well, we'd better get to the plans for your party, or Celia will form a new committee."

We discussed various ideas. Miss Gordon had suggested a "South of the Border" motif. We vetoed that. Jenny said that most members of the committee wanted a spring theme. Jenny herself favored garlands of papier mâché flowers and colorful mobiles. Robin Rouen would have found Jenny's ideas tedious. But then it wasn't his party. I agreed to go along with whatever the committee wanted.

Stacy had discovered the bookcase. Jenny tried to redirect her to the toy box. And failed. So she hunted through the shelves until she found a clothbound book with pictures of animals. She settled herself on the floor and showed the pictures to Stacy.

There was a muffled noise in the hall. Fortunately, Jenny didn't notice. If anyone had a legitimate reason for coming to the nursery, they'd either open the door now or knock. But our intruder did neither.

I edged to the door. I could hear someone breathing. I thought about the large attic above. Was it the brain of the house, the nucleus of Stonehaven's malevolent will? Or was it the hiding place of a creature attracted to the nursery by the sound of strange voices? Our voices.

I opened the door. And faced Tom Parsons. His presence was a relief after the beast I had conjured in my imagination.

Relief was short-lived, however. He said, "Pretty baby you've got in there."

I slipped into the hall and closed the door tightly behind me. "What do you want?" I whispered, hoping that Jenny wouldn't hear us.

Tom Parsons radiated innocence. "I came up to fix a leak in the plumbing."

"Go away! I have a guest. This is the wrong moment to bother with fixing anything."

"If you say so," He grinned. And he ostentatiously tramped down the stairs.

I went back into the nursery. What if he came back? Best to get Jenny and Stacy downstairs fast. I had no idea what Tom Parsons was up to but I didn't want to find out.

"Who was that?" Jenny asked.

"The plumber. Come to make repairs. Would you like to go downstairs now? We could see if Mrs. Parsons has any chocolate cake on hand."

But Jenny was reluctant to leave the nursery. She continued looking at books. Stacy was rolled up in a ball on the floor, contentedly gulping milk from her bottle.

Jenny came across *A Child's Garden of Verses*. When she came to the photographs, I took them and showed her the picture of Andre's mother.

"I'd forgotten how lovely she was," Jenny said.

Then I showed her the next picture, Laura with Andre as a boy. Jenny visibly stiffened. She stared at the photograph for a full minute before she said, "Mrs. Piedmont remained beautiful, didn't she?"

I was quite sure that it was really Andre, not Laura, who made the picture interesting to Jenny. Why this fascination? Was she so obsessed with Andre that she found even a childhood photograph of him irresistible?

But Jenny didn't look like a woman admiring a lover. She looked scared to death.

The door opened, banging into the wall. My first thought was that Tom Parsons had returned. Instinctively, I moved to protect Stacy. But it wasn't Tom.

It was Andre. Enraged.

"What are you doing up here, Tamara?" he shouted. "Why didn't you warn me that you would be here?"

"I would have told you that we were going to be in the nursery this afternoon but you've been avoiding me. I never got the chance to let you know. And anyway, I didn't think you were concerned with where I went or what I did anymore."

Andre saw the photographs in my hand and snatched them away. He looked at Stacy but ignored Jenny.

Then Andre literally went berserk. He roared at me, "Get that baby out of here! Do you hear me? Get her out!"

"But Andre, don't be silly. We were just having a pleasant——"

"Don't you hear me?" he continued, shouting, "I said to get her out." And he twisted my arm.

He didn't have to repeat himself. Jenny grabbed Stacy and ran. She would never come back to Stonehaven again. I was certain of that.

But my immediate thought was for my arm. It ached acutely. "Andre, stop! I can't stand the pain."

Andre looked startled, as if he hadn't realized what he was doing. He dropped my arm immediately. I knew he regretted hurting me. But it was too late for that.

"I find you unrecognizable," I said. "Are you still my Andre? Or have you already become someone else?"

We stood quite far apart. And neither of us tried to close the gap. We stared at each other, without affection. But with self-pity and with fear.

Chapter XVII

The chill of the north country had permeated the walls of Stonehaven, penetrating Andre and me. We had become partners in a minuet, moving distantly and formally, polite but not cordial.

Mutual anger had subsided but a feeling of mutual betrayal remained. We faced each other across a thick hedge of regret, finding it easiest to avoid each other as much as possible, and to be on our guard when we were together.

Sometimes I asked myself if the atmosphere within the house didn't seep into the bones and bloodstreams of human beings. After all, we lived night and day within a capsule of evil. Perhaps malignancy is somehow catching.

Although Stonehaven could perpetuate winter within itself, it had no power beyond its doors. Spring continued its slow progression in Woodlands. The branches of the willow tree turned to gold and one morning I caught sight of a bluebird. For me, the only world that mattered now was the world outside, away from the intricacies and complications of human relationships.

I had learned that I could exhaust my body and numb my mind by walking. And in the process, I had come to be a cultist, a true devotee of Nature. I had reached the point where I felt a kinship with the hunted animals of the woods: the bear, the deer, and the partridge. Glady would I have changed places with Daphne, when in her flight from Apollo she became a laurel tree.

One afternoon I returned to the house and found Celia Gordon waiting for me. My hair was wet from the rain; I felt lonely and tired and my face must have showed it, for Celia immediately said, "You look terrible."

"Just worn out. I've been in the woods."

"You're getting to be as crazy as Tom Parsons. You'll wind up living in the woods like he does, if you're not careful."

"Does he live at the cottage?" I asked.

Celia's stare was penetrating. "Minnie told me you'd found it. Bet she fed you nonsense about ghosts being seen there. The place is haunted all right, but by her husband."

"She told me that he looks after it."

"As much as that lazy good-for-nothing looks after anything."

I led Miss Gordon to my special room. She paused in the doorway, her entire body pointing, accusingly. Crispin was lying in a chair.

"Crispin, go away!" I shouted. But he wouldn't budge. He gazed fondly at Miss Gordon. Then he stretched, arched his back, and jumped out of the chair. He seemed most anxious to wrap himself around her legs.

"Crispin!" I screamed. I ran to him and picked him up. He

gave me a puzzled look, as if he couldn't understand what all the fuss was about. I put him in another room and closed the door.

Celia's indignation knew no bounds. "It's all Minnie's fault. She's supposed to hide the cat when I come. Provoking woman! I'll tell her a thing or two."

"It's lucky that you saw him in time."

"It certainly is. Otherwise, I'd spend the weekend in the hospital. Now, about the cottage. Tom Parsons doesn't live there. He and Minnie own a nice house, halfway to Orinville. Minnie saved for years to get it. But since she sleeps-in at Stonehaven most of the time, Tom probably camps out at the cottage whenever he feels like it."

"It's clear that he's not afraid of ghosts."

"Ghosts would be afraid of him, the mean old ape. Tamara, I can see that you're as gullible as Minnie. Any spot that's had a hanging is bound to get the reputation of being haunted. The story no doubt started when some drunk staggered through the woods on a summer night, fell over his own feet, and decided he'd been pushed by a ghost. I sent you to the Orinville library. Your research there should have convinced you that there are no ghosts, no curses, no goblins, no supernatural anything."

Celia Gordon, the proverbial closed mind. I wasn't about to argue.

"How is the party coming?" I asked, to change the subject.

"That's what I came about. I wanted to make sure the decorations are going to be suitable. We don't want anything eccentric, young lady. This isn't New York City."

"Jenny's designing the ornaments. I think you'll find them most appropriate."

"That's a relief. I've been running myself ragged. If I didn't oversee all the preparations myself, nothing would be done right. Norah Webb was supposed to bake her special peach pie but now she's got to go to Cooperstown to take care of her husband's sick aunt. And Joe Keely's arthritis is acting up again so he can't tend bar. Which won't stop him from drinking. Anna Fremont's bursting out pregnant and the doctor has told her to stay home that night but she won't listen. She insists on coming and I'm sure she'll dance every dance. Probably deliver the baby right then and there. Thank God we've got a doctor coming, even if he is a veterinarian. Better than nothing."

"I'm sure it will work out, Celia, and everybody will have a good time."

"If you don't mind, Tamara, I'm going to run along and see Minnie. Got to find out if she left that cat of yours in here on purpose to get even with me. Minnie says that sometimes I hurt her feelings."

Poor Mrs. Parsons. Miss Gordon went stalking her with great determination. It was a confrontation I was glad to miss.

I was so tired I just wanted to go to bed, but it was too early. There was still dinner and a long evening ahead. But perhaps that was just as well. I would be even more exhausted later. I had to be bone tired in order to sleep these days since I knew that Andre never came to our bed at all anymore.

The following morning was Easter Sunday. A calendar wasn't needed to show that it was a holy day. The sun proclaimed it by pouring cold, dazzling light throughout the woods. The April air hadn't made up its mind whether to be mild or frosty. So it was alternately a bit of both, sweet and sour.

My spirits revived and I thought that perhaps I should celebrate the day outdoors. A rock, covered with branches of pine, would make an excellent altar. Then I would have a church of my own in the wilderness. My grandmother might have considered this too pantheistic for her taste, but it seemed appropriate to me.

However, I decided in the end just to walk and enjoy the weather. The radiant sky made the woods appear open and innocent. Impossible to believe in evil spirits today. On the contrary, it seemed likely that I might meet a picture-book angel, with yellow halo and white feathered wings. But no devil's disciple would dare be out. The clarity of the light would drive him away.

The locals were all in church in Orinville. I hadn't wanted to go without Andre for fear people would talk. But, as usual, he was nowhere to be seen.

Celia Gordon, firmly Protestant, had waved to me this morning on her way to the Presbyterian Church. Her car, still coughing and choking despite the change of seasons, had passed me as I was about to enter the woods.

Earlier, Elsie, ripe as an autumn apple and dressed to kill, had left Stonehaven in a car crowded with girls her own age.

Minnie Parsons had dragged her reluctant Tom to Our Lady of the Tears although I couldn't imagine him actually going to Mass. I had seen the Hoopers' car on the road too. I was sure that it was on its way to the Baptist Church. The car picked up speed as it passed Stonehaven.

I knew I was safely alone in the woods so I decided to explore the cottage. The woods lost the quality of innocence in the thick of the forest. Overhead, the trees interlocked their branches, muting the sunlight. Again the air was damp and, today, almost hot. No birds sang. They had abandoned this part of the forest and fled to the young trees beyond.

The cottage was waiting for me. I sensed, but could not prove, that it watched me. When I averted my eyes the feeling that I was under scrutiny increased. But when I faced the cottage squarely, the feeling diminished. It was as if the cottage wore a false face, a mask which it removed when no one was looking and put back on when watched. I touched one of its outer walls to make sure the stones weren't a sham cut from construction paper. But they were real enough.

This time the door was open. And I went in. I was relieved yet disappointed by the ordinary appearance of the interior. I had expected something fabulous, out of the Arabian Nights. And all I found was a simple summer cabin.

It consisted of two rooms, a central one, where I stood, and a smaller one, behind a partition. In the main room the light was dim and the air musty. The cottage could have used a good spring cleaning.

Not that it was messy. I was surprised at how neatly it was swept. But it had been closed tight for too long. It needed its windows open so that the fresh air could get in.

The furniture in the cottage had been reduced to fundamentals. There was an old wooden table and bench, a chair, a worn rug, one folding cot, and a hot-plate. The only signs of human habitation were ashes in the fireplace and a few dirty dishes in the basin. The dishes would have to be washed in cold water drawn from the pump outside.

And that was it. The cottage was interesting only in its facade. Its interior was devoid of individual personality.

I thought about this for a moment. Perhaps the cottage was like a Greek temple, and important events took place in front of it, rather than inside it. The cottage itself might merely serve as a backdrop, a stage setting. That sense of being stared at as one approached might not emanate from the cottage at all. It might come from the air, or a rock, or a tree outside.

A tree? That was it! The cottage probably wasn't really on the exact spot where Geoffrey had been hanged after all. Most likely the precise locale was in front of the cottage. The ground itself, where the tree stump had been, was haunted.

I was as delighted with myself as if I'd pieced a jigsaw puzzle together. Just to make sure that the cottage was not potent in its own right, I opened the partition door, which divided the two rooms. And felt terror.

It took me a while to absorb the contents of the room, to bring objects into focus. My eyes resisted what they saw; my nerve endings refused to transmit the message to my brain. It was like being in an auto accident. One minute, the world is normal; the next minute everything is wrong. And it takes time for one's body to comprehend the change.

At last, I was able to take in the scene around me. The rustic cottage was rustic no longer. Its floors and walls were painted jet black. An overstuffed chair of blatant scarlet squatted in one corner. The only other piece of furniture in the room was a chair made of wood, elaborately carved, with a high back and strong arms. It had been gilded. It looked remarkably like a golden throne. Spread-eagled on the floor was a black lambskin, no doubt meant to be used as a rug.

There was only one other thing in the room, and it was this that had terrified me. It was the portrait of Geoffrey Piedmont.

Facing no competition, free of rivals, the painting dominated the room. It had never quite done that amidst the portraits at Stonehaven. I stared at Geoffrey; he stared back, enclosed within his beautiful frame.

He looked very real. His mouth was turned up in a half-smile which I'd never noticed before. But was it a smile? As I looked closely, I could see that the smug mouth wasn't grinning; it was gloating. In Geoffrey's face, the Piedmont eyes lost their glamour. They bulged slightly under fat lids. An altogether cynical and unpleasant face.

I had seen that self-satisfied expression somewhere else recently. Where? Then I remembered. On the child Andre's face, in the photograph taken with his mother. I was no longer terrified. I was desperate.

But the picture wouldn't let me go. I couldn't take my eyes off it. The centuries had not diminished the portrait's powers.

It shimmered with life and energy even in the semidarkness of the room.

Geoffrey had been a genius, I felt convinced of that. For he had experienced life with superhuman intensity. It was the luck of the Piedmonts that this intensity resulted only in evil.

Geoffrey released me. I was free to look away. Two candlestick holders in the shape of gargoyles stood on the floor beneath the portrait. Each held a candle burning red. I was reminded of the gargoyles in the library at Stonehaven.

Then I understood. This was a religious scene. The painting was an icon; the rug, a symbol of the sacrificed lamb; the candles represented immortality. But adherents of this religion did not practice Christianity. They mocked it. Theirs was a religion that exalted the devil's own representative, whose portrait basked in exaltation on the wall of this room.

Chapter XVIII

I bolted. I was out of the cottage, over the wall, and running along the path before I could think clearly again. Gradually, the forest grew brighter. Birds sang. But I didn't care. I just wanted to get out of the woods. I didn't slow down until I reached the road to Stonehaven.

Mrs. Parsons was back from church. I went directly to her. "Do you remember when I asked you to take Geoffrey Piedmont's portrait down and get rid of it?"

"Certainly, I remember. Why? Do you want it put back, ma'am?"

"Absolutely not. I want to know what you did with it."

My voice sounded harsh and accusing. Mrs. Parsons was alarmed. She thought hard for a moment.

Then she said, "Now I recall. I gave the picture to Tom."

"To Mr. Parsons? Whatever for?"

"I was going to have the portrait stored in one of the attics, ma'am. But I didn't feel right, doing that to a Piedmont. The picture might become damaged up there. Tom knew I was worried about something. When I told him what it was, he insisted on taking the painting."

"You had no right to give it to him, Mrs. Parsons. The picture doesn't belong to him."

"There was no way to stop him. I argued with him, told him what you just said, that the picture was Piedmont property. But he wouldn't listen. He became angry. I didn't dare say another word. He told me not to fuss, that he'd put the picture up on the wall of a small study on one of the upper floors. It would be safe and out of the way. There was little chance of your running into it so you'd be happy. He said it would make the best solution all around. I decided that he was right."

"What if I were to tell you that I just saw the portrait. And it wasn't in any study. It's hanging on the wall in that cottage in the woods."

Mrs. Parsons cringed. "Don't say that, ma'am; I don't want to hear it. Tom has been up to no good, I can see that. What's going to happen to him?"

I didn't bother to answer. I didn't care about Tom Parsons. But what about Andre? Had he been spending all his time at the cottage? He would look suitably regal on the throne-like chair.

I had to face up to the truth. It was too late for Andre. He had joined the accursed. There was nothing further I could do for him. I would stay for the party. I owed Celia Gordon that much. Then I'd return quietly to New York. I'd forget Andre. Someday, when I was remarried, I'd look back on this period of my life and be thankful that I got out in time.

But there was one thing I had to do immediately; phone Jenny.

"Jenny?"

"Yes?"

"This is Tamara."

"Oh?" Jenny sounded wary. I couldn't blame her. She probably expected another invitation to Stonehaven.

"I didn't call to ask you back here. I phoned specifically to tell you never to come near Stonehaven again."

"Are you in trouble, Tamara? Can you get over here to talk?"

"I don't think I'm in any immediate danger. But don't you come back here, under any circumstances. Somebody might lure you here, tell you that there's an emergency, and that you're needed. Ignore them."

"Can't you give me any details?"

"I wish I could. But I don't have enough information to be specific. Besides, whatever's going on in Woodlands may not concern you in the least. But I don't want you taking any risks. So keep away from Stonehaven."

I rang off. Mrs. Parsons stared at me as if I'd gone mad. "Do you feel unwell?" she asked.

"I feel fine. But I've got thinking to do."

"Why don't you lie down on your bed. You haven't been getting enough sleep lately. When a person's tired all the time, it has a bad effect on them."

"I don't think I can nap now. But I could use a rest. Would you bring a glass of warm milk to the bedroom for me?"

"With pleasure. Lie down and I'll be in with your milk in just a minute."

I went to the bedroom. As usual, it was deserted. Right now, Andre might be in the cottage. I preferred not to think about what he would be doing there.

I undressed, put on a nightgown, and lay down on top of the bed. I thought about reading a book. That often helped relax me. But I knew that I'd never be able to concentrate on the words. I would find myself going over the same paragraph three or four times.

I forced myself to close my eyes, and saw Geoffrey Piedmont's face. So I opened my eyes again. Perhaps it would be best not to sleep. Nightmares aren't soothing.

There was a knock at the door. That would be Mrs. Parsons with my milk.

"Come in," I called.

I leaned back and tried closing my eyes again. It was no use: Geoffrey's face sprang to mind.

I opened my eyes once more. And looked straight into the Neanderthal face of Tom Parsons.

I was outraged. I couldn't speak. I just stared at him. And he stared at me. He scanned my body critically, weighing its pros and cons, like a farmer debating whether or not to purchase a horse.

Then he grinned. "Wife tells me that you went to the cottage today, and now you're tired. So I volunteered to bring

your milk to you. And here are some home-baked cookies."
And still grinning, he left.

That settled it. It was time for me to leave Stonehaven. I
got up, dressed, and began packing. I would borrow a car,
drive it to the nearest town with bus service to New York.
Then I would telephone the house and tell Mrs. Parsons
where I'd left the car. I'd go back to my apartment in New
York, and get in touch with a lawyer immediately.

I pulled open a dresser drawer to get out my sweaters.
There was a scratching sound at the door and a gentle mew.
Crispin. I didn't want to leave without saying good-bye to
him. I let him in.

Next to him stood Andre.

"Where do you think you're going?"

I was afraid to answer. Geoffrey Piedmont stared out of
Andre's eyes, controlled Andre's movements. Andre was
nothing more than a wax figure now, a shop window mannequin on display. A vessel for Geoffrey's exploitation.

"Stay away from me," I said. "I know who you are, even
though I don't know precisely what your plans are."

"What kind of nonsense is this, Tamara?"

"Your lips move and your eyes see. But your body's a
husk, a discarded snake's skin. It's refuse. It makes a good
structure for camouflage, provides form and substance for a
powerful incorporeal force. What are you really, Geoffrey;
are you energy? Or do you have a shape which can't be seen
by the naked eye? Are you neurons and atoms, matter or an-
timatter? Or are you some sort of life-devouring vampire? Is
that why you need a fresh body every generation? Because
you're a psychic parasite?"

The man in front of me said nothing. He stared at me, in
disbelief. As if he found me unrecognizable.

"Geoffrey, I've been to the cottage. And I've seen your
portrait there, on the wall. I don't know what you want of
me, but if you try to overpower me now, I'll scream. Mrs.
Parsons is afraid of your henchman Tom, but he hasn't got
her totally intimidated. She'll come when she hears me, and
bring other servants with her. You'll have to confront them
all. So, I warn you, it would be best to leave me alone."

The face that looked like Andre's crumpled. Normally
pale, it turned paler yet, making him look like a ghost.

"You saw Geoffrey's picture in the cottage in the woods.
Are you sure, Tamara, are you positive?"

©Lorillard 1973

Micronite filter.
Mild, smooth taste.
America's quality
cigarette.
Kent.

KENT

WITH THE FAMOUS MICRONITE FILTER

DELUXE LENGTH

King Size or Deluxe 100's.

Kings: 16 mg. "tar," 1.0 mg. nicotine; 100's: 19 mg. "tar," 1.2 mg. nicotine;
Menthol: 18 mg. "tar," 1.3 mg. nicotine; av. per cigarette, FTC Report Sept. '73.

Try the crisp, clean taste of Kent Menthol.

The only Menthol with the famous Micronite filter.

"There can't be two faces like that."

"And you think that the curse has claimed me, that I've been possessed by Geoffrey."

"I'm quite sure of it." But, was I really? I wavered. Andre seemed very much himself.

He grabbed my hand. I made no effort to pull it away.

"I have not set foot in the cottage since I was thirteen years old, Tamara. And I haven't seen Geoffrey's portrait since you had it removed from its place on the wall in this house."

"How can I believe you, Andre?"

He let go of my hand. "You can't and I'm not surprised. Robin Rouen was right. I ought to have told you the entire truth long ago. Give me until tonight, Tamara. I'll need that much time. Then I'll explain everything. Then, if I can't convince you that the curse hasn't touched me yet, I'll let you go. Please, give me a few hours."

"I ought to go right now. You might be setting a trap for me. But, fool that I am, I'll stay. You'll have your chance to explain."

"Good. I promise that tonight, Tamara, you will know as much as I do."

Chapter XIX

Dinnertime came and went. I spent it completely alone in the enormous dining hall. It was a black, moonless night. The air was moist, reminiscent of the air at the cottage, but it was cold. Flames burned in the fireplace to drive away the chill.

The large windows in the dining hall were useless. They were like blackboards wiped clean. All Woodlands seemed to be waiting, most likely for a cloudburst of cold spring rain.

As I gloomily ate my supper, I reminded myself that this might be the last time I would have to endure dining at Stonehaven. Time dragged. It appeared to me that the entire kitchen staff was working in slow motion. Boredom destroyed my appetite. Finally, dessert arrived. A rich chocolate cake. I forced down one bite and left the table.

I ought to have felt tension and anticipation. But my emotions had been subjected to so many assaults over the past few months that they had gone into a defensive hibernation. I went to my special room and waited.

A half hour passed. I realized that I ought to keep busy and since I had collected materials for making party decorations, I began indolently forming flowers. It was unlikely now that I would attend the annual party. But the flowers would at least serve as mementoes to remind the local inhabitants that I had been part of their lives for a brief time.

I worked for two hours. By then the floor of the room was strewn with enormous red paper poppies and daisies of bright yellow. How I loved that shade of yellow, the color of forsythia, jonquils, and daffodils. In essence, it is the color of early spring.

Another half hour passed. Most likely Andre wasn't coming. I ought to have known better, but I was disappointed. Eventually I would have to rouse myself and see about getting my luggage to a car. But inertia had set in. Compulsively, I continued with the flowers.

I realized that I had made many more flowers than would be needed at the party. The carpet on the floor had been transformed into a garden. Or a jungle. To an observer I would have appeared to be a mad Ophelia, going to my doom in a stream surfeited with blossoms. Or an inmate on leave from a mental hospital, forever cutting flowers instead of paper dolls.

Andre finally came. He looked at the flowers and then he looked at me. Someone followed him into the room; I saw that it was Tom Parsons.

"Then it was a trap," I said softly.

Andre averted his eyes.

Tom Parsons edged Andre out of the way and stood in front of me. He was happy. His eyes twinkled, which made him look, incongruously, like a merry ape.

Gently, he took my hand and pulled me to my feet. I had lost the capacity to resist him. The skin on his hand was rough and dry. It reminded me of an animal's hide. In absolute silence he led me out of the room. I looked back at Andre. He stood still, a robot whose mind and will were shattered. Poor husband. He'd never had a chance. Geoffrey always triumphed.

It was quiet in the hall, our footsteps made little noise. Where had the servants gone? The soundless walk in the dampness made me think that perhaps Stonehaven had, in its enchantment, become a water world. I remembered old fairy tales about palaces under the sea. Would an octopus or a sting ray swim out to meet us as we rounded the next corner?

But Stonehaven was rooted firmly in the earth of Woodlands. We arrived not at the bedchamber of Neptune, but at the door of the library.

So the nocturnal revel would take place here, not at the cottage. I wondered what it would consist of. And what part I would play. I was resigned. I only hoped that it would be short and reasonably painless.

Tom Parsons gave me a little shove to get me moving. As I entered the library I mockingly told him, "Abandon all hope, ye who enter here." Then I was inside the room, and the door behind me was slammed shut.

I was alone with the gargoyles to keep me company. The lurid walls of the library reminded me that at the time this room was created, blood-letting was a common practice. It was not a comforting thought.

It took me a moment to get the courage to look up at the ceiling. What if something were pinned up there, watching me? I recalled my impression the day Jenny visited, that something might live in the attic above the nursery.

There must also be an attic above this monstrous room. Perhaps that was the creature's lair. Did it get out at night and hover above the room? Was I being given to it by Andre and Tom Parsons as a present?

I had to know. I looked up, expecting a whir of wings but there was nothing visible. Just books piled ever higher to the bare ceiling at the top of the room.

Then why had I been led here? I looked around. On a table near the magic collection was a portfolio. I walked over to it. It was the one Robin had come to Stonehaven to find. Had it been left here for me? Or had Andre carelessly tossed it on the table the day he had come across it?

I looked at the first engraving. It was the woodcut Andre had shown me. I put it aside. Then there was an Art Nouveau etching titled: Warlock. It had been done in the Aubrey

Beardsley style. The next picture was derived from an H. P. Lovecraft story. The picture was called "Ghoul Feeding." I stopped; I'd seen enough.

I lifted the portfolio. Its contents were distinctly unpleasant and I wanted to hide it, to shove it out of the way on some high shelf. Valuable or not, I didn't care. It would be best if no one ever found it again.

But something fluttered to the ground as I picked it up. I put the portfolio back on the table and bent down. Two pages, stapled together, lay there. They had been badly mutilated, but I could still read them.

They were pages torn from a book, Dr. Emma Piedmont's book. I remembered a day spent in that other library, in Orinville. How angry I had been when I found that a portion of the book I was reading had been ripped out. I had wondered why anyone would have done such a thing.

Now I knew. These pages covered the history of Edward and Laura Piedmont. And their son Andre.

Dr. Piedmont verified what Mrs. Parsons had said about the marriage itself. It had not been a happy one. Laura Blake had arrived at Stonehaven a charming girl. Within ten years she'd become an alcoholic. Another decade and she was dead. Suicide. One morning she had opened her mouth, put a pistol in it, and pulled the trigger.

Shortly afterward, Edward Piedmont also died, of a rare form of cancer. Dr. Piedmont asserted that this in no way validated the existence of a curse. I read on.

As the Piedmont marriage declined, Laura's parties became frantic. She took lovers. Finally, it was whispered that the parties had degenerated into orgies. Edward Piedmont retired to his cottage in the woods, during the last summer of Laura's life.

Andre's childhood must have been pitiable after all. I paused to think about it. When I glanced up, it seemed that the gargoyles had moved closer. Perhaps the walls of the library would slide forward, until they met, crushing me like a victim in an Edgar Allan Poe story.

But it was just an impression. The gargoyles remained immobile. Although I did have the uncanny feeling that if I turned quickly, I would find not a gargoyle but a human head, suspended from the bookcase behind me.

I looked. Again there was nothing. Perhaps the scarlet walls had a hypnotic effect on me. I continued reading.

"It is past time for professionals to investigate the detrimental results of excessive intermarriage among the rich," Dr. Piedmont lectured. She pointed out that although Laura Piedmont's depression was exacerbated by the death of her daughter Ann at the age of six, it was first manifested when her son displayed symptoms of severe mental disorder. "It is absurd," Dr. Piedmont stated, "to attribute this disorder to the curse, when it is clearly the product of genetic malfunctioning."

I read the remaining paragraphs.

"It is merely an unfortunate coincidence that the boy was born with a hair birthmark on his cheek, which had to be removed surgically. The rumor, that he later babbled in a strange language which he claimed to have invented himself, deserves little credence.

"His sadistic and rebellious behavior had a biochemical causation. It is sheer nonsense to suggest that he murdered his little sister, as has been alleged. It is a fact that she died of pneumonia, not of suffocation. As to reports that he gloated at his mother's funeral, such reports are mere hearsay.

"The boy's nervous system achieved a stable balance as he grew older. Now at the age of thirteen he appears perfectly normal, with above-average personableness and intelligence. If anything, his case refutes the theory of an existing curse, for he appears to have reversed the traditional order and outgrown the symptoms of a diabolical possession with the onset of adolescence."

Dear, sensible Dr. Piedmont reducing the curse to an allergic reaction. And herself destroyed by torture and starvation. There was only one paragraph left to get through. I was tempted to skip it. I had learned what Andre had wanted me to learn. That the curse had afflicted him early, in a particularly virulent form. But I decided to finish reading the page anyway. Silently, I read on.

And was literally jolted out of my chair.

"We refer, of course, to the younger son, Philip. Andre, the older boy, has been considered a model child from birth. The boys, although eighteen months apart, bear such a startling resemblance that from a distance they are often taken for twins.

"After their parents' deaths, the boys were sent to separate schools. Both are high achievers, with bright futures ahead. If they lead normal, reasonably successful lives, perhaps the myths surrounding the Piedmonts will be put to rest. Undeniably, old superstitions die hard. But we believe that the transformation in character of Philip Piedmont proves conclusively . . ."

A man's voice behind me completed the sentence, "Proves conclusively that there is no such thing as a Piedmont curse."

Then the man himself walked around to the front of the table where I sat reading. He was tall. With silver hair. And intense blue eyes.

He smiled at me and said, "Allow me to introduce myself; I'm Philip Piedmont. The family's black sheep. And Andre's brother."

Chapter XX

Ironically, my first reaction was relief. The curse had spared Andre. Almost immediately I was inundated by other sensations: fear, disorientation, and confusion. The stranger waited politely for me to speak. But I couldn't form a single cogent sentence. So I simply said nothing.

Tom Parsons came in and leaned casually against a bookcase. He said, "Philip, this woman's turning mute. When I brought her a glass of milk this afternoon, she was speechless, same as now."

Philip laughed. "It's just me, Thomas. I have a devastating effect on women. She's struck dumb because I'm irresistible."

Like Andre, Philip was striking in appearance; yet the brothers didn't look exactly alike. Up close, no one would have taken them for twins. In part this was due to differences transcending a basic resemblance. Andre's mouth was always tense; it resisted smiling. Philip, in contrast, was relaxed. Taller than Andre, his body was loose, and he was completely comfortable with it, like a dancer. The skull-like conformation of his head was very marked, perhaps because he was extraordinarily thin. His hair and eyes were the same as Andre's. But the mouth was radically different. The lips were thick. They gave him away. Philip was self-indulgent and insensitive.

Andre was much better looking. But Philip hadn't been kidding. He was irresistible. I felt wary and hostile, my defenses clamped into place. Philip quite consciously exerted a pull on the ancient and hidden passions which exist in me and in every human being.

My continuing silence amused Tom Parsons. "Look at her, Philip. Just sitting there. You've only to snap your fingers and she'll go off with you. For a day or a month or a year. Whatever you want. Like all the rest."

"Now, Tom, easy does it. Remember, she's my dear brother's wife. Tamara, that is your name, isn't it? You have beautiful hair. I've always liked that particular color." He walked around the table and stood close.

I watched him. He was making a fool out of me. He knew that he was returning dormant impulses to life and he thought it was funny. I didn't like to be manipulated. Or insulted. I decided to fight back.

Perhaps I could divert his attention. I asked, "Have you been in Woodlands all along? Or did you just arrive?"

He understood perfectly what I was trying to do. But he looked at me with respect. On whatever rating scale he used to evaluate the resistance level of potential conquests, I was a high scorer.

"She wants to know where I've been, Tom. Shall I tell her?" Philip walked away. It was easier to view him objectively when he wasn't too near.

Tom answered, "Why not?"

Philip grinned. "Honesty is the best policy, and all that. Very well. Would you like to hear an account of my travels, red fox."

"How did you know that I'm sometimes called that? Did Andre tell you?"

Philip stopped smiling. "My sainted brother and I rarely discuss personal matters. Until this afternoon, we weren't on speaking terms at all. But I have other sources of information. I know a good bit about you. And I've seen you myself, when you've walked in the woods."

"Were you hiding here in Stonehaven all winter?" Perhaps my fantasies about creatures secreting themselves in the upper rooms and attics weren't far from the truth after all."

"Stonehaven is my home. I don't have to sneak into it. I come and go as I please. My brother found that out. As first-born son, he is the official heir. Stonehaven belongs to him. Since I'm not respectable enough for Andre, he had me banished. All done legally. But it didn't work. True, I spent most of the winter away from Stonehaven, but I'm back now, in time to enjoy the spring."

"Does Andre support you?"

"He has, occasionally. But not for several years. I live quite well on an inheritance my sweet mother left me. She had doubts about whether I'd ever settle down and be a good law-abiding citizen. So she saw to it that I had ample money. My father would have cut me off without a penny. Women, I find, are more compassionate than men."

"Why didn't Andre tell me about you?"

"Ask Andre that. Knowing my brother, he probably thought his lawyers had settled matters so that I'd never return. Then he could pretend to you that I didn't exist. My inheritance is supposed to be discontinued the day I set foot in Woodlands. Apparently, Andre thinks my greed outdoes my love for my native land. He's wrong again. But, then, he always did underestimate me."

"You mean that as of this day you're poor? Wasn't it foolish to give up your entire fortune just to prove to Andre that you're independent, that you can defy him. I would have thought you were more clever."

"Tamara, I am not fond of my brother, but I wouldn't risk losing a copper penny just to provoke him. Stonehaven is my ancestral home; I'm a Piedmont, and I love it here. Most of all, I love my Woodlands. If I'm away from it too long, I grow profoundly homesick. I'd give up more than gold to be here."

"Personally I wish the estate were yours, particularly this house."

"Now you sound like Andre. He's here only because it's his duty. Our model child grown into a model man. But he hates it. Why should he get to remain while I have to leave? Andre doesn't know how lucky he is to be master of this precious piece of earth."

"Yes, Andre does hate Stonehaven and I don't blame him. But you can't say that he hates Woodlands. He loves it."

"Not in the way that you and I do. We worship the woods. Neither of us can resist it, can we? We have that in common, anyway, Tamara. Well, now my travels are over and I'm back home to stay. I've had quite a hectic time these past months. Ask Tom. I've been everywhere. Except in Hell."

There was a gutteral grunt from Tom. He was chuckling. "Life's dull when you're not around, Philip. No jokes. Just that serious, long-faced brother of yours, acting like he's the boss and giving everyone orders."

"My brother," said Philip, "is a bore and a pompous ass."

"How dare you," I said, "talk that way about Andre. You insult him because you're jealous. Not only of his possessions. You hate him because he's gentle and sensitive, characteristics you clearly lack."

Tom frowned. But Philip seemed actually pleased. "See how loyal she is, Tom; how she defends Andre. He doesn't deserve it but I like her for it."

While we talked we were actually communicating on two separate levels, one obvious and one covert. Anyone looking in on us would have seen two people engaged in a straight-forward conversation. What they wouldn't have seen was the invisible erotic energy exuded by Philip. Or was he a magnet, deriving such energy from women?

Perhaps this subterranean sensuality might form only one superior dimension of the man. Possibly he could also hear sounds past the range of human hearing, or see colors of the spectrum beyond the capacity of the human eye. A genius. The Ubermensch. Like Geoffrey Piedmont.

I had to exercise full self-control. Just to have a chat. "Philip," I said, "you can damn Andre to your heart's content and I can't stop you. But surreptitiously you've accomplished one good act. You've taken the onus off Andre. You are the reincarnation of Geoffrey."

Philip smiled. It gave him the look of a grinning skull. "You're not the first person to have that impression, Tamara. And I'm glad to be of service in cementing your dissolving marriage. Perhaps now Andre can stop brooding and return to the marriage bed."

He continued, "But you read my Aunt Emma's book. I'm cured. The first man in history to successfully ward off a case of the Piedmont curse."

"It's not pneumonia."

"Who can say? Perhaps all along it's been due to a heredi-tary virus infection. But I'm immune. Admittedly, an early touch of Geoffrey never leaves its victim completely sound. I haven't turned out to be the honorable upstanding citizen my aunt Emma so hoped I'd become, in order to prove her argument against the curse. I do still get into scrapes. And I have a very strange sense of humor. But this doesn't mean that I'm in league with the devil. I'd bear in mind, Tamara, that a good hypocrite can often put on a good act."

"What is that supposed to mean?"

"My brother might be more sanctimonious than sanctified."

"It's true, isn't it, that Andre never set foot in the cottage, and that you did?"

"Yes."

"That's all the proof I need of his innocence."

Tom Parsons and Philip exchanged looks. Philip laughed.

"Tamara, I see why Andre chose you. You're a constant source of amusement. But you're really wasted on him. He's too earnest to enjoy you. Did you fancy evil rites and revels at the cottage? Did you imagine that witches take turns sitting in the scarlet chair? Or perform a little danse macabre before the golden throne? Did you assume that ghosts promenade in front of the door? My poor red fox, you're gullible indeed."

"How do you explain the bizarre appearance of the cottage?"

"It was done as a joke! Tom and I concocted the idea. The explanation's as simple as that."

"It's a bizarre sort of joke."

"That's precisely the point. After my brother turned me out and sent me into exile, Tom came to my assistance. He decided that the cottage would make a perfect hideaway. I could live there from mid-March to early November, if necessary. But if Andre found out, there'd be the devil to pay. We wanted to make sure that voyeurs, lovesick couples, and stray tourists would leave us alone. Tom created the room behind the partition. He designed it effectively. It guarantees that intruders only barge in once. After all, look what it did to you. It practically drove you away from Woodlands altogether."

"What about the portrait? Was it used simply to add a gruesome touch?"

"Now the portrait is special. I'm fond of Geoffrey. He's the most prominent member of my family. You and Minnie Parsons were all for consigning him to an empty room. I couldn't have that. It seemed to me that Geoffrey and I had both been banished from our rightful place. Therefore, it struck me as fitting that we should share a common fate. So I had Tom bring him to the cottage and hang him on the wall. He looks good there, doesn't he?"

"I can't imagine a more appropriate place for him."

"There, you see; I have excellent judgment. And I've used it more than once in your case. I could have walked down the driveway and introduced myself to you that day you returned from Jenny Hooper's and almost caught me chatting with Tom. But I decided to spare you quite such a precipitous meeting. Besides, I knew Andre wasn't ready for it. The shock would have caused him pain. So I went into the woods and let him fabricate an explanation for you. I understand that it wasn't very convincing."

"No one could have survived the blizzard that day. Not in the woods."

"No one, Tamara? Certainly, not summer hikers with middle-aged spread. But mountain climbers survive far worse conditions. And I've been on expeditions to Everest and K2. I have first-rate equipment. Tom brought me snowshoes and cramp-ons and I made it to the cottage easily. Then I lit a warm fire, heated my dehydrated food, climbed into my arctic sleeping bag, and took a nap. It was a cinch."

"Then it was you, and not Andre, whom Elsie saw talking with Robin."

"Correct. And, being an old friend, he kept my existence secret. Robin's a kindly sort who didn't want to see you get hurt. He knew that Andre's lies and evasions would eventually alienate you. So he prompted Andre to tell you the truth. Which made Robin persona non grata to Andre. But that's Andre for you. No gratitude. And he's damned uncharitable. Robin had done Andre numerous favors in the past. From the moment he became my friend, Andre barred him from Stonehaven."

There was one more question I wanted to ask. But I didn't have the nerve. It was how well Philip had known Jenny Hooper.

"I won't answer that one," Philip said.

"Won't answer what?"

"I won't answer the obvious unspoken question. I told you I was well informed. I know everything that goes on in Woodlands. You'd like to know if I am the real father of

Stacy Lynn. For a while, you were convinced that Andre was her father. If you can pin the blame on me, then Andre goes scot-free. Brother Philip becomes the complete scapegoat. Andre and Tamara live happily forever. I think I'll leave you just a little insecure."

Tom Parsons said to Philip, "It's getting late. We'd better get back to the cottage."

"In a minute, Tom. You know, Tamara, it's a good thing Andre came begging me to show myself to you today. I'd already decided to meet you and I wasn't planning to wait much longer. I thought I'd confront you on a woods walk. Or in the nursery, when you were admiring that touching photograph of me as a child. But, without preparation, you might not have enjoyed making my acquaintance. And I did hope to make our first visit together as pleasant for you as possible." And he came very close.

I didn't trust myself. To avoid looking him in the face I stared at the floor. I watched Philip dig the toe of his shoe into the rug. It seemed quite possible to me that inside the shoe was a cloven hoof, belonging not to the devil's agent but to the great God Pan.

I forced myself to look directly at Philip. He blocked my way to the library door. Tom Parsons had closed in on me from the other side.

I said, "Meeting you would never be pleasant. Not under any circumstances. I'm leaving now; my husband would like to know what you've told me."

Both men stood still. Neither spoke. I wasn't sure they were going to let me leave. I behaved with bravado. But I knew, and so did they, that I really didn't want to go. My self-control was starting to crack.

Luckily, Philip decided not to challenge me with a test of wills. He said, "Tamara, I see that you are the sort who nobly stands by her man. I think it's stupid to believe in such rubbish, but Tom and I won't make you stay. However, I will point out that you are giving up an interesting evening with us in order to spend a dull time with my brother."

"I'm never bored when I'm with your brother."

"That old theme again. I've heard it all my life. How Andre Piedmont is blessed with all the virtues, while Philip is his bad little brother. Watch out, Tamara! The curse has never been predictable. Personally, I think Geoffrey would like to make Andre his next victim. It would be an excellent joke."

I didn't bother to answer Philip. Because I didn't dare. I had to get away from his presence fast. I left the library. In the hall, I found Andre, waiting for me.

Chapter XXI

"Are you going away with Philip, Tamara?"

"Of course not. What a ridiculous idea."

"Really? Then you're unusual. Philip's never had the least trouble getting any woman he wants."

"I can understand that. He's charismatic. But, fundamentally, I don't like him."

"Oddly enough, Tamara, that has very little to do with it. Philip succeeds with women when he's interested in them. Their attitude toward him is irrelevant. I've known women who've detested him. Yet, they've lived with him; even given him money. And they hated him with equal intensity at the beginning and at the end of the affair."

"So that is why you didn't want me to meet Philip."

"In part. I didn't want to test your loyalty against his magnetism. But basically, I wanted to erase him, to cross out his life. I see that I've been foolish. Philip exists. I can't wish him away, pretend that he was never born. But he's been a torment to me since childhood."

"I know. I read what Dr. Emma Piedmont said about his early years."

"His childhood coincided with my childhood. Mine was unhappy, due mainly to him. He destroyed my parents. They were convinced that he was the prototype of Geoffrey. That's why my mother killed herself. She couldn't bear to see Philip reach manhood."

"Poor Andre. I wish you'd told me all this sooner. It would have spared us recriminations and mistrust."

"I couldn't face it. Not while there was a chance that Philip would stay away from Woodlands. I was counting on his venality. I really believed that he'd rather give up Stone-haven than be disinherited."

"I guess he has some scruples after all."

"He has a mystical attachment to Woodlands. Sometimes I believe that he must touch base here from time to time, or else die."

"Like a whale surfaces for air?"

"That's right, Tamara. But I suspect, in reality, it's just an umbilical tie to the place where he was born."

I studied Andre, comparing his face to his brother's. Andre actually looked like a supernatural being. In him, the Piedmont physical characteristics had combined to achieve esthetic perfection. He might have been carved in alabaster by a Renaissance sculptor. Philip, in contrast, looked gross. His face was flawed, both by a prominent skeletal structure and by an ugly mouth. This mouth was a serious defect; it was like a thick wound in juxtaposition to the other Piedmont features.

I said, "Andre, I don't care about Philip. I feel like dancing, like drinking champagne. I was sure the curse had got you, and now I'm free of that fear. I'm not going back to New York. I'm going to stay here with you."

"It's not that simple, Tamara. Philip won't go away. He'll stay on in his damned cottage, and he won't let you alone."

"Please, Andre, not so much melodrama. You make the whole thing sound like a repetition of the temptation of St. Anthony, with me cast in the role of the saint. I can protect myself from Philip."

"Perhaps. But you don't really know him; I do. Philip has always been the winner. As a child, he managed to charm many adults into spoiling him, no matter what he did. Later, at school, he won scholarships without half-trying. He was also a gifted athlete. I never successfully competed with him in anything, even though I had the advantage; I was older. When I was still quite young, I gave up struggling against Philip and turned inward to music and books. If I hadn't had the consolation of literature, I might not have survived."

"If Philip was the winner, why is he jealous of you? He is; I can tell by the way he talks about you."

"Because I have Stonehaven. He wants this house more than he wants anything. And then he's had to come begging me to bail him out of trouble occasionally over the past few years. Which I did. To Philip, needing help is humiliating. He likes to be generous and squander his money on friends. But then he's doing the favors and others are under obligation to him."

"When I met you at Robin's, you seemed to be looking for someone. Was it Philip?"

"Yes. Philip had gone off on one of his safaris for girls. This time he'd picked one so young her father was ready to take him to court. Statutory rape. Robin and Philip were inseparable last summer. They were in the middle of magic experiments, something to do with alchemy. I'd heard from Philip that there was going to be a party, and I went, hoping he'd be there, so we could talk about the pending lawsuit. But I forgot about him, and everything else, as soon as I saw you. Do you remember? It was like a magic spell."

"Like witchcraft. My feelings haven't changed since that night."

"Nor mine."

"Then stop worrying about losing me to Philip. The Woodlands party is next week. We'll go and celebrate. We'll forget about the past few months. We can pretend that we've just arrived at Stonehaven from New York. That we're starting anew."

"The past is real, Tamara. Neither you nor I can pretend it didn't happen. I tried to do precisely that with Philip and what a fiasco I created. Besides, Philip is going to the party himself. He told me so this afternoon. He wouldn't permit us to enjoy ourselves. I know that Philip plans to embarrass me at the party, in front of the entire population of Woodlands."

"How can he do that?"

"I don't know and I wouldn't care to speculate. But I'm sure he'll devise something effective. He wants to turn me into a figurehead, to destroy my authority with the local people. Then I'd have Stonehaven in name only. He'd be the real master."

"I don't think he can get away with that. You work very hard, Andre. I know how seriously you take your duties here. Surely, the local people respect you for it. They'll side with you in a confrontation with Philip."

"Don't be too sure. They may respect me, but they're afraid of him. They remember his childhood all too well. They know what he's capable of. If you don't believe me, then ask yourself why they didn't tell you about Philip. I can guarantee that it was not out of deference to me. Even the gossips kept his existence a secret from you because they knew that's what he wanted."

"I hadn't thought about that."

"So you see, I can't possibly go to the party. I don't dare risk a public confrontation with Philip. I'd probably lose. I'd do it if it were just a matter of my honor. But my father expected me to watch over the interests of the people of Woodlands and that means preserving them from Philip even if I lose my self-respect in the process. Besides, there is another reason I'm going to skip the party. I don't want to leave Stonehaven completely unguarded. All the servants will be gone from the house that night. Who knows what Philip and Tom Parsons might try to do? Perhaps they'll decide to slip into the library. I once caught Philip in there, drunk, doing his damndest to conjure up the spirit of Geoffrey."

"Will you be safe here alone with Philip and Tom Parsons?"

"I've sometimes managed to cow my brother in the short run. I still have control of the purse strings, remember, and Philip is generally open to bribery. I'm not weak, I don't mind facing Tom and Philip alone; I just don't want a public spectacle."

"Then I'll stay here with you. We'll confront them together."

"No, Tamara, you must go. One of us has to represent Stonehaven. Since I can't, it's your duty to attend the party."

"I don't care a hang for my duty. But, if it's important to you, I'll go."

"Anyway, it will give you an opportunity to prove your own strength."

"Prove my strength?"

"Against my brother. I won't be around to stand in his way. He'll have you all to himself. And it there's one woman in the world Philip would want, it's my wife. He'll do his utmost to get you, Tamara. Be brave for my sake."

I said that I was completely confident that I could manage Philip. But actually I wasn't at all sure that I could.

I had become a battlefield, contested by one uncertain angel and an arrogant demon out of Hell.

Chapter XXII

For the next two days, Mrs. Parsons avoided me. Finally, I managed to corner her outside a broom closet. Her eyes were miserable and she pouted. She looked like a little girl about to be punished by a strict parent for an infraction of the rules.

"Why did you lie to me?" I asked. "You've caused me a great deal of avoidable unhappiness, Mrs. Parsons. You, of all people, should have told me about Philip."

"I wanted to tell you. But your husband would have been mad at me if I did. It was his place to let you know about Philip, not mine."

"You're right. My apologies."

"I can follow instructions," Mrs. Parsons said. "Mr. Piedmont told me to keep my mouth absolutely shut. 'When it comes to Philip, mum's the word,' he said. I knew he had your welfare at heart. He thought, ma'am, that you'd be a happier woman if you didn't find out about his brother. And knowing Philip as well as I do, I think your husband was right."

"I suppose Andre told you that Philip was gone for good."
She nodded.

"Well, he was wrong. Philip is back."

"I guessed that when you told me about seeing the portrait at the cottage. It sounded like Philip's idea of a joke."

"It was most considerate of Andre and you to want to keep me sheltered. But I'm a big girl and I can take the truth. So no more secrets, all right?"

"No more secrets," Mrs. Parsons said. She looked very happy. Keeping silent must have put her under a great strain. She was delighted to be free again to gossip to her heart's content.

Two days before the party I went into the woods. I knew I was taking a chance, that I might meet Philip there. But I couldn't very well surround myself with bodyguards or spend the rest of my life hiding in Stonehaven. Besides, my own strength would be the decisive factor in resisting Philip. No one else could protect me.

It was a fantastic day. Crispin walked with me a short way, and then moved boldly off, in search of rodents. He looked like a rare white miniature tiger, off hunting. The fate of any passing mouse was sealed.

A recent drop in temperature had left roads and paths icy and frozen drops of water, in pearl shapes of crystal, were trapped in treetops and bushes. The pine trees thus were decorated with Nature's own ornaments and lights. It looked as if elves had come the night before and prepared the entire woods for a Christmas in the springtime.

I felt as if I were experiencing two seasons simultaneously and I was enchanted by my winter–spring wilderness. By tomorrow, the frosty drops would melt, but today a king's ransom in aerial gems was strewn about the woods. I took the branch of a birch tree in my hand. Its ice ovals shimmered, pure water transformed into prisms of color: pink, blue, yellow. No exhibition of Russian jewels by Fabergé could be as beautiful. I flicked my tongue out to taste an ice drop. Unlike diamonds of the earth, this diamond of the air was delicious. It was hard, cold, and spicy, a confectioner's bauble.

"You understand why I love Woodlands," someone close-by said, startling me. For a moment, I thought the person who was suddenly there was Andre. But it was Philip. He was melancholy and slightly aloof today. I felt no fear because the woods soothed him, draining him of abnormality and making him a benign hiker off on a stroll.

He said, "Magnificent day, isn't it? And you are a nymph; I knew you were. Were you sent ahead by springtime to put the woods in order? You ought to have an apron, filled with blossoms, and wildflowers to shake out over the earth."

He started walking and so did I. It seemed a perfectly natural thing to do.

"You seem markedly different today," I said.

"I am. The woods absorb all tensions. In return they ask only to be adored. But tell me, Tamara, aren't you afraid to be alone with me. Andre has no doubt warned you to beware of my evil powers."

I smiled. "You don't seem evil right now."

"I'm not. I've leashed my lecherous tendencies. Out of respect to you, and out of respect to Nature. She is glorious today."

"Beloved Woodlands," I said.

Philip looked at me. Then he looked away. "You must see this forest in the autumn. That's the best time. Last fall I was in a café in a village in the south of France. It was mid-September. I was sitting alone watching the Mediterranean Sea below when a group of tourists came in. They were quite taken with the little village, and they kept talking about it. They liked its being settled precariously on the cliffs above the sea. They thought the red roofs on the stone houses quaint. They admired the beautiful old church in the center of town. But do you know what I was thinking of, the whole time the tourists praised the village, Tamara?"

"Yes?"

"Woodlands. I would have traded that entire village, its sun and its sea, for this patch of cool forest. I knew the leaves would soon be gold, orange, and red in Woodlands. The ferns would turn ochre as they died while the sumac would change to bright red. Whole hillsides of Woodlands would blaze in fall's different colors."

"I know. Once, when I was a child, my grandmother took me to Vermont on vacation. There, I saw the woods as you describe them. I remember thinking that walking under the treetops must be what walking through a Gothic cathedral would be like. The leaves had the luminosity of stained glass in the sunlight. They evoked awe and wonderment."

Philip said nothing, but he studied my face.

"Sometimes I wish I could live in the woods," I said.

"You should. Other nymphs do. Forsake the world and follow Bacchus."

"Now you're teasing me."

"Not at all. You'd do well at Aphrodite's banquet, serving the mead and nectar."

All of a sudden I was acutely aware of Philip's attractiveness again. I didn't trust myself to walk farther with him.

"I have to go back to Stonehaven," I said.

"Too bad. I thought we could spend an educational afternoon together. I'd give you an Audubon tour of the woods. I know everything about plants, birds, and rocks."

"No, I'd best get back."

"I see. Well, begone then! But I'm sure the time will come for us to walk together someday."

"Don't be too sure of that. Time, they say, Philip, is on the side of the angels."

He laughed. "If that were true, Tamara, I wouldn't stand a chance."

I laughed, too. "The devil take you, Philip."

And I watched him vanish into the woods, a tall elf surrounded by ice drops winking in the sunlight.

Then I went home to change. I had made a snap decision to drop in on Jenny Hooper.

Jenny did not smile at me, not even when I gave her a mammoth red paper rose as a gesture of goodwill. I had pruned the decorations I'd made and brought her the best to take to the party.

She led me to the living room and sat stiffly, hands folded in her lap, like an old-fashioned schoolgirl awaiting her turn in a spelling bee. I could hear the wall clock ticking. The house was exceptionally quiet.

"Where's Stacy?" I asked.

"Napping."

"Jenny, I may as well tell you that I've met Philip."

"I'd already heard that news."

"Andre was able to keep Mrs. Parsons from telling me about his brother. But I can't understand why you didn't talk to me about Philip."

"I had two reasons," Jenny said in a quiet, unapologetic way

"What were they?"

"First, it wasn't my business to tell you what Andre didn't want you to know. I'm not a busybody."

"And the other reason?"

"Philip himself. I can't pretend that I'm not afraid of him. When I was a child my father used to scare me with threats that Philip Piedmont would get me if I weren't good."

"Makes him sound like the local bogeyman."

"He was, Tamara. And he was only a child himself at the time. Yet, he was already notoriously cruel. He liked to hurt animals. Once he killed my favorite cat; I cried for days."

"Did you see much of him?"

"Very little. My father kept a rifle loaded in case Philip came on our property uninvited."

"Don't you think your father was being too dramatic?"

"Not at all. For generations Woodland's children had been nurtured on stories of Geoffrey Piedmont, and Philip was made in his image. For awhile it actually seemed that Geoffrey was reliving his prior life in our time."

"But Philip changed, didn't he, Jenny? At adolescence."

"He became a handsome and charming young man. The entire population of Woodlands was delighted and relieved."

"So relieved that they forgave him?"

"Certainly. Contrary to popular opinion we don't hold grudges or go in for blood feuds here in the mountains. So everyone welcomed the reformed Philip with pleasure. Some people even preferred him to your husband. They said that Philip was more generous, that he had a sense of humor, while Andre worked too hard and was formal and unfriendly."

"You didn't feel that way, did you, Jenny?" And then I realized that I'd asked a loaded question.

Jenny's eyes were without expression. If she felt a strong attachment to either Philip or Andre she concealed it well. She ignored my question completely.

"I suppose it is strange that people took to the rejuvenated Philip so readily, Tamara. But underneath their acceptance of him was a residue of fear. When word got around that Philip had been banished from Woodlands, many people hoped it was true. I, for one; I'd never really forgotten my poor murdered cat. I didn't talk about Philip to you or anyone else for the same reason that people don't generally mention the hydrogen bomb. It's there but they'd rather not think about it."

"Perhaps now that everything's out in the open, it would be safe for you to come back to Stonehaven."

"Perhaps, but I'd be afraid."

"I can't say as I blame you. Not with Philip likely to pop out of the shadows at any time. But his presence here has cheered me immensely. I'd become very suspicious of Andre, especially after the way he reacted to you in the nursery at Stonehaven. Now, thanks to Philip, I'm optimistic again. I know for certain that Andre is safe from the curse."

Jenny did not react to what I said. She looked at me blandly. For the first time I felt awkward with her. She treated me as if I were the minister of a new church, come to convert her. I was presuming on her patience, taking up her time, an interloper.

I decided to cut our conversation short. "I've got to get

back to Stonehaven. Sorry I missed seeing Stacy. Take care, and I'll see you at the party."

"I'm not going," Jenny said.

"But you've helped organize it! What do you mean you're not going?"

"I'm not, and that's all, Tamara. I've made up my mind that I want to stay home."

"Jenny, I don't understand."

"I'm not going to talk about it with you: I've already told Celia that I won't be there."

"And she accepted that?"

"She had to. And you do, too."

"You sound very defensive, and there's no reason for it. If you want to stay home, that's your privilege. It's just that now I won't see you at the party. I'm disappointed."

Jenny relented and smiled. "I'm sorry, Tamara. But for personal reasons I just can't go."

Personal reasons! The sort of vague excuse one gives for taking a day off from the office. Driving back to Stonehaven I asked myself what these "personal reasons" could be. There was one possible explanation. Jenny and Andre, the only two people who were absenting themselves from the party, were going to meet in secret.

Yet this explanation had one loophole. Why would the two agree to see each other on the one night when the entire population of Woodlands would notice their mutual absence? Celia Gordon would immediately come to the same conclusion I had, and she would tell everyone.

Would Andre or Jenny take such a risk? It seemed doubtful. Then I thought of something and my buoyant mood dissipated. I was depressed, weighed down as if by a metallic weight.

What if Philip had told me the truth. What if the curse had initially attached itself to him and then rejected him. What if the curse had then taken Andre, and Andre had seduced Jenny, because evil takes pleasure in corrupting good.

Was there something special about the night of the party? Some magical imperative? Perhaps it was the only night a certain plant would bloom. Or the moon would be in phase for particular incantations. Then Andre and Jenny would have no choice. The spirit of Geoffrey would compel them to meet and perform the necessary ceremony for the ossasion if they were lovers.

I wanted to cry. Here I was back with suspicions and fears again, after a very brief respite. I felt reasonably sure that the explanation I'd just concocted was nonsense. But I couldn't be sure. And now I would be on guard, watching for signs, waiting for revelations. I was back in the paranoid mood Stonehaven thrived on. The damned house would be titillated once more.

Chapter XXIII

The day of the annual Woodlands party arrived. There was suppressed excitement in the air; instead of their usual invisible efficiency the servants made their presence distinctly felt. I lay drowsily in bed during the morning and listened to them laugh and shout to each other. Predictably, the weather was rainy.

At least it was reasonably warm. Mrs. Parsons, ever an optimist, said, "Thank God, ma'am, there's no ice. Therefore, everybody in Woodlands and Orinville will come. Since the party's inside, rain doesn't matter." This statement reflected a lifelong accommodation to the climate of the north country.

By late afternoon the house began to empty. I stood at the window when a troop of young girls left. They giggled and looked around to see who was watching. Only the groom from the stable and the mechanic from the garage took any notice of them; but two men were better than none, and the girls flirted shamelessly with them.

Even Mrs. Parsons was eager to be off. After every other servant had gone she appeared in my doorway and said, "Everything's in order now, ma'am. I hoped I could leave early."

"Go now," I said. "It's a special occasion."

When it was time to dress for the party I chose carefully. I did not want to make an ostentatious appearance as Lady of the Manor. For this reason I had arranged for an inconspicuous car, rejecting the Mercedes as inappropriate. After mulling over my wardrobe, I decided on a simple blue knit dress with a sterling silver necklace and bangle bracelets for accessories.

The curving road to Orinville was easier to drive now that the winter ice had melted. The town's main street was dark, abandoned even by ghosts. The library was an empty tomb, its doors shut tight. I remembered standing under its high, vaulted ceiling, gloomy and foreboding even in the daytime, and I shuddered. A solitary light gleamed in the launderette, deserted on this special night. Each machine stood idle, watching the street from its single round eye, like a mechanical cyclops.

Traffic grew heavy by the time I reached the parking lot of the local restaurant. It was prosaically named, according to a flashing neon sign, "Jimmy's Place." I squeezed my station wagon between a red convertible and a pickup truck. I could hear loud phonograph music in the square, anonymous building next door as I got out of the car and merged with the boisterous crowd. Like a wave, we swept into the restaurant.

It was a roadhouse typical of thousands found along American highways. Comfortable, but without charm, it was a complete nonentity. Only our homemade decorations gave it a touch of uniqueness. A wooden bar with formica top and chrome rail extended the length of one room. A jukebox, lights bubbling, stood next to it. The second, and larger room, had red plastic booths and tables with black leatherette chairs. Hung along the walls were a number of scenes of deer feeding on wintry mornings, or hunters jovially consuming a hearty breakfast of pancakes. A phonograph located next to an infrequently used piano pumped out rock music. The door of the ladies' room had a picture of a hen. The men's room door sported a rooster.

A figure disengaged itself from the raucous semidarkness and I recognized Miss Gordon's purposeful walk. She looked as stringy as ever in a white beaded dress. Her short black hair, done for the occasion, looked perfectly awful; the permanent had left tight little curls like miniature corkscrews all over her head. She had decided that I was her protégée and clearly meant to introduce me to everyone in the room. There was no escape; she was implacable.

"There you are, Tamara. Ignore the noise. Later we turn

down the phonograph and turn on the lights. By then the teen-aged kids are placated so they stay. Otherwise, we'd have gangs of them roaming the town." She led me along at her determined pace, a mother managing a recalcitrant child. "Sorry Andre couldn't come tonight. But I've heard that your brother-in-law is coming." This mention of Philip upset me.

Miss Gordon grimaced, a grimace which was supposed to be a smile. Her sharp nose twitched. She had caught my reaction to Philip Piedmont and knew that I was far from indifferent to him.

"Sorry I couldn't tell you that Andre had a brother," she said casually, as if she had neglected to pass on the correct ingredients for a recipe. "I wanted to tell you about him and about the cottage. But they wouldn't let me. People are scared of your brother-in-law. I didn't think it my place to ride roughshod over everybody's fears. They assumed that if he wanted you to know he existed he'd see to it that you found out."

"A likely story," I thought. Celia Gordon would never keep a piece of gossip to herself to spare anyone's feelings. So how had Philip managed to bully her into keeping her mouth shut? She didn't scare easily. Miss Gordon interrupted this intriguing train of thought to introduce me to an elderly couple.

"This is Pop Modjeska and his wife Anna." They were farmers who supplemented their income by running a summer boardinghouse. From the look of them they served good food. About the same height and weight they looked like Tweedledum and Tweedledee. "Nice to meet someone from the old house," Pop said in a Central European accent. His wife grinned, repeating what he had just said.

Thus baptized I was taken around to meet everyone. I met so many people that their faces scarcely registered; besides, as a result of close intermarriage there was a strong family resemblance among these mountain dwellers. The crowds, noise, and darkness were overpowering, so that the room, not the dancers, seemed to revolve. Faces appeared, then reappeared. Dancing couples almost collided with us as we crossed the floor; clusters of guests formed and reformed to make my acquaintance. Through all this, Miss Gordon did not once stop talking. Like a nonstop Greek chorus, she judged everyone.

"You've got to meet Paul Rieger, over here; he's running

for county assessor next year; cheats everybody who walks into his store. There's Jenny Hooper's cousin, Sam, just got out of jail again. See that boy with the nice short hair, that's Johnny Powers who works at his father's gas station, luckily enough. His father's a drunkard and would lose the business in a month without his son's help. Johnny's marrying Jenny's cousin Marion as soon as she graduates from high school this June." Miss Gordon's attention was diverted by three silver-haired women in Sears Roebuck suits, corsages pinned to the lapels. Within minutes I'd not only met them face to face, I'd learned their darkest secrets behind their backs. Miss Gordon hurried on triumphantly.

Mrs. Parsons waved. She was wearing her Sunday best, black with pearls. The primitive drum beats of the music didn't suit her, for no one looked less primitive than Minnie Parsons at a party in Orinville. She paused indecisively and then spoke quickly, taking the plunge. "I wanted to tell you that I had one very special reason for keeping Philip Piedmont a secret." Her bright blue eyes glittered. She moved very close and said softly, "I had no choice, ma'am. It's my husband Tom. He would have punished me if I'd told." Her voice lowered to a whisper. "A good beating would have been the mildest thing he'd have done to me."

I was shocked and stopped her from any further confessions by saying, "Forget it, Mrs. Parsons. Say no more." She stood with her head cocked to one side, like a bird, doubtful and piteous. She was ready to cry.

To my horror, Celia Gordon snapped, "That's right, Minnie, shut up! You've got a big mouth. Who wants to hear about your troubles?" Mortified, I started to tell Miss Gordon what I thought of her. "Celia!" I bleated, but somehow she had vanished. Before I could locate her in the crowd, a whistle blew, shrill and persistent. The lights went on. Minnie Parsons was gone, too.

There was a moment of confusion before a bald man wearing glasses banged on the piano for quiet. When the room was still, he shouted, "Okay, everybody eat." Murmurs of agreement and encouragement rose up from all sides and soon I found myself part of a pushing, gleeful mob. There were men in wrinkled suits and women in bright pinks and blues. A few children were present, brought along because of the babysitter shortage; easy to see why—all the sitters were here. Adolescents abounded, dressed in cheap versions of "the latest" from New York. Everyone of all ages moved steadily toward the buffet table, set up along the far wall, opposite the bar.

I didn't feel isolated, for they were hospitable to strangers. Being in their good company raised my spirits so that I felt at peace for the first time since I'd come to Woodlands. These were practical, down-to-earth people, with everyday concrete matters on their minds, who had no time for superstitious nonsense. After the Byzantine complications of the Piedmont family I found the humdrum conversations around me refreshing.

"And I said to her, get out of that dress and into something else, Jane, the color doesn't suit you at all." "Well, Dick, the rain's good in the springtime but if this keeps up, it's going to be too much. Need a little hot sun." "How's that calf of yours doing?" "So I said, who needs that from the school board. Tax money here, tax money there. When I was a kid, we learned without this fancy stuff."

The food was fine; prepared with skill and enthusiasm even though nobody had bothered with grand style. There was turkey and ham, thick rich cream from the dairy, pastel Jell-O molds, stuffings, dressings, and desserts, home-baked by county fair prize-winners, the star cooks of the region.

After we'd eaten, someone brought out a harmonica. The crowd sang old songs that I remembered from childhood. Then the dancing began again, but this time the music was slow and old-fashioned. Jack Hooper came up to me and shyly asked me to dance. Clearly he felt uncomfortable with any woman but his wife Jenny. I smiled to myself; Jenny's clumsy but loyal knight.

"I'm surprised you're here," I said, "since Jenny didn't come."

"Jenny figured someone was needed to keep an eye on things at the party," he answered. I considered this cryptic remark but the music ended before I could decipher it. Afterward, I was too busy to bother with it, because I was not allowed to sit out one single dance.

I lost track of the men who took my hand and led me to the dance floor that night. They chose to honor me so that it could never be said that the locals didn't know how to treat a lady. I remember an octogenarian who left me breathless after a quick stomping polka. Then came a series of long-haired boys, nearly mute. The local veterinarian moved me along in an obsolete fox trot, complete with monologue on last year's rabies epidemic. He was followed by three farmers in succession, an energetic volunteer fireman, the local dentist, and the high school English teacher. He was married to the Orinville librarian who had stared at me impassively through thick glasses that day when I'd asked for Piedmont family history.

I grew tired and was on the point of begging for mercy from my partner, a fat man who stepped on my toes frequently, when suddenly the room became quiet. A viola played a sweet waltz. By then I felt like the heroine in *Red Shoes* who is compelled by magic to dance forever, when she wanted only to rest. A cello-rich voice which brooked no argument said, "My turn," and before I could stop myself I was in Philip's arms. As he moved me gracefully across the floor I saw that we were the only couple dancing.

Perhaps it was the darkness or the drinks which made me forget where I was. It seemed that the walls of the building melted, become ephemeral, and we were transported through them, dancing, to a green clearing in the woods. I forgot that Andre existed. Only Philip was real, under a round moon on a warm summer night. The shadowy trees were well-wishers observing us while the stars competed with each other, crowding the skies to see us. We ourselves were clothed in fragile, fantastic costumes in imitation of the delicate figures in a Watteau painting. The king and queen of the flowers, we waltzed as we held court.

The piercing noise which permeated this dream was strange, quirky. It jarred our translucent dream world, causing it to shiver. How long had we been dancing? A few minutes? Perhaps an hour? The noise might be a cat's cry, the frightened wail of a lost animal blundered into a fairy tale. Or perhaps it was Oberon's coach arriving, forced to stop suddenly and screeching to a halt on the rose-scented air.

But it wasn't either of those. The sound was undeniably human and definitely a scream. I drew back and stared at Philip. His blue eyes were murky and his lips crude.

I spun around in time to see Jack Hooper run across the room. He plunged into a cluster of murmuring people. Where had I heard that solicitous tone before? Then I remembered, at my grandmother's funeral. I pushed through the crowd.

Jenny stood there, a Jenny transformed. Her serenity and

quiet confidence were gone. Her hair hung lank and uncombed on her shoulders, her face was wild.

"Jenny!" Jack shouted and shook her as if he could help her by hurting her.

The voice that came from Jenny's throat was hoarse, unnatural. It ranged from shout to whisper. It said, "Our baby, Stacy. She's been taken from her crib, Jack; she's gone." A gasp passed contagiously from one person to another around the room.

With fear rising to panic level I remembered Andre's fury when he came upon Stacy at Stonehaven. Was kidnapping the end result of that rage? Then I heard another scream. "Odd," I thought, "it sounds very close. No wonder it's close; it's mine," I realized as the room started to spin, and by the time I'd fallen to the floor the room was very black and there was silence all around me.

Chapter XXIV

In the blackness I made my way through the woods. The rain, though not fierce, was steady. It didn't matter. I was wrapped in a poncho, had a warm sweater in my knapsack, and I'd worn wet sneakers before. Everything I had on, blue jeans, crew socks, and even a sweatshirt, had been given to me by a generous boy scout who happened to be big for his age. I'd insisted on joining the search party after they brought me around and I didn't want to waste time by returning to Stonehaven to change clothes. The searchers agreed, but they found me a nuisance.

The sound of heavy boots crashing through shrubbery came from all directions. Flashlight beams illuminated the rain, striping the trees and earth. I could hear the occasional shout, "Have you got her?" and the response, "No, just scared up a rabbit."

Rabbit! Stacy was like a little rabbit herself. I could picture her easily; deceptively cuddly and angelic looking but sniffing out mischief as she crawled along; the sort of baby I'd like to have myself someday. I told myself to stop this maudlin sentimentality or I'd start crying and then I'd really be a burden to the searchers.

I forced myself to keep my mind on what I was here for: to find Stacy. I hadn't come along tonight only because of anxiety. After all, my endless walks in the woods did qualify me as a minor expert on the terrain, although I had to admit to myself that I didn't know the woods at night and I'd best stick close to the other searchers.

I buried the image of Stacy but had less success with Jenny. Jenny the strong, the stoic, had collapsed at the party, gone to pieces. It was Jack who finally got through to her, using a combination of tenderness and rebuke. "Think about Stacy," he'd told her, "not yourself." And this did the trick. When she had pulled herself together, Jenny told us what we needed to know. It had started out a normal sort of evening. She'd put Stacy to bed at the usual time, then took up her knitting and watched television. She'd heard a slight noise an hour or so later but barely noticed it. It was only when she made a routine check that she found the nursery window open and the baby gone.

At first Jenny was calm and practical. She assumed that Stacy had managed to get out of the crib herself, so she looked into all the obvious places—the open closet, the bathroom. Then she went outside to the yard but there was no sign of Stacy. She went into the house to call Jack at the party but the telephone wires had been cut. That was when Jenny panicked and did absurd things, like unlocking the basement, opening the hamper, and even looking into the refrigerator. Finally, forcing herself to use her head, Jenny took a flashlight and went into the yard again. In the damp earth, underneath the window of Stacy's room, she found a clear shoe imprint, the mark of a man's boot.

Jenny grabbed a raincoat and, in the night silence of Woodlands, walked to the road and waited. Ten minutes later a truck tunneled out of the blackness. She waved; it stopped for her and the driver dropped her off at Jimmy's Place, where the search party was organized.

There were varying theories about what must have happened, although everyone agreed that no one would kidnap Stacy for ransom money; the Hoopers were far too poor. Most people talked themselves into believing that the crime had been committed by an outsider. A madman, probably from the city, had driven by, seen the light, and somehow sneaked into the house; the troopers set up roadblocks as far away as the throughway. I exchanged looks with Jenny; we both knew that the crime had the stamp of Woodlands.

My feet sank into the spring mud as I walked and I recalled Tom Parsons hovering around the nursery the day Jenny had visited Stonehaven with Stacy. He had leaned squarely against the door with an insolent smile on his face, a little too interested in Stacy to suit me, for he wasn't the sort of man who liked children. Then, of course, there was Andre who had lashed out furiously at us, actually ordering Jenny to get Stacy out of the house.

A hand gripped my shoulder. I jumped, startled, but relaxed when I saw it was one of the searchers, an apple-cheeked boy from a nearby farm. "Sorry to frighten you," he said. "I went to Stonehaven like you asked me to, but nobody was there. The house is closed up and dark."

"Thank you," I murmured, distracted. So Andre was gone, and after he'd told me it was vital to keep Stonehaven guarded against Philip during the party. "But of course," I tried to reassure myself, "by now he's heard that Stacy is missing and he's out looking with everyone else." However, I couldn't convince myself that this explained Andre's absence from the house.

Despite the enormous supper I had devoured at the party, I was growing hungry, the combined result of chill and exercise. I leaned against a boulder, opened my knapsack, and put on my sweater. Then I ate one of the sandwiches provided by the good wives of Orinville for the searchers. The coffee in my thermos was burning hot; it scalded my throat deliciously, reviving me.

I stared at the sky. Great swirls of cloud rushed across its surface. The rain had stopped and the moon was out. A clearing trend was on the way. I flicked off my flashlight to save the batteries and placed it carefully in a niche in the rock. "Damn," I muttered as it fell to the ground anyway. "Please don't be broken," I whispered, as I knelt down to retrieve it. I reached around on the damp ground and my hand, touching something soft, recoiled instantly. Tentatively, I reached out again, scared to death that the limp softness was Stacy. I was relieved when it turned out to be a blanket.

I located the flashlight and switched it on. Its glow revealed a blue bunny embroidered in the corner of the blanket.

So now I knew for sure. This was no crazy, spur-of-the moment kidnapping. Stacy wasn't in Orinville or on the throughway either. She was here, brought to these woods by someone who knew that most of the local people would be away at a party tonight. What sort of person would deliberately subject a baby to the rain and to the strangeness of a night in the forest?

There was only one shelter in the woods and it made a logical hiding place on a cold wet night: the cottage. I had hoped that I would never have to see it again, but the need to find Stacy outweighed my fear.

I was on the verge of calling to the other searchers to tell them that we should look in the cottage, when I noticed how quiet it had become. They had moved on and although I could catch up with them, it would take time. The stillness caused me to consider whether it would be the searchers who would answer if I shouted or if the response might not come from someone dangerous, someone I didn't want to confront yet.

It was time to set off. "Here I go," I thought, "to the hanging place of Geoffrey Piedmont." I bumbled along, changing direction, finding my way and then losing it again. At this rate I'd never locate the cottage. I crossed a clearing and veered sharply to my left when about fifty yards later I suddenly froze. I'd heard a noise behind me and it wasn't an animal rustling through the bushes: clearly this had been the clump of a boot.

I looked ahead for cover as all hunted animals do. A few feet in front of me was a huge rock. I crouched down and inched toward it. I would gladly have metamorphosed into an earthworm at that moment. I heard another footstep, well behind me but distinct. I was too frightened to look around so I didn't move but sat exposed, like a rabbit to the fox's eyes. The rock ahead was close enough to touch; I could feel its pitted lichen-covered surface with my fingers. Somehow this gave me courage, like holding a good-luck charm, and I risked a backward glance, then sagged with relief. There was a wall of dry stone behind me and in all probability the sound of someone walking came from behind it. Most likely, he was watching the open fields which lay on that side of the wall.

It occurred to me that I might actually hold the advantage since the kidnapper occupied the peculiar position of hunting me and being hunted by the searchers at the same time; thus, he couldn't concentrate his energies completely on me. "In reality," I reassured myself, "he doesn't know I'm here at all because he can't see over the wall. He wouldn't have gone clumping around so loudly if he'd thought anyone could hear him." I wasn't convinced by this sensible line of reasoning but it gave me the courage necessary to scurry for the rock.

In a minute I was safely behind it but I had made noise. There was a tense moment before I risked a wary look from behind my rock. Something round hurtled at me and I bit my hand to keep down a scream. It flew into an arc and then plopped to the earth: an apple core. Instead of throwing grenades, my enemy was enjoying a snack. The humor of this didn't escape me but my lips were too tightly drawn in terror to smile.

I peered around again and this time my heart almost stopped beating, for standing on top of the wall was a man and in his hand was a hunting rifle. I couldn't recognize him as he was a featureless black shape against the night sky. But immediately, I pulled back, out of sight. Still it was not fast enough since I could hear him coming slowly closer. He was oddly casual for a man pursued by a search party. He even whistled very quietly to himself as if he hadn't a care in the world. I contemplated making a break for it, but he was no doubt a first-class shot who would kill me before I'd gone two feet. The light-giving moon was a blessing when I followed him but no blessing when he came after me.

He was very near my rock. Then, to my surprise, I heard his footsteps going away. Had it been a false alarm? I was trying to pull myself together when a whispering voice said, "So it's you, is it?"

My hand rushed to my mouth and I thought, "This is it." I bit my knuckle until I tasted blood. My body pulled itself taut, in preparation for the explosion of a bullet, and when a nearby owl hooted I knew it was sounding my funereal music. But there was no shot and the owl hooted again. Feeling like a happy fool, I realized that the man's "So it's you, is it" had been directed to the owl, not to me. He had heard my clumsy movements but the presence of the bird provided adequate camouflage.

I relaxed and waited. Just when I hoped I could continue

clinging to my rock until dawn, the footsteps started away
and I had no choice but to follow, since there was a good
chance the man would lead me to Stacy. He used his flashlight and moved normally while I dumped my backpack,
abandoning food and coffee, and stuffed my pockets with
candy bars. I hooked my flashlight and canteen to my belt
and followed at a discreet distance.

For some way nothing occurred and I even told myself
that I had a talent for playing private detective. But suddenly, with shocking speed, he swung around, his light revolv-
ing smoothly, and I braced myself to run. The yellow glow
never reached me. Again I was rescued by the abundant
wildlife of Woodlands as the light fixed on two gentle deer,
munching, and held them blinded and terrified in its steady
beam. The man chuckled comfortably. "Too bad I can't risk
the noise, you two," he said softly. "It's a good night for
jacklighting and I could get me a venison dinner out of season."

This time I recognized the voice. The man was Tom Parsons and I couldn't imagine anybody worse.

As we walked, it because obvious that he was heading
toward the cottage. For this I thanked him. I might never
have found it by myself but Tom Parsons knew the night
woods like an animal, and was leading me straight to it.
When I was quite sure of my surroundings, I let him go on
alone because it was safer.

The stars were fully out now, sparkling overhead, and the
moon looked like a hard, polished marble. After a reasonable
length of time had elapsed I reluctantly gave up star-gazing
and set off. The moist air grew heavy, giving this portion of
the woods a tropical atmosphere peculiarly its own, so that
once again I felt transported to a South American rain forest.

The huge trees witnessed my progress along the stony path.
This part of Woodlands had never been used for lumbering,
and thick trees blotted out the night sky. These same trees
must have lined this path on the day Geoffrey Piedmont was
taken past to be hanged.

Without warning I was at the edge of the small clearing
which holds the cottage. By day the exterior of the cottage has
a certain fey charm; at night it looks grotesque, a squat, mis-
shapen offspring of Stonehaven. No candle or kerosene lamp

burned in its black window; no noise broke its silence. Only a
gentle wind, rubbing itself against the new buds on the trees
made any sound.

There was no sign of Tom Parsons, and I began to worry.
Perhaps he hadn't come here after all. I decided to crouch
down behind the stone wall which surrounds the clearing and
wait. I must have dozed off because the sky turned instantly
from black to pearl instead of lightening in successive stages.
Although it was still hard to see details, outlines could be
sharply delineated.

I knew I had to go into the cottage but I hesitated despite
its deserted look. No matter what dangers existed out here,
the woods provided basic protection: camouflage and space.
The macabre little hut offered no escape route; it was tightly
enclosed with only one door and small, shriveled windows.
Whatever was in there could keep trespassers inside with it. I
drew closer. The dawn light exaggerated the clumsiness of
the building and turned door and windows into features on a
mock face, so that the cottage seemed like the head of a
monster whose body, embedded in the earth, was even now
struggling free.

"Nonsense," I said to myself as my hand touched the
doorknob. Vividly, I hallucinated that the moment I opened
the door the huge forked tongue of a serpent would lash out,
knocking me backward across the ground to the wall. I was
astonished at the clarity of this image and I drove it away by
consciously replacing it with another—a vision of Stacy, lying
dead on the cottage floor.

"Get hold of yourself," I lectured. "You're acting insane.
You've waited long enough to know if anyone was inside,
and if anyone had come out of the cottage you'd have heard
them. The building has no supernatural powers and you're in
no danger yourself, but Stacy might be. So you must open
the door and go in."

Thus, semifortified with common sense, I let myself in.
Curtains were drawn effectively over the windows so that it
took me a while to get used to the dark. I lit my flashlight
and shot the beam around the room quickly. It was empty
and the simple wooden furniture looked dusty and unused.

But I knew the other room was waiting and I would lose
my courage if I delayed. A few quick strides and I was at the
connecting door. I pulled it open. I had fancied discarded
witches' cloaks or the remains of animal sacrifices, but noth-

ing had changed. My flashlight caught the portrait in its beam; it was still in the same place on the wall. The light caught the gilded chair and sheepskin rug. I felt like laughing; after all, the room really was silly, a cheap carnival trick, a joke.

Which is why I was taken unaware and screamed involuntarily, for when my flashlight lit the remaining chair, it encircled Tom Parsons, relaxed and comfortable, feet crossed, his rifle leaning against the chair arm. His eyes didn't blink in the blinding light and on his face was that familiar nasty grin.

"Enjoyed your hide-and-seek game, Mrs. Piedmont?" he asked, obviously amused, as if I were a casual visitor who had dropped in for coffee.

Trying to control my trembling voice I asked, "Where's Stacy?"

He smiled and didn't answer; I asked again, "Where's Stacy?"

"You mean the little girl they're all out looking for tonight? Why ask me? How should I know?" he countered.

"I think you do know and I'm not leaving until I find out."

He uncrossed his legs and stood up, throwing off a peculiar odor all his own: a smell compounded of whiskey and sour milk. Then he slowly walked over to me and, frightened, I backed away instinctively.

"You see, Mrs. Piedmont," he said, his manner abrasively tender, "I could get mad at you for what you're implying. I come here nights to be in the woods I love and you come sneaking along, acting like I'm a kidnapper."

He edged yet closer. "So it was you who followed me here. Thought you were smart, didn't you? But I knew that was no owl tramping down the bushes in the forest. I thought it might be you and I decided to let you follow me. We haven't been alone together much, Mrs. Piedmont. You avoid me. But we're together now and a long way from anybody."

I was silent a moment listening to the wind. How I would dearly have loved to hear the voices of the searchers, but there was no human sound outside. Whenever I'd met Tom Parsons before, my muscles had involuntarily tensed, ready to run. But there would be no running this time.

"Where is Stacy?" I repeated firmly. "I'm going to find her. Tell me or else I'll leave."

He was delighted with this worthless threat, and literally pinned me to the wall. "I don't want you to leave," Tom Parson's voice crunched. He threw his arm against the wall, using his body as a barrier to escape. "You're pretty, you know, very pretty. I see why Andre likes you."

Then, enjoying my terror, he ran his hand slowly along my face and down to my shoulder. This he gripped painfully hard. There was a static moment while he carefully considered what move to make next in this playful little game, when suddenly his other hand enveloped my mouth, choking back sound and breath.

"The fun's over," he whispered. Someone was approaching the cottage, and not at all surreptitiously, but openly; the way the owner of any house walks up to his front door.

"Are you there, Tom?" It was a man's voice; Andre's.

"Coming," Tom called, and ominously to me, "Shut up." There was no need to repeat the command; I kept quiet.

Andre said impatiently, "Who are you talking to?"

"Nobody," Tom answered. "I mutter to myself now that I spend my time alone here in the woods. Getting old, you know."

"Well?"

"Well, what?"

"Don't try to back out." Andre's voice was hatchet-sharp. "Where's the child? Or don't you believe in keeping up your half of the agreement?"

Tom Parsons rocked back and forth. Though I couldn't see it, I could imagine the self-appreciative sneer on his face. I wanted to cry out to Andre for help, but I controlled the urge. He and Tom were talking like shrewd business partners, negotiating a deal.

Tom mumbled something that I couldn't catch and then there was a scuffle. The door slammed and Andre shouted from the path beyond the wall, "Double-crosser! Get moving because when I get back with the others . . ."

The phrase "the others" hung on the air. The words had an eerie connotation. Did nameless strangers hide among the trees, observing us unseen? Tom merely grunted.

I heard Tom Parsons step out on the porch and I stiffened, expecting him to return. But a long time passed and he didn't come back; he had lost interest in me. So I crept out of the dark room, blinking my eyes in the rectangle of light which the open door admitted. It was morning. The misty air was rose-colored and the birds sang gloriously as they always do at break of day in springtime. The dew reflected the sun's glow and sparkled, for the earth was softening with the season.

But Tom Parsons remained, an ugly residue of the night. I felt depressed and exhausted, for nothing was resolved since Stacy was still missing. Then I saw how quiet Tom was. He was staring at something ahead.

I walked to the doorway to see. Tom Parsons made no effort to block my way; he ignored me completely, so I stood on the porch. A tall elfin figure came toward us. He walked directly to me and reluctantly I went forward to meet him. It was Philip. The morning light made his hair a dazzling silver. A still bundle was in his arms. Was it being given to me for burial?

But Philip's eyes were curiously gentle. I flinched when he handed the bundle to me and could barely bring myself to look. My hands trembled and then steadied, for the baby was alive and uninjured. Stacy was simply sleeping; under the pink, rippled sky she seemed a dreaming cherub.

"Take her home," Philip said quietly. "And Tamara?"

I lifted my head. I didn't want to stop looking at him.

"Watch Andre. He's dangerous."

The black mood building up in me all night erupted. Without another word I left, to take Stacy back to her mother.

Philip said nothing, staring after me as I moved away, but Tom Parsons was eloquent. He laughed, without pause, a loud, merry laugh that followed me until I was too far to hear.

Chapter XXV

Stacy and I were royally escorted to Jenny's house. I was the heroine of the hour. The searchers praised me and Jenny embraced me, her face ravaged by the night's events. A hag's drawn lines and shadows had been superimposed over her young face.

A reporter from the *Orinville Gazette* came to interview us. He asked the key question, Where did I find Stacy?

I lied, saying that I had found her near the big rock where her blanket lay. There had been no sign of the kidnapper. I owed Andre the courtesy of protection, at least until I received an explanation from him as to what sort of agreement he had made with Tom Parsons concerning Stacy.

As I lied I watched Jenny. The look on her face gave her away; she knew I wasn't telling the truth. What else did she know? Did she know why Andre had come to the cottage to get Stacy? I wanted to ask her point-blank. But she would never tell me. I would have to confront Andre directly.

In the meantime Stacy was content to lie in her playpen, surrounded by toys, with Jack Hooper guarding her. From now on, he would keep his rifle handy.

I felt very weary. I couldn't cope with another thing until I got some sleep. I needed to be alone. Or did I? At the moment I would have liked to sit quietly with Philip. After all, he had probably saved Stacy's life. The searchers formed an honor guard and saw me back to Stonehaven.

Two days later it was the first of May, that month when the springtime of poets and lovers frees the Catskill mountains of winter at last. The weather turned playful. Even Stonehaven became somnolent like a beast resting in the heat of the sun.

It was the time for pretty girls to put flowers in their hair as a signal to young men that they were ready to be courted. Children ought to have danced around a maypole, as they did centuries ago. I would have liked to go back to medieval times when such a day would have lured pilgrims out for a holiday tour to a cathedral town. I wanted to join them as they went off on horseback, singing songs and telling stories, to cross the green countryside and ride toward the sunlit sea.

My body craved light and warmth and I could feel it storing radiance and health to help face the battering winds that would return all too soon. In a little more than half a year from now, there would be deep snow again.

The light turned golden and day long outstayed the night. Buds on the lilac bush smelled like lemons. Soon the purple blossoms would come out, coating the air with a rich fragrance. Breezes would bring the scent into my bedroom at night, lulling me into false dreams of well-being.

Jonquils bloomed, as yellow as the yellow in a child's paint-box. Nature had dressed forsythia shrubs in the same shade and used the most delicate green to color the new leaves and grass.

The woods had become a concert hall, a stadium, filled with elusive musicians. They sang, trilled, croaked, and rang melodies around the treetops. Occasionally they showed themselves. With spring, our plain little northern birds had become as brilliant as canaries or parakeets. They were like tropical jewels: bright orange with ebony wings, pale blue, yellow-green, and red, luminous in the sunshine.

All the little animals were out. Striped chipmunks took time from their busy lives to stare at me from bright dark eyes. Indifferent to the point of contempt, the grouse didn't even bother to move as I approached. Deer were abundant, pausing before flight to observe me, looking for all the world like statues on a suburbanite's lawn. Then they were off and gone. Despite their size, they could hide as thoroughly in the woods as any smaller animal.

Spring is the happy time for the deer. Their babies are born into a paradise of food and warmth. It is a temporary Eden.

Still, in May, the hunter's days seem far off. The woods are gentle. Even birch trees share in the joyous mood. They lose their sheen and blaze, scrubbed bone-white, in the sunlight.

For two days I waited for Andre to tell me the truth about Stacy. But he showed no indication that he had a confession to make. I decided that I'd been patient long enough and went to find him.

He was going over the accounts. Under such mundane circumstances it was hard to connect him with a kidnapping.

"I have to talk to you," I said.

Andre looked up, preoccupied with forms, facts, and figures.

I recounted every detail I could remember about the night of the party. When I was finished, he put his head in his hands. Then he lifted his head and looked at me. Andre's face was drawn, reminiscent of Jenny's the other night. Woodlands was aging its loyal inhabitants before their time.

"Again, you think I'm cursed, don't you, Tamara?" Andre said.

"I certainly want to know why you went to the cottage that night."

"To bring Stacy home to her mother."

"I don't believe you. It sounded like you had an arrangement with Tom Parsons. My guess is that you were both involved in a plot to capture Stacy. I can't imagine why, but I'm sure you had your reasons. Tom double-crossed you, didn't he? He didn't keep his part of the bargain. Instead, Philip talked Tom Parsons into turning Stacy over to him, so she could be brought back to her mother."

"I am not the prince of darkness, Tamara. I don't sacrifice infants. Nor am I an enchanted Gypsy king who steals babies. I was not going to make Stacy a changeling."

"Then what were you doing?"

"All right, Tamara. I admit that I lied to you when I said that now you knew the entire truth. Nothing I told you was false, but I did hold back on certain facts because I didn't want you involved in a dangerous situation."

"Secrets again. If you lied to me before, how can I tell if you're being honest now?"

"I didn't lie to you. I just left out certain things."

"What?"

"About two years ago, gossip got around that Philip had seduced Jenny. As a joke. It happened on a hot summer day when she went into the woods to pick blueberries. Philip found her. He was at his most magnetic that day. Jenny went home in tears to her Jack and he forgave her. He knew that it wasn't her fault."

"Do you know if this really happened?"

"I have no proof. But nine months after the gossip started, Stacy was born. When I saw the baby I decided that Philip probably was the father. As you know, she has the Piedmont face."

"Yes."

"Luckily, both Jenny and Jack adored Stacy. They would; they're decent people. The Hoopers see Stacy for what she is: an innocent babe. But my brother has a strange sense of humor."

"What do you mean?"

"From the time Stacy was born, Philip and Tom Parsons have been altogether too interested in her. That's why I was so upset when I found Jenny, Stacy, and you in the nursery. I sensed that without your realizing it, you three were courting disaster, although I never knew exactly what Philip and Tom were up to. Finally, the night you met Philip, Minnie Parsons came to me. She was alarmed because of a conversation she'd overheard between Philip and Tom. They were conspiring to kidnap Stacy. It seems that Philip, unbelievable as it may seem, is actually fond of Stacy. He feels cheated of his paternal rights. He decided on a humorous prank. Both he and Tom would take Stacy into the woods, to the cottage for a few weeks, so Philip could have his daughter all to himself for a while. 'Visiting rights,' he called it."

"He couldn't be so cruel."

I told you before; you don't know Philip. He didn't consider whether his little prank would hurt Stacy and he didn't care if it hurt Jenny."

"What did you do, Andre?"

"I got hold of Tom and told him what I knew. I threatened him. Not with arrest; that wouldn't scare him. I told him I would never let him set foot in our woods again if he went through with the kidnapping. He knew that I meant it. He's always had free use of our forest up to now. But I told him that I would post armed guards in the woods to keep him out. He would sneak past them, of course, but he'd be forced to hide constantly, to be on the defensive every minute. He was persuaded that it was in his own interest to leave Stacy alone."

"Then why did Philip and Tom Parsons take her?"

"Tom was afraid of Philip. He asked to be allowed to talk Philip out of the plan in his own way. I consented. That and that alone was our agreement. At first, I was all for getting Philip into the house and confronting him with my knowledge of the projected kidnapping, right then and there. I wanted him to understand that if he pulled it off I would hand him over to the police, and he knew where that would lead: to a maximum security cell in a prison for the criminally insane. But Tom stopped me. He couldn't face Philip's vindictiveness. After all, it was Tom's own wife who had alerted me to their plan. And he did discuss it with me behind Philip's back."

"You made the mistake of listening to Tom, didn't you?"

"Yes. I never spoke to Philip at all. I agreed to let Tom protect himself by manipulating Philip whatever way he could. I didn't really care, Tamara, how he did it; whether he cajoled, or argued, or simply made Philip see that kidnapping wouldn't be a very sophisticated joke."

"But he wasn't able to discourage Philip, after all."

"I don't know how hard Tom really tried. I didn't trust him. It struck me that the night of the party would be the perfect time for them to carry out their vicious stunt. That's why I stayed here at Stonehaven. When I heard that Stacy was missing, I knew immediately what had happened. I hoped that Tom and Philip would bring her to Stonehaven. When they didn't arrive, I went to the cottage; it seemed the obvious place to go. You heard my conversation with Tom, my reference to our broken agreement. I left to get the others, the searchers."

"But by the time you'd found them, I'd already gotten Stacy back."

"That's right. I heard that you had found her near a boulder. I assumed that Tom and Philip had realized that their plan was too dangerous, that I would expose them and that, therefore, they left Stacy in the woods for the searchers to locate."

"Andre, I don't honestly find your explanation plausible. Philip didn't leave Stacy in the woods. He returned her to me. Why would he do that after going through a great deal of trouble to kidnap her? And why would he reveal himself to me if he'd been involved in taking the baby? Wouldn't that be dangerous for him? I could link him directly to Stacy if he were brought to trial for kidnapping. It doesn't make any sense."

"No, it doesn't, but I'm telling you the truth, Tamara. The only reason I didn't let you know any of this sooner was to keep you safe. As it is, you went to the cottage alone, ready to face Tom Parsons, in order to get Stacy back. You don't seem to realize it, but you're a brave woman. Even foolhardy. I was afraid that Tom and Philip would set a trap for you if I informed you in advance of their plan. And knowing you, you would have jumped right into it, unhesitatingly."

"Andre, will we ever be rid of paranoid suspicions?"

"They're endemic at Stonehaven."

"Haven't you any idea why Philip would take Stacy only to bring her back to me? If you could answer that one question, then your explanation would make sense."

"I have no idea what my brother's motives are. Tamara, he is the reincarnation of Geoffrey Piedmont. That means he's capable of any crime, providing it's bizarre enough for his tastes."

"Philip said that I should watch you, that you're very dangerous."

"Naturally; he wants you suspicious of me. I warned you that he would do his best to lure you away from me. So far, he hasn't succeeded. It's taking him longer than usual." Andre paused. Then he said, "Tamara, maybe that's the answer."

"What?"

"Perhaps Philip decided to call off the crime when he heard that you were out looking for Stacy. He wants you and he saw that if he carried through his kidnapping game, you'd hate him forever."

"Andre, do you mean that because of me, Philip is now reformed?"

"In the process of reforming, anyway." Andre took my hand and held it tight. "Tamara, be more careful. Don't take any risks. Philip is reliving Geoffrey's life."

"What are you getting at, Andre?"

"That girl, that other girl, in the eighteenth century; the one at the Manor. Remember, Geoffrey seemed to reform. And then the girl refused him. You know what happened to her, Tamara."

How could I ever forget. I was on the verge of panic. Ready to scream or run away. Anything to evade Philip. But as I watched Andre, I thought I saw a slight smugness around the mouth. A self-satisfied little smirk.

My own experience contradicted Andre's account of the kidnapping. A gentle Philip had handed Stacy to me after an enraged Andre had demanded her from his confederate, Tom Parsons. Servants of the devil are notorious for their guile. Andre might have thought his explanation up that very minute. He had no proof. Quick thinking; another renowned Satanic trait.

"Andre?"

"Yes?"

"Did Jenny suspect that there might be danger the night of the party?"

"I don't think so. Why?"

"She was the only person besides you who didn't attend the party."

"A coincidence, Tamara, that's all." Andre's face was innocent, like a knight from a medieval romance. My Sir

Gawain. He looked ready to ride off in search of the Holy Grail. But his innocence was marred by that slight smugness which I still fancied I saw at the edge of his lips.

Chapter XXVI

The grounds surrounding Stonehaven had taken on a formal appearance. They had lost their wintry bleakness. And gardeners were now busy imposing order.

Stonehaven looked like a wild thing trapped in a grid formation. It would have preferred untended fields of wild-flowers. They would be out soon. Within a week maiden pinks would border the dry stone walls of Woodlands. Devil's paintbrush would add drops of orange to the grass. Purple thistles and yellow dandelions would abound. There would be plants with delightful names, like butter and eggs, with its flowers of yoke yellow and milk white. And there would be daisies, charming daisies, covering the hillsides.

Stonehaven's hill had become a field of gold. It was a mass of cultivated jonquils. I viewed it critically, however. It was too tame. Philip, also walking among the flowers, agreed. Andre's accusations against him seemed ridiculous today, for he waved, smiled, and walked casually up to me. He showed no sign of sprouting either fangs or poisonous tendrils. Under the mellow sun he looked natural and ordinary, a most maligned man.

"What do you think of our gardens?" he asked.

"I don't much care for them. But I should start painting again. Wildflowers."

"If this land belonged to me, Tamara, I'd let the grass grow high and the weeds run riot. Why do people hate weeds? Give me fields of dandelions and clover."

"Whoever planned this garden has a regimental mind."

"Then you admit that my dear brother has a fault. He designs the landscaping of the grounds himself, you know. He is unimaginative and unoriginal. Wait until the summer comes.

It gets worse. All hedges are squarely trimmed. There are swan shapes formed by marigolds and lilies. A distinctly dull rose garden. And a stupid maze that a six-year-old could find his way through in a minute. It's made up of neatly clipped bushes."

"If you're going to insult Andre, I'm going to leave."

"I'm only asking you to recognize a slight flaw in your hero. I'll even give him the benefit of the doubt and concede that the gardens are probably done so poorly simply because Andre is overworked and can't give them his full attention. Of course, he could import a landscape designer from New York."

"I think it's nice that Andre would rather plan the grounds himself."

"Very well, I promise to stop criticizing your husband. After I make one more point. Notice those daisies along the driveway. They look like soldiers lined up in neat rows for battle."

I couldn't deny it. "Or like pieces of plastic," I said.

"See, I've wrung the admission from you, Tamara, that Andre is less than perfect. Look at Stonehaven! The poor old house looks miserable. It wants to see untutored fields up to its doors. At least it can console itself with the pine trees. They do it justice."

"I don't like those trees. They frighten me."

"Really! Why?"

"They are completely unchanged by the springtime."

"Perhaps I've overestimated you, Tamara. Nature is winter as well as spring. To belong to her cult you must admire her in all her aspects. She nurtures some plants in summer, and others in winter. The pines are her lords of the snows."

"I like most pines. I just don't like those particular ones surrounding the house. They've taken on the character of Stonehaven and I find them ominous."

"Are you sure it isn't just that you don't like winter? Perhaps it's too desolate for you."

"Pine trees are the symbol of winter. If I thought winter were desolate I would hate anything representative of the season, including pines. But I like winter. I never feel that it's bleak. I sense that the woods are rich with life during the cold months. But life is lived secretly; it's muted. To us the animals and plants look dead but actually they are busy. In their own private way. In the springtime they live publicly again."

"You are a marvel, Tamara, that is exactly right. And not too different from people who bustle about outdoors in June and retire to their houses to live quietly in February."

"Like moles hibernating."

"I didn't overestimate you; you are one of Nature's daughters."

Philip looked at me fondly. I felt, once again, a tremendous attraction to him. It would have been easy to stand close to him, to touch him. I wanted to. The way a child wants a special toy for Christmas, one for which there is no substitute.

Then Philip did a surprising thing. He walked away. The spell was broken. I felt no tension. Philip had given me back free will.

"How's Stacy?" Philip asked, changing the subject to allow me time to pull myself together.

"She seems fine. Philip, there's something I have to clear up."

"Why so somber? Has my brother been telling lies about me again? Making me out to be the big bad wolf while he's teacher's pet."

"He did tell me a wild story; I can hardly believe it. Frankly, Philip, Andre told me that you and Tom Parsons kidnapped Stacy, that you meant to hide her in the cottage. He suggested that you probably backed down and returned her only because you knew I would never forgive you if you didn't. He also said that you are Stacy's real father."

"Well, well, so Andre told you that, did he." Philip sounded grim. "It's patently absurd. Stacy is charming but I don't normally seek out the company of infants. Why on earth would I want to kidnap her? To bounce her on my knee and to say googoo and dada for days at a time? Tamara, does that sound like me? Do I strike you as the type destined to be a good family man?"

"Hardly."

"There, you see; Andre was talking nonsense. As to Jenny, why would I have seduced her? She's not pretty in the least."

"She's a remarkable person. Perhaps you were attracted to her because she has strength of character."

Philip laughed. "Come now, Tamara. You sound like a Victorian. I've never been interested in any woman because

of her character. Until you, that is. But then, you're different;
you're a wood sprite."

"I wonder. I once showed Jenny that picture of you as a
child, the one with your mother. She became extremely agitated."

"And that's supposed to prove that we were lovers. Let me
suggest another interpretation, it makes just as much sense.
When Andre and I were children, we could have passed for
twins. Our features were softer, the physical differences between us were blurred. These differences have grown greater
over the past few years. For all you know, Jenny thought she
was staring at a picture of Andre. It's Andre who sets her
heart beating. Not me."

"I refuse to accept that."

Philip became angry. "Tamara, use your brains. You heard
Andre, not me, connive with Tom over Stacy. It's Andre, not
me, whom Jenny reacted to violently on her visits to Stonehaven. Tom is not under my control. He's his own master. So
don't ask me what he was up to with Andre. I met Tom in
the woods and talked him into handing Stacy over to me. He
was very secretive. I took Stacy away for safekeeping. I decided to give her only to you. It was my way of showing you
that I'm not an ogre. But I see I was wasting my time. I
should have handed her to the nearest searcher. My brother's
tongue was dipped in honey. He can talk you round to anything he wants."

I covered my ears and said, "Stop it!"

Philip pulled my hands down and gripped them. "Tamara,
my brother has never received such loyalty before. Can't you
see him for what he really is: a lying hypocrite. A devious
fraud. I'm no saint. Everyone knows that. But at least I'm
straightforward. Andre is cursed. He's been ordained as Geoffrey's successor. And he'll destroy you, Tamara, if you stay
with him. Leave him and come with me."

Time stopped. Then, as a tape recorder unwinds, the centuries slid past in reverse order. And with them went the surface accoutrements of civilization. Finally, it seemed that
Philip and I stood on the edge of a hot, marshy plain. I was
stripped of conscience and of moral inhibitions. Soon even
my physical being was gone. I was a whirlwind of base passions, of disorganized hungers. And Philip, too, was reduced
to a mass of primitive instincts. We had become two halves

of a greedy pleasure principle compelled to couple ourselves, to merge and become a single unquenchable force.

It was the laugh which saved me, a merry laugh, bouncing through time, restoring the normal order of things, and leading me back to the present again. Here was Woodlands once more.

And here was Tom Parsons, laughing.

Philip was furious with him. "What are you doing here?" he growled.

"Why, I came for you, Philip."

"You could have waited a little longer. You've behaved foolishly, Tom. You've put me in a punishing mood."

Tom Parsons didn't seem to care. He went right on barking laughs in his hoarse voice. At last, after gasps and sputters, he stopped. "Don't be mad, Philip. But I was watching you. And it was funny. Her such a high-minded lady. With her touch-me-not airs." He gave me a lewd, contemptuous glare. "You women; underneath your manners and modesty, you're all she-goats."

"Shut up!" Philip snapped. "This one is different. If you insult Tamara, you'll regret it." I didn't doubt that Philip could think up a nasty revenge.

"All right," said Tom, "I'll be polite."

"You'll be more than that," countered Philip. "You'll be the essence of courtesy and correctness."

"Come, an old man's got a right to make little jokes."

"Not at Tamara's expense." Philip turned to me. "Don't worry about Tom. He'll do as I say. To my regret, I must leave you. But I'll find you again. Next time we will be together without interruption." Furious, he left. The air where he had been was shot through with tension even after he was gone. Like his other emotions, Philip's anger was on a heroic scale.

Tom Parsons grinned. "Shall I escort you home, Mrs. Piedmont?"

"No thank you. I'd appreciate your going away and leaving me alone."

"Now that wouldn't be polite. But if you say so I'll do it. Still, I can't help but laugh, especially when I think about your red hair."

"What's funny about my hair?"

"Just that she had red hair. The girl in the legend. The one that Geoffrey loved." His grin widened.

Then I did panic. I ran. Andre's wild guess was true. Or was it? What if Andre had put Tom Parsons up to saying it to turn me against Philip? Whom could I trust? Was there no way to get to the truth, no way to find out which of the Piedmont brothers should be believed? I couldn't think of any. Therefore, I would have to rely on my intuition, my judgment. It seemed hopelessly inadequate but it would have to do.

At least I had gotten away from the immediate danger: Tom Parsons. In the far distance I could hear his boisterous laughter.

Chapter XXVII

By the time I'd reached the nearest road I was exhausted. Much as I loved my precious woods they were clearly dangerous. They had become the setting for grim encounters. I ought to avoid them from now on. But I didn't know if I could. Without doses of woods walking, I no longer felt alive. The woods had become a habit.

A car came winding along the road toward me. It was battered and blue. It slowed and then pulled alongside me. Celia Gordon popped her head out of the window and ordered me to stop.

"You're out of breath. Why were you running?"

I managed to say, "No reason, I just like to," between gasps. Celia Gordon was the last person I'd confide in. A loudspeaker system would be preferable.

"Get in the car, Tamara. I'll take you home."

"Thanks. I've had enough exercise for one day."

"More than enough from the look of you. You'd collapse walking back to Stonehaven. You've succumbed to the local disease: woods fever. Now your case is as bad as Tom Parsons'."

I hoped she didn't notice that I shuddered at the mention of his name.

"I've been anxious to get hold of you to tell you that we're all proud of you for tracking down Stacy."

"I didn't track her down. I stumbled upon her."

"No matter. You're the one that found her. A night in the woods might have killed her. It was damp and cold. If she didn't freeze, the bears might have got her."

"Bears don't normally bother babies, Celia."

Miss Gordon sniffed a loud rebuke. She didn't like to be contradicted. "Jenny's your friend for life now. She won't hear a word against you. Eternally grateful, that's what she is."

"That's not necessary. Anybody would have done their best for Stacy."

"Anyway, Stacy's not the main reason I came looking for you. I've been circling the woods for an hour, hoping you'd walk out." She braked the car to a jarring stop and scowled. "You are going to give a party," she said.

"What?"

"You heard me. The kidnapping killed the annual party. Demolished it. It ended all right because of Stacy's return but the evening was soured for everyone. Now, unless you help, everyone will have to wait a whole year until there's another big party. The people of Woodlands can't afford two in a row. But the Piedmonts are rich enough to pay for a big party all by themselves."

"You mean that you want me to imitate my mother-in-law, Laura."

"Why not? You can do it. You being an artist. Give Stonehaven a touch of Blake festiveness again."

"I don't know, Celia. I'm tired and preoccupied."

Her nose twitched. "What are you preoccupied with?" she asked.

"Never mind. You win. I'll give a party."

"Fine. Make it soon. The end of May. I'll tell everyone."

"I'm sure you will, Celia."

"You'll need a theme. It's got to be a costume party. I don't have anything definite in mind, but as soon as I get an idea I'll call you. It's got to be something clever. To compete with Laura's parties. I remember one fabulous costume ball when everyone came dressed as pirates. There was a big wooden boat with sails set right on the lawn. It had a bar with a fountain that sprayed real champagne. Laura drank her share of it, you can bet on that. But it was a wonderful party, all the same. Everyone got phony pirates' booty as prizes. The locals will be excited when they learn that there'll be a party again at Stonehaven. We've all missed the fun. The house has been solemn too long."

"Could it ever be anything else?" I asked as we drove up to it. I couldn't imagine a motif that would suit it. Its many windows looked at me like the multiple eyes of a fly. Its bulk seemed to pant slightly in the sun.

"Laura was good at disguising it," Miss Gordon said. "Go back to the Orinville library. They've got a book of photographs taken at her parties. Perhaps it will help you come up with something."

"That's a good suggestion." I sounded depressed even to myself. With so much on my mind already, I would now be faced with planning an elaborate party. And the initial step would be to return to that dreary library in town a second time.

"Cheer up," Miss Gordon urged as I stepped out of the car. "I thought you had more self-confidence," she added, misinterpreting the cause of my listlessness. "Don't worry; you'll do a good job on the party. I guarantee it. It will be the night to end all nights at Stonehaven." And pointing her nose at me, she smiled a crooked smile. And pulled off in her car.

I went into the house and looked for Andre. He was in his study, hard at work. I knocked at the door. He looked at me and frowned.

"What do you want, Tamara? I'm very busy."

"I've just seen Celia. She wants us to have a costume party here at Stonehaven. To make up for the fiasco at the annual party. I wanted to find out what you think of the suggestion."

To my surprise Andre perked up. "I'm all for it, Tamara. What an excellent idea."

"I hardly expected such enthusiasm."

"Why not? You wanted us to start fresh, put the past behind us, and celebrate. We couldn't do that at the other party but we can at this one. We'll drink to our mutual relief that the curse has left us untouched."

"Yes," I said, dubiously.

"And now, if you don't mind, I've got to get back to work." I was being dismissed from the royal presence.

"Do you have any ideas for a costume party?" I asked.

Andre looked noble and long-suffering. "I'm absorbed in

important things, Tamara. We've got tax complications. Be a good girl and get to work on the party yourself. But don't bother me now, please."

I left Andre's study, feeling none too kindly toward him. I didn't like to be patronized and Andre had certainly been supercilious. How had Philip described him? As pompous and sanctimonious. Perhaps he was right.

It was the next day that the rumors started. They began as whispers, barely spoken. Turning a corner I would catch the words, "Did you hear?" only to find the corridor ahead of me empty. Or groups of servants would cluster, heads together, and scurry at my approach to return to their labors.

Once when I bent down to give Crispin his morning milk, I heard two gardeners talking outside the open window.

"Ted says he saw it last night."

"Ted says he sees lots of things."

"Still, it's Maytime. You know that."

"True. You never can tell. Think I'll stay home nights."

At the combination general store and gas station, I heard two stout women gossip.

"Effie saw it three years ago."

"I don't believe it."

"I do; spring's come." Then they noticed me and became quiet, moving closer, to form a solid bulk blocking the counter.

For the sake of security, I kept out of the woods. But one night I felt such a craving that I threw open my bedroom window and leaned forward, staring at the irregular line of treetops which marked the beginning of the forest. I was alone, and much as I missed the woods I felt that the woods missed me too. We were like lovers, separated by hostile parents, wanting only to be together.

It was a beautiful night. The moon was a slice of orange melon in the black sky. The rhythmic sounds of frogs and insects made the night's noises. I wanted to leave the house immediately and feel the cool grass under my feet. I resisted and returned to bed.

But the next day I couldn't hold back any longer. I set out for the woods at a run, unable to contain my impatience. Just outside the woods, I was stopped by an old woman.

She looked a creation of the forest, a product of wood and moss and stone. Bent with age, her arms were stiff as branches, her skin brittle as an autumn leaf, and her hair like strands of willow tendrils. She had a basket over her arm, filled with mushrooms and violets. And when she spoke her voice was the croak of a frog.

"Don't go into the woods!" she said.

"What?"

She repeated herself. Her command was given in the warning tone of a soothsayer, prophesying the inevitable dangers of the Ides of March.

"Why shouldn't I go into them?" I asked.

She shook her head. It creaked like a tree in the wind. "Stay out; it's the Woodlands springtime." And saying no more, she turned and walked down the road. Her feet, reluctant to move, gripped the earth like rocks at each step so that her progress was slow and feeble.

Up close, the woods were glorious. Many new leaves were a soft brown, a pastel version of autumn's splendor. Soon they too would be green. I wanted to see them now before the monotony of summer set in.

But, nevertheless, I went back to Stonehaven. And I stayed there. I didn't have the courage to disobey the old woman.

It was Elsie who administered the coup de grace. She came to my special room the following morning while I arranged branches of forsythia in a white porcelain vase. A sunbeam transformed the forsythia into golden light and caught motes of dancing dust in its path.

"May I speak to you?" Elsie timidly asked.

I observed her. She'd changed. She was no longer a saucy wench; she was subdued and pale. A lily instead of a rose.

"Something's wrong, isn't it, Elsie?"

She fumbled, not quite willing to talk.

"Tell me. Perhaps I can help you."

"I don't need help. I've told my story to Mrs. Parsons and she insisted I come to you with it."

"Well then, go on."

"Last night I had a terrible fright. Mrs. Parsons said I could go home early, but by the time I washed my hair, and got to talking with a friend, the next thing I knew it was almost dark."

"Yes?"

"Well, Mrs. Piedmont, I wanted to visit Lenore Wilson who lives on the other side of the woods. I knew it was getting late and I ought to have stayed here at Stonehaven rather than risk going into the woods at night. But I didn't want to waste time here when I could be off having fun."

"Why didn't you ask someone to drive you?"

"I did. But everyone I asked was busy. If I'd left earlier there would have been plenty of rides. So it was either walk or stay home. I left, carrying a flashlight. It was still twilight when I reached the woods."

"What happened?"

"It got dark very quickly and I was scared. But I walked fast and tried not to think about spooky stories I'd been told about these woods. Then, half a mile from Lenore's, I heard a laugh. I've never heard a sound like it before. It was as loud as a fire engine's siren. I don't know why it didn't wake up everybody in Woodlands."

"What did you do?"

"I stopped and stood still. I was too scared to do anything. Then I saw lights. They looked like the sparkles of fireflies, but in many bright colors. The laugh stopped. Then I heard whispers. They must have been speaking a foreign language, because I couldn't understand what they said. Next a shimmering silver light appeared. I got smart, turned off my flashlight and hid behind a big rock. I didn't know what else to do."

"Had the moon come out? Was the light coming from it?"

"No. Don't you remember? It was cloudy last night. You couldn't see the moon or stars."

"That's right. It finally rained. The sound of the thunder woke me up before dawn."

"Well, this light glowed behind the trees. Then it came out. It was like a halo, an aura, and it was all around an odd-looking man. He was dressed like an actor in a movie. He had tights, and shoes with buckles. And he was wearing a big white wig."

"What did he do?"

"Very little. He just walked around a few times. Then he went back into the woods. The lights and the whispers followed him. It became very quiet. I ran all the way to Lenore's house. When I told her parents what had happened they didn't believe me. They hadn't heard any noise and they know how well sound carries in a woods. They calmed me by giving me brandy and sent me to bed. This morning Lenore's father drove me back to Stonehaven. I told Mrs. Parsons everything and she believed me. She said that there've been lots of stories about a ghost in the woods. He's seen on warm nights. She told me to watch my step. As if I needed to be told that. You'll never catch me near the woods again. Ever."

I didn't walk in the woods again that spring. I didn't dare.

Chapter XXVIII

Mrs. Parsons burbled. "A party at Stonehaven. Isn't that wonderful? I told Celia that it will be like old times again."

"I've already been working on the arrangements. I may as well; I have nothing else to do these days now that I've given up walking in the woods."

"Very wise of you, ma'am. Though Elsie has been known to exaggerate."

"No doubt. But I think I'll err on the side of safety and take her story at face value."

"It's up to you. So we're going to have a masquerade. They were always the best sort of parties Laura Piedmont gave."

"I wish I could think of a theme for this one."

Mrs. Parsons' eyes grew misty. She was recalling festive nights at Stonehaven. "There was one time, ma'am, when everybody came dressed as lords and ladies. It was something to see. The jewels were worth a fortune. The setting was supposed to be France."

"In the *ancien régime*, I assume."

"Mrs. Piedmont was Marie Antoinette. She came dressed as a shepherdess. She looked beautiful. She wore a hand-embroidered dress and carried a staff made of mother-of-pearl. Around her neck was a big diamond on a chain. Everybody had wigs, powdered white. And wore dancing slippers with buckles. They danced the minuet while we servants watched. It was splendid. People had tiny masks on and pretended they didn't really recognize each other. Then at midnight they stripped off their masks." Mrs. Parsons blushed.

"What is it?"

A rather nervous giggle escaped from her. "Nothing. The party did get a bit scandalous at that point. But all in all it was a magnificent occasion."

I had the impression that it was an evening the guests were unlikely ever to forget.

"You're Cinderella," Mrs. Parsons said.

"What are you talking about?" I asked. For a moment I thought my old friend had lost her reason.

"Give a fairy-tale ball!" Mrs. Parsons said. "You're an ideal Cinderella."

"Oh, I see."

Mrs. Parsons stared dreamily. "You arrive in a golden coach, then you step out, assisted by your footmen in green. Your husband is the prince. He takes you by the hand and leads you to the marble floor of the ballroom. I can see your gown now; white satin and lace, with blue spangles that flash as you dance." She sighed, lost in a romantic fantasy derived from past girlhood dreams and scenes from the late show on television.

"I'm not sure that Andre would quite like the idea," I said, as gently as possible.

Mrs. Parsons returned to reality. She said, "I suppose you're right. Since he's a man, he'd probably prefer something less romantic. But, ma'am, I'd give anything to see a fairy-tale ball. It would be lavish and spectacular, like a movie."

"Don't worry, Mrs. Parsons, I promise you that whatever theme we choose for the party, it will satisfy your taste for the dramatic."

But I wasn't sure I could keep that promise. If I didn't find a motif soon, it would be too late. I would have to hold a common garden party, and nobody would get to come in costume. So that afternoon I went back to the Orinville library to learn what ideas my mother-in-law had had in her day.

The library was essentially unchanged. However, it was not quite as gloomy as it had been in the winter. Springtime pressed itself against the enormous building, looking for a way in. It managed to penetrate a few cracks in the wall, sending in stalks of sunlight. And it soared joyously when it found a partly open window. But it was too flimsy to win the battle against the darkness of the domed ceiling, the dimness of dusty light bulbs, and the crypt-like atmosphere of the book stacks.

The librarian with the slightly crooked face was again behind the desk. A splash of sun turned her thick glasses to
light. I couldn't see through them to her eyes. I was afraid
that if she took the glasses off, gutted holes would show in
place of eyes. Perhaps she found the idea of being sightless,
in this library without Braille, funny. It might strike her as
amusing in the same sense that she found Dr. Edna
Piedmont's morbid fate good for a laugh.

But she turned her head and shook off the light; I could see
her eyes clearly. Next to her she had two books. She handed
them to me unbidden. I took them and went to the reading
room.

On the way I stopped and turned. The librarian had left
her desk and was standing in the aisle watching me. When
she saw me in turn observing her, she walked mechanically
back to her work. A human wind-up doll.

I was more relaxed than on my previous visit. That had
been a shocking experience. Now I felt hardened, jaded. I
could find out that Laura Blake and her kind were descended
from a race of giant fanged toads and I wouldn't blink. Since
I was prepared for anything, I found nothing.

The first book was simply a large historical survey of
clothing. I perused it quickly. I stopped at the pages covering
the Napoleonic era but somehow I couldn't imagine the
ladies of Woodlands in dresses with transparent tops, designed
to reveal bosoms. Scratch one historical costume party
based on the theme of the Napoleonic Wars. I was equally
unimpressed by ancient Romans in togas, American pioneer
women in bonnets, and flappers of the 1920s. With a ho-hum
to myself I shut the book.

The other was better. It showed Laura Piedmont on every
page, photographed against the backgrounds of her parties.
In the first picture she was a Chinese empress, with shining
hair. The face was young, the smile genuine. The book's brief
text noted that the party was "famed for its elegant Man-
darin cuisine."

With each successive picture, Laura's face grew more de-
jected, her dark eyes expressed more pain. It was like
watching a sequence of takes in a film or a magic lantern
show, where the character depicted turns from an erect star
to a crumpled wretch in seconds. For behind Laura, there
was always Stonehaven. The house, though primed for its
role as backdrop to the party, never looked benign.

Its lawns were often festooned with flowers. Once, it was even decorated with false turrets and an artificial moat so that it could serve as Richard The Lion-Hearted's castle for Robin Hood and his band of Merry Men. To no avail. Stonehaven still looked like Stonehaven.

In the final photograph of the book, the exterior of the house had been trimmed with toys and its shutters were painted pink. It was supposed to be a doll's house. It looked grotesque. Laura stood on the lawn, dressed as a little girl in white pinafore and Mary Jane shoes. The slim body could conceivably have belonged to a child but the face, never. The face was desperate, mouthing a mock-smile. I was looking at a woman eager to die. I said "Amen" to myself, closed the book, and left.

A fruitless day. All I had gotten out of my trip to the library was an insight into the agony of a once-gentle lady, now past help.

As I drove back, it was Stonehaven, not Laura, I considered. The house had refused to cooperate with her. It had remained formidably true to its own nature and would not change for my party either. Whatever theme I finally chose would fall flat. It would not help to primp or paint the house. Who could feel gay and cheerful on the lawn with that miserable pile of rock exuding hatred? One might as well try to enjoy oneself with a recent airplane wreck lying in the garden. Why bother with a party at all under such conditions? I would have called it off then and there if Celia Gordon hadn't phoned me the minute I was back in the house.

"Tamara?"

"Is that you, Celia? Look, there's something I want to tell you."

"It can wait. I've solved the problem."

"What problem?"

"You know, the theme for the costume party. I've told everybody that you're having one. If you weren't able to reach me it's because I haven't been off the phone for a minute."

"I see."

"Everybody's pulling out their sewing machines. They can't wait to hear what sort of clothes they should make. You're the talk of the county, young lady. You could run for supervisor, you're so popular."

I was trapped. There was to be no reneging now. I had no choice but to ask Celia what she had in mind.

"A Hawaiian motif," she shouted into the phone, hurting my ear. She waited, expecting me to make some laudatory comment.

"Tamara, are you still there?"

"Yes I am," I said. "Unfortunately," I added to myself.

"It's going to be great! We'll have poi and punch. I have a cousin in Hawaii and I'll write her tonight for advice. We want everything authentic. How about orchids brought in by helicopter from New York? We can hang leis all over the outside of the house and for a grand finale we'll hold a hula contest. You Piedmonts will give the winner a two weeks' paid vacation to Honolulu. How's that?"

"I'm overwhelmed."

"Good. Then I can tell everyone that we'll have a Hawaiian party. They can start making their grass skirts now."

"Hold on, Celia. Your idea is terrific. But I've already chosen the theme," I lied.

A silent quiver of indignation pulsed through the telephone wire.

"I've been working on the plans, Celia, and I can't possibly alter course now. It would be too expensive."

"Well, what is your plan?" Miss Gordon asked.

I hadn't the slightest idea. "It's a surprise," I improvised.

"The party's weeks away and you're keeping its theme a surprise?"

"Only for today. I promise that I'll call you tomorrow with the news. You'll be the first to know."

"Well, I never ... What a crazy business! Listen, you better come up with something good by tomorrow or I'm going to tell everyone that we're having a Hawaiian Islands evening." And she hung up.

She meant it too. I knew I'd better wrack my brain or poor Mrs. Parsons' fairy-tale spectacle would dissolve into a ukulele nightmare.

Jenny Hooper solved the problem. I met her at the general store that afternoon. It was a dingy little place, specializing in chewing gum, magazines, day-old milk, and cigarettes. But it was the only store for miles.

I had been taking a drive for lack of anything better to do, and to help myself think. Jenny was buying a knitting pattern-book when I entered the store to get pocket tissues.

"Tamara!" she exclaimed, and came over to me. Her greeting was forthright and friendly. She looked as serene and self-contained as an early Quaker woman, bearing witness. I wanted to trust her but I couldn't quite. Not while she and Andre might be cursed lovers. A corrupt soul can hide behind a deceptively pure countenance.

Jenny took no notice when I pulled away from her. "Tamara, I want to thank you again," she said.

"Please don't. I only did what anyone in my place would have done for Stacy."

"I'm not so sure that just anyone would have risked the night woods to help her. But I won't embarrass you by praising you. I just want you to know that if you're ever in trouble, I'll do whatever I can to help." Her smile was sweet and her voice warm with sincerity. It was hard to associate her with evil. I found myself growing friendly against my will.

"I'm in trouble now," I said. "If I don't come up with a motif for our party, Celia Gordon's threatening to do things her way. And you know what that means."

Jenny laughed. "You have my sympathy, Tamara."

"If she gets her wish the epitaph for this party will be 'And a dull time was had by all.' By the way, where's your daughter?"

"My mother's moved in with us, Tamara. To keep an eye on Stacy. Stacy's never alone now, not even for a minute. Jack's also thinking of buying a German shepherd to protect us."

"You're right, Jenny. Guard Stacy well! I have a feeling she's not out of danger yet."

Jenny nodded. For a brief moment, fear shattered her composure. Then she was herself again. "Tamara, you understand that Jack and I can't come to your party. I wouldn't want to leave my mother alone with Stacy at night. And Stonehaven itself would get on my nerves."

"I understand, Jenny. Don't apologize. I'd rather you didn't come. I'd only worry about Stacy."

"Come and see me soon, Tamara. I've been working in the garden every day and I'd love company. Stacy's starting to walk. Jack's got home movies of her first steps. She falls as much as she stands; it's a sight to see."

"I'd like to come; I miss her. But I'm afraid I won't have any time until this blasted party's finished."

"You must be busy, planning a party on such short notice. I've just thought of something. Why don't you exploit the way Stonehaven looks. Why fight it? Why not turn it into a haunted house?"

"What?"

"It's not Halloween but so what? Have a haunted house party. Your guests can come as ghosts, goblins, or any supernatural creature they fancy. Have the party inside the house. Then you won't have to worry about decorating it. It's quite gruesome enough as it is."

Jenny's suggestion clicked inside my mind. It was just right. I'd take the idea further. I'd use it to defy the supernatural; no, better yet, to ridicule it, put it in its place. I'd strike back at Stonehaven, exorcise the devils that dwelled within by laughing at them. Mockery would serve as a healing factor, provide a catharsis. Perhaps the devil would be persuaded to abandon Stonehaven in disgust.

I hugged Jenny, feeling gratitude and affection. "You," I said to her, "are a genius." And I ran out of the store, jumped into my car, and zoomed back to the house, to see Andre.

Chapter XXIX

"A haunted house?" Andre mulled the idea over for a minute, putting aside a book he'd been reading. "I like that. Perhaps we can put the demons to rest, once and for all."

I watched Andre closely. Was he laughing at me? Smirking? Up to something evil? He seemed completely honest. I certainly hoped he was. There was nothing in the world I wanted more than to know that Andre was trustworthy, untouched by the curse.

"I'll help you with the party, Tamara; together we'll combine into an unbeatable force. We'll see to it that the ghosts are banished forever."

"Andre, do you mean it?"

He looked at me in surprise. "Of course. We'll apply the

old slapstick, let the spirit of the Marx Brothers loose. No monsters could stand up to that."

His enthusiasm was contagious. "What should we do?" I asked.

"Something vaudevillian. Everything will be scary until midnight. Then we'll unleash an orchestra of clowns dressed in mock vampire and werewolf costumes, and they'll turn the rest of the night into a spoof."

"Good idea, Andre. Or we could invite comedians to slip into the party from the beginning and mingle with the guests. Whenever the party turned gloomy or eerie, they could pull silly stunts or make jokes."

"You mean, dance with lampshades on their heads, Tamara, or blow whistles?"

"Why not?"

"Perfect. The night will be devoted to pure old-fashioned corn. It will be one long horse-laugh."

"Let's start slowly and build," I said.

"Right. The guests will arrive together, at one time to find a silent house, mysteriously glowing with candlelight."

I laughed. "I'll scrounge through attics, looking for old candlesticks."

"I'll scrounge with you. We'll have the entire dining hall lined with banquet tables."

"And the guests won't see us at first. We'll wait until they're milling around, bursting with curiosity, and then we'll make a grand entrance."

"Let's add one more touch, Tamara. Let's import an organ. The organist can play weird music while everyone dines!"

"And then at twelve o'clock, the witching hour, we'll turn on the lights."

"We'll let the house blaze with light. Our comic musicians will rush in."

"Flowers will be brought in and displayed."

"Yes. The brightest flowers we can buy, Tamara."

"We'll take off our masks. And then, Andre, we'll just be goofy and stupid . . ."

"And crazy and foolish until morning. Tamara, you're a gem." Andre touched me. He had a capacity for tenderness. Philip didn't. Would the successor to Geoffrey Piedmont be gentle? Ever? I didn't think so.

I laughed.

"What? Tamara, here I am, at my most appealing, and all you do is laugh."

"I'm sorry. But I just had a mental picture of Celia Gordon, dressed as a witch."

"She certainly looks the part. I can see her, too. Complete with accessories—peaked hat and broomstick."

"And complaining every inch of the way. Andre, if she comes as anything else, I'll never forgive her."

"How about Mrs. Parsons as the Woman in White?"

"Splendid. She can carry an Irish harp."

Crispin came in and stared at us as if we'd gone mad. He wasn't used to seeing us free of our habitual gloom.

"But Andre," I said, "what in the world will we come as?"

Andre stroked Crispin's soft fur and scratched him behind one pointed ear. "Tamara, you would make an excellent cat."

"A cat?"

"Certainly. You needn't bother with a costume so grand that it outshines our guests' apparel. After all, this party will be for the denizens of Woodlands alone. No outsiders. We'll invite only those people who have been directly touched by the evil influences at work in Stonehaven."

"Then I will come as a cat. It's a simple costume to put together." Crispin mewed. "In honor of you, pet," I said to him, "I'll be a white cat."

Andre came close to me. "All you'll need is a mask with pointed ears, tights, and a furry fabric for your middle. You'll make a marvelous cat. Graceful and sensual. Just like any real feline." He imitated a cat's low growling purr and nipped my ear playfully. I began to lose track of my thoughts.

But there was one question I had to ask.

"Andre, what kind of costume will you wear?"

"Me? I think I'll pick something appropriate to the occasion. Tell you what, I'll come as the devil. What could be more suitable?"

I felt a barely discernible pinch of fear. Then Andre embraced me and I forgot to be afraid.

That same day formal invitations to the party were sent to everyone in Woodlands, with handwritten notes attached telling them to wear supernatural costumes. Celia Gordon received a personal call from me as well. She was most adamant that I had made a mistake, rejecting her Hawaiian suggestion. In the end, after I apologized to her, she gave a loud sniff, and was, thereafter, resigned.

Mrs. Parsons, on the other hand, was euphoric. Her one regret was my choice of costume. If only I would consent to come as the ghost of Cinderella, the party would be complete. But I held my ground, despite her entreaties, and insisted on coming as a cat, that most notorious of witches' familiars.

So, in the midst of a springtime that would go down in local history for its beauty, I was as busy as it was possible to be. Not since the spring of '34, old-timers assured me, had there been a season like this. Each day was sunny, each evening cooled by a brief, gentle rain.

Bushes foamed white with apple blossoms. Cherry trees amassed flowers of palest pink. Lilac bushes wore the royal purple. Bumblebees were back, their black and yellow bodies furry in the sun. Lawns were starred with yellow. Dandelions and buttercups by the thousands thus turned the earth into a great green sky, illuminated by golden torches reflecting the sun. Nests were woven and spun. Dappled fawns played in the woods.

The people, too, came alive with spring fever. Their faces took on a glow, their voices were gayer; they whistled or sang. And they talked incessantly about the party. Sewing machines hummed as costumes were chosen, made, discarded, and run up again. Girls bribed other girls to find out who was going to wear what. Gossips gossipped, and busybodies snooped. Everyone was happy.

Happiest of all were Andre and I. Every morning Andre ordered me out of bed. He would throw open the window and expound on the beauties of Nature. Then breakfast would arrive. We ate on trays in our bedroom, planning the day's schedule. We joked and laughed and chatted, like newlyweds on a honeymoon.

Next, came a period of major activity. There were endless details to see to, endless arrangements to be made. Then came lunch, followed by a bustling afternoon, and finally, dinner. Evenings we kept for ourselves.

One day, Andre called to me as I unpacked crates. My hair was tied in a kerchief to protect it from dust, my clothes were dirty, my face smeared with grime. I must have looked like a ragamuffin, a dirty urchin from a Victorian slum.

"You've got to see this, Tamara," Andre shouted.

"I'm coming," I shouted back. I ran along the hall, past Mrs. Parsons who was arguing heatedly with several gardeners about floral displays. She wanted everything to be exactly right for the party.

I hurried along, dismissing servants' questions by saying I had no time. I stopped when I reached the dining hall and stared. Andre was alone in the enormous room. When he saw me he said, "Look!" and pointed to a newly arrived musical instrument. The organ was here.

"Fantastic," I said, walking all around it.

"Isn't it something, Tamara."

"But who in the world can play it?" I asked.

Andre smiled. "Don't worry, I've arranged for someone to come up from New York City. A master musician, I'm told."

The organ stood in splendid isolation. It was gigantic in size, ornately carved, a rococo fantasy out of *The Phantom of the Opera*. It belonged in a carnival, providing musical accompaniment to an antique carrousel.

I played a chord. Immediately the room throbbed with sound. "It looks immensely complicated," I said. "Where did you find it?"

"In a wonderful shop in New York. They sell all kinds of old instruments. They had a glorious old piano with ivory keys. Its legs were solid mahogany. Thing must have weighed a ton. I considered buying it for Stonehaven. Let's put the organ in the nursery. I'll sneak up there and play Bach when we have visitors down here. That will impress them."

"Or scare them away. But you can't spend the day here admiring your latest acquisition, Andre. There's dozens of crates to unpack."

"Get the servants to help you, Tamara. I feel an inspired mood coming on. Time for a genius to create." He moved purposefully to the organ.

"Oh no you don't," I said. "The servants have their own work to do. We've got to set them a good example."

"I see I have no choice; I'll have to get back to my new toy later." He patted the organ as if it were a St. Bernard dog and followed me out of the room.

A truckload of crates had arrived the day before. All they contained were candlesticks.

Andre whistled. "Madame, I am amazed at your perseverance. Where will you put these?"

"I mean to have Stonehaven inundated with light."

"Don't we have enough candlesticks in the house?"

"No. Besides, these are simple wooden ones. I plan to use them to light the rooms in the upper stories. I scoured the attics and found a number of remarkable candlesticks for the dining hall. Some are sterling and others are bronze. By the time I'm finished, Stonehaven will look as it did in the eighteenth century. It will bask in candlelight."

"It's a good thing you didn't decide to cover the walls with tapestries," Andre said. "Stonehaven would look like a cloth factory."

"That's not a bad idea," I teased. "We've still got time to get the rooms covered in silk or velvet."

"I draw the line, Tamara. Stonehaven looks archaic enough as it is. No more trappings."

And we went back to work. That evening at twilight Andre and I walked together in the gardens. We picked a blossom bouquet to put in our bedroom and watched the night come. We waited until the stars were hard needlepoints of light before we returned to the house, to see our bedroom window become a mural depicting the night sky.

Two days before the party, activity at Stonehaven reached fever pitch. The inhabitants of Woodlands scurried to and fro putting finishing touches to their costumes. Mrs. Parsons frowned from overwork. Andre and I were giddy from the confusion.

The weather was so grand that I felt my old craving for the woods come upon me urgently. I had been absorbed enough in party plans to repress it until now. But today it wouldn't be denied. I kept seeing myself deep in the woods, looking for birds, admiring wildflowers, drinking from clear mountain springs.

I stopped work and hurried to the garden. I was still afraid to walk in the woods but I could at least enjoy part of this perfect day outside. The sun was hot on my face but a charming breeze cooled my cheeks and kept me comfortable.

I sat under an apple tree. Its trunk was friendly, a benign chair back. I could look through the blossoms in the tree to the clouds, the lush blossoms of the sky. From marshes to hilltops the earth was a maiden hymn to springtime.

I felt like a miniature creature in Nature's vast garden. Was I lying under a tree or at the base of a petunia? Was I Thumbelina at rest in a flowerpot on the windowsill of a kindly old gentleman's house? I closed my eyes and imagined the old man out picking a pretty nosegay of wildflowers for me.

I asked for nothing rare. The common colors would do; pink, yellow, and white; and the common shapes; bells, stars, and laces. I would have liked to lie back and hold them up, matching them against the delicate blue porcelain bowl of the sky.

I felt safe, under the complete protection of Her Majesty, Nature, queen of all seasons.

"You are really under the protection of Venus," Philip said.

I looked up, startled to find him there. Since I'd been preparing for the party with Andre, I had practically forgotten about his brother. But, of course, no one could overlook Philip when he was close.

Late spring had intensified his powers. He seemed to draw sustenance from the warming earth. He looked as pagan as a Greek God. Perhaps he really was Apollo, for the sun seemed to love him. It caressed him and brought a burst of sparkling silver to his hair. Though he kept his distance I could feel the pull of his body, radiating energy. A Sun King.

He was dazzling. I had to avert my eyes.

"Tamara," Philip said earnestly, "don't look away; don't be afraid."

He was pleading with me. I stared at him. And was bewitched.

"I'm going away," Philip said.

"Away? But I thought you loved Woodlands."

"I do. But I have to leave for a while."

"Where will you go?"

"Eventually to Spain. Possibly to Greece. I'll come back to Woodlands in the fall. And then I won't leave it again."

"You'll be here in the winter," I said. I could picture him, changing with the weather. In the era of the snows he would become a tall elf, sculpted in ice.

"It's a long time to winter, Tamara. Come with me now. I know a white sand beach that stretches for miles. No one ever goes there. We could have it to ourselves. The water of the bay is turquoise. You would love it."

"Would I? I like green woods and mountain streams."

"What about cities, Tamara? I can take you to one that rivals ancient Baghdad. Its roofs are jade and the inhabitants speak a language unchanged since the days of the Druids. They brew a fine white beer that tastes like champagne."

"I told you, I like the woods."

"Then we'll find you a woods. I know an exotic one. It consists of lemon trees bearing fruit. And it houses fabulous birds and beasts. Unicorns roam free there under southern stars. Or if you'd prefer something more prosaic, I know a German forest that was young in the time of Charlemagne. I'll take you there and show you the special plants, and name you their special names."

Pictures came into my brain, covered my eyes. I saw myself walking across secret fields with Philip, hiding in ruined temples, burrowing through caves. Then Philip touched me and I felt intense, quick pain, as if I'd received an electric shock. Philip was like a vibrant life force, sucking power from the sun.

I wasn't tempted; I was afraid. Philip overwhelmed me. I wanted to be with Andre who was scaled to my level, who was of an order that I could understand. Andre, like myself, was merely mortal.

Philip said, "Tamara, when we return to Woodlands, you'll experience it differently. You'll have learned what plants to look for, what animals to find. You'll realize that it's the most precious place on earth. Only if you come with me, can you ever really be mistress of Stonehaven."

"I won't go with you," I said. "I love Andre, not you. I don't even know you; you're like a sweeping force that leaves me in turmoil. I feel that if I go with you, I'll return to Woodlands this fall an old woman. I'll be burnt out, destroyed for flying too near the sun."

Philip's eyes were whirlpools, ready to absorb my soul. His body exuded white heat; it glowed like a flare. I thought that he was going to punish me for refusing him by turning into a whirling dervish of flame and roaring over me.

But he merely stood still and spoke. His voice, however, was hard, unforgiving.

"Very well, Tamara. You've had your opportunity. I won't ask you again. But I warn you, you are making a fatal error. Do you know why my brother is suddenly happy and loving? It's because he has a surprise in store for you at your party. I offer you your only chance to escape to safety."

I felt trapped. If Philip were telling the truth, I was doomed. I would be alone at Stonehaven with the reincarnation of Geoffrey Piedmont. But, as I thought about Andre, I decided that I would not renege on my choice. I loved him. I had to trust that he loved me. I would not abandon him.

I said strongly, "I'm staying here, Philip. That's my final decision."

"Then I'll see you for the last time at your party. I'll come to bid you farewell. Good luck, Tamara. You'll need it. I'm afraid you're going to pay for your sentimentality."

With that parting comment, he was gone. The sun went behind a cloud. The day suddenly turned a mournful gray.

Chapter XXX

It was the day before the party. Andre opened our bedroom door, shouted, "Surprise," and thrust a large box into my arms.

"What's this?" I asked, hurrying to untie it.

"Your costume has arrived," he answered.

Quickly I tried it on. It was a thick cream-colored satin leotard. The white stockings were opaque. The shoes were heavy leather and somewhat orthopedic. If it weren't for the mask, the costume would have suited a nurse. The mask had peaked ears and wire whiskers. I pulled it on. It improved the over-all effect. The costume even sported a cat's tail made of cotton, looped over stiff wire.

"How disappointing," I said as I looked in the mirror. "I'm sure I could have done better if I'd had more time."

Andre pulled my tail and laughed. "Be careful, Lady Crispin; don't gouge anybody's eye out with this."

"You know, Andre, I think I look rather like the Cowardly Lion."

He snorted. "Nonsense. You look just fine. If I'd thought of it in time, we would have had the costume treated to glow. Then you could have come as a cat's ghost. Very mysterious."

"Enough about me. What about you? You've been keeping your costume very secret."

"No expression of curiosity, please. Or you'll be down to eight lives. You'll see my costume at the party, and not a minute sooner. It's to be a surprise."

"Very unfair. After all, you know exactly how I'll look."

"It's my prerogative as master of Stonehaven to keep you in suspense, Tamara."

"It's lucky that I only have to wait one more day. Otherwise, I'd search your closets."

"You wouldn't find my costume. I've got it well hidden."

"Andre, there is one thing I should tell you before the party. Philip plans to come."

I was relieved to see that Andre didn't care.

"Don't worry about Philip anymore. Tomorrow night is for you and me, Tamara. Philip can't affect that. He doesn't count. So change out of your feline attire and let's get back to work. There's plenty left to be done."

And, side by side, we labored, until the middle of the night.

Next morning brought spring's finale; it was the end of May. June meant the start of Woodland's cool, brief summer. Within days the air would swarm with mosquitoes. The afternoon sun would burn hot enough to allow swimming in cold mountain lakes. Rain would fall, the thunderbursts of summer.

Swallows, masters of aviation, flew across the pond, their wings cutting the air like scissors as they dipped for insects. Hawks, a study in slow motion, circled the skies. Huge, lumbering turtles went walking. Snakes napped on ledges of rock.

Children reported a disquieting find. A dog's skeleton, victim no doubt of winter snows, was found on the path near the cottage. Something had probably dragged it there, out of the woods. Its flesh was completely gone. Its bones were dry and its teeth were ominously large in its skull. A thick leather collar was still attached to what had been its neck. An ill omen for the party.

Everyone's work was done. For the moment there was a lull. Occasionally, a servant was seen hurrying to rectify a mistake or add an extra finishing touch.

It was as if a net had been thrown over Stonehaven, locking people into place, keeping them at rest. In a few hours they would again race and dash, to see that details were in order, flowers properly arranged, and food set upon the banquet tables. Even the candles were all in place, waiting for the matches that would ignite them into life.

I was exhausted. I lay in bed. It was time for a nap. The white cat costume was folded neatly on a chair. A tray with empty teacups was on a table nearby. There was nothing for me to do but stare dreamily out the window at a sky of lapis lazuli. The weather had held. Tonight would be perfect, the last of the fresh, flower-glazed evenings of springtime. Complete with full moon.

There was a knock at the door. Assuming it was Andre, I called, "Come in." There was another knock. I got up and went to the door. The hall was deserted. But a large white box tied with lime-green ribbons was on the floor. I picked it up and brought it in.

A small envelope embossed with the Piedmont seal was taped to the box. Enclosed was a note from Andre. It said, "Darling, the cat costume doesn't do you justice. Wear this tonight. For me. Love, Andre."

"What on earth?" I said, as I lifted the costume from the box. I had never seen anything so beautiful. It was an elfin creation fit for Fantasia.

I held a long gown, sheer as a new-spun web when it shines in the morning sunlight. The gown was green, pale as a young leaf, just unfurled. There was a slip to wear beneath it, a silken petticoat the color of an emerald. The sleeves of the gown were long and full. I swear they were made of Queen Anne's lace.

For my hair there was a crown of dried wildflowers, intricately woven. And for my waist, there was a daisy chain. Velvet dancing slippers, the shade of spring's first blade of grass, were meant to grace my feet.

The entire costume was handmade. The fairies must have labored over it, sewing fine seams. I examined the workmanship with awe. Some stitches were so neat and tiny that I fancied mice seamstresses had been busy at their tailoring benches.

These were clothes straight from a bard's ballad, meant to drape Maid Marion, Barbry Allen or Guenevere. Mrs. Parsons had got her wish: I was transformed into Cinderella, after all.

But I felt a slight fear. Had the costume been created with love or vengeance in mind? Was it a Medean gift that would

turn to flame when it touched my skin? I ran my hand along
it. The gown was pleasurable to feel. It was soft and inert. I
couldn't resist it. Dangerous or not, I had to wear it tonight.

I had faith; the gift was from Andre. I would do as he
wanted and come to the party as Springtime herself. I put
the costume away. I was too tired to stay awake any longer.
I went back to bed and closed my eyes. Soon I was asleep. I
dreamed that I was alone and lost. First, I was in the deepest
woods, then I sailed the most distant seas, and finally, I stood
amidst the tallest mountains. They were capped with snow. I
was isolated beneath the cold, impersonal stars.

When I awoke it was twilight. The sky was passing
through successive shades of blue. Before long, it would
reach blackness. The earth was darkened already. Leaves
formed an ebony mosaic; shadows merged. A few brave stars
had come out and were feebly trying to twinkle.

It was the hour when the night animals grow active in the
woods. Deer move freely, their bodies blocks of shade under
the muted sky. Cool winds were blowing up, to replace the
static air of the day. It was time for the party to begin.

I stood in the hall, an incongruous figure; Springtime come
to make my final rounds before the promise of summer murdered me. It was strangely quiet. I had expected that by now
the house would be filled with guests, that it was time for my
entrance. Where was the raucous laughter, the hilarity of a
party? Where were the servants who ought to have been passing back and forth, carrying drinks on silver trays?

Perhaps in my anxiety as hostess I had dressed too soon.
The guests would probably arrive en masse fashionably late. I
hurried to the dining hall just in case there were any bewildered early arrivals. They would expect to find company and
discover that they were alone with the servants. It was
enough to intimidate anybody.

The house seemed larger than usual in its emptiness.
Treating it as a haunted house had not brought it down to
manageable size. Instead Stonehaven had expanded, as if released from spatial restraints. In the swelling process the
house had lost its solidity. It seemed buoyant, like a ship at
anchor. As a result Stonehaven felt as if it were itself a
ghost, the insubstantial remains of a once-living house.

My velvet slippers made little sound; barely a whisper in
the noiseless house. I reached the dining hall and went in

without pausing, the quicker to help any stray, befuddled guests. There were none.

Massive wooden tables lined the wall. A cornucopia's worth of food was spilled across them. There was something for everyone, from the simplest fare to food that would satisfy the most discriminating gourmet. Chilled champagne was ready to be served. But where was the wine steward? Where were the servants? Where were the comics Andre had hired to make us laugh? The room was ready and waiting. All the candles glowed, butterflies of light in the cavernous room, still a shadowy blue.

For a moment I didn't know what to do. All my careful plans were wasted. All my work was undone. I thought about returning to my bedroom to await Andre. Perhaps he knew what had gone wrong.

But then the music started. Not the artificial silly songs I had requested to keep our guests amused and help them mock evil spirits. This music was Gothic, medieval. With a jolt I realized that the organ was no longer in the dining hall. The awesome sounds were coming from another part of the house. The library.

I went there. And saw the scarlet walls and leering gargoyles again. There was the organ. Great rolling notes made the room quiver. As suddenly as the music had started, it stopped. I could feel, even if I couldn't hear, pieces of sound trembling in the air.

A man stood up and came to me from behind the organ. We were surrounded by candles, their wicks still virgin, untouched by flame. But our faces were bright under the glare of the electric lights.

"Robin Rouen," I said softly. "Friend or foe?"

"Friend, red fox, on your side, always."

"Why are you here? Andre told me the party was only for local people."

"I don't believe he quite put it that way. Surely I am an honorary resident of Woodlands, not an outsider. I, too, have been touched by the evil influences at work in Stonehaven. That qualifies me as a bona-fide guest."

"True, you are one of us."

"Would you like to hear more music?"

"No, Robin. I don't understand why the house is empty. Do you know where Andre is? Or other guests?"

"Patience. They'll appear before you when they're ready. That means you have time to admire my costume."

Tonight Robin was literally dressed as a magician. On his head was a shiny black top hat that might have been snatched from the head of a 1930s movie idol. His spade-beard was neatly trimmed. He wore an old-fashioned tuxedo with starched white shirt-front, black tie, and tails. His kid gloves were spotless. And he carried a cane.

"I'm surprised that you didn't pick something more dramatic," I said.

"I thought of coming as Bluebeard as I did at my last party. Even dyed my beard cobalt blue. But I decided not to risk it again. I had all the little children and dogs in the village scared for days."

I smiled. "You're still the same old character, Robin," I said fondly. Then I remembered the trance he had gone into in this same library on his last visit. We were alone here again. I stopped smiling. I wanted to leave, to insure that we conversed with someone else present.

"Let's find Andre," I said.

Robin studied my face. He nodded. "Afraid to be alone with me, I see. Well, I deserve it. You go find your husband. I'll stay here. I'd stand out too much if I joined your other guests. They'll all be dressed colorfully and here I am, clothed with discretion. But remember I'm here; your resident magician in a haunted house." And he gave me a stiff, formal, stage magician bow. Then he returned to the organ. I could hear him playing an ancient and brooding melody as I walked down the hall.

Night had come. Except for the library, no electric lights were turned on in the house. I picked up a candleholder in the shape of a serpent. It watched me from its ruby eyes. I lit its candle and carried it aloft. It would help me face the dark stairs.

I went up the central staircase. Not to the top floors; I didn't have the courage for that. Besides, as far as I could tell, the upper part of the house was deserted.

I went back down. Still the organ music reverberated from the library. I walked to the kitchen. The gigantic room was empty. By now it ought to have been filled with a frantic staff of servants, under Mrs. Parsons' direction. She was nowhere to be found.

The great copper cauldrons were unused, the stoves were

turned off; even the sinks were scoured clean. Freezers the size of trucks were locked. Pots and pans, polished and glowing, hung from hooks on the wall. Cupboards and pantries were shut.

The room looked deserted, a fraud, a fake kitchen which had never been used for the preparation of food. I considered whether the kitchen was at fault for this illusion. Perhaps Stonehaven had become the Sleeping Beauty's palace. Perhaps I was awake early from a sleep of centuries, out of kilter with the rest of the house which had not yet shaken off the magic spell. I looked around the room to see if grass grew between cracks in the floor, or if a cook lay snoring under a kitchen chair.

Then I noticed the round clock on the wall. It was nine-thirty. The party should have been in full swing. Yet it was dead quiet. The organ had stopped.

Then there came the sound of a violin. It was very sweet, for it played a sentimental tune. I went to the huge double doors of the kitchen, doors that could open to admit sides of beef, and sturdy tables of oak.

I went outside and stood on the lawn, which was mowed and gentled to the texture of moss. I looked first at the house behind me. It was a dark, obscure shape, a backdrop for its windows. The candles had given them glory. The windows seemed to hang in space, rectangles of yellow light; the candles within them like damned souls flickering and dancing in the night.

Then I looked in the opposite direction. And felt astonishment. Below me, down Stonehaven's hill, pastel lanterns by the hundreds shimmered in the tops of trees. Tables were set up, under canopies of circus colors. And all the people of Woodlands were gathered. They stood disguised, under a giant blood moon that hovered just over the trees. It was round and ripe. A Sicilian orange, which, if punctured, would drench the crowd with cold, spicy juice.

Chapter XXXI

———◆◆———◆◆———

The guests were rooted to the earth like statues. Quietly, they watched my approach. Above veils, or behind masks, their eyes were expressionless. I had a long way to go to reach them. Suddenly, a funny little man leaped from nowhere, landing beside me. It was the solitary violinist.

A smidgen under five feet tall, he had a wrestler's strong body. His dark eyes were sad. His hair formed a thick cap of black ringlets framing his face. Lanterns cast circles of light which brought out the colors of his jester's costume. His tights were violet, his jerkin scarlet. He played "Greensleeves" while he danced and hopped, leading me past groups of silent observers.

Here were the young, hoping to be fed; there, the old, seated on wrought-iron benches. We did not stop until we reached one man standing alone, a tall elf whose pale hair and face were colorless, a ghost transfixed by a moonbeam. It was Andre, dressed as a wicked monk in robes of fiery red.

I stood under a lantern that sprayed yellow light. It had the touch of Midas, it turned me to gold. The lantern made Lazy Susans of the daisies round my waist and changed the flowers in my crown to marigolds and dandelions.

Andre raised a glass of champagne. It was clear and frigid as starlight. "A toast," he said, "to Springtime, who honors us with her presence." Then he broke the glass against a tree trunk. It shattered into a thousand diamond fragments, which fell glittering to the ground.

This must have been a prearranged signal, for the guests now laughed and talked with animation. Servants moved in and out among them. Plates rattled as food was served.

"Andre, I don't understand," I said. "Why is the party being held outside?" He looked wary but would have answered, when Celia Gordon approached. She looked exactly right. She was disguised as the eternal crone. She wore high-buttoned shoes, a black frock, and a peaked hat which

197

lengthened her chin and pointed her nose. The archetypal witch.

"Marvelous," I said to her. "And you've got every detail perfect. Down to a broomstick."

"It was my mother's, Tamara. Good thing I can carry it in one hand. Frees the other to hold a martini." And she took a strong sip of gin and vermouth.

Then she tilted her hat at a rakish angle and eyed Andre with disapproval. "Hmm, red robes. You need more than that to look like the devil. Where's your pitchfork and pointed ears?"

"A very conventional view of Satan," Andre answered. "I had in mind something older, more obscure, more powerful."

"An evil force that goes back to the Stone Age," I said. I imagined a primitive forest. In a cave a small group of barely human beings bent forward, awaiting their deity.

"Older than that, Tamara," Andre said. "Evil was born with the earth at its creation."

"Don't talk about evil," a woman's voice said. "Not a fit subject for a party." It was Minnie Parsons. "Have you eaten yet, ma'am? The food is scrumptious!" She was dressed as an affable Halloween ghost. A simple white sheet cut out at the face was draped around her plump body.

"I had a mask, but I took it off," Mrs. Parsons said, smiling. "It got in my way and I didn't want to miss anything."

"You look beautiful," she said to me, her face becoming tender. "If only I had had a dress like that when I was young."

"They probably wore togas when you were young," Miss Gordon said acidly.

Minnie Parsons stopped smiling. "You were no beauty yourself, Celia; when was it? Back in the Civil War. The Yankee belle, they called you, didn't they?"

Miss Gordon became irate, an avenging Mother Goose. She trembled, pointed, and snapped, "That isn't funny, Mincie. Now go away before I lose my temper. I'm going to give Tamara a tour of the party."

And she led me off, saying, "You won't recognize half your guests. They've done a darn good job on their costumes." We wandered into a make-believe world, a wonderland of surrealistic sights.

The violinist had joined an orchestra of strolling midget

musicians. Couples swayed gracefully to the music or bobbed mechanically, like dolls on a music box. Close-by, a Kodiak bear, seven feet tall, growled a song to his partner, a petite creature, with the beautiful wings of a butterfly. A pair of vampires whirled past. The female half smiled at me. She had dyed her pointed teeth a feminine shade of rose.

Surrounding the dancers were other monsters enjoying the music in their own way. Some argued, some harangued. A huge, muscular Frankenstein, his face green in the moonlight, argued with a small, thin Frankenstein, its face a gruesome criss-cross of scars. The argument was settled by the big Frankenstein smashing the shorter one's skull in.

"May I have the time?" a tall bat inquired of me.

"I don't have a watch," I answered politely, averting my eyes from his ugly face.

"I do," said Celia, ever prepared. "It's ten-thirty."

"He doesn't look like he's wearing a rubber mask, Celia. His bat's face looks real," I whispered. She grunted in reply. Then she smiled, catching hold of a passing couple.

"You remember Pop and his wife Anna from the other party, don't you, Tamara?"

"Certainly," I said. A rotund Tweedledee and Tweedledum. At the moment they were greedily devouring lobster. Pop extended his hand. But I couldn't bring myself to shake it, for he was the image of a squat, hairy toad. So was his wife. They grinned in unison and nodded their heads.

"Nice to have a party at the old house again," they croaked together. Then they returned to the engrossing business of cramming food into already swollen bodies. I watched with fascination as they ate. They were insatiable, their torsos puffed like balloons. Occasionally, they would pause and gaze at nothing, their faces in agony from starvation.

A zombie walked steadily across the lawn, looking neither right nor left. Tall and emaciated, it held a tray blindly in front of it. It swerved suddenly and made for me. Miss Gordon removed a plate of food and a glass of wine from its tray and handed them to me.

"Why thank you, Paul," she said to the zombie. "You also met him at the last party, Tamara. Paul Rieger. He's running for county assessor, and he owns a store." She whispered loudly, "Cheats everybody who comes into it."

The zombie must have heard her. But he remained as impassive as ever. Miss Gordon dismissed him with a snap of her fingers and he turned abruptly, knees rigid. Mechanically, he began his strange goose-stepping progress back across the lawn. He did not alter his course, forcing people to scurry out of his way.

"Eat your food!" Miss Gordon ordered.

I wasn't hungry, but I was very thirsty so I drank the champagne, which bubbled and flowed in my glass like a small trapped brook. It tasted like spring water from an uninhabited woods.

A man came up to me and said hello. He wore no mask and his face was familiar. It was the local veterinarian, wearing a homemade devil's costume. He looked perfectly normal. A relief.

"I came as the devil because half the people in Woodlands already think that's who I am," he said, smiling. Others around us laughed.

A woman's voice called from behind a leonine mask, "Last of our cows died and it was your fault."

A female vampire in lilac pantsuit and pearls shouted, "It was a sacrifice," and growled and snapped like a dog does when threatened.

The veterinarian only laughed. A centaur in the surrounding group whinnied in response.

"I'm proud of this get-up," the veterinarian said to me, and he showed his costume off for my approval. It simply looked like dime-store red flannel, poorly sewn together.

Then I saw his feet. Cloven hooves. They had a life of their own, jiggling restlessly while from the ankles up the man's body was still.

Celia pulled me away before I had time to react and we continued our strange odyssey.

"Johnny Powers!" Celia called. He waved. Seven dwarfs ran between us. They looked like costumed children, but I wasn't sure. Their merry voices quavered from old age.

Johnny reached us and greeted us politely. Miss Gordon viewed him with civic pride as one of the few young people able to meet her ethical standards.

Johnny's hair was still neatly cut and worn short. But only on the top of his head. His face and arms were a mass of hair, for he'd come as a werewolf. I had the impression that the hair did not stop at collar or cuffs but continued underneath the very proper suit Johnny was wearing. His entire body oozed thick matted hair, dark brown in color, and tightly curled. I tried not to think about it.

"A good boy," Celia murmured appreciatively after he'd left. "Such a hard worker. His wedding to Marion will be the event of the year. Except for this party, of course."

Miss Gordon gave me a different kind of wine. It was pink and tasted strongly of woodruff. I drank three glasses in a row, for it made me thirsty. Afterward I felt passive, vulnerable; time slowed.

"Wouldn't you like to dance now?" Miss Gordon asked, pushing me into the arms of an old man before I could reply. He was dressed as Father Time, with flowing beard and white tunic. Suddenly I recognized him. It was the same old man who had led me in a merry polka at the last party. Now he gave me a wise, sad look as we waltzed, as if he had a secret he must keep to himself.

My next partner was the local dentist, who chatted away. He made a most gregarious Beelzebub. Then I danced with a farmer who wore a witch doctor's mask. Shaking a giant rattle while he chanted to the moon, he whirled me across the grass.

I did a spin with the high school English teacher, husband of the Orinville librarian. He was garbed as a warlock. His wife stood close by, watching us; the moonlight turning her glasses white. She was dressed in her everyday clothes but around her shone an incandescent glow. When she walked away I could see a metal key in her back and hear it click as it unwound.

A volunteer fireman dressed as the devil pushed through the crowd and aggressively danced me around. He talked of the new yellow fire engine bought for Orinville. Then he reminisced about fires. His voice trembled and his eyes dreamed as he described flames rising, matches glowing, sparks igniting the trees.

In hushed tones, he said, "Someday the whole woods will burn and if I'm lucky I'll live to see it. Just think, the whole woods on fire." And his orange costume itself turned to flame, a cold blue-tipped painless fire, a portable Hell.

And so I danced on and on. Young men, old men, they all whirled me round, taking a polite turn with their hostess and going back to their friends for good talk and good drinks. Were they all human? I didn't know. Some seemed monsters or animals pretending to be people. In my listless state, I made a superb dancer. Everyone pushed me here and there, in their own way, at their own pace.

Finally, the Kodiak bear took me in his huge paws and danced me wildly across the lawn. Tall as a young tree, his head blocked the moon from my view.

I heard snatches of conversation as we passed groups of guests. Jigsaw pieces of dialogue from the mouths of beasts. "Corn come up pretty good this year," a farmer said. When he faced me, I saw that his eyes were glazed with a wild madness and his hands had become claws.

"Not bad," his companion agreed, "but it's too early to tell." He ran his furry tongue across charred lips.

"And I said to her, Emmy Lee, I never saw such a hat in my life and worn at church, too. Do you know what she answered?" A woman in a purple dress spoke, bending to whisper the rest of the story to a friend. Her head was the head of a fish, with bulging eyes and silver mouth. I could see her scales glitter, all wet in the moonlight.

"She's starting school this fall, aren't you, Norma Sue?" a proud mother said, patting her daughter's head.

"Yes, ma'am," the little thing replied. She was dainty and charming, with blond ringlets down her back. She wore a white pinafore and patent leather shoes.

I waved to her as I danced past. Eyes bright, she smiled. In her mouth were the pearly teeth of early childhood. Except for the canines. These were two inches long and sharp as daggers. The smile on the little face grew wider as the girl watched me. Eyes gleaming, she followed me. Wherever the bear moved me, there was the child, lips stretched like rubber in a perpetual grin.

"Been to the shopping center in New Jersey?" a sea serpent hissed the question to its mate, a mermaid, whose breasts were pale blue under a violet lantern.

"Where is it?" she bubbled.

A giant cyclops overheard them. It affixed me with a stare from its one unblinking eye and answered the mermaid, "Thirty miles past Orinville. Good buys in the fabrics department." Immediately it spun around, for I had danced by, and it wanted to keep me in sight as long as possible.

Two elderly women dressed as witches were exchanging recipes. "Rosemary, that's what you take," the first said.

"A velvet purse, lined with thread, by the half-moon," the

other opined. "Remember, it's good velvet you want. The best. Bury the purse in the garden."

The two women were joined by a third, a brunette dressed in the outlandish costume of a stage Gypsy, complete with bandanna, gold earrings, and fiery dress. She shook her head. "A potion works best. That's what He uses. Try this." And she held out a small vial filled with white powder.

The second witch sniffed and then coughed. "I'd smell like a goat if I drank that."

The Gypsy answered earnestly, "Not a goat. You'd smell like the sweat of Pan. I tell you, a potion works best."

The first witch said, "Rosemary, that's what you take. Try a little rosemary."

Now the bear began spinning me around so fast I could barely breathe, much less listen to my neighbors. A centaur cut in. He had the body of a magnificent roan stallion and the head of a Viking. His hooves trod the earth like thunder, his nostrils snorted fire. We went crashing about the lawn. The moon bounced overhead like a bright rubber ball. I felt it was dancing along with us in a black sky, the texture of moss.

We changed partners again.

I was dizzy. It took me a moment to recognize Andre. He held me tight, crushing the red velvet of his costume.

He stared at me curiously. "The party, Tamara, is a huge success. But you look numb."

I couldn't see. I had been staring at the sky until my eyes were blinded by starlight. The stars were out in force now to rival the moon. My eyes like telescopes, seemed able to focus on distant galaxies. If it were quiet I believed that I would hear actually the music of the spheres.

"It must be very late," I mused. "I must have been dancing for hours."

Andre chuckled. "The party's only starting."

Echoing his words, an enormous shower of flares boomed through the sky, beneath the syrupy stars that form the Milky Way.

"Fireworks," Andre said, his eyes mirroring starlight.

Another display immediately followed. It showed a scene from Hell painted by Hieronymus Bosch. Devils tortured lost souls. Slowly the picture faded until all that was left was one smiling demon. He hung in the sky next to the moon for a long time.

"You'd better stop dancing," Andre said to me. "You're on the verge of exhaustion." His voice was concerned, caressing, but he danced on and on, faster and faster. I felt pain, then fatigue, then nothing. My legs moved independent of my will and my brain was a vacant void.

With a shock, I found myself thrust into Robin's outstretched arms. My body throbbed as if still in motion although I now stood still. Robin stood before a table piled with exotic foods.

He had been about to dip into sauced sea cucumber when Andre flung me against him. Robin held me and stared at Andre. Their eyes exchanged some sort of message.

Then Andre lifted my hands to his lips. "The finale lies just ahead," he whispered. "I must leave you for a while. We will be together again soon, my Springtime." He squeezed my hand.

I winced and let out a small cry. Then Andre released my hand and walked off. I watched him go, a tall elf in scarlet robes which billowed in the night wind that had just sprung up. He went to the house, to Stonehaven itself. I wanted to shout, to call him back. The house was deserted, dangerous, no place for Andre tonight. But I was too numb to speak.

Robin soberly raised my chin. My eyes shattered, broken like glass. I could see three, four, five faces of Robin, through the fragments of my eyes. All the faces stared tenderly.

"Do you know, red fox, that your eyes are huge black holes in your face? Best avoid the champagne, girl."

Then my knees crumpled and I realized that I was too tired to stand any longer. My velvet slippers already looked old and worn, grass stains streaking them with extra layers of green.

"Hey, hey," Robin said, as I buckled, "a seat for my lady." I was gently pushed into an iron lawn chair. It was hard and uncomfortable but a Turkish cushion was placed behind my back.

Robin gave me food and ordered me to eat. I tasted an orange avocado sprinkled with mustard grains. Piled on my plate were slices of blue bananas with lumps of sugar shaped like pearls; ruby fishes and chops of meat; spiced grape leaves and olives the size of eggs.

Robin snapped his fingers and a goblet of mead the colors of a tropical rainbow appeared in my hand. I drank the mead. It was cool and sweet and cleared my head. I began to feel better. By the time I'd eaten the last morsel of food on my plate, I was fully restored.

There was a blast of music, the triumphant sound which greets a magician on the successful completion of a trick. "Thank you, maestro," Robin called to an invisible conductor.

Then he took my arm and escorted me round the lawn. "Your guests are certainly having fun," he said, waving his silver-tipped cane. I studied everyone we met. Now they looked perfectly normal, real people merely wearing false faces. A nearby trio, wearing Tyrolean shorts and feathered hats, were doing a jig. They wore large cardboard pigs' heads. But it was obvious that they were really three jolly farmers.

A girl in a paper witch's costume almost collided with us. It was Elsie. "It's a wonderful party," she said. "Just like Halloween." And then she was lost in the crowd.

The moon outlined Stonehaven with a ghostly light. It made me think of Andre. "Robin," I said, "we must find Andre at once. He went to the house."

"Now, now," Robin soothed, as if he were talking to a child. "Andre knows what he's doing. Anyway, you can't run off and desert your guests. You're their hostess. Come with me and we'll find a good place to watch the remainder of the fireworks."

Robin led me to the edge of a large crowd which had formed to watch the show. Great prisms of color periodically rocked the sky, temporarily turning night to day. Then a sparkling cat burst into view, scraping the earth with its claws, before vanishing into the air.

Around me the people of Woodlands expressed their delight. Their plain faces were beautified by the light from the fantasies shimmering above them. Children squeaked and chattered in their homemade costumes. They ran and jumped, and played with sparklers which splashed light, like firefly daubs, spattering the darkness.

"I never saw anything like it," a Frankenstein in green pancake makeup said to me. It was the Orinville pharmacist. He'd put his glasses on to watch the fireworks. The glasses looked incongruous; mundane and normal in contrast to his bizarre chartreuse complexion.

Suddenly the whole crowd went "Ooh" in unison. A huge

grinning skeleton of silver tap-danced in the sky. We could hear its heels clicking. Then it changed colors, becoming first a brilliant vermillion, next, a deep gold. Finally, it turned its back on us and continued to dance until it slowly merged with the night sky. Just before it disappeared, it gave us a sad little wave.

"Marvelous," Robin shouted, as the crowd applauded. He removed his top hat, thrust his hand in and pulled out a white rabbit. With a twitch of its nose, the rabbit was off, racing across the grounds while children stared, entranced. The fireworks show came to an end when the American flag was splashed against the sky.

The crowd was silent. There was no applause. I considered this strange on their part, considering their enthusiasm for the fireworks. Then I noticed through the slits in their masks that the eyes of my neighbors were filled with fear. Were their hidden mouths pursed in soundless screams?

A lone figure was approaching, across the lawn. Robin and I sighted him simultaneously. He was the focus of the crowd's gaze. His progress was casual and unhurried, yet stately. He reminded me of a monarch, out surveying his lands. He lacked only flattering courtiers and a golden coach, to look precisely like a Hapsburg Prince on a stroll. Except that this gentleman was encased in an aura of silver light.

His clothes were elegant. He wore shoes with buckles. On his head was a powdered white wig. When he was very close to the crowd, he stopped, smiled, and said, "Surely it cannot be that I go unrecognized."

His voice was slightly shrill, unfamiliar. The face, however, was Philip's. Moonlight etched his skull sharp as a poison symbol. But a witch behind me shouted, "It's the ghost of Geoffrey Piedmont. I know; I've seen it in the woods." A werewolf howled, "Save us! What will he do to us? We're caught." The witch cackled hysterically and then screamed. The scream grew louder and rose higher until it must have reached the far planets in the sky.

Chapter XXXII

For a moment the crowd was fixed in a fearsome tableau, a scene from Walpurgisnacht. Then the ghostly figure walked nonchalantly through the crowd, splitting it in two. The monsters reacted like exploding atoms. Tension broke. Released, then ran wildly in all directions, desperate to escape.

A bird-headed woman rushed past me, beak open, cawing. Two fat ghosts lumbered along. They practically knocked me down. I was trapped in a frenzy of fur, fangs, and claws.

Meanwhile, the luminous ghost continued strolling, indifferent to its own effect. It stopped before Robin and me.

"You've got a nasty sense of humor," Robin told it.

"Sorry," the ghost replied, "but I'm not feeling accommodating these days. I've had to sustain a severe disappointment recently." And the ghost's eyes shot blue anger at me.

"An excellent costume, Philip," Robin said. "You look authentically eighteenth century."

"And authentically ghost," he answered. "At least to judge from the crowd's reaction." Then Philip stared at me. "You look beautiful," he said quietly. "Out of place among these freakish creatures."

"I've got used to them," I said.

"Really, Tamara? Then you've been drinking too much."

"It's true that my head was in a whirl for a while, Philip. But Robin sobered me up."

"Were you drinking the champagne or the wine?"

"Both. The wine had a peculiar taste; woodruff, I think."

"Perhaps," Philip said, and smiled to himself, as if at a private joke.

Robin's voice was harsh. "Why are you here, Philip? I thought you were off on your travels again."

"I leave in the morning. I promised Tamara I'd come to her party tonight."

"To frighten and intimidate her?"

Philip pretended to be shocked. "What? A strange idea, Robin. That sort of thing's more in your line, isn't it? I assume you do still go into mystic trances."

Robin growled, beard trembling.

Philip added, "I, on the other hand, have full control of my faculties at all times, old scratch. I came tonight to act as guardian angel." He shimmered in an otherworldly light.

"You mean fallen angel," Robin said.

"Who are you guarding?" I asked.

"You, Tamara."

We three were now alone, the lawn around us completely deserted. In the distance a faun bleated a mournful song on his pipes. The moon bleached the life from Philip as I watched. He grew paler and fairer, until he was almost transparent, a few streaks of silver composed in the shape of a man.

"Beware of false friends," he whispered sadly, in a voice almost too soft to be heard above the wind.

"Philip!" Robin warned.

"The magician rebukes me, Tamara. He thinks I'm a Judas, a traitor to Andre. And, in addition, a bad friend. Robin doesn't choose to remember that he sought me and, when he found me, begged me to teach him magic. How he flattered me, Tamara, hoping that I'd let him read the secret books. And, thanks to me, he has absorbed his lore, he knows his magic tricks. He doesn't need me any further so I'm expendable. It's my guess that he plans to use the knowledge he's acquired against you. Assisted by my willing brother."

There was a long pause. Then Robin said flatly, "You're a liar. I resisted the black arts; they're your special pursuit. I stayed with white magic."

Philip grinned. "We have your word alone for that." Then he turned to me. His voice was urgent. "Go now, Tamara. Please. Return to your lair in the city, run, like a rabbit runs from the fox. The city is filled with people. They'll form a protective wall around you. Go now."

Suddenly the night was cold; the wind had a chill at its core. "I don't know what to do anymore," I said. "I am so sick of mysteries and secrets."

"I'll solve the mysteries for you, I'll tell you the secrets, Tamara. At another time. But you must leave Stonehaven." It hurt my eyes to look at Philip, for he glittered like foil as the moonbeams converged on him, pinpointing him in their light.

"Tell me everything," I said.

"Not now," Robin spat out the words and stretched an arm between Philip and me. It startled us, for it was like a gate suddenly closing between expectant lovers.

Before I could speak, a third person joined us. It was Mrs. Parsons, huffing and puffing, after a strenuous run.

"I've got a message for you, ma'am," she said, between gasps caused by lack of breath. "From your husband. He wants you to meet him at Stonehaven."

"Why?" I asked. "Why can't he come out here?"

"I don't know," she said, shaking her head in puzzlement. "He cut off my questions. All he told me was that you had to come to him. He said it was imperative."

Philip tried to touch me. Robin blocked him. Philip said, "Don't go, Tamara. It's a trap. Stay here where you're safe." I could scarcely hear him above the whistling wind for his voice had grown weak.

Mrs. Parsons implored, "Your husband needs you, ma'am. If you'd seen him, you'd agree. He sounded desperate."

"Don't listen to her," Philip countered. He had faded to a silvery wraith. "Go home to New York."

"Go to your husband, ma'am," Mrs. Parsons said.

I simply stood, pulled both ways, unable to make up my mind.

Then Robin pushed me violently in the direction of the house. I looked at him. His face was impassive. In his black clothes he looked like a spy or thief, up to no good in the nighttime. A mysterious dark stranger, conjured up from Tarot cards by a Gypsy fortuneteller, a man who was no longer my friend.

Like a moth, I was drawn toward the light. It was Philip I wanted. I turned to him, hypnotized, when Robin again gave me a violent push. I staggered. Mrs. Parsons gasped, pressing her hands into prayer position. Robin pointed his cane at me.

"Go!" he bellowed like Svengali giving an order. "Ignore Philip. Get to Andre. Then you'll be safe."

Andre needed my help. This fact broke through my lethargy, my passivity, my ambivalence. I turned and ran. Ran as I'd never run before. Like a deer, like a wildcat. I sped, while above me the sky's canopy burned with shooting stars. The velvet slippers became seven-league boots. I barely heard Mrs. Parsons screech behind me that Andre had told her he would be in the nursery. Her voice scarcely carried on the wind that trailed me.

I passed clusters of guests who ignored me as if I weren't there. Perhaps I'd become invisible, moving so quickly, experienced by others only as a blast of cold air whirling by. And then I was at Stonehaven.

I was afraid to enter. The candles had burnt out in many rooms, for there was no one inside to keep them lit. Thus, there were dark rectangles among the glowing windows. They looked like missing teeth, giving the house the debased, battered look of a pugnacious fighter no longer quite sane.

I went in. Silently I moved to the central staircase. Here and there I passed a room in shadow, still feebly lit. And some that were fully black. I was afraid to call to Andre, for I didn't know what would answer.

On the stairs, something square loomed. It was an old trunk. On top of it, there was an antique silver candlestick, which held a burning candle. I looked at the candlestick. Georgian design. Eighteenth century.

I opened the trunk. Inside was a wardrobe of clothes to suit the fancy of a rich gentleman of eighteenth-century France. I felt brocaded fabrics, touched leather shoes. The clothes were folded neatly. Waiting.

I shut the lid of the trunk and picked up the candle. Grasping the banister in my other hand I slowly mounted the stairs. I had the strange impression that the stairs would wind upward forever, that I was on a treadmill from which there was no escape. By the time I'd found my way to the nursery I might have climbed to the roof of the world. Could it be that I stood on a mountain top in the Himalayas, my cozy Catskills vanished forever?

My foot touched a loose floorboard. It creaked. I stopped. Was I mistaken or did the house bend slightly to hear the sound? I moved more carefully, placing each foot gently before the other, like a tightrope walker, ascending a wire.

There was a crash, a boom of sound, somewhere below in the bowels of the house. It sounded very far away and muted, as if a bomb had been dropped under water. The house quivered. For a moment I thought Stonehaven was in pain. Then I realized that it was laughing.

I arrived at the nursery door, and could hear no sound.

Andre didn't come to see who I was, nor did he call my
name. For some inexplicable reason, I thought of Laura
Piedmont in her silly little girl's costume. The house had punished her for mocking it with parties. It had changed her into
a pathetic rag doll.

I opened the door. The nursery was black, quiet as the
tomb. I didn't want to go in. It was like entering a disguised
gas chamber, a pseudo-nursery, created not for babies, but
for death.

I went in, whispering, "Andre?" Only the wind, playing at
the window, answered me. I took courage and called Andre's
name again, loudly. Great shadows sprang to life as I moved
the candlestick in my hand back and forth.

There was nothing to see but furniture, toys, and the curtains drawn across the windows. There was the familiar
bookcase; there were the rain slickers on pegs; there, the little tables; the doll house, balls, blocks, and teddy bears. And
there, sprawled on the floor was an immense puppet, its legs
and arms askew. It wore a bright red monk's robe. My candlelight revealed hair of silver.

This time I forgot to be cautious; I screamed Andre's
name involuntarily. I ran to him. But I never reached the
body on the floor. Because of the laugh. It stopped me. It began softly, then it grew louder, stronger, until it filled the
room, and escaped like gas or like fire, pouring down the
staircase, to the floors below.

It seared my throat, my eyes, almost burst my eardrums. I
was forced to drop the candlestick to cover my ears with my
hands. The laugh began merrily, then it grew hysterical, and
finally, became maniacally intense.

The laughter bounced off the walls, reverberated from the
ceilings, penetrated my bones. Then it was inside my head,
pushing my mouth open, pouring out of my throat. I threw
my head back and disgorged its wretched booming sounds
until my body ached.

Against my will, I laughed and choked until my nervous
system shattered. As I sank into blessed unconsciousness I
seemed to see the laugh take shape and color. It was like a
Cubist painting in pink and purple, filling my eyes, sliding
into my head. Then it shrank and finally it was diminished to
a point of light. Then that, too, went out and I lay in beautiful blackness, seeing, hearing, and feeling nothing at all. A
merciful oblivion.

Chapter XXXIII

At some point I began to dream that I was in a small boat adrift on a great sea. Huge waves splashed across me, trying to push me overboard. The little boat jerked and bounced in the water so that my muscles grew sore and my bones raw.

Then there were the little colored lights. They annoyed me. They flickered against my eyelids. I kept trying to raise my hand and wave the lights away. I fancied that they were bugs, trying to gnaw through the lids and eat my eyes—as a friendly gesture to save my sanity by making me blind. For the head of Medusa might be close by.

The bouncing motions became smoother; they grew rhythmic. Now I dreamed that I rode a headless horse of ebony black. We crossed a canyon which twisted its way between enormous lunar rocks. Next, we waded through a golden river. Suddenly, the horse, like Pegasus, flew above the earth. Then it soared to the stars.

I looked at those stars. They were white lights far in the distance. I was seeing the real sky, not the trickery of dreams. I was awake. Someone was holding my feet while someone else held my arms. They were carrying me along a path lined with huge trees, centuries old. They were remarkably strong, moving me quickly and easily as if I were a mere rag doll or a large puppet. Puppet! I had to get to Andre. I began to struggle.

Gently, they placed me on the ground. A familiar voice said solicitously, "Now you just rest until you feel better, ma'am." I had been rescued by dear Minnie Parsons. She let go of my arms. I smiled at her gratefully. She smiled back, generously.

My other savior bent over me. A scowling crone. It was Celia Gordon, efficiently in command. "Just relax," she ordered, pouring brandy down my throat. I choked because it burned.

"How did you get me out of the nursery?" I asked. And then I sat up. "Andre," I said. "We've got to go back for him. He's been hurt; he's in danger."

The two old women said nothing. Celia's face was impassive, Minnie's blank.

"Is he dead?" I asked.

Still they didn't move but remained inscrutable. I felt cold; the wind had an arctic touch despite the season. I listened to the scurrying noises in the woods around us. Were they made by small animals or by dwarf demons sent from the devil to spy on us?

All at once Celia's bright crow's eyes took on a sparkle in the starlight.

"If something's happened to Andre," I said, "I want to know."

They continued to stand still and say nothing. I wondered if their feet had taken root in the moist earth. Perhaps, like trees, they would stand here deaf and dumb forever, or at least until someone came with an axe and chopped them down.

Then Minnie Parsons' impassivity collapsed; her face decomposed, melted by laughter. She gave Celia a friendly nudge with her elbow.

"Let's tell her."

"No. Shut up, Minnie. It's not your place to tell her."

"But I like her," Mrs. Parsons said.

"We have been friends," I agreed.

"And I've always wanted the best for you, ma'am." Mrs. Parsons pouted. "Celia, you've got to let me tell. She's a lucky woman. It's cruel to keep her uninformed."

"Lucky?" I said. "Then you must mean that Andre is all right, after all."

Mrs. Parsons giggled. "I mean much better than that." She turned to Miss Gordon again. "Please, Celia, I'm bursting with the news."

"Very well, then," Celia snapped. "I don't know why I let you talk me into these things, but I see that I won't have any peace unless you get your way."

The moonlight smoothed Mrs. Parsons' face, obscuring signs of age, thus giving her the look of a coquettish child. She trembled with excitement and leaned close, in order to whisper a secret.

"You've been chosen!" she announced, and looked at me

with delight, waiting for me to share her pleasure. She was like a little girl, issuing a friend an invitation to her birthday party.

I was suddenly aware of my heart. It pounded, pulsing signals of fear like radio waves to all parts of my body. "Chosen? for what?" I asked.

Mrs. Parsons chuckled warmly. Her eyes were points of light. They glittered, two heavenly transplants, stars glowing where once eyes had been. "You have been chosen," she said, "to take Stacy's place as Sacrificial Victim."

Sacrificial Victim! Immediately, the world did flip-flops, rolling over and over. I lay on a web of starlight while overhead the dark earth was studded with the javelins of tree trunks. Then the world turned right side up again and I lay on the mossy ground looking up at two very old women.

Mrs. Parsons was in a chatty mood. "At first, I wanted Stacy to be Victim, ma'am. Such an adorable baby. But we can't always have everything we want, can we? Besides, you'll do quite well." And she cheered up again.

"You're a sentimental fool, Minnie," Celia snapped. "Let me explain. You never get anything right. It's decreed, Tamara, that every ten years we must have a blood sacrifice."

Minnie Parsons interjected, "I did all I could to see that the honor fell to you, ma'am." She gave me her friendliest smile, looking like a child who's just won the neighborhood hopscotch contest.

Now Celia was angry. "If you interrupt one more time, Minnie, I'll tell Him that you couldn't keep your mouth shut, that you were giving away secret information."

Mrs. Parsons, already pale in the moonlight, turned a sickly gray. "Don't say anything to Him, Celia; I couldn't stand that. There's no telling what He'll do."

"Then hold your tongue," Miss Gordon said. "We must have discipline." She looked at me. "Symbols are very important to us. We must get all our rituals exactly right. His own child is always the first choice for Victim. Well, you ruined that, Tamara. And from the time you did, I wanted to see you pay for it."

"How did I ruin it?"

"By getting so fond of Stacy. Jenny Hooper's such a fool. He thought she'd be relieved to let one of us raise the baby for her. He said that she couldn't possibly want it, not after the things He did to her that day in the woods."

"Blueberry picking," Mrs. Parsons said. "She went into the woods on the wrong day to pick blueberries. He found her there. She tried to escape but He wouldn't let her go. Not for a long time."

"That Jenny," Celia spat contemptuously. "See no evil, hear no evil. Lived in Woodlands all her life, and she never guessed what was going on around her."

"Blueberry picking," I said. "Andre told me about the rumors. That Jenny was seduced by Philip when she went into the woods to pick blueberries. So Andre was telling the truth all along. Philip is the reincarnation of Geoffrey Piedmont."

Celia nodded, her head bobbing up and down as if controlled by the wind. Then she said, "Yes, He is Geoffrey, born again. Stacy was His, conceived only to die. But, unexpectedly, Jenny loved her and then you protected her. Because He wanted you as his consort, He decided to spare Stacy."

"Geoffrey thought that you would love Him if you believed it was Andre who bore the curse," Mrs. Parsons said. "My husband Tom and I did everything we could to help Him. We lied to Andre and hoodwinked him all the time." She laughed. "And we did a good job. Admit that at times you did suspect that Andre was cursed."

"That's true," I replied. "But no matter what happens to me now, at least I know that Andre is innocent."

Mrs. Parsons ignored this. "So my husband Tom had to give Stacy back to Him so that He could give Stacy to you. Which was a shame, in a way, for Tom went to a lot of trouble organizing that kidnapping. And returning Stacy did no good; you still loved Andre." She shook her head. "I can't understand that, ma'am. How could anyone prefer Andre to Geoffrey? Geoffrey could have forced you to love Him, of course. But, instead, He chose to let you make up your own mind."

"Yes, Tamara, He did," Celia said. "I've never seen Him respond like that to any other woman." Her voice was bitter. "He talked of no one but you. All He thought of was you."

"We were jealous," Mrs. Parsons said.

"He neglected us," Miss Gordon agreed.

"He's so clever," Mrs. Parsons stared dreamingly up at the moon. "He understood that the Victim must wear green during the Sacrifice so He designed that dress you're wearing. He ordered it made for you after your final refusal of Him. It was sewn of spider's thread, then hidden in a cave, and, finally, smuggled to Stonehaven from beyond the Irish Sea."

"It arrived on the first night of the full moon," Celia said. "We must get our symbols just right. Very important."

"So clever," Mrs. Parsons cooed, still preoccupied with praising her hero. "Geoffrey knew that you wouldn't listen to Him tonight if He told you to go into Stonehaven. You didn't trust Him anymore. So He pretended instead that the house was dangerous, that you ought to keep away from it. Isn't that funny? That convinced Robin that the house was the safest place for you to be. He believed me when I said that Andre wanted to meet you in the nursery. So Robin sent you to the house. Not knowing that some of our group were waiting for you there."

"Did you kill Andre?" I asked, ready for the worst.

"Mercy, no," laughed Minnie Parsons. "Why should we bother?"

"Not tonight, anyway," Celia said. "Tonight is reserved for the Sacrifice."

"The legend will be relived," Mrs. Parsons said. "Think of it, Celia! We'll be able to watch. I can't wait."

"It will certainly be more interesting than if Stacy were Victim. What with Him feeling angry and betrayed."

"He is mad at you, ma'am," Mrs. Parsons told me. "When I saw that the legend was repeating itself all over again, I decided that perhaps it wasn't so bad after all, losing Stacy. And then, it wouldn't be fair to deprive you of the great honor of being Victim. I wouldn't want to see you disappointed. I envy you. I'd change places with you myself except that by tomorrow you'll be dead. And I want to live so I can see other Sacrifices again in the future."

"I'm also glad you'll be Victim," Celia said. "Serves you right, rejecting Him. He'll show you, the same way He showed that other girl, two hundred years ago. And, besides, now we won't have to wait on you hand and foot, and treat you like a queen. That's what He would have made us do if you were His consort."

Both women snickered. Mrs. Parsons said, "You made a serious mistake when you remained loyal to Andre. Why there's nothing to Andre. Weak, that's what he is. I ought to know, I was baby-nurse to both boys and I was with Laura when each of her children was born. How I prayed that Geoffrey would send us an heir. My mother used to tell me not to get my hopes up. She said that you could never count on it. Some distant branch of the family might be blessed this time. But He didn't cheat us. The minute Philip was born, I knew He had come again."

"She called me immediately," Celia said, "and I went over to Stonehaven right away. Laura was weeping. I went to the crib and peeked in. Without question, it was Him. The hair birthmark was very clear. I can't describe how I felt when I opened the babe's mouth and saw the swollen tongue, twisted and tied."

Minnie Parsons said, "Our faith was confirmed."

Celia added, "We knew that the curse was stamped powerfully on this child. Geoffrey had laid His hand upon Him. We were saved."

"Hallelujah!" Minnie Parsons shrieked. The wind bore her cry away, the sound of a banshee howling at the stars.

"It's the Eve of the Great Festival now," Celia said. "Tomorrow He must leave. But He'll be back with us in the fall and then He'll never go away again." Her intelligent eyes went blank. She had drawn a shade across her thoughts. She had memories of Philip she preferred to keep private.

"No, He won't go away again," Minnie Parsons assured herself. "We miss Him when He's not here. Nothing seems to happen, life is so boring and monotonous." She gave one convulsive shiver and then lost herself in a carnal fantasy of Philip.

"Minnie!" Celia warned. "Keep your mind on business."

Reluctantly, Mrs. Parsons returned her attention to us. "He must stay here, after He comes back to us this fall because He has to assume His rightful place." She added casually, "That's when we'll probably murder Andre."

I said, "Your plan shows Philip's true character. He's really contemptible, not grandly evil. He's a pretender who usurps his brother's estate by force. Philip's sleazy. The great villain can devise nothing more glorious than a cheap coup. Whatever Philip does to him, the moral victory will belong to Andre."

The women exchanged amused looks. Minnie Parsons' eyes were bright; Celia's crackled. They were enjoying a rich joke.

"Go ahead, Minnie, you tell her," Celia said.

"Andre won't win any victory, ma'am, moral or otherwise. Andre's going to look the fool."

"Why?"

"Would you like to know a secret?" she asked. I could hear the wind. It pulled playfully at Mrs. Parsons' white hair. It was waiting to hear the secret, too.

Her eyes glowing with the excitement of good gossip, Mrs. Parsons bent forward and brought her lips close to my ear. She waited a moment, enjoying the delicious tension which precedes a revelation.

Then she whispered, "Andre's not a Piedmont at all."

The stars showered us with drops of light. The moon pounded us with beams. We were creatures of the night, chattering away; telling tales, spinning yarns which I could scarcely believe were true.

"Mrs. Parsons, are you lying to me?"

"She's telling you the truth, Tamara," Celia said.

I half-expected the moon to fall or a comet to flash across the sky. Surely some great natural catastrophe should follow Minnie Parsons' words.

But Mrs. Parsons was nonchalant. She repeated, "Andre isn't a Piedmont." Then she said, "I was with Laura for years. I was her special confidante. She came to me for advice when she quarreled with her lovers. I ran her errands and arranged locations for rendezvousing. One day, she told me that she'd fallen in love. With a musician. It went on a long time. He was Andre's father."

"Andre's pure Blake," Celia said. "Remember, Minnie told you that the so-called Piedmont face really developed from the Blake line of descent."

Mrs. Parsons shook her head. "It was sad, ma'am, seeing Laura fight the curse. Against her better judgment she became reconciled again with her husband, Edward. She really had no choice. The curse determines such matters. Without wanting to, Edward and Laura conceived a son: it was Philip."

Celia was contemptuous. "Edward actually wanted Laura to have another man's baby. He was relieved when Andre was born. Silly Edward. He thought that Andre could protect Woodlands from the results of the curse. Therefore, he kept up the pretense that Andre, not Philip, was the true heir to Stonehaven. The man rejected his own son and gave his affection to a stranger's child."

"Andre will just have to be put aside," Minnie Parsons said. "A nuisance; Andre's practically not worth the effort. But it must be done."

She was about to say more but paused since some creature was tramping loudly through the shrubbery. It was making noise enough for a bear. Or perhaps it was a prehistoric animal newly hatched from its egg, out exploring. The bushes parted. A Neanderthal face stared at me.

"Tom, my old Tomcat," Mrs. Parsons gushed, running up to him and clinging to his arm.

"Get away!" he said, roughly shoving her aside. "I've got no use for you tonight. There's something better here." And he grinned at me. His teeth were sharp and pointed. He had the mouth of a wolf.

Mrs. Parsons whimpered. Then her natural optimism reasserted itself. "Well, you are the lucky one again, aren't you, ma'am. You'll enjoy Tom. There's none like my old Tom. He knows all the right tricks." And she rubbed her arm lovingly where her husband had bruised it, in pushing her away.

"I hoped things would end like this," Tom said to me. "Geoffrey would have had us worship you but I wanted you to be Victim. You had it coming, you with your touch-me-not attitude. We'll humble you. We're going to the cottage now. Our rituals begin in front of it. The first part of the Festival belongs to the moon, and the winds, to Nature and her earth, to all the growing things. Later, we'll go inside the cottage to the scarlet chair and the golden throne. We must do homage to Geoffrey's portrait during our final acts of worship."

"It's getting late," Celia said. "Punctuality, Tom. Go ahead and tell the others that we're coming. It's time."

With an unintelligible grunt, Tom was off.

Minnie's voice rippled the words, "It's time." Carefully, she composed herself, getting into the right mood. Her face became pious in the extreme. She looked like a peasant woman going to church.

Celia grabbed hold of my arms; Minnie took my feet. I couldn't get away from them. They gripped me with hands as strong as bear paws. We started off. In minutes we had reached our destination: a luminous pentacle in the shape of a star, drawn on the earth before the cottage. It marked the precise spot where Geoffrey Piedmont had been hanged for unspeakable crimes, committed two centuries ago.

Chapter XXXIV

Tenderly, they lowered me to the earth, taking care to place me in the exact center of the pentacle. Then they joined the others who formed a perfect circle around me. They were members of a religious congregation more ancient than any other on earth.

From the look of them they might have been a group of Puritans, a committee of judges, or possibly a class of students, waiting to graduate, for they wore plain black robes. I had expected them to look freakish, eccentric. But they appeared perfectly normal, a band of the persecuted faithful, safely at service in the woods.

I recognized many of them. The old farm couple was there, Pop and Anna. Their faces formed a somber double image. I saw Johnny Powers, as respectable as the valedictorian of a high school class. The local veterinarian politely nodded his head to me. No cloven hooves in sight. He wore shoes which were solidly anchored to the ground, his devil's costume discarded. The dentist was respectful as a deacon; no smell of brimstone attached to him. The high school English teacher gave me a courteous bow. His wife, the Orinville librarian, was there. The moonlight smeared her glasses with light thick as paint.

And Elsie was there, lovely blooming Elsie who had seemed so afraid of ghosts. She stood next to the volunteer fireman. His other neighbor in the circle was the old man who'd come to the party as Father Time. The rest of the group I didn't know, although their faces were vaguely familiar. I must have seen them at their work, shopping, or on their farms; nodding their heads in deference to me as I passed.

In all, a neat, tidy group which kept silent. Elsie detached herself from them and went to the edge of the woods. When she came back she held a small bouquet of violets. She had removed her robe and wore a fragile white tunic. It transformed her from a shepherdess into a nymph, a dryad, at play under a waterfall of moonlight.

Solemnly, she showed me the violets. They were graceful forms colored gray by the stars. Then she handed the bouquet to Celia Gordon, put her robe back on again, and returned to her place in the circle.

Celia crushed a violet between her fingers and held the rest of the bouquet above her head. She began to sing. I was amazed. Her singing voice was different from her speaking voice. No raucous croaks. Instead, she sang with an old-fashioned trill, as if she'd once been on the stage. I could imagine her as a young woman, surprisingly attractive in a long dress ruffled and flounced, doing a vaudeville routine of sentimental airs.

There was nothing sentimental about the song she sang now. It was in a language sadly beautiful. The song incorporated the calls of tropical birds, the sibilant hisses of cobras, and the growls of the great cats. How far back did the music go? For how many thousands of years had groups like this met in the woods to sing this song? Tom Parsons sounded the best. His animal snarls were real. Overcome with feeling, he bayed at the moon. He had a profound understanding of this music, invented when man was groping his way toward becoming a distinct species, when he had not yet lost touch with the other animals.

Celia waved the flowers in the air and the group danced. They moved formally, in a kind of ballet learned at the court of some disciple. Who was he, that prince of long ago? Had he composed the celebratory music himself, on behalf of his initiation into the congregation?

The dancers stopped. And waited politely. Celia threw the violets to the earth and crushed them under the heel of her boot. When they were maimed and shredded, she stood still, then raised her arms. In her hands appeared two small rabbits. They shivered, terrified. She put them into a cage. I knew that the poor scared creatures would have to wait awhile before their turn came to be sacrificed. Something more exciting than animal torture was planned for tonight.

Celia clapped her hands, a signal for the group to go mad. They babbled in tongues, sang songs, shouted. Their black robes kept their bodies hidden but their faces were clear to see. In the moonlight they looked like disembodied heads, their faces sculpted to express the full range of bizarre emotions.

Shrieking and crying, they rolled about the ground. Some wept to the wind, others shook their fists at the stars. They were like a troop of lunatics turned actors, performing on a stage. Elsie laughed hysterically, then joyously stuck her tongue out at the moon. The veterinarian went down on all fours and imitated animals. First he pranced and neighed; then he clawed; finally in ecstasy, he bashed his head against a tree, pretending he was a horned goat. His face reflected his delight in the blood that flowed.

Only Celia Gordon stood at rigid attention while she hummed, conjuring the devil with a tune as old as Hell. Minnie Parsons knelt in the moonlight, her face fanatic in its reverence, her hands folded in prayer, while her mouth, as if it had a life of its own, spewed one continuous cry of pain.

Tom Parsons alone was immune to the hysteria. He grinned at them all as if he thought them a pack of fools, wasting energy which ought to be conserved for the rites that would follow. He snapped his fingers, and the night turned black; the moon vanished. The dancers grew calm and then fell down, exhausted.

Out of the sky there came a star, a silver light which fell to earth and lay quivering, a broken piece of the cosmos, a glittering meteorite from space. Then the moon came out again. It dissolved the star into points of light. The light coalesced again, this time into a tall elf dressed in monk's robes of radiant white and carrying a gnarled staff. Philip had arrived.

He was completely translucent, flickering on and off in the darkness like a glowworm, a mere vessel now for his powers. They poured out of him and flowed directly to the rest of us, heightening our senses, infusing us with his erotic force. I had the shocking realization that I might actually enjoy the horrors planned for me tonight.

The entire group fell to their knees as one in worship. They chanted a Latin prayer backward. Then they rose together and each produced a candle of green, red, blue, yellow, or orange. These they waved about, weaving odd patterns in the air. First, the colored lights shaped a snake's head, next a laurel tree. Then they described a river's current, the pull of the tides, and, lastly, they outlined the rotation of the planets around the sun.

Philip raised his staff. "Friends," he said, in a strangely gentle voice, "we meet tonight to celebrate the Great Festival, just as our ancestors have done for so many centuries. We have survived the burnings and tortures of our enemies, and the ridicule of an ignorant world. We have survived, and we have kept our secrets. No thought, no action, is alien to us. The ancient Gods who fired the Maenads, gave wisdom to the Gnostics, and provided courage to the Catharists to go unflinchingly into the flames still dwell with us here and now, within our circle. Their wisdom, their power, and their ecstacy will be celebrated tonight and we offer to them the homage due them, the music which soothes them, and the blood which refreshes their spirits. And so, friends, let us rejoice in their survival, and our own."

Philip took a carved wooden flute from Tom Parsons and blew into it. It made the sound of the north wind. He shot lightning bolts from his fingers and the thunders boomed in answer from the sky. He sang and his music was the wild laughter of the loon.

Then Philip clapped his hands and the group fell to their knees again. At his whim, they danced, whirling in their black robes while the wind danced with them and the night watched.

They melted, merging together to form a dark sea; its waves rose and fell in the starlight. Then they became the pitted landscape of the moon's surface. Now they parted, were separate entities once more, but they no longer seemed human. They were wolves, and deer, vultures, and toads. They brayed at the moon, crowed to the stars. At Philip's command, they turned into trees the size of redwoods, and boulders big as icebergs in the frozen Arctic Ocean.

In the end, when Philip was ready, they became simply his followers once again, mere individuals of a religious congregation, whispering Geoffrey's name in place of an "amen."

Then they moved in on me. I understood what a wounded deer experiences when hunters come close to watch its death throes. Geoffrey's thralls stared at me with expressionless faces, but their eyes gave them away. For their eyes were sly. Voyeurs and sadists on a holiday from restraint.

Philip was the unquestioned master; therefore, it was his duty to approach me first. He floated, a platinum strand of light carried on the wind. Then, as I watched, his body settled into a mass of solid flesh once more. He became simply a man, tall and pale, with a pronounced skull-like head, self-indulgent mouth, and hair the color of silver. On his right cheek, there was an irregular patch of black hair, a birthmark. The robes he wore gave him the look of an oversized white plaster saint, a cheap carnival souvenir.

Then he touched my hair and the illusion that he was only a honky-tonk fraud was dispelled. He said, "Firebird!" and the name turned my hair to fire. I could smell it burning, see it smoking. Philip snapped off a lock of flame and twirled it playfully in the air. He tossed it to Tom Parsons who separated it into three balls of fire, juggling them with the skill of a circus performer.

My scalp began to burn. I screamed for help, instinctively shouting Andre's name. Philip, in a final gesture of pity, a memento mori of his affection for me, snapped his fingers. The fire changed back to hair. I felt no pain. I was healed.

Philip immediately regretted his moment of weakness. "You called for Andre," he said. "Within an hour you won't remember his name." He stepped aside.

Minnie Parsons came forward, holding a shriveled mandrake root. She touched my arm, my forehead, and my knee with it. Her round face was like a balloon, suspended above her black robes. It swayed with the wind, bobbing and nodding, as if detached from her body. Such a cheerful good-natured face. It might have belonged to a nanny, a favorite aunt, or any dear old soul.

She whispered, "Don't worry, ma'am, the night will pass quickly. You'll be over your suffering soon. It's worth a little pain to be the Chosen One. A sublime achievement. Oh, how I envy you." And smiling warmly, she gave me a friendly pat on the shoulder and rejoined the others.

Philip snapped his fingers and Tom Parsons came to his side. He waved his arm and Celia Gordon came forward. The other members of the congregation joined hands and began a slow circle dance around me. Celia, looking very serious and responsible, walked slowly to me, meanwhile reciting a poem in Middle English. It told of meandering by moonlight through a forest of oak trees. I had never heard it before. It was sad and rather lovely.

When she was directly in front of me, the dancing stopped. Celia finished her poem and then waited in silence. She looked duly worshipful, as if she were about to seat herself in the pew of the Presbyterian Church of Woodlands.

Carefully, she raised her arm, concentrating hard. Philip pointed to it and whistled three notes. Something flashed into her hand. It was a tiny odd-shaped object, a miniature replica of the woodcut of the half-man, half-woman. It glowed like an electrical coil. It was a brand.

Celia lowered her hand to the level of my eyes. She moved the brand toward them.

"They're going to blind me first," I thought, in a panic. "To make me completely helpless. Then they can be as cruel as they like and I won't even know in advance what's going to be done to me." I screamed, as I had never screamed in my life. The sound must have been carried by the wind all the way to Orinville.

I struggled. If I couldn't save myself, I would at least lash out at them. I couldn't face the night's ordeal. I would rather force them to kill me now. So I tried to injure Celia, to provoke her to murder. It was no use. I couldn't move. Philip had tied me with invisible ropes. Now, to punish me for kicking out at Celia, he paralyzed my legs.

When I threw my hands over my eyes to protect them from the sizzling brand, Philip forced me to pull my hands back down to my side. When, as a last resort, I lay down and tried to roll away from Celia, he commanded my reluctant body to sit up again. It did.

And so I waited with no more power to resist than a steer brought to slaughter. The members of the congregation waited tensely. They braced themselves for a Bacchanalian release. I closed my eyes. The brand had the hot, slightly scorched smell of a clothes iron.

I took a deep breath and wished I were dead. Then I heard Celia Gordon shriek. For a moment, I thought her crying out was a necessary feature of the ritual, the preamble to putting the brand against my skin. But the shriek went on and on, accompanied by a strange spitting and growling. Had Philip decided, after all, to save me and to destroy Celia Gordon in my place? It was a grim sort of joke, very much in Philip's style.

I opened my eyes. Some animal was attacking Celia, digging its claws into her cheeks. It was small but powerful. It had pointed ears and a curling tail. I thought at first that it was a wild creature of the woods, disturbed by the group's mad behavior and so launching what it perceived as a counterattack. Perhaps it presumed that its young were in some way threatened by the congregation. Then the animal made a most familiar sound. It mewed.

"Crispin!" I shouted. "Beautiful cat, it's you."

When they heard these words, the celebrants of the Great Festival looked bewildered. Then they became confused and frightened. Their unanimity dissolved and they would have panicked completely if Tom Parsons hadn't roared them into submission.

"Keep your places," he bellowed. "Hurry, Minnie; get them back in order."

"I can't, Tom," Mrs. Parsons wailed apologetically. "I must help Celia. She can die from a cat's scratch."

Luckily, as far as she was concerned, Tom didn't hear her. Otherwise, she would have been severely chastised for her disobedience. But Tom had put his head to one side and sniffed repeatedly at the wind, as an animal does to catch a scent. I looked at Philip. He ignored the frenzied dissolution of his little band. His skull-like head was very white, in contrast to the blackness of the woods behind him. He looked like a pirate's symbol, the Jolly Roger, torn down from the mast.

Poor brave Crispin. He would now probably replace the quaking rabbits in their cage. But Philip gave no orders to that effect, did not interfere in any way. He paid no attention to Celia either, even though she was convulsed with pain and cried helplessly. Like Tom, he, too, was preoccupied with something else.

However, Philip hadn't forgotten about me. I still couldn't move.

As I watched the collapse of the group I found myself growing curious. The congregation was disintegrating, becoming a crowd of individuals. A little cat had them thoroughly intimidated.

Pop and Anna, holding hands, ran to the steps of the cottage. Then, still feeling vulnerable, they climbed over the surrounding wall. From time to time, their heads would pop up together. They wanted to keep track of what was going on.

Elsie, in her hysteria, forgot that I was the Chosen One and ran to me, crying, "Help me, Mrs. Piedmont; please don't let your cat get near. It's inside the star." Observing my incomprehension, she shook me, as if to jolt me out of a deliberate stupidity.

"It got inside the pentacle," she said emphatically. Then,

clearly deciding that I was an absolute fool, she let go of me and ran aimlessly, without hope, around the perimeters of the star.

The pandemonium grew worse. People cried, raved, and twisted their hands. Some prayed. We might have been survivors of a shipwreck, trapped in a lifeboat about to hit a rock. For some inexplicable reason, we were all victims now.

In the midst of the chaos, Celia Gordon remembered her mother's teachings, pulled herself together, and took charge.

"Rosemary," she shouted above the din. "I have a potion with rosemary. Have you forgotten your first lesson as novices? 'Always look to the woods for an answer to any problem.' Bring me some coriander and I can heal myself."

Hearing this, some members of the group broke away from their brethren and went into the woods. But those who were left foundered in abject terror. They rolled on the earth, climbed trees, or simply stood still, and shook with palsy.

"Stop it!" Celia screamed.

Minnie Parsons, wringing her hands and almost in tears, feebly begged everyone to listen to her dear friend's advice.

"It will be all right," Celia told them. "Catch the cat, skin him, and put him inside the pentacle. Then you'll all be safe once again. And your powers will be restored to you. Hurry!"

When they heard these words, the group became a pack; they turned in force and went for Crispin. He saw them converge on him, their tongues hanging out, their eyes rolling. They crept toward him on all fours. He held still, back arched, claws ready. A graceful warrior encircled by deadly enemies.

He was calm. He calculated precisely the right moment and then he jumped. He was above their heads and over their bodies in seconds. Before they could stop him, he was a distant shadow, a Halloween cat etched against the full moon. As he rose, higher than I would have thought possible, he emitted one triumphant meow. It was a war cry. A victory song. In a dazzling burst of starlight he landed far away from us. He was somewhere in the woods. The pack pursued him, of course; but cats implicitly understand Nature's secret paths and hidden ways. I knew that Crispin would be safe in the woods.

It wasn't long before the pack returned, depressed and empty-handed. Those who had gone into the woods to look for coriander also came back. But they had found what they wanted. Celia took the herb and added it to her potion. She drank half, pouring the remainder into a silver beaker shaped like a dragon. Celia held the beaker against her cheek and gray smoke poured from the dragon's mouth, caressing her skin. The potion worked, for the scratches disappeared from her face as I watched.

She turned to stare at me. Her lips were puckered as if her mouth had been soured by a citrus taste. She hated me. I was to be held responsible for Crispin's attack.

To my surprise her face suddenly crumpled, losing the viciousness which had kept it firm. In an instant, she looked very old, her face a ruin of its former self. The jaw went slack, the cheeks wrinkled, and the eyes became vague. I couldn't imagine what had caused this transformation. Until Tom Parsons spoke.

"Geoffrey, they've come. It was their smells, mingling together, which I caught on the wind."

"I was waiting for them," Philip said. "I had hoped this confrontation wouldn't come tonight. But I see that it was inevitable and I welcome it."

The invisible bonds which held me vanished. I stood up. And found Robin by my side. He was still dressed as a magician. This costume gave him the look of a swarthy charlatan, a huckster, a confidence man escaped from a carnival.

"Did you bring your shell game?" Philip sneered. "Where's the rinky-dink piano music to accompany your act? Where's your tent? Your assistant? If you didn't bring the entire panoply, you'd better go back for them. You arrogant fool! To think that you imagine yourself my adversary. You don't even represent a challenge. It will barely be an effort, defeating you." And Philip struck the ground with the gnarled staff.

Robin choked, gasping as he struggled with the unseen hands which were strangling him. Then Philip raised his arm and Robin was spared, although for a long minute his face remained distorted with pain.

Then Robin stood straight as a general. He faced Philip's contempt without cringing. "I know my magic isn't strong enough to match yours, but I will do my best against you. I propose a duel to the death."

I was flabbergasted. Could this be Robin, the exhibitionist and clown? The moonlight coated him with a broad band of white, making him look tall and strong, a black avenging spirit. With dignity, he raised his cane; its silver tip changed into a diamond, twinkling like starlight. He pointed it directly at Philip's heart.

Just for a second, Philip's body went rigid. Robin smiled. Then Philip collapsed to the ground, but as he fell, he caused Robin's cane to split in two. The diamond was turned into a piece of coal. Robin bowed his head and waited to be punished.

Then an enraged voice shouted, "Try your magic on me, brother. I'm ready for you." Andre! He had materialized in front of the cottage. His robes, which had been vivid red under the lanterns at Stonehaven, looked dark as blood here in the woods. His face was in shadow, the cowl pulled over his silver hair. He pointed accusingly at Philip.

Philip smiled. It was the same smug smile found on the face of Geoffrey Piedmont in the portrait. Slowly, emulating his brother, Philip pulled the cowl of his white robe over his head. The two brothers were like twin chess pieces, the one light, the other dark. Their differences were obscured by the night, so that they looked identical; duplicate images. Under the moon, the two replicas stared at each other with intense hatred.

Members of the congregation grew bold. Feeling less demoralized, they crept forward, hoping that the night revels had merely been interrupted, not halted. With luck there might be three Victims for the Sacrifice instead of one. That would make up for the delay.

"You are the opponent I was waiting for," Philip said to Andre. "Not your blundering friend." Robin stood by, helpless. I expected Philip to destroy Andre immediately with a spark, a puff of smoke, or a column of fire.

But time passed. Andre and Philip remained in full combat. Philip concentrated on Andre remorselessly as if he wanted to puncture Andre's skull through sheer power of will and burn through to the brain. Andre, however, did not back away nor did he lower his eyes. The intensity of his stare matched Philip's.

Finally, Andre said, "Go ahead, brother; pull something out of your bag of tricks."

Philip shouted in frustration, "Damn you, I can't. Brother, our mother protected you. Without even realizing it. I can't do anything to you. You're immune to my power. You carry the antidote to my magic in your genes."

Andre shouted in triumph, "Then let's settle this as equals. In battle."

Philip raised his staff. Instantly it became a sword with blade of silver, its hilt an emerald carved with runes. It might have been King Arthur's sword, Excalibur, or a treasure of the Knights Templar. It trembled a little in the wind, quite dazzling our eyes in the moonlight. It was a magnificent object.

Philip waved it. It flashed once, spurting golden fire. Then it shriveled and died. And became only a charred piece of wood. Philip examined it briefly, then threw it away. Then he went to meet Andre. The two men grappled with each other and fell to the ground.

The members of the congregation cheered their leader, shouting Geoffrey's name over and over as if in so doing they could communicate their own strength to him. Tom Parsons decided to offer more tangible assistance. He lifted a rock and held it poised over the heads of the two fighting men. He had to be very careful. The brothers did not hold still. A wrong move and it was Philip's head which might be smashed in by the rock.

But it was only a matter of minutes before the men paused long enough for Tom to bring the rock crashing down on Andre's skull. I screamed, hoping to confuse or disconcert Tom. My scream alerted Robin, making him forget his humiliation. He ran to Tom, shoved him and forced him off-balance.

Tom Parsons tried to crack Robin's forehead open with the rock but succeeded only in grazing him. Nevertheless, Robin was hurt. He slumped into unconsciousness. Tom turned back to Andre and Philip. This time he made his decision quickly. He was taking no further chances of being interrupted again.

The muscles in his arms tightened. I could see that he was ready to swing the rock down, that he was going to squash Andre's head as if it were a melon. There was nothing I could do. If only I had some way of stopping Tom.

Suddenly a voice drawled, "Stop, Tom Parsons, or I'll kill you." It was Jack Hooper. He spoke casually, but there was no question that he was serious. For his hunting rifle was pointed squarely at Tom Parsons' head. This was magic which Tom respected. He put down the rock.

Jack's presence imparted a sense of concrete reality to the

scene which had a dampening effect on the spirits of the congregation. He looked like a frontiersman, a no-nonsense Daniel Boone, whose narrow imagination circumscribed the limits of fancy permissible to the group.

And intensifying this effect was Jenny. He'd brought her with him. There they were, two work-a-day pioneers whose world flatly excluded magic. It was the final disaster as far as the celebrants of the Great Festival were concerned.

The very sight of Jack and his rifle, instead of keeping them still, sent them rushing hysterically into the woods to hide. In the ensuing tumult Jack Hooper did shoot, but I doubt that he aimed to kill, for no one was hurt.

While this was going on, Philip extricated himself from Andre. Like a serpent, he slithered on his belly between the legs of his followers and so escaped. Andre rushed after him, followed by Jack Hooper, who had the best of reasons for hating Philip.

Jenny came to me, serene and strong once more. "Are you all right, Tamara?" she asked.

"I think so," I replied.

"Andre sent us a message during the party," Jenny said. "It informed us that you were in danger and asked us to help. Jack and I knew you could probably be found here at the cottage. We came as quickly as we could but we were terribly afraid that we would arrive too late. Andre got in touch with us because he suspected that he might be killed before he could rescue you. But, luckily, Philip's followers didn't take him seriously and they only knocked him unconscious, to see that he didn't get in their way. Robin found him in the nursery, revived him, and, by taking a short cut, they managed to get here before Jack and I."

When she was through speaking, Jenny's face tightened in fear and she gripped my arm. The congregation had returned and was regrouping in a circle around the pentacle. Taking no notice whatsoever of us, they lowered their heads, then raised them again briefly, looking up at the sky in a kind of salute. After that they went limp. The life went out of them.

Tom Parsons sniffed the air. "He's dead," he said. And began to cry. He looked almost comical, a sobbing ape.

"Did Andre kill Him?" Celia Gordon asked. I shuddered, contemplating her capacity for revenge.

"No," Tom shook his head. "Far worse than that. He died practicing His Art. Deep in the woods. First, Geoffrey drew the pentacle. He took the gnarled staff and outlined it in the earth. He was going to step into it. Another minute and He would have been completely protected. But He was denied permission to be safe."

Minnie Parsons whispered, "Because there was no Sacrifice?"

Tom nodded. "Geoffrey thought He'd be forgiven this one mistake. It was the first in His entire career. He was wrong."

Minnie shook her head. "No one can circumvent the rule. There must be a sacrifice. When no one else can be found, the leader Himself becomes the Victim."

"Geoffrey was granted a beautiful death," Tom said. "He deserved as much. He was a singularly great man."

"Describe how He died, Tom," Minnie begged. "Since you alone saw it, share it with us."

Tom stopped crying. His brutal face went slack. He was lost in a mystic vision.

"It all took place quickly, as if time were compressed. Like a film speed-up. It was magnificent. First Geoffrey recited the ritual oath. Then He raised His left foot and brought it to the edge of the pentacle. But, before He could enter, the leaves on the ground near His right foot shot into orange flame. Geoffrey screamed and stepped back on His left foot. Instantly the leaves surrounding it changed to silver fire. Now Geoffrey was rooted to the earth and couldn't move. Suddenly a wind, swirling like a miniature tornado, rushed to Him. It bore all the leaves from a mile round. The leaves poured over Him. Those covering His right side blazed like autumn, those surrounding His left burned like hot frost. Each leaf became a single lick of flame. All kept their places; the colors did not merge. The orange and silver fire was divided in half by an ochre seam. The leaves kept coming until Geoffrey's body was hidden in a cage of fire. I couldn't see Him anymore. Before me stood only a burning bush, both hot and bright enough to turn that small part of the woods bright as day. It blotted out the stars and made a bit of sky overhead pale blue. I have never seen anything as fair as that fire, crackling sweetly as if it were a harmless tame thing produced by a few twigs on the hearth on a winter's day. Scalding leaves like copper. Searing leaves like white-hot steel. I watched until the fire faded and finally burned itself out. When it was over, there was nothing left of Geoffrey but a soft ash. The wind gently took the ash and carried it away, spreading it over Woodlands in a fine rain."

For a moment the members of the congregation stood in awed silence. Then they realized what Geoffrey's death meant.

Never one to forget duty, Celia turned to the waiting group. She was resigned to her loss; still, she sounded bitter. "It's all over," she told them. "Woodlands is finished. We're leaving and we can never come back. But you can still stay here. So go home and live out the rest of your mundane, boring little lives."

Guiltily, almost on tiptoe, the little group disbanded. They crept home, cowards from that day forth. Ashamed of their pasts, spiritual lepers to friends and neighbors.

Minnie Parsons, looking wan, trembled like a frightened child. "What will we do now?" she asked.

"Pull yourself together," Celia snapped. "Be proud. There are other Woodlands. We'll start again. Just as we have for untold centuries. We'll dedicate our lives to Geoffrey. We'll mourn Him, another martyr for our cause."

Tom Parsons nodded.

Minnie Parsons looked around, taking a last view of the Woodlands she loved. She was like a refugee, driven permanently from her home. "Good-bye," she called to the surrounding woods, her voice shaking. "Remember us. Remember Geoffrey."

In tears the three old people, backs hunched with weariness, went away. They were never seen in Woodlands again.

By the time Andre and Jack Hooper returned, Robin was just coming to. He sat up, put his head in his hands, and groaned.

"It's all over, old man," Andre said. "We were on Philip's trail but we lost him. We've just been told the good news though. He's dead."

Robin's only comment was a moan.

"You okay?" Jack Hooper asked.

"I'll survive," Robin said. The dawn light made him look pink. Gone was the magician of the night. Back again was my lovable, harmless old friend. "I don't think I have a concussion," he said. "But what a clout! Remind me never to leave New York again."

Chapter XXXV

Hours later, Andre, Robin, and I, making a motley crew in our disheveled costumes, sat in the library, opposite Jenny and Jack. The gargoyles, listening to us, looked friendly now. Amusing anachronisms of the Renaissance.

A quick trip to the doctor had established that Robin was indeed all right. Although he would have quite a lump on his head for a few days.

And now it was our turn for at least a minor festival, for we had much to celebrate. It had been decided that Stacy deserved to be present for the occasion. She slept peacefully in a crib in the corner of the room.

We were exhausted, as a result of the night's traumas, but silly and giddy with relief. Besides, we had toasted each other a number of times by then and were all half-drunk.

Andre said, "I knew Philip had a grisly plan in mind for Tamara when I saw her costume last night. I'd never ordered it. As far as I knew, she was to make her appearance as a slightly medicinal-looking cat. And suddenly, there she was, dressed as a fairy princess. Besides, I'd assumed that the party would be held indoors. When I saw the guests on the lawn I knew my brother had taken command. Rather than oppose him right then and there, Robin and I decided to play along with Philip, trusting that we could trap him at some point later in the evening."

"As usual," said Robin, pouring another round of champagne, "we underestimated him. But, fortunately, we were able to arrive at the cottage in time to prevent Tamara's being injured."

Jenny smiled. "It's Crispin who really deserves the credit for that."

"Yes," I said. "He delayed the group until you arrived, Robin." I smiled at the cat. He was sitting on a red velvet cushion which rested in a shaft of sunlight. Sedately, he

234

licked a white paw. Then he held still, expecting to be admired. He looked like a primitive ivory carving. "I promise you a bowl of cream every day for the rest of your life, Crispin," I said, smiling at him. He took this in, blinked, and went to sleep. The night's exertions had tired him out, too.

Andre said, "With all due respect to Crispin, Robin is the hero of the hour as far as I'm concerned. If he hadn't found me and brought me to, he would have had to go to the cottage by himself and face Philip alone."

"Which would have led to total disaster," Robin said, "since I could never have defeated Philip. I'm glad I was able to be useful, though. It soothes my conscience. For such a long time I'd sided with Philip against Andre. You see, I'd got so damned fascinated with magic that I began to believe everything Philip told me. And, as you all know, he could be extremely persuasive. He got me thinking that Andre had persecuted him. And it did look that way, what with Andre barring his own brother from the house where he'd been born, and the countryside he loved. Then, I have to confess, Tamara, that I was growing very fond of you when Andre dragged you off from my party last summer. I was jealous. Philip noticed and encouraged it. Besides, I felt a basic contempt for Andre since he knowingly got you into the middle of the dreadful Piedmont mess. He should have known better. I felt that, if he truly loved you, he would have stayed out of your life."

"I'm glad Andre didn't share your point of view," I said. "We were in love. It was no time for false heroics."

"It was like a magic spell," Andre added.

"It turned out to be a lucky bit of magic in the end," Robin said. "But you must admit it didn't always seem that way. I saw how unhappy you were that day I visited Stonehaven, Tamara. Your unhappiness convinced me that the supernatural was genuinely evil. It created hideous misery for good people like you. That's why I grew strong enough to give magic up."

"You showed courage," Andre interjected. "There is probably nothing more fascinating, once you get involved with it, than the occult."

"The freer I became, the more I hated Philip," Robin said. "I came to see that I'd been hypnotized, that I had let myself be drawn into a kind of slavery. If I hadn't broken away when I did I would have wound up one of Philip's followers, a full member of the congregation. Completely corrupted."

"I thought you already were," Andre said. "That's why I hated you. I considered you to be a traitor. My loyal friend gone over to the enemy. I believed that you were in Philip's power completely, that you'd gladly sold your soul for the sake of a little occult knowledge. I was mistaken."

"It took some doing to convince you that you'd misjudged me," Robin said.

Andre smiled at me. "Robin bombarded me with secret phone calls and letters, Tamara, warning of danger to you and offering to rescue you from Philip. I desperately needed an ally. Eventually I realized that Robin was not Philip's dupe, that he sincerely cared about you and had broken away from my brother's control."

"In the old nick of time," Robin said, laughing hugely at his own joke. "Finally, Andre and I met in private and made plans to thwart Philip. After mutual apologies, of course."

"Tamara," Jenny said. "I want to apologize. I should have told you all about Philip. But I couldn't bring myself to talk about him, not after that day he found me in the woods." She looked inward and remembered. For a moment horror welled up in her soul and emerged in her eyes. Then Jack reached over and touched her hand. A compassionate and loving gesture. It drove the memories away.

Andre changed the subject. "It's over now. We're all safe. And I, for one, intend to rejoice at the good news. Here's a toast to my father, whoever he was. With gratitude. I feel as fortunate as the royal bastard. Was illegitimacy ever so welcome?"

We all laughed.

"And you, Jenny," Andre said. "When is the new baby due?"

Jenny patted her expanding stomach affectionately. "Not so soon that I won't have time to recover from last night's exertions. What are your plans now, Andre?"

Andre put his arm around me protectively. "I think that Tamara and I deserve a change of scene. We'll go off on a trip to Europe. Then we'll come back and spend a little time in New York. After that, we'll return home to Stonehaven. After all, we have to provide Stacy with a few playmates and Woodlands with a few heirs."

I stood up and opened one of the narrow latticed windows

in the library. It was like unrolling a scroll showing a pastoral scene. Another perfect day. Birds sang, settled into domesticity now, well finished with their migrations. The air was slightly pink still, the earth moist from dew. It was a soft, drowsy morning of pearl. Summer coming in.

"Look, everyone," I said, "the weather's glorious." As I stood there I heard a faint rumbling deep in Stonehaven. The damned old house was chuckling. It seemed kindly now, as if it enjoyed our company. Freed of nightmarish fancies, it was simply a large Gothic house. People would probably come from miles away to see it and admire its antique beauty. They'd never know that it was once a dangerous animal, whose teeth and claws had been removed, an architectural Samson shorn of its malignant strength.

"Stonehaven is a tamed dragon now," I said. "A pet. We did exorcise its ghosts and demons after all, last night."

"By the way," Robin said, shaking the last bottle of champagne to get at its remaining drops, "what will the local residents say when they notice that there's been an exodus of some of their leading citizens?"

"Another unexplained mystery," Jenny responded, "that's all. They're used to strange happenings around here. They'll concentrate on keeping the facts from outsiders. Eventually, everyone will have to learn to live without wild goings-on. It will take a little time, but someday Woodlands will be no different than any place else."

"Anyway," Jack added, "only a few leaders of the Congregation are gone. Many of the members, like Elsie, were recent recruits who hadn't had the opportunity to do much damage yet. They'll keep their mouths shut and lead exemplary lives from now on. They'd better; their neighbors will be watching them closely."

Robin said, "I, for one, am returning to the simple unvarnished life of the city. Whoever said that nothing happens in the country? You people lead fantastic lives out here. I can't keep up with you."

"You'll come back again for visits, won't you, Robin?" I asked. "After all, you're going to want to see your godchildren someday."

"Godchildren," Robin mused. "A pleasant idea. It will bring out my latent avuncular instincts. I will visit you then, from time to time. I'll give the children piggyback rides and perform magic tricks for them."

"Robin, I am shocked," I said. "I thought you'd sworn off magic. It isn't good for you, you know."

Robin sighed. "You're right, Tamara. I am done with it." Then his eyes took on a sly twinkle. "However, there's much to be said for white magic."

And, waving what was left of his broken cane, Robin removed his high black top hat. Then he reached one white-gloved hand in.

"Ahh," he said, drawing out a magnum of fine dry champagne. "Ladies and gentlemen, allow me just this one last example of my art before I renounce it." Our delighted laughter drowned out the pop of the cork. Then we eagerly held out our glasses for the last toast of the morning.

More SIGNET Gothics You'll Want to Read

☐ **HOUSE OF DARK ILLUSIONS by Caroline Farr.** A nightmare lingered in the shadows of the great stone house. Would it engulf Megan and her newfound love . . . ? (#T5579—75¢)

☐ **A CASTLE IN CANADA by Caroline Farr.** Horror lurks in a mist-shrouded castle and love's dream becomes a nightmare of terror. . . . (#T5211—75¢)

☐ **THE TOWERS OF FEAR by Caroline Farr.** Ali Cavanagh came to Storm Towers expecting a pleasant vacation, but she soon found herself immersed in a terrifying web of mystery; a web that tightened around her, threatening her life . . . (#T5138—75¢)

☐ **BIANCA by Florence Stevenson and Patricia Hagan Murray.** Could an old house destroy a beautiful marriage? What was the forgotten tragedy which brought sorrow to all who dwelt within the aged mansion? (#T5434—75¢)

☐ **THE CURSE OF THE CONCULLENS by Florence Stevenson.** A beautiful young woman ignores intimations of seduction and doom—to become the governess in an accursed Irish castle. (#T4903—75¢)

☐ **THE DEMON TOWER by Virginia Coffman.** Set in Napoleonic Italy, this Gothic novel of suspense tells the story of a wealthy orphan who journeys to the home of her mysterious aunt, only to find herself held prisoner there and destined to be the bride of a hateful man. (#T4974—75¢)

EVOKE

THE

WISDOM

OF

THE

TAROT

With your own set of 78, full-color cards—the Rider-Waite deck you have studied in THE TAROT REVEALED.
